EXECUTIVE PRIVILEGE

EXECUTIVE PRIVILEGE

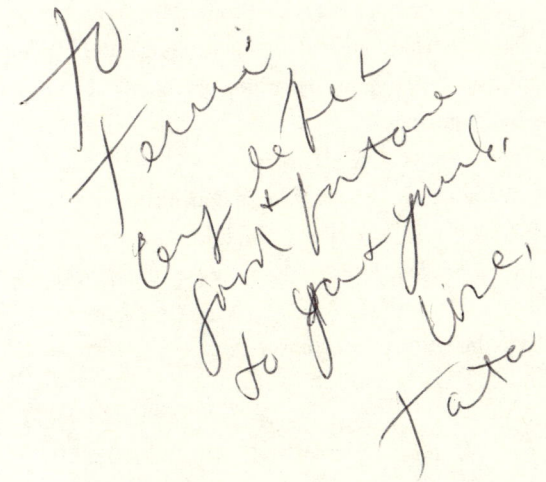

Tata Bosboom

Copyright © 2001 by Tata Bosboom.

Library of Congress Number: 00-193220
ISBN #: Softcover 0-7388-5434-4

All rights reserved. No part of this book may be reproduced or transmitted in any form or by any means, electronic or mechanical, including photocopying, recording, or by any information storage and retrieval system, without permission in writing from the copyright owner.

This is a work of fiction. Names, characters, places and incidents either are the product of the author's imagination or are used fictitiously, and any resemblance to any actual persons, living or dead, events, or locales is entirely coincidental.

This book was printed in the United States of America.

To order additional copies of this book, contact:
Xlibris Corporation
1-888-7-XLIBRIS
www.Xlibris.com
Orders@Xlibris.com

CONTENTS

CHAPTER 1 9
CHAPTER 2 12
CHAPTER 3 18
CHAPTER 4 21
CHAPTER 5 24
CHAPTER 6 26
CHAPTER 7 31
CHAPTER 8 37
CHAPTER 9 42
CHAPTER 10 51
CHAPTER 11 57
CHAPTER 12 60
CHAPTER 13 64
CHAPTER 14 69
CHAPTER 15 73
CHAPTER 16 79
CHAPTER 17 82
CHAPTER 18 84
CHAPTER 19 89
CHAPTER 20 93
CHAPTER 21 97
CHAPTER 22 101
CHAPTER 23 107
CHAPTER 24 112
CHAPTER 25 118
CHAPTER 26 125
CHAPTER 27 130
CHAPTER 28 134

CHAPTER 29	137
CHAPTER 30	145
CHAPTER 31	155
CHAPTER 32	158
CHAPTER 33	163
CHAPTER 34	168
CHAPTER 35	178
CHAPTER 36	186

For mom, Rose and Jo,
three great ladies.

I also want to thank those people in the arts and sciences whose opinions and expertise helped shaped some of the ideas for *Executive Privilege.*

CHAPTER 1

Madeline Chambers sat in the back seat of her sleek sedan preferring it in place of the highly visible limousine. Discretion was the order of the day. Slim and curvy, Madeline could easily pass for a much younger woman, and very often did. Her graying hair was dyed a gentle blonde, and her elegant hairstyle framed a perfectly shaped face which was a canvas displaying those delicate features that had enchanted men for over fifty years: clear blue eyes, high cheekbones, full lips.

She was a beautiful woman.

As she leaned against the headrest with a half-mast gaze, she watched the young man in the passenger's seat, not taking notice of him before. His dark hair showed no gray and when he turned to the driver, she admired the clean curve of his strong jawline. *Ahh, youth,* she thought, *there's nothing like it!* She closed her eyes and listened to the passionate voice of a modern day Piaf crying out her song. It was her favorite tape, and the men in front knew enough not to distract her with idle conversation, but the second it stopped, her driver filled in the lull.

"I'd suggest you put your seat belt on, ma'am."

"I find them very restraining."

"Then this is a restraining order." He tossed a smile in the mirror.

"By whom, Mitch?"

"By the driver."

"Let's not forget that I'm in the driver's seat." She enjoyed the banter.

"Touché, but we're moving at a fast clip."

"Good, that's the only way to have privacy, stay ahead of the pack."

The car exited the highway and glided through the quiet secondary roads. If anyone followed on this overcast morning, her experienced driver would easily lose him, but so far, all seemed well. She looked through the tinted glass at the blackened crusts of snow. A week ago it was gloriously white, crisp and new. Today it was ugly. The smudged gray sky was an appropriate cover, casting a somber spell over everything. In the distance the tall buildings were shrouded in mist.

They continued their circuitous route toward an apartment complex known for the amenities it offered its upscale tenants. It was managed like a four star hotel, a far cry from a nearby building where government staffers pooled their money and played house in secret pads, giving it the name of Brothel House instead of Bethel House. No, Parker Place was a Mecca for young people who coveted power and money and who weren't afraid to work for it. After putting in a long day, they came home to jog, work out at their fitness center and eat pasta at restaurants within the complex. They fell into bed, sucking on their bottled water, only to start the routine all over again the next morning.

On any given day the buildings were almost empty, except for staff and those tenants who worked out of their apartments. That was the main reason it was so perfect for Mrs. Chambers, who made this trip whenever her schedule permitted. A ripple of excitement shot through her sleek body as she thought ahead. But she sat perfectly poised not revealing a scintilla of her excitement.

They were quiet now as she feigned an interest in the papers she shuffled, her mind was on other things. She began to doodle, scribbling, "Clever? You bet I am." She answered her own question with the confidence of a woman used to getting her own way. Suddenly, she addressed the young man.

"What is your first name?"

"Rolland, ma'am, with two L's."

"Rolland," she repeated in a throaty voice. The driver clenched the wheel, throwing a sidelong glance at the young man who looked straight ahead.

As they neared their destination, she reached over and picked up a slouchy hat, dipping the wide brim seductively over her right eye. She craned her neck and peered at her reflection in the glass partition, turning her head at an angle and sucking in her cheeks like a Vogue model of the Fifties, darting an eye toward the young man in front. She felt him watching her in the mirror.

The car swung into the building's parking lot, the wheels crackling over the damp pavement until it eased into its usual spot. The doors flew open as the men jumped out. The younger man opened Madeline's door and offered her his hand, which she held onto longer than necessary. Their eyes met as she casually swung her shapely legs out of the car, her coat opening, revealing them in sheer, dark hose. She watched him look, and was amused, *How simple men are,* she thought.

She reached in her bag for a pair of sunglasses and slipped them on, confident no one would recognize her.

As they stood and talked, she ran her hands down the sides of her belted raincoat, smoothing the beige fabric, smiling directly at him revealing small, sharklike teeth. "Thank you, gentlemen," she said. "I'll call down when I'm ready to leave, and Mitch, why don't you get the elevator."

The driver ambled ahead, walking toward the service entrance as she and the younger man slowly followed. *Why haven't I noticed him before?* she thought, giving her young escort the once-over behind the dark glasses as he reached for the door, allowing her to enter. His left hand grazed her back as he guided her in and a thrill shot through her. She turned for a second and looked out as the door slammed shut, not knowing that this was her final look at the outside world. Not knowing that this was the last day of her life.

CHAPTER 2

For the first time since joining *Maison Russe,* I missed work. I opened my eyes to stare at the small lavender flowers covering my Laura Ashley drapes. I had seen monkeys climbing up those floral vines, overrunning my frilly room. I lifted my head from its damp arc, straining to see. But even with blurred vision, I knew the monkeys were gone.

I tried to open my mouth, but couldn't. I worried that my lips would tear if I tried, so I just fell back on my pillow flip flopping between chills and fever, knowing that my hair would turn into a bouquet of ugly ringlets.

The glass on my nightstand was empty so I probed my tongue along the seam of my flaky lips, but I had no saliva. I remembered my grandmother's advice on a long, family car trip, when I was dying of thirst and being a pest.

"Think of sour lemons," she whispered in my ear. It worked! So, I envisioned myself sucking a puckery fresh sour lemon and it worked again, unleashing a natural spring under my tongue, enough to free my lips. I quickly closed my mouth on the smell of rotting garbage. I needed mouthwash. I threw off my covers and shivered under my damp nightie. And when I tried to get up, the room spun, but I held on, fighting off the dizziness, and finally, I stayed upright. I held onto the furniture like a drunk, and slid against the wall inching my way to the bathroom where I drank a gallon of water, gargled, washed and smeared Vaseline over my flaky lips. I gulped down an aspirin and changed into a dry nightie. I postponed a trip to the kitchen for a cup of tea, and headed back to my dark bedroom. It looked so dreary and glum I wondered what the day was like, so I drew apart the heavily lined draperies for some much needed sunlight. There was no improvement. It really *was* a dreary day. I stood there for a minute watching a shiny, black sedan pull into the parking lot. My vision was blurred, but I remained, curious, looking through the slats. *Who could that be?* I wondered. Then I remembered my next door neighbor, Frank Landry. He was the "Psychic to the Stars." He boasted a celebrity clientele, but with our conflicting schedules, I rarely saw him. I did, however, catch him on television one night. I knew he saw clients at home and this could be one of them. When the car doors flew open and I saw the tall, slim blonde who emerged, I knew I was right. She wore sunglasses and a slouch hat pulled down, but she looked familiar. Had I seen her in the movies? On TV? I couldn't be sure from this angle, but I was certain that she was "somebody." I reached for my Nikon, a constant companion when you're in the antique business, and I pressed the button. The telescopic lens hummed out and I slipped it between the slats of the blinds and shot several times as the trio stood there. Seconds later they disappeared inside the service entrance of my building.

I began to shiver, so I plopped down on my bed and burrowed a hole in the soft mattress. It was a lost day anyway, so I figured I might as well sleep.

It had been years since I felt this sick, and as I lie there I remembered the monkeys, the green lights and the music. I had spent Christmas vacation at grandma's farm, nestled in her goose down bed burning with fever, too sick to enjoy anything. My chest ached from coughing, and the monkeys were there, jumping and swinging on grandma's flowered curtains. Green lights flickered as an organ grinder played his tinny music for those monkeys, who were all over the room.

I could still smell the pungent odor of the hot mustard plaster glued to my chest. It was as potent as having raw horseradish grated beneath my nose. My eyes teared and my nose ran as I shook my head from side to side trying to escape it. Snot, like glistening candles hung from my nostrils, while I hacked away like a barking seal. Grandma wiped my sore nose with a stained cotton hanky and poured liquids down my throat. She held me to her, singing Russian lullabies in her soft accented voice, and my eyes began to close. Overnight, my chest cleared and the coughing almost stopped. I felt better, except for the gluey sputum that dangled in mid air before breaking off. But grandma's home remedy worked. The next day I was as good as new and the monkeys were all gone.

I haven't seen my grandma in years, but I think of her whenever I discover a beautiful icon or religious painting at some obscure shop or country auction. She alone opened my eyes to that splendor, allowing me to hone my visual skills at an early age. For being a simple farm woman, grandma had sophisticated taste, a sharp contrast to her life. She emigrated from Russia and she had tried to learn the American ways by going to night school in the 1930's, but she was forced to stop when she bore her sixth child; my mother. Somehow she trained her eye and became a lover of beautiful things. Her taste was impeccable.

She still lives alone in the same house she lived in as a bride, renting out most of the land to her neighbors who help her with chores. Her favorite pastime is chatting on the phone, but unfortunately I no longer have the time or patience to make those calls to her; to listen to the same old stories; and to constantly fill in lapses of memory. One day I just stopped calling. "Can't you spare ten minutes to call your ninety-year-old grandmother?" my mother reprimands. I give her my litany of excuses which she relays to grandma, and the old lady understands and sends her love to me, anyway. One day I'll drive out to the farm and beg her forgiveness, it's the only thing to do after such an embarrassing lapse of time.

I was brought back from my reveries by my telephone, so I cocked my ear to listen. "Andy." My boss's cultivated voice sang out to me. "Where *are* you?"

I grabbed the receiver, and remembered I had never called him.

"Karl?" I was careful to keep my lips apart hoping they wouldn't catch again like Velcro.

"You're late," he said.

"I'm as sick as a dog," I said, as I explained my dilemma. I had spoiled him by being a workaholic, and now he would have to do all my work.

"Since you've never been out before, I'm forced to believe you," he laughed. "Call me if you need anything. By the way, an Iranian businessman with a taste for Faberge trinkets is stopping by. We're slowly educating them."

I loved Karl, who grew up rich and still had a casual attitude to all things costly. He enjoyed them, but never revered them. Trinkets, indeed!

"If I can't handle the sale," he continued, "I'll set up an appointment with you. You know P.R. is my forte."

"Partying is more like it." I made a weak attempt at teasing knowing that he was the best in the business. He just didn't like catering to the whims of the spoiled rich, whereas I didn't mind.

Karl hung up with a, "Feel better, luv, call if you need anything." He had my work to do. We were the only ones who knew the combination of the safe and security system. Even Karl's lover didn't know. God, how I love this business, which was certainly inspired by my grandmother.

I was raised listening to stories about Czarist Russia and Faberge Eggs. I sucked up everything that my grandmother wove into glorious tales. As I matured I wanted to know more, finally making it my life's work, becoming the director of Russian Art and Antiques at two prestigious auction houses; one in New York, one in London. One day Karl Merriam of *Maison Russe* called and made me an offer I couldn't refuse. I have never regretted a minute of it. We've made brilliant discoveries at country auctions and tag sales. I do regret not sharing my triumphant moments first hand with my grandma. That information trickles down to her from relatives and I know she's proud of me. *Instead of being grateful to her for jumpstarting my career, I have given her short shrift. Have I become so selfish and self-centered? Or has being around all this money changed me? Or am I ashamed of my humble background? There are perils of constantly being exposed to wealth. You must remind yourself that this is not real life, that this is not how most people live. Oftentimes, I forget.*

I must have dozed off for awhile, because suddenly I was awakened by a tapping on my wall. Perhaps somebody was hanging up pictures. Tap . . . tap . . . tap. It became louder. *My God! Was somebody coming through the wall?* I sat up, startled. The tapping became rhythmical and was joined by the persistent squeak of the bed. Soon, other sounds mingled; moans, groans and grunts, and I realized the tapping was a headboard banging against my wall. I sobered immediately. That woman, the one I had seen, is having sex with the clairvoyant. I thought he was gay, but he obviously isn't. What a great cover! Was he a male prostitute? A woman tells her husband she's off to see her psychic for a reading and she has sex with him instead, for a fee which hubby pays, and nobody's the wiser. This guy doesn't even have to know the future. I had been missing all this by going to work every day. Staying home was proving to be exciting.

I got out of bed steadier than I had been and slipped into the space between my armoire and my bureau. I planted my ear firmly against the wall and felt the vibration of the bed. The lovers were in the throes of wild, intense sex. She was gasping, making low animal sounds. I began to see Frank Landry in a different light. After listening to this I decided he wasn't so bad after all. The worst part was that I was enjoying my role as a listening Tom. The sounds were enough to draw pictures in my head, and having been celibate for a while, it didn't take long for me to conjure up some very erotic images. My hand slid between my legs as I felt a pressure build, but I stopped; curiosity got the best of me. I had to find out who she was. I shivered as I flattened my body against the cold plaster. Any closer and I would have been in their room. I strained, desperately trying to hear a name, hoping he would call it out in passion, but everything was unintelligible. I heard voices but not one stray word or phrase, only the rutting sounds which didn't go with the image of the regal blonde I'd seen. By this time I was so involved in this soap opera I had forgotten I was sick. I left the cold wall and sat on my bed listening to her passion and abandon with envy, wishing it was me. I stared into space a long time thinking about my former love, a great guy who just didn't fit into my lifestyle. I went to cocktail parties, he went to Bosnia.

I sat there listening, until there was absolute silence. Then my imagination took hold as I visualized them naked and sweaty, sipping champagne from crystal flutes; or licking it from each other's genitalia, spent from their lovemaking, dozing off entwined in each other's limbs.

I thought of my own nonexistent sex life; I let a perfectly good man slip away because of superficial reasons. The pickings are lean in Washington for those of us interested in marriage. I'm entirely surrounded by gays or married men looking to cheat. My sex life was now reduced to eavesdropping on my neighbor's trysts, I was disgusted with myself.

Feeling sorry for myself, I had to get away, so I wrapped myself in a fleecy robe, put on some scuffies and shuffled out to my kitchen. My stomach growled, perhaps tea and toast would silence it. I filled the kettle and waited for it to boil, puttering around my kitchen. Then I remembered. I'd never picked up my morning newspaper outside my door. Paper delivery was one of the amenities in my building. I knew the lovers would be sleeping, so I quietly turned my lock and cracked the door, just wide enough to retrieve my paper. I was expecting the hallway to be empty and I was startled to see the dark blur of a man shooting by, heading for the stairs. He must have heard my lock, but he didn't turn around, so I only saw his back; dark hair and a dark suit with bulgy pockets. As he turned into the stairwell, I caught a glimpse of his sculptured profile before the door slammed shut and he slipped from sight. I had never seen him before and I didn't know who he was or where he came from, but there was one thing I did know; he was not the psychic.

CHAPTER 3

Rolland Nichols stood beside the sleek car, his hand resting loosely on the door handle, waiting to climb in out of the raw air. His head was turned, looking the other way giving his partner privacy while he used his port-o-potty. They had sat in the car for over two hours waiting for Mrs. Chambers. They chatted, read, did puzzles, and now they were hungry. His partner called to him covering the urinal and wedging it under the lip of the front seat. "She's taking longer than usual," Rolland said, climbing into the car, his big frame settling into the passenger seat. He checked the time while his partner lifted his hips in an effort to zip his pants. They hoped their charge would call soon, they were hungry. The second she called they would make a dash upstairs and accompany her home. That done, they would be free to eat a late lunch at some fast food joint.

"Do you really think she's seeing a seer?" Rolland asked, curiosity getting the best of him.

"Who knows what she does. The guy's reputable, he's got a celebrity clientele here and in New York. People pay big bucks to listen to that crap."

I wish he'd look into his crystal ball and tell her we're starving. Do you have any more granola bars?" Rolland asked.

"Sorry, we ate the last two." They were silent for awhile, Rolland wondering if he should say anything about Mrs. Chamber's subtle message to him as they left the car. He knew she was coming onto him, but he was trained not to react. He was, however, flattered and now curious about her personal life.

"I'd love to be a fly on the wall," he murmured.

"A while back, the place was bugged." His partner filled him in. "Bugged, long before her first visit. But the bugs were found, every last one of them. It had to be a pro doing it. It was a clean sweep. Either she's no dope or the psychic respects client confidentiality. We never did it again."

"Did the old man know?"

"He ordered the bugs. As long as she's discreet, he figures it's all right. She's a helluva woman, and she's done her job for him. Rich, powerful men love power more than anything else, so as long as he has what he wants, he looks the other way. Doesn't mess with the status quo."

"I'll never know," Rolland replied, his stomach growling. "I'm beginning to think we should call."

"And have the wrath of Madeline upon us? No way."

"But she's never been this long, and last time, when she was running late she called down."

"Hey, you want to call, call, but make sure you spell your name again," he said sarcastically.

"I could get away with it. I have the feeling she's coming on to me," Rolland said, baiting him.

Mitch tossed him a look. "She flirts with every man."

"You too?"

"Look, all I'm saying is that you'd better be careful, if you like your job. She'll ride your cock and you'll be out of work."

Rolland gave him the once over. "You're still here, Mitch, does that tell me something?"

"Just don't be fooled by the fair hair and fine bones; she's one tough lady. Are you aware that nobody knows the truth about these visits?"

"You know that?"

"Yes, I know."

"What else do you know?"

"Nothing."

Rolland wondered what else Mitch knew about her, but he wasn't deterred. He had confidence in his good looks and he was determined to call. He reached for the car phone and punched in the number which was written on a card. The phone rang several times and Frank Landry's voice told him that he was not able to take this call; please leave a message. "This is Rolland Nichols, waiting for your client who is running late today. You can appreciate our concern. Please pick up." The telephone clicked off, nobody answered. Rolland held the phone, thinking of his next move. His partner's beefy body shook with quiet laughter at the naiveté of the younger man.

"I still think we should check," Rolland said.

"What could happen?"

"A kidnapping," Rolland answered, eager to make points with Madeline. He was intrigued by her.

"Rolland, drop it . . . she's getting laid. Instead of once, it's twice. And that's what's taking so long. *Capisce?*"

"No, I don't *capisce*. I'm going up," he insisted.

"Do you have a key?"

"Yes," he joked. "She slipped it to me for emergencies."

"Get out," his partner laughed, poking him in the side with his elbow. "You'll use a credit card. Go on, beat it, I'm willing to call your bluff. Go!" He shifted his frame as the eager young man left the car and briskly walked to the service entrance. Mitch watched him and shook his head. *Shit, I think he's got the hots for her.* He shook his head, thinking of the flirting she did with him just to get her way and extract a vow of silence from him. He became her pawn, protecting her secret life. Never crossing the line as much as he desired. John Stanger refused to play her game and was retired while he, Mitch, was still on the job with the most fascinating woman he had ever met. He shook his head, half grinning. *It'll serve him right. When Madeline finishes with Rolly, he'll never be the same, I know.* Suddenly, his two way radio crackled with Rolland's voice. "Mitch, Firecracker's in trouble, get Dr. Foster, A.S.A.P., and get your ass up here!"

CHAPTER 4

For the past hour, I heard voices and the crackling of a two-way radio. A strange feeling gripped me. Something was wrong! Somebody rang my doorbell, startling me, but I was afraid to answer, to get involved. I stood paralyzed near my door, afraid that someone might hear me with only two inches of wood between us. Like a frightened mouse I backed away and scurried on tip toe back to my bedroom. If they charged in, I would pretend I was near death, not having heard or seen anything, when in fact I was beginning to feel better. I didn't know what had happened, but these mysterious goings on scared me, yet piqued my curiosity, and I was certain the man in the hall had something to do with it. It was better if they thought that nobody was here.

I carefully moved a slat of the Levelors and peeked through that little slice of light. The sedan was still there. Quietly, I dragged over a chair and worked it between my furniture, waiting there like a gossipy old crone. Then I saw it; a silent ambulance pulled into the parking lot. The back bay doors hissed open, the attendants wheeling out a stretcher, a doctor following . . . something dreadful must have happened next door, but to whom? I heard no cries for help, no screams, nothing being thrown around, all I heard were sexual sounds. I was at the window when I heard my doorbell ring again. My breath quickened as I huddled in my corner afraid to answer. I felt safe there, and besides, I didn't want to miss anything. After watching for awhile and hearing the muffled sounds next door, I was dying of curiosity, determined to see it through. Suddenly, the exit door of my building flew open as a stretcher was wheeled out with a body bag on it. I blinked to make certain of what I had seen. "My God, what's going on? Who's in that?" I whispered. Waves of nausea swept over me in a sickening rush and terror froze the red tide beneath my skin paralyzing every inch of my body, I was glued to the spot, watching the attendants at work. Slowly the terror melted, allowing me to back away from that window which let me peek into the life and death of a stranger. I was overcome with guilt. Somebody had died, and I did nothing! Could I have prevented it with a call to the police? The blonde, the psychic, the man in the hall. Was it a *menage à trois* that went wrong? "Who are these people?" I quickly came to my senses and I grabbed my camera. *Please let there be film left.* I had no time to check as I focused, stopping in mid-motion as one man looked up; my heart raced with excitement then relief when he turned his head and scanned another part of the building. Quickly, I zeroed in on that mysterious group and shot repeatedly until they heaved the stretcher into the back, the wheels collapsing on contact. The doors closed, and the film ran out.

The silent ambulance slowly backed up then turned toward the exit, followed by the sedan. They drove slowly. There was no need for urgency. It was a clear sign to me, that I was right; the patient was dead.

◆ ◆ ◆

I didn't know the real story and I may never know it. But if the blonde was a celebrity, I was hoping to hear something on the news. My pictures told a story; but what story? If she was a star, the tabloids would be interested. I was giddy at the thought. A strange glee swept over me just thinking about it, thinking about making money so easily. I forced myself to get started. Once the news was out, this couldn't wait, I had exclusive pictures every tabloid would be bidding on. A paranoia gripped me. I took my precious camera to the bathroom and hid it among the stale smelling laundry in my wicker hamper, afraid that someone would steal it. I locked the door and stepped under the shower as needles of hot water pelted my body, invigorating me. I had to find a fast, reliable place to develop the precious film. The Photo Express was off limits for this job, I couldn't take a chance on them disappearing or having some lab rat selling a stolen set. So, whom could I trust? My head ached trying to think of somebody who could work fast and be discreet. I wanted them developed tonight. I had to be ready when the news came out.

I was so deep in thought I didn't care about my hair which was curlier than ever. I stepped out of the shower, dried off, and pulled on a pair of faded jeans and an old shirt. I was shocked at the pale face looking at me in the foggy mirror, my eyes looked bigger and darker against the white mask. That 24-hour bug ravaged me. But now I had a goal, and that little bug was not going to deter me. I slapped on lipstick, rubbing some on my cheeks. I started to look better. Make up really works! I retrieved my camera from it's hiding place and paced the floor, holding it to my chest, trying to think. In my heart I knew who I should call, but I didn't want him to think it was personal, although I really missed him. Still, his image crowded my mind. I squeezed my eyes shut, hoping to make him disappear, but he wouldn't. His name was imprinted across my vision, and no matter how hard I tried, I knew he was the only one for this job. I would risk the rejection. After all, business is business. I took a deep breath, swallowed, and made the call.

CHAPTER 5

Lucien Champier had just gotten his key in the lock when he heard his telephone ring. He struggled with it, coaxing and wiggling it gently, trying to finesse it past whatever blocked it's path. He was patient, handling it carefully, hoping it wouldn't break. "This needs WD40 or I need a new lock." He knew that, but he was never around long enough to have it done. Slowly and carefully, he tried again and this time it worked. By the time he got inside, the phone had stopped ringing and the message light was flashing. "Shit!" He grimaced at an unpleasant thought. "She's too much. I can't take it!" He stood there looking at the machine, shaking his head as he thought about the evening spent with Samantha Dewar, the senator's daughter, who was obsessed with the Tom Sellick look-a-like. Tall, dark, mustachioed, Lucien was a dead ringer for the handsome star.

"How about a little conversation, Sam. Are you capable of doing that? Or is drooling all over me the only thing you can do?" He threw his leather jacket on the sofa. Nothing went well tonight, all he wanted to do was get away from cling wrap Samantha— as far away as possible. He knew of her drug use and he was bored with her offers of it, claiming better sex. He was disgusted with her frequent trips to the bathroom, sniffing a line of coke from the marble sink counter. He tried it all, but it was in his past now and he didn't want to go back. But sober or high, Samantha Dewar was boring, and worst of all, the sex was boring. She needed more than a pretty face to hold this man.

He plopped down on a chair and yanked off his clunky boots, wiggling his toes with relief at the freedom they felt, the rest of him should feel this free, but this relationship worried him.

Samantha had threatened to kill herself if he ever left. He escaped tonight, pretending to have an important assignment to clear up, but what about tomorrow, and the next night? His lie was a first step in fighting her emotional blackmail, *Tomorrow, I'm gonna beg for an assignment out of the country, away from Sam's reach.* His spirits lifted by the thought.

He stood looking at the answering machine unable to replay the message. *If I don't respond to her nighty-night call, she might come over, to see if I'm with somebody, then I'll be stuck for the night.* He gave the button a light tap, and stepped back, afraid of hearing her voice. He was startled to hear Andy. "Lucien, I need your professional help. Please call me at 343445566. I'll be in all evening waiting to hear from you. I hope you're back in the country; oh, there may be a scoop in it for you. Thanks, Lucien." He played it again, standing motionless, trying to get a handle on it. He wished the call had been more personal, she sounded so businesslike, but her voice still gave him a rush that he had never felt with anyone else . . . and the news of a scoop interested him. He checked his watch. It was ten-thirty. *I'll call in the morning,* but he continued standing there staring at the light, which was now a green speck glaring back at him. "I could pretend I'm still in Bosnia, she'd never know." But he felt so relieved that it wasn't Samantha, and so curious that it was his old flame, that without further hesitation, he tapped in her number . . . surprised that he still remembered it.

CHAPTER 6

I kept my conversation with Lucien strictly business, and he was interested in helping me for "old times sake," but I must admit that when I heard him, I had a slight contraction in my private. I wondered if he felt anything. Probably not, after the way I dumped him, perhaps when he sees me? I remained in my casual clothes, knowing he liked that; I secured my precious film, got in my car and drove to the working class area where he lived.

As I drove past his small apartment house, searching for a parking space, I saw him at the third floor window, watching. It was this kind of consideration he always showed me, that made me love him once. A warm feeling came over me and settled in my groin.

After struggling to park my BMW in a tight spot, I sat for a minute and took a deep breath, after all, I had just gotten out of my sick bed. When I looked up, he was walking toward me. An electric shock ran through me. Dammit, that old feeling was back. I must be very careful tonight, friendly but correct. As I struggled out, I felt my curls bounce. I knew he would like that, as well as my beatup clothing.

"God, you're the same old Andy. I wouldn't believe it. You always reminded me of Orphan Annie."

"I suppose that's a compliment but it's just for tonight," I nervously said.

"You did it for me?"

"No," I replied sassily, feeling better every second. "No, I showered and had no time. Lucien, how are you?" I extended my hand. He held it for a moment looking into my eyes. We missed each other, I knew that without having to hear it. I made no attempt to kiss him, it wouldn't be fair, after having gotten out of my sick bed. There was an awkward silence, as we stood, neither of us making the first move. *I shouldn't have come, I should have gone to the Photo Express.*

"Well, Andrea, . . ." his voice trailed as he spoke in a business-like tone. "Shall we?" He tried my doors to make certain that they were locked, afraid it wouldn't be there when I returned and for some reason, I didn't care.

We went inside and walked up to his third floor apartment. Food smells still hovered, even though it was far past the dinner hour. I was out of breath when we reached his door which he left ajar. He opened it, allowing me to enter, noticing my breathlessness. "Gee, Andy, the good life has you out of shape."

"I'm just getting over a bug."

"That was thoughtful of you."

I didn't answer, because I didn't know if he was being sarcastic. "Thanks for seeing me, Lucien." If he had refused, I couldn't blame him. I had been ruthless. Such a loving man should never have been subjected to the rotten things I said and did to get him out of my life. I shudder to think of it. I was so impressed with my new importance and my new lifestyle, and he didn't fit in. I hang my head in shame whenever I think of it.

My eyes scanned the spartan living room. Although he made a decent living as a photographer for the Washington Tribune, the room was sparsely furnished with just the bare essentials. A table, a few chairs, a leather recliner and TV, a leather sofa. Lots of books and bookshelves, no curtains, just blinds. A small area rug covered the dull wooden floor which ringed it. I glanced toward the small kitchen, which was neat and orderly. No stacks of dirty dishes, but Lucien always ate out. He ingeniously made a small darkroom from part of his bedroom, and that's what I had in mind. "Sit down," he motioned. "Let's get down to business. I received this cryptic message, now what's this all about?" I sat on the edge of the sofa and leaned toward him.

"I missed work today."

"That's the scoop?" He was clearly amused.

"Yes, because something strange happened." I handed him the roll of film with a brief explanation of what had happened. "I think I have a story in these pictures."

"OK, let's get on it." He reached for the film and with a sweep of his hand said, "Make yourself comfortable." He laughed, knowing how much I hated this place. With that, he disappeared into the darkroom. I sat back on the sofa, and thumbed through a trade magazine, hoping he had locked the front door. I rose to check, and found that he had. He did it for me, knowing how I felt about the neighborhood. That old feeling overtook me again and somehow it didn't matter where he lived or what he wore. Being in this dumpy, little apartment with him just magnified my loneliness. I belonged with him, not with the spoiled rich who needed me as a tool, a knowledgeable conduit to guide them to buy authentic art. But how did he feel about me? He gave no indication.

"Andy," he called, as I rushed to the darkroom. "Come on in, it's OK, I'm finished." I opened the door on total darkness, careful not to mess up the film. Suddenly the light went on. "They're drying," he said, wiping his hands on the towel. We were standing very close to each other in his small, self-styled darkroom as he clipped a picture on a frame. He had blown it up. "Look, do you recognize her now?" I dug in my bag for my glasses and looked closely at the picture of the woman and her two escorts. He said nothing as he watched me, nodding his head, prompting me to see what he had already seen, trying to instill in me some magic vision. "Look who wound up in the crosshairs of your lens." I continued straining my eyes and then I stepped back, looking at the grainy textured photo from a distance, and suddenly it came together.

"I can't believe it!" I whispered as I plopped down on a high stool before my trembling legs gave way. "I can't believe it," I repeated as I continued staring at the woman in the sunglasses. She was now recognizable and I now knew who she was! She was

Madeline Chambers, First Lady of the United States! I sat there slack jawed staring at the picture, not believing it.

"You have some scoop, Missy," Lucien said, breaking the silence.

"*We* have some scoop," I croaked, my mouth as dry as the desert.

"Does anybody know you took these?"

"No."

"Does anyone know you were home?"

"My boss."

"I'm afraid you're gonna have the Secret Service all over the place. What was she doing there anyway?"

"Having sex."

"Having sex?"

"Yes, I told you about the psychic and the man in the hall."

"Was this a *menage à trois*?" He continued the questions.

"I don't know. I heard a woman having great sex, and then I saw the ambulance and the body bag, all there on film."

"And there were no police?"

I shook my head 'no.'

"Then she wasn't murdered," he said.

"No, but I thought she was some TV personality."

"No, you bagged a big one."

I found myself watching his mouth as he spoke. He had beautifully shaped lips, and I remembered them well. He touched my upper arm.

"Look, would you like to stay here tonight?" I became flustered. "You could say you spent the day with me, 'cause if you make a sale, the paper won't reveal the source, but guaranteed, the Secret Service will investigate. I'll get you off the hook."

I tried to remain cool, but I was becoming mush. "I'm thrilled to hear such concern, but I can't stay."

"Still not good enough for you?" He dropped his hands.

"Come on, that isn't it." He looked hurt, but I couldn't tell him that if I stayed, I'd be under him all night. He brushed past me and I followed him to the living room, where he had already turned on the TV.

"Let's see if there's a news flash." We stood there side-by-side waiting for a program interruption, but there was nothing. No news flash, no announcement from the White House . . . nothing! Lucien and I were among the select few who knew the truth. We knew that the First Lady was dead.

Several days had passed without any announcement from the White House. On December 6, the First Lady appeared on television. She had the honor of lighting the Christmas tree at the annual tree lighting ceremony at the White House.

CHAPTER 7

Frank Landry, "the psychic to the stars," looked startled at the two men who towered before him. The little man's eyes widened when they identified themselves as Secret Service. "What's this all about?" His voice was caged with apprehension.

"May we come in?" Mitch Levett asked.

"Yes, of course." He stepped aside after inspecting their credentials. "Is anything wrong?"

"No, not at all." The agent answered, pleased that they had frightened him, he'd be more cooperative now. "We appreciate you taking the time to see us."

Frank looked at his watch, "I expect a client at noon."

"We'll be long gone," Mitch assured him, segueing into the heart of the investigation. "We understand you were in New York on Thursday."

"Yes, I maintain an apartment there, I also see clients."

"We know that."

"I'm sure you do." He laughed, a little more relaxed now.

"What is your relationship with the First Lady?"

"We are friends. Madeline is my friend." Mitch knew he used the old first name trick to show how well he knew her. "Come inside." The men saw him roll his neck, looking up at them was beginning to strain. So Frank walked to his formal living room followed by his visitors.

The room was exquisitely decorated with antiques and oriental rugs. Fine paintings graced the walls. Exquisite accent pieces were placed about, an ivory carving, a red cloisonné vase, a jade figurine . . . and others adding color and harmony to the pale yellow room. The men looked around appreciating its beauty. "Business must be good." Rolland Nichols laughed.

"I must be good. I bought all of this on repeat business."

"Touché."

"May I get you something to drink. Coffee or tea?"

They refused the offer and sank into the plump goose down sofa. "You don't see too much of this anymore, everything is foam rubber." Mitch said as he patted the sofa. Frank remained standing, nervously getting to the point.

"Madeline's life is an open book, she lives in a fishbowl. The poor woman has no privacy, and she has a right to it. I am able to give her that. When I'm in New York, which is about once a month, I let her use this apartment."

"What does she do here?"

"Don't ask, don't tell." He rolled his eyes and made a limp wristed gesture.

"Was she seeing anyone?" agent Nichols asked.

"No, of course not."

"But she might be?"

"Don't put words in my mouth. I really don't know. She told me once that she liked to read, meditate, listen to tapes . . . daydream."

"Or have sex?" Rolland interrupted.

The little man with the sad brown eyes and receding hairline stared unblinkingly, wondering which road to take. Finally he said, "Possibly. I really don't know. She never told me. I'm never here . . . she has a key. I know she uses the place under the pretext of seeing me for a reading. Look, I give her a day of privacy, what's wrong with that?" He was visibly nervous, beads of perspiration covered his forehead.

"Mr. Landry, the First Lady won't be needing your place for a while."

"Why?" He was clearly upset by the news.

"Because she can do all of those things you mentioned at home," Mitch continued. "She can read, meditate, listen to music."

"Is anything wrong?" Frank interrupted.

"No. It's a decision that the President and the First Lady have made."

"My God, does the President know?" He looked stunned.

"Yes, Mr. Landry, they're going into an election year and discretion has become a popular word around the White House these days. I'm certain you understand."

"My God," Frank whispered, biting his nails. "My lips are sealed. Nobody knows anything. Madeline's inner circle believes she's a client. She refers them to me, but they know nothing else."

"Is the First Lady a client?"

"No, she's my friend. She refuses to have her cards read. She just laughs at my warning about a dark haired man. I see danger but she just laughs."

"They would prefer having no contact with you until after the election. A hint of anything scandalous is dangerous in an election year. She'll hold onto the key, until things get back to normal." The men weren't ready to give up the key.

"Thank you, Mr. Landry." They rose as Frank, once again looked up at them. He trailed as they headed for the door, suddenly Mitch stopped in his tracks. "Do you know who she is seeing, it's very important."

"Did I say she is seeing anyone?"

"No. But you're a psychic, you know more than you're telling."

"Thank you for the vote of confidence." Frank was weakened by the flattery as Mitch continued. "We must be careful of blackmail. Anything leaked to the press can undo everything the President has worked for, and he's gotten some pretty good programs through the House, and if you think this meeting is unsettling, imagine what it'll be like if something goes wrong." Frank held up a finger to stop him. "I did find an Arab newspaper in my wastebasket."

"Recently."

"Last month, my cleaning lady is Haitian, so I found that

rather odd. Madeline had an interest in Arab causes, that's why I warned her about the dark haired man, but she found that hilarious."

The agents jotted in their notebooks. "Anything else?"

"I'm not in the habit of going through the garbage, I just happened to see a newspaper. I had just come back from New York and I hadn't read it that day. I scavenged it thinking she left it. Naturally, I couldn't read a thing."

"Did you save it?"

"No."

"Too bad."

"But there was something else. The other day, all my messages were cancelled on my answering machine. I missed all my messages, and I must have had them. I go away for three days, I have messages, believe me. I don't know who did it; perhaps Madeline? Oh, well, they'll call back." The men nodded sympathetically not willing to tell him they had done it to cancel agent Nichols call to him.

"Is that it?" Mitch said.

"Yes."

"Thanks again, Mr. Landry. I'm sure we can count on your discretion."

"It's my business. And you might remind the First Lady to be careful, you might also remind her that she promised to invite me to THE Inaugural Ball."

"We'll be happy to do that," Mitch said as they walked down the carpeted hallway toward the elevators, but he muttered, "Don't hold your breath."

As they neared the bank of elevators, Rolland Nichols stopped in his tracks. His partner continued walking, only to look back and discover Rolland planted in one spot. Something was holding him there. "What? What?" Mitch said.

"We never checked the neighbor. Remember, a newspaper in front of the door when we arrived, and none when I returned . . . and no answer when we rang."

"So."

"Let's have a look." The young man turned and headed for Andy's door while Mitch reluctantly followed. "We'll get to lunch, don't worry, it'll only take a minute." As he zeroed in on Frank's next door neighbor, they pushed the buzzer, waiting for a response. There was none. Without hesitation Agent Nichols removed a set of keys and tried several until the door knob turned allowing them to enter a sunfilled apartment. It was a woman's place, with beige area rugs. A fireplace dominated one wall, with two beige and white silk loveseats facing each other. Art objects in ivory and coral were placed about while crystal vases sparkled, catching the blinding sunlight. Impressionist paintings and Russian icons complimented each other in that eclectic room. "Nice stuff," Mitch commented feeling at home. They looked around and discovered Andy's work space with the Post-it fringed computer. "Here's a card," he said reading it. "Andrea Evanovich, Executive Vice President, *Maison Russe*, Wisconsin Avenue. This explains all the good stuff here. This is a very expensive store!" He waved the card, then gave it to his partner to look at. "All the exclusive antique stores are on Wisconsin Avenue." The message light on the answering machine was on. Mitch tapped it and heard Lucien's message. "Andy, call me at home the second you get it. I'm arranging a meeting with somebody very interested in meeting you. Bye."

"He didn't leave a name, so it's someone she knows very well. It isn't business, otherwise he would have called her there. What do you make of it?" he asked Rolland, who pressed the button and replayed the message. "It doesn't mean anything, but it could mean something. Somebody is interested in meeting her. She's with a prestigious store, maybe it's about antiques."

"Then they'd meet in the store."

"Wait a minute." Mitch grabbed the card his partner was holding and punched in the telephone number of *Maison Russe*. The telephone was answered by an operator with a clipped English accent. Very classy, Mitch thought. She put the call through to Miss Evanovich's office. "Miss Evanovich," Mitch said in a broad Texas accent. "Bart Dudley here, in town visiting. Your name was given to me as the little lady to see if I wanted some fine jewels. I was in lookin' for you last Thursday." He said nothing more, allowing her to fill it in.

"I wasn't in. I'm sorry I missed you, I hope . . . " He interrupted with, "I hope you weren't sick, it was too nice a day for that." It stopped her in her tracks, the question didn't set well, since last Thursday wasn't a very nice day, that she could remember, so she quickly replied, "No, I was at an auction bidding on some marvelous pieces. When can I expect you to come by to see them?"

"Tomorrow, 'bout two, I'll be by tomorrow. I thank you for your time." Mitch hung up, not fully satisfied with his act. "I think I screwed it up. I shouldn't have asked her if she was sick, we just should have assumed that."

"It's a good assumption, Mitch. She wasn't at work. Her newspaper was missing when I came back. I think we should look around." They checked her medicine cabinet, checking her prescription drugs, but found nothing unusual. They made their way to the frilly bedroom, where everything was neat and orderly. They snooped in drawers holding silk and lace panties. And looked in the closets. They stood at the window and looked out on the parking lot where their car was parked in exactly the same spot it was in five days ago, they eyed each other. Rolland opened the armoire where the Nikon rested among the linens piled neatly on the shelves. "That thing loaded?" Mitch asked as his partner turned on the camera, number one flicked on the digital screen. "It's loaded, but it's on one."

"So she just loaded it."

"Depends."

"I think we should keep an eye out for Miss Evanovich."

"Fine, but we don't have the manpower to make it a full time job. We're the only ones who know, so we'll be doing the snooping."

"We'll manage," Mitch said as they put the camera back on the shelf and left the apartment, passing Frank Landry's noontime client in the hall.

CHAPTER 8

When I got home that evening, I had a strange feeling that somebody had been in my apartment. It was nothing I could put my finger on, it was just a feeling. My telephone rang and I listened to Lucien's voice, quickly picking up the receiver.

"Jeez, Andy, I've been waiting for your call!"

"I just got home."

"Oh. I left a message earlier, I didn't want to call at work."

"My message light isn't on."

"Well, I called. I wanted you to know I spoke with Eddie Wallace. He wants to meet with you tomorrow."

"Great." I was thrilled. Eddie Wallace was the Herald's finest investigative reporter and he wanted to meet with me. I knew then, that I had a great story. Lucien gave me the details and hung up. I was sorry he did. I was hoping he'd invite me to dinner, brief me before my meeting tomorrow, but no such luck. I pressed my replay button, curious about the message Lucien said he left. My messages were lined up. This call, his previous call, a telemarketing call, and a call soliciting money for the homeless children's toy fund. They were all new but my light wasn't flashing. A chill ran up my spine. Somebody *was* here and played back my messages. They may even have a tap on my line. I left my apartment immediately and went down to call Lucien from the lobby phones. He wasn't there, but I left a message telling him of my suspicions. I reluctantly returned, not happy to spend the evening alone in that apartment.

I looked forward to tomorrow, and my meeting with the legendary Eddie Wallace.

◆ ◆ ◆

Lucien trusted one man with this photo scoop; Eddie Wallace. The meeting was veiled in enough secrecy to arouse this news legend's curiosity. Tough, curmudgeonly, fair and honest, Eddie was a man who faced jail rather than give up his sources. A man like this, a man of such integrity is not a large commodity in any business these days and certainly not in Washington. I was excited to meet him and I became less enthusiastic about selling the pictures to a tabloid, and more willing to give the photo scoop to Lucien and Eddie. I knew I could trust them not to reveal their source.

Although the White House never announced anything, I still felt something was wrong. Call it a hunch, a sixth sense, but in my heart of hearts I felt they were hiding something, because suddenly the First Lady's appearances came to a screeching halt. They had the usual excuse; illness.

When I got to Lucien's, Mr. Wallace was there. They had been waiting for me, but instead of a lecture on punctuality, he shook my hand firmly. I liked him immediately, this big, bear of a man, heavy featured with one long furrowed eyebrow. I was aching to tweeze a small space in the middle to separate them.

They had been studying the pictures. "I see who I'm looking at, and I ran a check on the tag number you gave me." I looked concerned. "Very discreetly. I did it personally and the sedan is part of the presidential fleet. So that checks. But it could be anybody in the body bag."

He blew a hole in our theory, but I was adamant. "I know what I saw. I saw her arrive and then I saw her leave in a body bag. Otherwise why all the secrecy, it's as if nothing happened in my building."

"She might have left by the front door, have you thought of that? With her disguise, nobody would even notice her. She might have slipped into a car, that her secret service guys called for. Then they go out the back with the body. The woman was on television, she is not dead!"

He gave us food for thought; but my instincts were stronger than logic and I parried with him. "Why would she leave by another door?"

"Ohhh," Eddie said smiling, "I thought you'd never ask. Because maybe the guy she was with died. It happens, guys croakin' in the saddle. What if that happened and her guys had to clean up the mess, they'd order another car to pick her up out front, get her the hell away from this area. She probably had sex. Rumors have been surfacing about Madeline for years *and* with an election year coming up, you better believe the opposition is dying to make a slip of the tongue, and that's why they have to be careful."

"He has a point." Lucien agreed with him.

"Then who was in the body bag? The psychic is still alive. I asked the concierge if he's back from New York and he said yes, nothing more. The building's staff doesn't know what happened."

Eddie pointed a finger at me. "OK, maybe she whacked the guy. Her men moved the body, dumped it somewhere. You know, like Vince Foster. Ever think of that?"

"We of the press know Mrs. Chambers had a taste for younger men. She's flirted with many of us," Lucien added.

"The man in the hall looked younger, and by the way how did you escape her clutches?" Lucien was noticeably handsome.

"By playing dumb." He answered my question but Eddie didn't want us getting off the track. "Andrea, did you see the man come out of that apartment?"

"No. I saw him in the hall, but . . . why did he take the stairs instead of the elevator?"

"Elevators are slow, he might have been in a hurry, maybe he was visiting someone on a lower floor. I'd love to say this is the scoop of the century, but I'm afraid you have no story. You don't know who was in the body bag and you didn't see the mystery guy leave that apartment. You saw him walking in the hall."

"I know what I saw, I know what I heard and I saw how it ended," I stubbornly replied. He was annoying me. I wanted Lucien to love me again, I wanted him to have this scoop and this man was tearing everything apart.

"She was on television! Lighting the tree! And the White House says that she's sick as a dog with the flu"

"I know. That's the only thing that throws me."

"Well, that's a helluva lot to throw you with."

I quickly added, "but I also know someone was in my apartment."

"Was anything missing?"

"No. But Lucien left a message on my answering machine, and somebody played it. The light never flickered and when I replayed, there were several new messages."

"Is it possible the machine malfunctioned? After all, it is a machine."

"I suppose so, but it never happened before." I decided not to tell him about the Texan's call. He'd pooh-pooh it unless he saw the man make the call.

I was no match for Eddie Wallace, who needed facts not hunches. I could see that Lucien felt sorry for me, and suddenly he came to my aid. "Andy, does your building have security cameras?"

"Yes, at all entrances and exits."

"Then they must store the videos. Okay, let's take a look, we know what she wore, let's see if she left the building by another exit, while her agents cleaned up a mess. Let's test your theory, Ed."

Eddie quickly agreed. "We're not above doing a little detective work ourselves to ferret out the truth." He rose and paced the floor planning the scenario, "Okay, okay. We have an assignment. We're doing a piece on the security in luxury buildings, and we expect them to be the best. We don't involve Andrea, we don't even know Andrea. We're doing a story for the Herald."

The next day Eddie and Lucien appeared at the concierge's desk displaying their credentials, asking to see a cross section of security tapes for a story the Herald was doing on modern building security. The manager was so impressed by the dynamic duo, he immediately gave his approval. It was good for his reputation to have a well run, secure building. He escorted them to the building's security office, where a man was on duty at all times monitoring the numerous T.V. screens which taped all of the building's entrances and exits. When they asked for several tapes to view; one on a weekend, two during the week, the surveillance tapes for Thursday, December 3rd were missing.

CHAPTER 9

"Mr. President." Charlie MacIsaac addressed the silver haired gentleman sitting at the oval office desk. His refined manner and impeccable dress were befitting a man who held the highest office in government. MacIsaac, his chief of staff, stood before him, hands clasped behind his back. He rocked back and forth on the balls of his feet, showing his uneasiness at the unpleasant subject he was about to bring up. It was the "Madeline Problem," and it worried him. "I think it's about time we discussed our problem. I think it's time we drop a hint to the public . . . you know, that the First Lady is gravely ill." The president looked up, sliding his glasses to the tip of his nose, peering over them. His blue eyes took on the color of his steel gray suit. He blinked several times to clear his vision before focusing on his young confidante. They could have been father and son.

The President was reflective for a moment collecting his thoughts. "I dread this moment, I dread this moment!" He sighed, shaking his head.

"I do too, Sir, but it must be dealt with."

"Charlie, this is going to be a media circus," he said, removing his glasses, setting them down on the large, handsome desk. He was worried about the feeding frenzy of the press if they caught wind of some impropriety. "No, Tom, everything will be handled with dignity, I'll see to that. I have everything planned down to the last detail. I know how hard it's been for you, but try not to think about the coming days, try to concentrate on other things, like your reelection. That's your goal. There's nothing you can do for Madeline."

"I know Charlie, I *have* been thinking of the coming year, it's kept me sane." His eyes misted as he lowered his head, his jaw hung slack and Charlie MacIsaac realized how much he aged since he took office four years ago.

"I've never had such a devastating week in my entire life, and you're right, I can't change a damn thing. The only thing I have now, is this office; I have to win in November for her. I've *got* to keep my promises to the American people, and I've got to push those programs through the House." He became alive speaking about them. "I've got to finish what I started and I pray every day that the good Lord sees me through." It sounded like campaign rhetoric but Charlie was relieved to finally hear him speak so enthusiastically, he was a tough old bird, and Charlie was proud of his strength and endurance. He was glad that the strange events of the past week didn't make a basket case of him.

Thomas E. Chambers barely squeaked into office four years ago, but with his winning ways, he had become very popular, charming the press and the populace with his straightforward, no nonsense approach to problems. "He walks with kings and still bears the common touch," The Times wrote of him. The Washington Tribune championed his causes. "Thomas E. Chambers has the qualities it takes to become one of our nation's greats." They knew that any hint of scandal would be devastating in an election year. They remembered the unflattering "if you lie with dogs you wake up with fleas" that an ultra-conservative paper wrote about the President. Many thought it was about his political allies but Charlie knew they were referring to Madeline. The restrictions on her private life made her all the more likely to create mischief, a sign of her independence, but a powerful man who couldn't control his errant wife wouldn't wash with the average male voter.

The President's hand trembled as he signed a letter and rested his pen. It was the only sign of strain that Charlie had noticed. "This has been a nightmare for me, and yet I'm carrying on as though nothing has happened; when indeed everything has happened. My private world has collapsed. I tell lies to everyone, telling them that Madeline is ill, or telling the help that she's away . . . ill."

Charlie was moved by the man's fortitude and quiet resolve. He placed his hands on the desk, leaning forward, speaking with quiet passion. "I want you to know how deeply I feel for you, Tom. Don't let my business attitude fool you. I'm hurting inside. But this is something we've got to deal with. You . . . Thomas, you are a great president, there's no doubt about that. You've won people over who used to despise you! There's too much at stake to be dragged down by this." The President seemed not to be listening. A faraway look crept into his eyes, much to Charlie's annoyance. *Oh no, not again, he's thinking of her.* He could see it coming; the adulation of Madeline. The President was starting to reminisce during every private conversation they had. It drove the young man wild. *There's work to be done and he's fantasizing about Madeline,* but he took a seat, and indulged his commander in chief by feigning interest, knowing there were very few people the President of the United States could discuss his personal life with. So, Charlie clenched a fist, digging his nails into the palm of his hand to prevent him from yawning with boredom. *Christ,* he thought, *he knows the circumstances, why doesn't he just write her off.* But he remained silent, while Thomas Chambers came alive.

"I was a lonely widower, with no children. All I did was work, work, work! My brother and his wife literally begged me to come visit in Ohio, and one weekend I did. I surprised them. I don't know if they really liked that, but they acted happy to see me. I was a full fledged senator and I was treated with great respect. I was treated like royalty at their country club . . . and then I saw her." He sighed, closing his eyes, reliving the moment. "She was in lace, looking like a *Florentine Bella* in the *quattro centro,* the most beautiful woman I had ever seen. The woman of my dreams. My perfect woman . . . with those beckoning blue eyes, but her attitude was unequivocally dropdead." He laughed, shaking his head in admiration. "She confused me and I liked that, and that night I made a vow that I would win her, and I did, and I paid dearly for it. That vixen wielded her seductive powers over me until . . . " His voice broke and it took him a minute to gain control. "Madeline could have toppled kingdoms. I was a seasoned politician and she made mush out of me, as she did every other man she met. They flocked to her, but she married me, and I made her the First Lady, I did that!" Charlie nodded, thinking about the man's unfortunate coup; about the rumors and innuendo surrounding the woman who stopped at nothing to get her husband elected, and subsequently had become bored with the role. He was surprised that a blackmailer hadn't come forward in the past four years. But he knew Madeline was clever; somehow she would have eliminated him. *What the hell, if he insists on making a saint out of her, so be it.* He was just glad the flashbacks were coming to an end. He had heard that story a hundred and one times.

"Are the men outside?" the President asked, coming out of his reverie.

"Yes, Sir."

"Show them in, please, I'd like to thank them." The young man rose and went to the door, opening it and waving the two men inside. They had been waiting in the corridor and they nodded their greetings and stood at attention until they were invited to sit down. "Are these men trustworthy?" the President asked his chief of staff as though they were alone.

"Absolutely, Mr. President." Charlie stuck to protocol. "They've taken care of every detail."

"Then thank you, gentlemen. I'm very grateful for all you've done. You've been with Mrs. Chambers since she became First Lady?"

"I have, Sir," Mitch Levett replied. "Agent Nichols replaced John Stanger who retired to private life about six months ago."

"My wife was a beautiful and vibrant woman, married to an old man." Charlie's eyes narrowed wondering where this conversation was heading. "My wife had become impatient with me. I'm an old man and a very busy one, I had no time for her anymore. I think her affair was a way of getting back at me for neglecting her." Charlie rolled his eyes. He was blaming himself, making excuses for her. *Shut up, Thomas,* he thought. *You're the President. You don't have to explain to anyone.*

"Which of you found her?"

"I did, Sir." Rolland Nichols raised his hand like a schoolboy. "I called my partner immediately, he phoned the doctor and the paramedics on our cell phone. We did everything we could to save her."

"Yes, Sir, everything. And it was all done discreetly," Mitch added.

"Thank you, yes, Dr. Foster said she had had a massive coronary, and it was just too late."

"All we could think about was trying to spare you any embarrassment and getting the bod . . . your wife out of there unseen. Our allegiance is to you," Mitch said, causing the President's eyes to mist as he looked directly at the men.

"I value your loyalty." He spoke sincerely to the men whose quick thinking prevented a scandal. "Although she looked like one, my wife was no longer an ingenue, and her body finally deceived her, that's what really happened. Do you know who the gentleman was?"

Charlie was becoming uncomfortable with the questions. *Why doesn't he just shut up, not be so damned curious?* "Not yet, Sir," Mitch said. "We were able to get hold of the surveillance tapes for that day, but we have nothing so far. We're checking further with A.L.A., the Arab Liberation Alliance. It's a group that the First Lady was sympathetic to. She entertained members of the group at several White House luncheons. And she lent her name to several fundraisers."

"I know," President Chambers answered. "Is there any reason to believe she was involved with one of them?"

"The psychic Landry found an Arab newspaper after one of the visits."

"Then find him. I want to know who this man is."

"We're getting the member list and the luncheon guest lists."

"Do it! If he stayed with her and got help, she may still be alive. I want him found!" He held their gaze, furrows deepening across his scowling brow. This was an order! Now it was up to them to find him and they knew what they had to do when they found him. "Was there evidence of intercourse?" His voice was quietly controlled but it was such a painful question, Charlie began to feel a twinge of nausea. He wondered if his boss derived some kind of masochistic pleasure from asking these questions. He rose, taking charge.

"Yes, Sir. That's why we should make the announcement before a blackmailer gets involved." The others nodded in agreement. "We can't continue to use the lookalike. The agency was sworn to secrecy. They were told that the First Lady was ill, and you didn't want to disappoint millions of children who look forward to the tree lighting. It tied in with our plans, but we can't continue the charade. The household staff thinks she's away, we're telling people she's ill, it's madness to continue like this. Enough time has elapsed to throw off any hint of scandal."

"He's right, Sir," the others agreed, leaving the President to ponder his thoughts.

"Then take care of it, Charlie. Do what you must to protect my wife's good name."

Shit, Charlie thought. *What good name?* But instead he assured his man that nothing was overlooked and the few people who knew the truth could be trusted. "Frank Landry was back in town, unaware of what really happened. As far as he knew, the First Lady used his place in return for celebrity referrals, as far as he knew, she left there alive."

The President rose, slightly nodding in understanding, looking vulnerable. The most powerful man in the world, looked forlorn as he quietly told his chief of staff, "Charlie, call Dr. Foster, then make the announcement!"

◆ ◆ ◆

When they left the oval office, Rolland Nichols hung back while his partner was shown to the men's room. It was the first time he could speak to Charlie MacIsaac alone. As they waited in the corridor of that splendid house, Rolland removed something from his pocket and held it in a cupped hand. "I was first on the scene, using an emergency pass key and I found this." He slowly opened his hand revealing a small crush of glass protected by a silky web. "Nobody knows about this, not even Mitch, I thought I'd give it to you." Charlie squinted, quickly removing his glasses from his pocket. He stared at the small plastic bag which contained the crushed ampule. "It's Amyl Nitrate, she must have sniffed it before climaxing to get a better high. The only problem, is that it puts your heart in overdrive, the beats stumbling over each other, often leading to cardiac arrest. We've seen cases like this."

"Stupid bitch, it was bad enough she fucked around, she had to use this shit." His vehement language shocked Rolland. "I'll have forensics check it out on some pretext. Will this show up in an autopsy? They'll want one you know."

"Yes, it's going to show."

"Maybe I can talk to them, keep it from the President, he's suffered enough. By the way, did you sanitize the place?"

"Didn't have to, it wasn't a crime scene, she just upped and died in the saddle."

"And the Arab connection?"

"We couldn't find a clue. We're working on getting her luncheon guest lists."

"I remember those, and I couldn't figure them out, I advised against them, but you know Madeline. She always got her way."

When Mitch finally joined them, the three men made their way through those august halls toward the elevator which took them to the first family's second floor private quarters, which housed the large walk-in freezer storing the First Lady's body.

"Our cottage industry cryogenics" Mitch muttered to his partner, relieving the tension as they walked through a wall of cold blocking the entrance like an invisible barrier.

With so many sides of beef and poultry hanging like stalactites, and so many cartons of frozen foods packed on the shelves, nobody paid much attention to the long package placed against the back wall behind this frozen forest. It was clearly marked in red felt tip pen which read: *Property of the First Family. Choice parts of a Montana elk. Do not touch!* They lifted it, as puffs of frosty breath escaped their lips.

Charlie had told the chef that a family friend had shot and dressed the elk, the chef had looked forward to making Montana Elk pie for the President. He had found the menu served at Teddy Roosevelt's first formal White House dinner, which included Montana Elk pie. He had hoped Mrs. Chambers would return soon so he could discuss it with her and he was disappointed when Charlie told him that the first family was donating it to a homeless shelter. Charlie signed for it and the three men carried the package with gloved hands, back to the President's private quarters placing it on a huge plastic sheet which covered the bed. The busy holiday season was the perfect time to make this announcement. Charlie picked up the phone summoning Dr. Foster to the White House. They would have to pretend she died tonight.

When Dr. Foster arrived, they waited for Charlie to contact the President's press secretary telling him the shocking news. Shortly afterward he read his statement to the press. "Madeline Chambers, First Lady of the United States has suffered a massive coronary and has died this evening at the White House. Mrs. Chambers, who had a history of heart problems, wished to remain in the White House, attended by Dr. Lucas Foster, the first family's personal physician. Everything had been done to accommodate her wish and to make her as comfortable as possible in her final hours."

The announcement was made at 9 PM. The cover up had begun twelve days earlier. Everything had been done to remove her far enough away from the scene of her tryst to preserve a proper image. No more than ten people knew the truth; Andrea Evanovich was one of them.

CHAPTER 10

A light snowfall had started, making it a perfect night for our Christmas gala. A steady stream of taxis and limos discharged their passengers as glistening snowflakes sprinkled them like fairy dust as they hurried past the gold-tasseled doorman and into the shelter of our beautifully decorated store. In a dull city like Washington, we were the big ticket. Tonight, wives replaced girlfriends, but our lips were sealed.

As Karl and I air kissed arriving guests, they were immediately served by red jacketed butlers circulating with champagne on silver trays. "I love this store," a senator's wife gushed, clasping her hands. "It's like stepping back in time," . . . and in some ways it was. *Maison Russe* was a replica of the original Faberge store in Paris. High vaulted ceilings, pegged floors and a sparkling wheel of crystal hung overhead, dominating the room.

Art for sale covered the walls and the long showcases displayed jewels, which we were internationally known for. Many of the guests caught the flavor of a bygone era, a gentler time, and in keeping with that spirit, it was Karl's cardinal rule that there would be no pressure to buy. He allowed everyone to enjoy the evening of champagne, caviar and Balalaika music playing in the background. He allowed his customers this one free night, he would get them later. Tonight, with me at his side, Karl Merriam was a perfect host.

I saw Karl's lover watching us as we stood chatting with arriving guests. His eyes narrowed, he looked resentful. He would have loved being in my shoes, and he hated me for it, but it was Karl's decision that I be at his side this evening and that drove Mal wild. Later, as I passed him going to the ladies room, I stopped to speak.

"Are you enjoying the evening Mal?" The second I looked into his glazed eyes, I was sorry I spoke. The corners of his mouth tilted upward in an insincere smile as he hissed out his insults to me. "Well, if it isn't Handy Andy, the girl with the roughhewn intellect. Now tell me, where was it you learned this business? On Granny's farm or somewhere else in the Boonies?" He laughed for Karl's benefit, pretending we were having a pleasant chat. "How presumptuous of you to ask *me* if I'm enjoying myself at my own party. You're the donkey and don't you *ever* forget it."

He startled me with his viciousness. I felt the anger rise, but I remained calm. He would love me to lose control, make a fool of myself, but I didn't.

"I won't, Mal. But my so-called rural education has kept you in antiques and Armani. And when our boss needs an expert opinion, he calls me . . . not you." I abruptly turned and walked past a group of ladies in little black dresses lined up like crows on a wire. I wore red. It gave me the confidence and determination not to let this stupid man spoil our big night. He was dangerous and I must try to avoid him at all costs. He was jealous of me and my credentials, he was jealous that Karl doted on me in every phase of the business, but in spite of all that, I knew I would never be welcome in their lives.

When I returned, Mal had taken my place standing next to Karl who was still greeting late-comers. Not surprisingly, Karl ignored him and didn't include him in his conversation with a darkly, handsome man, he felt it wasn't good for business to let people know about his private life. After all, many female customers had a crush on Karl. As I neared, Karl waved me toward him, and I thought I had met the handsome man before. He was about forty, with a neatly trimmed mustache.

"Have we met?" I asked.

"Not yet, I've been waiting for you." He flashed his white teeth.

"Mr. Majdallani had an appointment with you the day you were out ill."

"I'm so sorry, sir."

"No, no . . . it was all right because he ended up canceling, and that's why he's here tonight, with the distinguished ambassador of the Ukraine." A big, rumpled man, whose eyes had Epicanthic folds, he was obviously of Tartar ancestry. As we shook hands I was certain I had seen the younger man before. Suddenly my imagination went into overdrive causing the hair on the back of my neck to stand out. Recognition finally flickered. Could he be the man in the hall? The demon lover? A spine tingling chill made my vagina contract. I rubbed my arms pretending I was cold, and I wondered. Could he have seen me when I opened my door for the paper? Is that why he wanted to meet me? As I readied to excuse myself he spoke in an accented voice, gently rolling his R's.

"Mr. Merriam has spoken so highly of your expertise, my dear, I most certainly will be a customer. Especially if a beautiful woman educates me."

"Sir," I bravely answered, "You are perfectly safe. We do no business here tonight."

"We can make an exception. I'll even throw in a nice little box," Karl laughed. Mal was desperately trying to join us but the big Ukrainian saved me.

"Madame." He spoke in his mother tongue. "I'm told you speak my language."

I lifted my glass and toasted him in Russian.

"Yes, your Excellency," I answered in perfect Russian. "But booze is the international language tonight." He let out a hearty guffaw, shaking his head in agreement while he threw down another vodka. No sissy champagne for him.

"You have heard of the Winter Egg?" He spoke slowly, in English.

"Yes," I answered.

"It is missing? No?"

"Not really. It was out of circulation for a while."

"Why?"

"It was in a very private collection."

"Is it still in this *very private collection?*" he mimicked me.

"No, it was sold."

"Can you obtain it for me?"

I knew he was testing me. "Your Excellency, you have it." He looked surprised, then threw his head back and laughed. "I'm certain you know what I mean. At any rate, it's back in one of your new countries, or so the story goes."

"Very good. This woman is up to date on knowledge. Where exactly does it rest? In the Ukraine?"

"My guess, and it's only a guess, is that the Winter Egg is in Russia. With all the renewed interest in the Czar, I have a feeling it's right there in St. Petersburg with Yeltsin. Some say it was his payback for his cooperation with the west." Bravely I turned my attention to the other man. "And you, sir, why did you cancel your appointment with me?" He smiled a perfect smile again and I could see how a woman could be attracted to him. He was tall, well built and extremely polished. Locking his hazel eyes onto mine.

"I no longer had a need for this kind of gift." He waved toward the showcases. "My lady changed her mind." Again flashing his white teeth against his dusky skin.

Because she's dead? I thought. Instead I said, "That's women for you. What did your lady choose instead?" I pursued it, taking him off guard.

"A . . . a . . . a Mercedes Benz." He smiled every time he spoke. Back and forth, he closed his mouth and smiled again. I no longer found him attractive, I found him a grotesque smile machine.

"Seems to me you got off cheap," Karl laughed. "He's in the cab and limo business. I'm sure you'll write that off as a business expense."

"I'd like to meet your lady one day, I will be happy to help you with your needs. I'm at your service." We exchanged business cards, and the Arab continued smiling. I hoped he never found out where I lived.

It was nearing 8:30 and guests were beginning to leave. Small clumps of people remained, and that's when I saw him enter. My heart did flip flops. I took a glass of champagne from a passing waiter and took a large swallow. It was Lucien with a beautiful mini-skirted blonde. My heart sunk when I realized they were together.

"Andrea, how have you been?" He walked directly to me with an outstretched hand.

"Fine, Lucien, long time no see, as they say." I shook it, wondering why he was so formal.

"You bet. Sorry we're hitting the tail end, but we were sidetracked. I'd like you to meet Sam Dewar."

"The senator's daughter?" Karl asked.

"Yes, Daddy couldn't make it, so we came instead." *Daddy was either drunk or screwing around,* I thought. We knew he was a philanderer, but he had good taste in jewelry and spent tons of money here.

"Karl, you remember Lucien Champier? Are you still traveling?" I pretended I hadn't known.

"Yep. I'm taking off tomorrow."

"Oh, Lucien, you said you'd try to stay." She batted her eyelashes and rubbed his muscular arm tossing her silky blonde hair. I wanted to punch her. "I really plotted to come tonight, making certain Daddy had another engagement. I want Lucien to buy me something wonderful for Christmas." She spoke in a breathless, sexy voice.

"Like an engagement ring." I blurted it out, watching him squirm.

She hopped up and down kissing his cheek. "Oh, that would be cool. I'd love it. I'm totally besotted with this man."

"We can see that." Karl was becoming bored with her little girl act, as she wrapped herself around Lucien like a sable stole.

Suddenly there was noise at the door as several drivers tried to enter.

"What's going on?" Karl briskly walked to the group.

"Madeline Chambers is dead," a driver informed us. "We heard it on the news."

"Oh, my God." Samantha clasped Lucien's arm.

"How? What happened?" I asked, watching the Iranian who stood a few feet away stonefaced and emotionless. He wasn't smiling now, and I thought he looked directly at another dark complexioned man.

"Heart attack at the White House."

"My God." I locked eyes with Lucien. Shocked guests were leaving, hurrying to get to a T.V. or radio, trying to hear the news. But it wasn't news to us. We were among the privileged few who knew the truth.

CHAPTER 11

"Mr. MacIsaac, I have an urgent call on line two." His secretary interrupted the weekly staff meeting. "It's Dr. Cranford at Walter Reed." Charlie quickly excused himself and took the call in his private office. He knew what it was. Dr. Cranford was the chief pathologist and was assigned to do the autopsy on the First Lady.

Shit, he thought. *He knows she was frozen, I'll have to tell another bullshit story.* "Hello, MacIsaac here."

"Charlie." Joe Cranford greeted him. "I need to see you in person A.S.A.P."

"I'm in a staff meeting. Can it wait until three?"

"No, Charlie, immediately." He lowered his voice. "It's something I can't discuss on the phone."

"I'll be right there." He hung up, told his secretary to hold all his calls and appointed his deputy to carry on.

A car drove him to the huge hospital complex, finding their way through the huge maze and finally arriving at Dr. Cranford's building.

He was expected and an assistant walked him to the doctor's private office, a messy hole in the wall. When the doctor came in, it all made sense to Charlie. Cranford was a small, unkempt man, who looked like he needed a good bath, especially his hair. Charlie could smell scalp odor in that airless room. He was almost afraid to sit down among the papers, books and magazines which were piled all over. But Cranford looked serious enough to pique his curiosity.

"What's this all about? Don't tell me Madeline was pregnant?" he laughed, adding, "Today, anything is possible."

"Charlie, I ran into a problem. So far I'm the only one who knows and I thought I'd better speak to you in person. I'm going to have to report this; Madeline Chambers was murdered."

"What?"

"She was murdered."

"But the heart attack."

"She *did* have a mild coronary, brought on by some crap she used. Probably Amyl Nitrate, there was a trace of it in her system... but she didn't die from it."

"Are you sure?"

"Charlie, I'm a board certified forensic pathologist. Nothing escapes me."

"That's what I'm told."

"Take it from me. Her life was snuffed out. She was suffocated. She was deprived oxygen."

"Were there any marks?" Charlie's breathing became shallow.

"No. The murderer could have held a hand or a pillow over her face while she was gasping for air. But it was out and out murder, and I'll have to report it."

Charlie almost blacked out. He held onto the sides of the chair afraid he would topple over. Dr. Cranford quickly rose and gave him a cup of water which he wouldn't have accepted under any other circumstances, but he needed it and gulped it down. His mind started to work on overdrive. How could he stop all this.

"I'm begging you not to report anything. This will crucify the President. The hell with the election. He may just blow his brains out. I can't be responsible for that." he pleaded with his eyes. "Put yourself in his place. He gave her this honored title of First Lady and she screws some guy using chemicals. Then he murders her for a sexual high. It's stuff that happens to hookers, not First Ladies. I'm begging you to work with me on this."

The pathologist was silent as he folded his hands and looked off in the distance. Charlie stared directly at him, waiting for a reply. After what seemed like hours, he said, "I'm putting my butt on the line. I could lose my license. But I'll be discreet for a while, but only if the two agents who found the body will be called in on the case. Just those two."

Charlie agreed to everything, knowing he was putting Cranford's career and credibility on the line. "Look, nobody is going to second guess you. Dr. Foster signed the death certificate. He said it was a coronary, so that's taken care of. Your pathology report just agrees with it. Leave out the murder and I'll get the two agents to pursue it discreetly. I promise."

"Okay. I'm going to write up two reports and give them to you. You can do with them whatever you will. But my conscience will be clear."

The messy little guy was honorable, Charlie thought, jumping at the offer. "Fine, that'll be fine, thank you. If it's ever discovered, I'll take the heat."

"By the way," Cranford handed him the reports. "She was frozen, probably to disguise the time of death." Charlie said nothing. "Ordinarily, I wouldn't have known. But there were still traces of ice inside. Another hour or two, and I wouldn't have known." Charlie remained silent. *He is good,* he thought.

"Okay," the doctor continued, "I won't ask any questions. Do you know why? I'm afraid you'll tell me."

A less nervous man left the office. *Whew,* Charlie thought. *That was close.* He went to the men's room and rinsed his sweaty hands, cupping one for a fast drink of water. He was beginning to feel better. He would file one report, the one which said she died of a coronary, the other one which told the truth, he would destroy. He would tell nobody, not even the two agents. He was certain Dr. Cranford would remain silent and not compromise his career and reputation. On the ride back, Charlie sat in the backseat of his car and closed his eyes. He began to relax a little. It had been a harrowing day. Thank God it worked out well.

CHAPTER 12

Two days later the First Lady was cremated, her ashes placed in a small, oblong, intricate silver casket. A black satin backdrop framed a photograph propped on a wooden easel. It was a head shot of Madeline, a picture of elegance. The service, which brought dignitaries from near and far, was held in a favorite old cathedral in Virginia. Charlie MacIssac escorted the president from sunny daylight to the dimness of the old cathedral, stopping for a minute to allow their eyes to become accustomed to the change. A cough echoed as the odor of incense permeated the air.

As they walked to their pew, the president looked from side to side scanning the faces, looking for that one face that would identify his wife's lover. He seemed to be asking himself, "Which one this time?" when he was seated in his pew with family and heads of state. Charlie took his own seat behind him, feeling the power of being confidante to the most politically important man in the world. He shared his grief and his secrets. He, Charlie had pulled off a perfect coup. Not even the members of the press were aware of what had gone on. He could relax now.

Eddie Wallace and Lucien Champier covered the 'invitations only' service. They too wondered who the mystery lover was and to what organization he might be connected. Women in love can be targets for unscrupulous men. As they waited in their seats in the back of the vast cathedral, Lucien scanned the congregation.

"I wonder if he had the decency to pay his respects," he whispered.

"It's by invitation."

"I know, but there are ways and means. Nothing has stopped him before."

"Look, a guy who walks out on a dying woman ain't worth poop. He could have made an anonymous call, then left. Don't hold your breath, he's not here."

"I wouldn't bet on it."

A burst of organ music interrupted him as the service began, the eulogy bestowing accolades on the First Lady. By the time they were through she was ready for canonization.

What hypocrites we are, Charlie thought, listening to the whitewash job being done. The President's cheeks glistened in the flickering candlelight and some sniffling was heard, but none of the women ruined their mascara; Madeline didn't cultivate female friends.

Motes of dust floated in a stray shaft of light which filtered through the stained glass windows. The soft organ music made a majestic backdrop for the touching words which were spoken. Charlie suddenly felt emotional, tears stinging his eyes, rolling down his cheeks. He was deeply touched by the eulogy. *I should be*, he thought. *I wrote it.*

◆ ◆ ◆

Before the service was over Lucien stood outside, ready to take pictures of everyone leaving. He took photos of the crowd milling about outside, waiting for the President to emerge. A Marine band played a dirge as the heavy, carved, wooden doors opened, and the ride back to the White House would begin, the President taking Madeline's ashes with him

Lucien and Eddie watched, listened and continued taking photos of the crowd. When they had taken enough of all the dark haired men who attended, they headed to Georgetown, for a much needed beer and hamburger.

"Okay, if Andy can identify him, then what?" he asked Eddie.

"Then we find out if he had ties to any group or if it was just a sexual fling. Remember, Madeline was a gorgeous woman, plus the power of the White House could be a heady combination. It's a mighty conquest for some alien, if indeed he is that. What about the man Andy met at the party?"

The waiter came over to take their order and they stopped their conversation long enough to order two beers and a couple of cheeseburgers. When the waiter left they continued.

"Andy wasn't certain it was the guy. She felt it might be, but as you always say, you gotta have proof."

The cold beers arrived to cool their dry throats. "Okay, let her look at these the minute they're dry," Eddie said. "If she doesn't recognize anyone, we're back to square one and Farid Majdallani. I had him checked. He's an upstanding businessman. He's had that taxi and limo business for four years. Funny thing though, he's never there."

"I'm told he's an elegant guy. I'm sure he doesn't hang out at a garage."

"Wherever he hangs out, we gotta find him."

◆ ◆ ◆

I sat there paralyzed with boredom. My head started to ache as I stared at those pictures, trying to place the face. Trying to jog the memory of that day, but nothing worked.

"I'm totally confused." I leaned back blinking and rubbing my eyes. I hadn't slept well the night before and I was tired. When I finally closed my eyes I still saw those faces.

"Remember, Andy. You've got to be sure," Lucien reminded me.

"I can't be. It was too fleeting." My eyes remained closed.

"What about Mr. Majdallani?"

"He could be, but I can't be sure. I just saw his back. I just had a feeling. He had an appointment with me to buy a gift, then he cancelled on that day. It could all be circumstantial. I can't be certain." I was silent and let my eyelids flicker. I saw Lucien watching me grapple with the enormity of the problem I had started. I could sense he felt sorry for me. Suddenly he was bending over me kissing my lips as a hundred dark celluloid eyes watched. He lifted me into his massive chest and wrapped me tenderly in his arms, his kiss more passionate and intense.

"Don't." I tried to pull away, almost passing out from the pleasure. It had been so long. But he was involved with another woman. I couldn't risk his rejection. I was no match for the beautiful, wealthy blonde who obviously adored him. I would die if he dumped me now. I struggled to pull away as his hot tongue flicked over my ear and neck. "Stop it, stop it." I pushed him with all my might, breathing like I had just finished the marathon. "Stop it, please. You're involved with Samantha. Please stop."

"I'm sorry. I forgot it was over with us."

"Never mind that, what about Samantha?"

"I'm not in love with Samantha. Can I be any clearer than that?"

"Then why are you seeing her?"

"She's a lay." I cringed, hoping he didn't say that about me. "She pursues me, and I can't get rid of her. Plus, she has a lot of connections which helps me in the business."

He knew I was stunned at his crude appraisal of their relationship. And he bitterly continued. "Andy, why are you looking at me so disapprovingly? You taught me to use people. You dumped me because I didn't fit in with your well connected new friends. How many of them are still around?"

I couldn't answer. I grabbed my belongings, I had to leave. Every word he said was true. He followed me to the door.

"Andy, I'm willing to take a chance with you, I'm willing to risk being demolished by you again. If that's not love, I don't know what the hell is."

I couldn't see the stairs as tears flooded my weary eyes. I ran out to the shelter of my car, where I leaned on the steering wheel and sobbed for what seemed like an hour. After what I had done to him, he was still willing to take me back. He deserved better. As I drove off, I looked up at his window, and he waved to me.

CHAPTER 13

Eddie Wallace was now convinced that there was a cover-up. If the First Lady died on December 3rd, why wait almost two weeks before announcing it, unless the circumstances were tawdry. But one thing bothered him. How did she manage to be at the tree lighting? How did they pull that off? What else might Mrs. Chambers be involved in? Did she bite off more than she could chew with some obsessive lover who refused to go away, who threatened to expose the affair? Was blackmail involved?

These questions haunted Eddie day and night. *There's more to this,* he thought, as he left his bed, going to his den to jot down ideas and to doze in fits and starts, sometimes startling his wife who would tap an empty space in the dark, not knowing if he was still beside her or sitting in his big recliner. One night as he thumbed through a People Magazine, he saw an article. The next day he made his move, gathering all the evidence and getting into work at the crack of dawn. Even then, the phones rang, faxes whirred and people gulped down gallons of coffee as a new day began. He knew his publisher would be there. He tapped on the glass door and walked into a big office with sun washed windows. Jack Stern looked up, "Mornin' Glory. Why so early? You have something ripe?"

"I have something I think is rotten. Something you're not going to like as a friend, but something you may love as a publisher."

"What, what?" He seemed impatient. His thin, wiry frame was poised for action as he grabbed a Bic and held it. His craggy face, which bordered on being handsome had a question mark imprinted on it. Jack Stern was born curious, and he inherited the right business, making the Washington Herald one of the most popular and well respected newspapers in America. For a man approaching his golden years he had an endless amount of energy. He was on the go for almost twenty-four hours a day, leaving some to think that he was battery powered. He waved Eddie to the sofa.

Eddie sat down, shoving over a pile of papers that were left on the leather sofa. The atmosphere was charged with vitality as sunlight filled the room. He clicked open his briefcase, telling Jack, Andy's story.

"Okay, okay, so what does it mean? Spell it out," Jack snapped.

"You need proof? I have it. I have photos; before . . . after . . . alive . . . dead, all in the same morning. Madeline Chambers died presumably in the saddle, in an apartment in Virginia. Her body was moved elsewhere, probably the White House, where they kept it a secret for almost two weeks. I don't know why or how; but it's something I would like to know."

"December 3rd, you said." Jack looked at a calendar. "But she was at the White House tree lighting after that, millions of people saw her on TV. Come on, Eddie, get real."

Eddie slowly removed a tape recorder from his briefcase and laid it on the desk with great ceremony, making a point of every movement, watching the boredom grow on Jack's face.

"Yesterday, I made a call and I recorded it."

"That's illegal."

"I know," Eddie said. "But I hesitated to come to you until I had that piece of the puzzle. Now hear this." He triumphantly pushed the button; immediately they heard a voice. "Famous people," the voice said.

"This is Charlie MacIsaac's deputy calling from the White House." Eddie Wallace hoped the operator would take it from there and lead him to the right person, otherwise he would just inquire about their services and try someone else, but he felt hopeful when her voice peaked with excitement.

"Yes, sir, I'll connect you to Mrs. Olson." Relieved at hearing a name, he settled back in his chair and began talking. Mrs. Olson was pleased but surprised to hear from the White House. Once paid, they said she wouldn't hear from them again. So she was happy to know they appreciated the good work and her discretion.

"The pleasure was all mine, sir. The First Lady was so ill, we were delighted you chose us to help."

"None of us wanted to disappoint the children," Eddie fibbed. "All of America was watching." He was beginning to enjoy this.

"Our double had a good time doing it. I also would like to extend my deepest sympathy to the President. I hesitated to write."

"I'll personally convey your message, but as you must know, we'll no longer be using your services."

"I'm aware of that. Mr. MacIsaac made it clear that it was a one time booking. And now that she has died, well, our lookalike is out of business."

They said their good-byes as a steady hum filled the room. Eddie snapped off the tape recorder, and slid a copy of People Magazine through a clear highway of mahogany with stacks of papers on either side of it. It stopped in front of Jack's nose. "See, Famous People, a celebrity lookalike agency in Jersey. People hire them for parties and special events. Take a look at the woman in the gown. She's a dead ringer for Mady Chambers. Charlie must have seen this and gotten the idea, because I saw it and got the same idea.

Jack Stern looked over the two page spread with lookalikes ranging from Cher to Woody Allen; some looked better than others, but the First Lady lookalike was so good, Eddie wondered why they didn't just keep her there.

"This is good work. But do you realize that you impersonated the deputy chief of staff?"

"She never asked my name."

"And," Jack continued, "You recorded a phone conversation without permission or the other person's knowledge. Eddie you're not a cop."

"I know."

"But I don't. Christ, what am I supposed to do with this?" dismissing the evidence with a wave of his hand.

"Pursue it." Eddie wrinkled his forehead like a grumpy sharpei puppy. "I'm giving you proof that the woman was dead for almost two weeks before it was announced. Why? The woman on television was a lookalike."

"So what? Churchill had a double."

"Don't you want to know what really happened, and why?"

"Eddie." Jack's voice was stern. "Does it really matter? It can only deepen the hurt for Tom Chambers, and he's my friend."

"I know that, Jack. That's why I came to you first."

"Or else what?" They eyeballed each other, still careful of crossing the verbal boundary; that area where it no longer remains friendly.

"Jack, you're an honest man, and so am I. 'In a profession of sleazebags, Eddie Wallace is an honest man. He can't be bought, bribed or threatened. He's a seeker of the truth and I am honored to welcome him to this newspaper.' Your words, Jack."

Jack Stern winced at the smooth assault which were his own words being hurled back at him.

"Okay, I said all that, and I meant it. But how can revealing that Mady Chambers screwed some guy on December 3rd, in some apartment in Virginia . . . How can that help anyone?"

Eddie knew he had his attention and hunched his body forward, tapping his forefinger to emphasize each word. "We think this guy was an Arab . . . probably an Iranian."

"Iranians are not considered Arabs."

"Whatever. You know what I mean! That woman was sympathetic to A.L.A.; she lent her name to fundraisers. She entertained them at White House luncheons. Did you know that?" Jack shook his head. "You know why? Because there was little or no publicity about it. She had them there when the President was away or involved with some crisis. I spoke with her scheduling secretary and those luncheon dates always coincided with the President's absence."

"For Christ sake, she was fooling around, she did that when he was away. The luncheons were probably a cover."

"True. But there's something more sinister here. A.L.A. is an educational and cultural group. They hand out scholarships, they help artists, they do a lot of good things. But they're also suspected of funneling money to terrorist groups based in Iran. Do you think Mady Chambers would be involved with that just to get laid?"

"Yes. If she was in love, and according to your source that's exactly what she did. You said your source heard them having sex."

"Yes. But I know there's more to it."

"Like some kind of conspiracy? Come on, Eddie. Do you think the President would allow that?"

"Allow it? She had him so mesmerized he probably didn't even know about it."

Jack rose and walked to the window absently scanning the street below, watching pedestrians scurrying about like ants. He finally turned to face his award winning journalist. "Again, I'm asking you. Do you really think that Tom Chambers would allow that?" Eddie was exasperated. Was Jack suddenly so thick?

"No. But he didn't know about the affair either. She was supposed to be seeing a psychic and she's boinkin' some guy. I feel there's more to it and I want your permission to go ahead."

"No, not yet. Give me a few days."

"One day," Eddie said, holding up a finger. "One day. And if you don't give me the green light, I guarantee it'll end up in the tabloids."

"Is that a threat?"

"No, a fact beyond my control." He gathered up his evidence and walked out, disappointed his boss didn't back him up on this.

"Ed," Jack called to him, stopping him in his tracks. "I have a compelling case for not running this story." Eddie turned to face him. "Tom Chambers knew about the affair. He discussed it with me. He blamed himself." Eddie said nothing more, he just turned and walked out. The second he left, Jack Stern reached for the telephone.

CHAPTER 14

The president answered his private line. "Hello Jack, good to hear from you. I'm fine, I'm fine... I'm right in the middle of something, can I call you back within the hour?" He hung up, thinking, *if Jack called, it must be important, and, most importantly it must be private.* He analyzed the call and the timing of it.

Jack was relieved. He was given a reprieve from the unpleasant task at hand. His sweaty palm left a moist imprint on the receiver. *God, how am I going to do this?* It was such a delicate matter... anything concerning Madeline was delicate with Tom Chambers. He hoped his old friend would understand, would forgive him for making this call. Jack was one of the select few who had immediate access to the president. Their long friendship and his staunch support made him an invaluable confidant, yet the president didn't confide in him this time. *Maybe it's all hogwash*, he wondered, *maybe it's nothing.* He hoped things would remain the same after this, but he had to get to the bottom of it before Eddie's source sold it to a tabloid.

An uneasiness started to wash over him. He paced the floor, not able to concentrate on anything. He went over a mental script, worrying about approaching the problem diplomatically. When his phone rang, he hesitated to answer it but it was his private line and he knew who it was. After exchanging greetings he was shocked at his own directness.

"Tom, you have to level with me because it's the only way I can help you." He lowered his voice. "Did Madeline die on December 3rd, in an apartment in Virginia? I won't ask you anything more."

The president hesitated, but he knew better than to lie to

him. "Yes Jack, she did. We had to do what we did to preserve the dignity of her position. It also had to be done to save me in an election year. Does it answer your question?"

"Thank you, I appreciate your honesty."

"But how did you know?"

"Nothing is sacred, Tom. People find things out. I'll do everything to kill it."

"Please. But how did anyone know?" He was pathetically stumped. "Could it have been the paramedics? They were the only two besides Dr. Foster and the two agents."

"No, it was somebody who lives in that building. They have pictures of Mady arriving and leaving in the ambulance. They have the license plate on the sedan. They have Dr. Foster. They have it all on film, shot from somewhere above."

"Can we buy them?"

"I don't know. We're dealing with an . . . honest man. But I might be able to kill it." Jack decided to leave it at that, don't explore the possibility of international intrigue. He felt this was enough for one day. He felt Tom Chambers had had enough.

◆ ◆ ◆

The president buzzed for his Chief of Staff, who immediately appeared.

" 'Oh, what a tangled web we weave . . . ' Everybody thinks that's Shakespeare, Charlie," he calmly said.

"I know. I've made that mistake myself."

"I just heard from Jack Stern. Brace yourself, Charlie. Somebody has pictures of Madeline at the apartment on the day she died."

Charlie squeezed his eyes shut, his face drained of any remaining color, trying to salvage hope. "So?"

"So it means, she's on film arriving and leaving in a body bag."

"They can't see her face, it could be anyone, we'll deny it."

"Anyone could blow up the picture and find out the car belongs to the presidential fleet, and those two agents were Mady's men."

"Then we have a problem."

"Not if you can get hold of the film and destroy it."

Charlie sat down; it would be a long afternoon and a longer than usual week. His mind started to work, trying to solve this new dilemma.

"Shall I offer payment?"

"Offer anything, but get those shots. I can't have my beautiful wife remembered that way. Please, Charlie, do something."

"I'll try." He felt anger at Madeline for creating this predicament, and now he, Charlie, was the only one who knew the truth of the murder and he was the only one who could solve this. It was getting out of hand. He wondered if he should call Jack Stern and find out who had those pictures, then he might be able to deal with it, offer payment or steal them. But knowing absolutely nothing made him feel helpless. For once, he had no plan . . . The enemy was anonymous. He had to forget about Jack Stern, he would never reveal his source. His only hope were the two agents. He would have to level with them, trust them. He would have to tell them about the murder and hope they could uncover something.

◆ ◆ ◆

Eddie grabbed his phone on the first ring. He knew it was Jack. As quick as a flash, he heaved his big frame out of his chair and despite his big, heavy shoes, there was a spring in his step. He was at Jack's door almost before the man had a chance to hang up. Jack looked up. "Close the door." His voice was all business, it didn't bode well for the project.

"I want you to drop it."

"Why, Jack?"

"I'm asking you as a personal favor . . . I'm beggin' you."

"Is there anything to it?"

"Yes." Jack knew enough not to lie to him.

"I respect your honesty. I'll drop it . . . but . . . "

Oh shit, here it comes, Jack thought.

"If it's anything more than an affair, I have to pursue it. Fair enough?"

"I'll buy that. Tom could have lied to me, but he didn't. Give the man a break."

"Again, if it's just an affair, I will. But if our national security was compromised . . . I can't." He stood firm and Jack knew that he meant it, and he knew he was right. He extended his hand as Eddie shook it. Two decent men inadvertently caught in Madeline's web. She was controlling men, even in death.

Eddie Wallace thumbed through his file of informants. If he could only find ONE to nail the truth about Madeline's death, it would help him decide whether to continue. Right now he was in a quandary. If she died in the saddle, he'd write it off. But . . . if there was more to it? Now, that was what great scoops are made of, and he needed a great scoop. He felt some younger journalists stepping on his heels. He needed a scoop.

As he looked for that magic name; any name connected to the funeral home, Dr. Foster's office, the paramedics or the medical examiner's office, he suddenly spotted a likely ally. A lab technician at Walter Reed Hospital, someone who helped him in the past. He checked his watch, and decided it was too early, it was better to call her at home from an outside telephone.

Several days later, she called from a pay phone. *I love this gal,* Eddie thought, as he jotted down her information. Their brief exchange at a busy mall suited both of them. Eddie discovered that Madeline's death was by suffocation; and the single mother earned some much needed cash.

CHAPTER 15

The two agents met with Charlie in his office. He had lunch brought in. Plump roast beef and cheese sandwiches on pumpernickel, with cole slaw and pickles, sides of crispy fries and onion rings. It was the best lunch they had eaten in weeks. When they were almost finished, he said, "Jack Stern called the President today. Somebody contacted him with pictures of the comings and goings of that day, you're all in it, plus the ambulance and the body bag. They know she died December 3rd in an apartment in Virginia."

The men held their last bite in mid-air, stunned at this new wrinkle which spoiled a perfectly great lunch.

"What do you want to do?" Rolland asked.

"Find the whole enchilada."

"It's funny you should mention it, because somebody comes to mind."

"Who?"

"A neighbor who lives next door to the psychic. We think she was home that day . . . We found a camera in her place."

"Then get on it. What above the lover, any progress?" He held back telling them about the murder. First things first.

"Yes, we did a lot of investigating," Mitch said, pulling out a sheaf of papers, looking at them before passing them along to Charlie. They were copies of the White House luncheons guest lists and contributors. The First Lady hosted four such luncheons for A.L.A., White House security provided some information on each guest, a standard procedure, the rest, they dug up on their own. There were about thirty guests at each luncheon. All businessmen from the Arab American Community, except for a few Ukrainian and Russian diplomats. Several of the guests brought women, but most attended alone. Five men were unmarried, which meant nothing in an affair. However, Mitch pointed out an interesting observation, "the Russian diplomats and these two guys," he pointed to two Middle Eastern names, "attended every luncheon. Why? As I recall, there was a lot of Arabic babbling and handshaking going on with these guys."

"Perhaps they're officers of the organization," Charlie said.

"A Ukrainian and a Russian?"

"Let's find out." Charlie gave them the green light.

They narrowed the list down to five Middle Eastern men. All were single and attractive and all of them did business in the Virginia/DC area. One man owned a restaurant, one a dry cleaning chain. Two owned taxi and limousine companies and one man owned an exclusive women's shop. He also had an import license. When they checked their home addresses, the women's shop owner, Ali Sahlool, lived at the same address that the First Lady had visited. It was also Andrea Evanovich's address.

"Bingo, I think we have a connection." Mitch said.

"It makes sense. Tell me, why didn't we see anyone suspicious leaving the building? Why was there nothing on the surveillance tapes we confiscated?"

Before the others had a chance to answer, Mitch crowed, "Because he lives there . . . "

"Right. When he left Madeline, he just went to his apartment," Charlie said.

"That's good work, but go easy and make certain. If they happen to find his body one day, we don't want it coming back to us."

So the men continued their investigation, with one hand tied behind their backs, without knowing the truth, that the First Lady was actually murdered

One afternoon as they entered Ali Sahlool's apartment, Rolland felt a flutter of excitement, a thrill he always had when entering someone's premises illegally. It was a gloomy place facing the shady side of the building. It was not as cheerful and sunny as the apartments they had seen upstairs. It was a man's place. Comfortably furnished with big leather furniture. A wine leather sofa finished off with brass nailhead trim dominated the room. There were leather club chairs on each side of it with matching ottomans. The deep raspberry Persian rug gave the room a somber, Mid-Eastern look.

They looked through papers, magazines, and books which were piled high on the shelves of the built-in bookcases, most were in Arabic. They tossed them on the floor in piles looking for some clue, Mitch groaning as he bent over to replace them on the shelves. The ornate silver coffee table held an empty coffee container, which they took for prints. He wouldn't remember it. But the living room, kitchen and bathroom held nothing of significance. They went to the bedroom looking for something to link him to the First Lady. It was equally somber. The bedcover and draperies were rich in deep reds, russets and olive, with velvet and satin pillows to deepen the luxury. They looked in drawers, in expensive suit pockets, under the area rugs, in the linen closet, but there were no love notes, no inscribed gifts, no intimate garments to be kept as souvenirs. The only thing they saw was "Casablanca", which was written on a note pad in a night table drawer. "Probably a reminder to pick up the video," Mitch suggested. There was nothing on his computer screen, they came up empty.

Before leaving they called the exclusive woman's store, "Minouche", and asked for the proprietor. "Mr. Sahlool is out of town," they were told, so they raced over, finding this a perfect opportunity to speak to the help. A hush covered the store as they entered, interrupting a sale. Several women were being shown suits for two and three thousand dollars. Sales help spoke in whispers, and Mitch broke the spell. In a loud voice he said his piece, flipping his badge for effect. He knew they'd want to get rid of him in a hurry. "A vender, Mrs. Burgess, has filed a complaint against Mr. Sahlool, the proprietor of this place." The saleswoman was aghast, as she helplessly looked around for support, all eyes were on her.

"On Thursday, December 3rd she sold several hand-knit sweaters to Mr. Sahlool. She was given a check which bounced. You know, it didn't clear, and every time she calls, he's not available."

The saleswoman left her customer and rushed to the back, telling the manager. They both came out holding an appointment book.

"Mr. Sahlool wasn't even here on December 3rd. He was in Michigan. He didn't return until Monday. See." She held the appointment book for him to see. "That lady is lying."

The men were crestfallen, they had pinned their investigation on this man.

"What did he do in Michigan?"

"He is opening another shop there."

"Did somebody else use his place?"

"Possibly. But what has that got to do with it?"

"A great deal," Rolland interjected. "That's where the transaction took place. What airline did he fly with?"

"Tops Air. I booked it myself."

When they checked with Tops Air there was indeed an Ali Sahlool on flight 231 to Detroit, Michigan.

"Now what?" Mitch said.

"We have to find out who stayed there, and we have to find out if Ms. Evanovich is the photographer and what exactly she knows."

"We know where she works, we know where she lives, the rest shouldn't be too hard."

◆ ◆ ◆

It was near one P.M. when they drove up to *Maison Russe*. They sat there awhile, trying to figure out the right approach, their growling stomachs interrupting their conversation.

"There she is," Rolland said, looking down at a picture of Andrea which they got at the DMV. Mitch hopped out and walked toward the store as Rolland turned on the ignition and pulled up slowly behind the cab Andy got into. When Mitch turned to look, both cars had disappeared and he found himself entering the beautiful store. Suddenly he was transported into another era, leaving behind him the problems of the past weeks. He envisioned the beautiful Madeline inside this place, her taste and elegance would have been perfect in this kind of setting. Yet, he was with her for four years and never remembered accompanying her here, it was odd. She certainly knew about this place, unless her lovers did her shopping for her.

He walked to a vitrine and gazed at the Faberge pill boxes, pins and jewel-encrusted ornaments from another time, wishing that somehow he could have given her a gift from such a place. All those years he suppressed his love for her, doing his duty, protecting her, and now, in death, he must do it again.

An important looking man stood behind one of the cases and Mitch walked over to him, showing his badge. "Mitch Levett. Is Andrea Evanovich here?" He saw the surprise on the man's face and quickly added, "It's about a robbery that took place in her building."

"Oh." Karl Merriam was relieved. "You just missed her. She left for lunch a minute ago."

"I'm surprised your help can leave on the lunch hour." He looked around at the few people being helped.

"We don't get the lunch crowd." Karl spoke without any hint of snobbery. "Andy didn't tell me she was burglarized."

"She wasn't, it was her neighbor. Some valuables were stolen on Thursday, December 3rd. I'd like to know if she saw or heard anything unusual on that day. I believe she was home ill."

"Yes. She's only missed one day in two years, that's why I remember it. She'll be back about three."

"Thanks, you've got a great store here. Tell me, did the late First Lady ever shop here?"

"No. She seemed to have a taste for modern pieces—Bulgari, Fred Joallier."

And cash, Mitch thought, remembering the many times her secretary returned gifts for cash.

"Come browse any time." Karl handed him his card.

"Browse, I'd like to buy . . . on lay away."

"That could be arranged," Karl said good naturedly.

They laughed as he left the store, knowing definitely that Andy was home on December 3rd. He would rendezvous with his partner and together they would try to set a plan in motion to get hold of that film.

CHAPTER 16

When I saw him, my legs turned to wet noodles. Lucien waited outside. He was so handsome in his navy blazer and sparkling white shirt . . . and a tie. He did it for me.

We embraced comfortably for the first time since our reacquaintance, and I floated into The Directoire introducing him to the *maitre d'*, who showed us to a good table. Lucien was impressed.

"You really rate."

"The store rates, we're a very good account." The French restaurant was elegantly furnished in the *directoire* period with striped wallpaper and lots of expensive fabric hanging all over. I always found the heavy brass chairs a little uncomfortable but after a drink or two I didn't notice. And certainly today, I wouldn't notice a thing. We engaged in small talk, not taking our eyes off each other. I hungered for him, and he knew it. Slowly he turned the conversation to the problem. "I wanted to see you, to get a first hand reaction."

"To what?" I naively asked.

"Tom Chambers and Jack Stern are old buddies. He asked Eddie to drop the story."

"Then they must believe it." Disappointed that this lunch wasn't more personal.

"They believe it, all right. The President knew his wife."

"Well, should we go to someone else with the story?" Andy said.

"If she was just fooling around, I have to agree with Eddie, it serves no purpose, other than gossip. But if it's something else . . ."

"Like what?" I wanted him to have this scoop. I didn't care about the money or about getting credit, and Madeline Chambers wasn't a favorite of mine . . . I wanted this to work for Lucien. My disappointment was evident.

"Eddie wouldn't tell me yet. But he was trying to get some info on the autopsy report. There was a rumor . . . and that's just it, a rumor, that Madeline was offed."

"Oh, no." I pooh-poohed that. "I heard it all, I couldn't help it, they weren't very quiet but she never called for help, she was having great sex."

"As I said, it's just a rumor."

The captain greeted us with menus and as we looked over the luscious fare, I settled for a light and delicious lobster salad, Lucien ordered veal. When the *maitre' de* approached our table I was startled at what he had to say.

"Miss Evanovich, I want to tell you that a gentleman was here inquiring about you and your guest."

"Who was it?"

"Presumably the Treasury Department."

"But why? We've done nothing wrong. My guest is with the Washington Herald. What did he ask?"

"Your guest's name." He looked at Lucien who sat expressionless, not volunteering anything.

"Did you tell him?"

"No. But they have ways of finding out. Anyway, I thought you should know." He walked away, stopping to chat along the way. He spoiled our lunch. Now we surely needed a drink.

"They're onto us, the Secret Service is part of the Treasury department." Lucien spoke quietly and calmly as he took my hand, kissing it. I felt something hard being rolled into my hand. "I'm slipping you this film in case things get hairy. Do you have a safe deposit box?"

"Yes, but that's the first place they'll look."

"Andy, act as if you're enjoying this."

"I am, you haven't held my hand in a long time."

"No fault of mine. Come on, loosen up, they have nothing. It's all circumstantial." He gave my hand a squeeze. "Loosen up."

"I'm afraid to."

"Why?" he laughed.

"Because I'm still in love with you." I blurted it out, I didn't care. I was ready to marry this man.

"Andy, pretend you're looking for a tissue or your glasses, and carefully put the film in your bag."

He ignored what I had said, which was worse than having an argument. I was embarrassed, I should have kept my mouth shut.

"Is it safe now?" he asked after I had slipped it into my bag using a tissue to dot my tearing eyes. I couldn't stand the indifference.

"Yes, it's safe." Without warning, he leaned forward, cupping my face in his hands, kissing my lips, slowly and tenderly. When I closed my eyes, the tears trickled down my cheeks, but it was all right. We were alone in that crowded room. We didn't care about people, propriety or the Feds. When you're in heaven, you don't care. When the entree was served we feasted on each other. I just couldn't get enough of him, I couldn't stop looking at his handsome face. We ate nothing and we said nothing.

"Do you have to go back to work?" he whispered, breaking the spell.

"One of these days."

"Then let's go."

"Your place or mine?" I signaled the waiter for the check.

"Yours," he replied," but thanks for giving me the choice."

CHAPTER 17

Agent Nichols had snapped pictures of Andy greeting Lucien with a kiss, but his weren't the only pair of eyes watching them.

The *maitre' de* had lied to cover his tracks. He had given Lucien's name to agent Nichols, remembering it from the introduction, but he wanted no trouble with the Secret Service.

Mitch Levitt was waiting for his partner's call in a small restaurant near *Maison Russe,* he was on his third cup of coffee when his cell phone rang.

"Hop a cab and get your ass over here. I need to check this guy out. Lucien Champier."

"Yeah, I know him. Works for the Herald."

"Now you tell me."

"Now I have a name. He's a Pulitzer prize winning photographer. Won a couple of other awards."

"A perfect fit. She lives next door to the mystery apartment, out sick that day. The boyfriend's a photographer at The Herald, and Eddie Wallace, the guy pitching this story is also with The Herald. How convenient."

"Convenient, but traceable." Mitch was encouraged.

"Get here ASAP. I'm not letting those two out of my sight. If I'm gone, I'll contact you." He felt certain that this was it. All they have to do now is find the pictures and the negatives and destroy them.

Ten minutes later Mitch came bounding out of a cab, looking up and down the street for Rolland's black car. He hoped he wasn't left behind, missing the adventure. At least this wasn't as boring as sitting around on surveillance. Relief flooded his face when he saw it. He ran over to it and yanked opened the door. Just as he settled in his seat, the couple left the restaurant.

"There they are. They didn't stay very long." Rolland Nichols hoped the *maitre' de* didn't tattle. They watched as the couple sauntered toward the parking lot, waiting until the attendant brought up Lucien's car.

As they drove off, Samantha Dewar was not about to give up the man she was obsessed with.

"Bitch! Bitch," she hissed, her face contorted with rage as she turned on the ignition and sped after them.

CHAPTER 18

I was bursting with desire knowing he felt as I did. Nothing mattered anymore, my job, my car, which was parked downtown, I didn't care. I didn't care about any of them. I'd get it tomorrow. Lucien would stay over and drive me to work in the morning.

We drove in comfortable silence, stealing sidelong glances at each other, flirting with knowing smiles. My breath quickened every time I stole a glance. The anticipation was better than any drug high. We were so involved with this silent mating game we barely thought of the film until I said, "I hope you have another set." Lucien quickly signaled me to be quiet. I got the message. The car might be bugged.

"Later," he mumbled, giving me a smile and a wink, not seeing a red car which came dangerously close to us. Suddenly, there was the hollow bang of metal on metal, plunging us forward, narrowly missing the car in front, our faces sailing toward the windshield. If we had air bags, we might have crashed in that stream of fast moving traffic. The car in front swerved into another lane, trying to ditch us, as Lucien held on to the wheel, pulling toward the shoulder. "Who's that idiot?" I screamed. The belt restrained me from seeing. Bang! They rammed us again. This was no accident, somebody was trying to kill us. "I'm calling the police." I reached for my cell.

"No. It's Samantha. I know her car. Don't get the cops involved." He slowed down as we bounced to a stop and parked on the shoulder, Samantha directly behind us. "Stay right here." He shot out running to the red Jaguar as I held my breath, praying she wouldn't ram me while I sat there alone.

She burst out of her car screaming, "Fucking, prick bastard, I hate you, I hate you." She was insane with rage, lunging at Lucien's face, her hands, tiny claws as her talons tried to draw blood. I had to help. I released the belt and opened the door. I heard his command. "Stay there!" he yelled to me. I quickly obeyed. This woman was nuts, I might make matters worse. I watched helplessly as she kicked at him, still screeching obscenities like a mad woman. I heard the slap which silenced her as she crumbled into his arms. He held her as her body wracked with sobs like a child.

The afternoon held such promise, and now Samantha . . . to spoil our day, our plans, our renewed relationship. Her timing couldn't have been worse, putting our fragile beginning in jeopardy. I had visions of her bursting through my front door with an ax, I know I'll have nightmares.

She quieted down and Lucien seemed to be whispering to her, looking into her red face, giving her his handkerchief to use. When he clasped her to him, I knew I was a goner and I started to cry, feeling sorry for myself. I realized I loved him so much and I no longer cared about anything but being with him. Sometimes we need to learn a hard lesson, and I had learned mine, but maybe it was too late. Now I would have to pay for my early stupidity. I reached for my cell and called Karl, trying to make sense between sniffles.

"Karl, I've been involved in a minor traffic accident, would you mind if I didn't come back."

"No, love. Are you all right?"

"Yes, but a little shaken. I'll tell you about it tomorrow." I would go home and cry the rest of the afternoon.

"A detective was in asking about you. He said there was a robbery in your building."

"Not that I know of."

I knew exactly who it was, and it had absolutely nothing to do with a robbery. It had everything to do with the film. This was the second time today that they had come snooping. As I hung up, I saw a black car pulled up behind Samantha's Jag. Two men got out and walked toward them, showing their badges. I couldn't hear anything but I assumed they were offering their help. I also felt that they were the ones who had been inquiring about me. I threw caution to the wind and bravely left the car and joined them. Sometimes you just get a feeling and you know, I hoped Lucien knew, too.

Those men had probably been following us, pulling over to watch the hysterics and jumping in at a good time, which was now.

"Yes." I heard one of them say. "We thought you had car trouble. Can we help?"

"You can help, all right. This bastard is cheating on me. Break his legs."

The men seemed amused. "Stop it, will ya, Sam. Andy's an old friend. We had lunch to catch up on old times. I'm giving her a lift, that's all."

"Yes," I interrupted as I approached. "I'm not feeling well."

"You're going to feel a lot worse, bitch!"

"No worse than you, when you sober up and realize what an ass you've been. You almost killed us, ramming our car. You should be arrested on assault and battery charges."

"Assault?" she laughed.

"Yes, assault with a deadly weapon, you ass!" I was beginning to like this. I turned to the men. "I wasn't well and wanted to leave, I barely touched my lunch." I knew if they had watched us, they would have seen that. Standing up to that spoiled brat seemed to take the wind out of her sails.

"What are your names again?" Lucien asked.

"Rolland and Mitch," the young man said.

"Okay, Rolland and Mitch. Suppose you take Ms. Dewar to her elegant family home in Wesley Heights. Her father is Senator Dewar, and I believe she needs an escort, there is no way she can drive. I also believe she shouldn't ever drive. I think her license should be revoked, she almost killed us. Sam, did you take a snort of something to put you in that rage? I won't press charges this time, but if you guys are government men, I'd like you to speak to the Senator. His daughter belongs in rehab, and he'd better give it his full attention now, before it's too late for her and before it gets out and screws up his re-election. That part should make him act." With that, he took my arm and steered me toward his battered car, examining the damage with his hands.

"Not so fast," Rolland called out to us. If drugs are involved here, do you mind if we search your car? I don't have a warrant, but we could keep you here awhile until we get one." We knew it wasn't drugs they were looking for.

"It's okay," I whispered.

"Really?" He wasn't sure what I had done with the film, but I nodded. Rolland looked through our car, while his partner went through Samantha's and I saw our intimate afternoon slipping away. It was not to be.

Suddenly Mitch, the older man, called, "I found a stash." He found Samantha's coke, then he looked in her bag and found more. Rolland found nothing in our car, but he asked to look in my bag. I gave it to him as Lucien started to sweat. He found nothing in my bag. Suddenly he patted our pockets.

"What's this all about? You want to do a strip search?" Lucien sarcastically said.

"You gave permission, sir, and I thank you for your cooperation. We'll make certain Miss Dewar gets home." With that, he walked off somewhat disappointed that he didn't get what he was really after. Mitch drove a sullen Samantha in her car as Rolland followed.

"Whew, that was close. I'm sure we'll see them again."

"And her too," I added.

"I'm afraid so, but I'll be damned if I'll let them spoil our afternoon together. I've waited a year and a half for this."

A thrill shot through me like an electric shock. It was the most romantic thing I had ever heard. He wanted me and he wasn't going to let anything stop him. Not some crazy woman, not the FBI and not the coveted film. It would all have to wait until we made love.

He stopped me from getting in the car. "If the car wasn't bugged before, it is now. Don't say a word in it. But where's the film?"

"I tucked it in my panties."

"Lucky film." He patted my buttocks. "And I offered them a strip search."

CHAPTER 19

"Where's Lucien?" Eddie roared, swooping through the partitions looking for Lucien. His co-workers were impressed. Several lifted their eyes to peek, others gawked, wondering what Lucien had done to bring the great Eddie Wallace downstairs, hunting for him in person. Finally, one brave assistant poked his head around. "He's out, took the afternoon off. Had a hot date or something, came in all dressed up."

"Shit!" Eddie banged the desk, then a light flashed. "I think I know where he is, thanks, son." He patted the young man's arm, rewarding him for his bravery.

He checked his watch and hurried up to his office. He felt energized and took the stairs two at a time, breathing heavily when he reached the top. But he felt good. His annoyance with Lucien's absence was abating, after all the man has a life. He headed down the hall with a confident stride, one of his colleagues calling out to him in passing, "What's up?" He waved him away. He closed his office door and looked up Andy's number.

◆ ◆ ◆

We had made love. Passionate, comfortable, satisfying love. The great hunger we felt for each other was mutually satisfied . . . for the moment. We were old lovers who never stopped loving each other, it just took time between then and now. We were positive about the future. We knew we would share it. We were dozing in each other's arms when Eddie called. When my voice instructed him to leave a message he roared, "I need Lucien now!" I handed the telephone to him.

"Luc, I spoke to an old friend with Interpol. I've uncovered some incredible stuff in this big web and I'm bursting to tell you."

"Say nothing." Lucien was afraid someone was listening but Eddie threw caution to the wind. "I think I know who the lover is."

"Say nothing, it can wait until I see you."

"Meet me at my office at seven. I can't wait to see your face. This is just the beginning, those photos were the tip of the iceberg. And are you ready for this? Madeline was murdered. See you at seven."

Lucien hung up, turning to me.

"Wait'll you hear this," he said.

◆ ◆ ◆

Mitch and Rolland heard it too. They had bugged Eddie's phone using the old 'problem on the line' routine, when Eddie was out. Nobody thought anything of it; since the phone company called beforehand. Charlie was magic. He could get almost anything done.

"I think we'd better have a talk with Charlie. The newspaper hound is sticking his nose into things that we don't even know about."

"You think she was murdered?" Mitch said.

"I don't know, but maybe Charlie knows?"

◆ ◆ ◆

"I swear on my mother's grave, I don't know."

"Your mother died?" Mitch asked.

"No, but I swear on it anyway." He threw his arms up in exasperation. "I'm leveling with you. I know nothing about this new wrinkle. Christ, is there an end to this?"

"I hope you are leveling with us." Rolland looked him straight in the eye and held his gaze.

"I am!" His voice rose. He had yet to tell them about the murder. "Look, sit down, have a drink or a coffee. There is something I'd like to discuss with you."

"Is this the other shoe?" Mitch said.

"Sort of," he answered, sweating a little. Mitch poured drinks. Having drinks with the chief of staff in his private office wasn't a bad way to spend the afternoon; that is, until Charlie continued.

"You're not going to like what I have to say, but I was sworn to secrecy. I feel that now I should take you in my confidence." There was an awkward silence as the men knew what was coming, waiting for more. Rolland's eyes narrowed as he and Mitch stared steadily at their target, waiting.

"The First Lady was murdered."

"We know, we heard it today. Eddie Wallace knows."

"What?" Charlie said in disbelief. "It's not possible, the pathologist took care of it."

"He lied on the death certificate?"

"Not exactly." Charlie took a big swallow of his vodka. "Madeline had had a coronary, but as she was lying there still alive, somebody snuffed out her life. Suffocation, the pathologist said."

"And you didn't think we should know about this?"

"I just found out about it myself," he lied, lifting his forehead, widening his eyes in innocence. "I'm not even telling the president, it would serve no purpose."

"You can only spare him so much, Charlie, if it was my wife, I'd want to know," Mitch said.

Charlie dismissed him with; "But she wasn't your wife, Mitch. She was the First Lady." Red blotches appeared on Mitch's face as he tried to restrain himself. His hands began to sweat. His heart began to pound faster, his breaths were harder to control. He had spent more time with the First Lady than he did with his wife and she had spent more time with him than she did with her husband. In spite of his feelings, he had always played by the book. He felt honor bound to do so. To be so shabbily treated, to be deprived of such crucial information in such a complicated case was more than he could take. Rage welled, and he was certain it showed in his eyes. He rose, placing his trembling hands palms down on the desk. He leaned forward; with veins popping, and he suddenly grabbed Charlie by his lapels.

"You little shit! I don't give a rat's ass if you are chief of staff. You should be fired. You're out of line, out of order, and out of your league. That autopsy was done before Christmas. You *just* didn't find out about it. You deliberately held back crucial information concerning the murder of the First Lady of the United States . . . who I might add, was in my care for four years." His face was dominated by guilt.

"But, but," Charlie sputtered.

"How do you think I feel about that?" Tears stained his cheeks. "She died in my care, because she wanted privacy to fuck some guy. And I'm gonna find him. The public doesn't have to know that, but I have to know. I'm going to get that bastard . . . and I'm going to kill him to clear my conscience." He shoved Charlie back into his chair with a thud, his lapels wrinkled from the iron grip. "You just found out about it, my ass." Charlie said nothing. It was better that way.

Rolland had never seen his partner lose control before. He knew he hated the Harvard bred yuppies who ran everything but he also knew Mitch didn't jeopardize his job or his pension with this outburst, because Charlie would never lodge a complaint. They knew too much. Charlie would bite the bullet, remain silent, and take the heat from all sides. He would continue his protection of the President at all costs, walking a tightrope every day, doing a pretty decent job of it.

It wasn't easy being Charlie.

CHAPTER 20

As Lucien turned the corner he almost knocked over the pizza delivery boy. He stopped short, steadying the young man. "Whoops, sorry pal." The little Mexican held onto the box. The tomato and onion smell got to him. "I'll pick some up on the way home." They had made love but hadn't eaten much, and he realized he was hungry. As he walked through the office it was still a beehive of activity. The news never stops. Several writers called out to him, surprised to see him on their floor. He found his way through the maze of partitions to Eddie's small cubicle where journalistic awards dotted the walls, including a Pulitzer.

"Come in," Eddie yelled, inviting him into his cluttered closet. Somebody yelled, "You want pizza?"

"Smells good, later," Eddie said.

"Later, there won't be any," came the reply. Eddie stood at his coffee maker pouring a mugful for himself and offering one to Lucien. The strong aroma of stale coffee kept hot, almost made him gag. But he accepted it, hoping that Eddie would accept the pizzas now.

"You remember The Snake? He's on Interpol's 'Red' wanted list." Eddie continued, not waiting for a reply as he stirred sugar and Cremora into his coffee. "He was a hot property at one time, blowing up ships, embassies and Army barracks."

"Didn't he die in some suicide mission?" Lucien waited as Eddie sat down, shifting his stocky frame in his chair until he was comfortable. He kicked off his shoes and elevated his feet on the wastebasket, the sour smell of his socks reached Lucien's nose. *Good thing I didn't eat,* he thought, hoping Eddie would get to the point so that he could leave.

"Well, according to my friend at Interpol, it seems the Libyans got sloppy, and Israeli intelligence intercepted a ciphered message to them from the super secret Iranian Intelligence. According to him, The Snake is alive." A chill ran through Lucien.

"You mean this could be bigger than a home grown tomato?"

"It could be; according to him, The Snake went undercover with a new I.D. and slipped into the U.S. He claims every immigration boss in the country knows, and a secret search is ongoing, but they're on direct orders from the White House not to go public until they try to get his I.D. and location."

"A silent manhunt? Who gave the orders?"

"Didn't know. He said he's probably right under our noses, but he's very slippery, using older, powerful women. That's his *modus operandi*. He secretly romances women who are married to powerful men. That's how he blew up the British embassy. He had a fling with the ambassador's wife. Of course, she never lived to deny it. He's an amiable seducer, presumably handsome, sophisticated and deadly... And I think he was Mady Chamber's lover."

"Do you have proof?" He felt clammy and uncomfortable.

"No."

"You're the guy who always needs proof."

"Journalistic integrity; we'll get the proof." Lucien was silent for a moment. The story scared him. They were playing for keeps with a madman. But he liked the angle and he was intrigued by The Snake. If they could nab him... what a coup, what a photo story... from start to finish.

"Do you suppose he killed her?" Lucien asked.

"We'll never know, but why keep the story quiet for so long, unless there's another angle."

"But why would he kill his entree to that world, his golden girl?"

"Maybe she wanted to break it off, or maybe she decided to discontinue those luncheons or fundraisers or whatever the hell went on there. The White House connection gave clout to that group. Maybe she knew too much or wanted too much. We won't know until we find this guy, if we find him."

It was now Lucien's turn to fill Eddie in on the events of the day; a man questioning the *maitre 'de,* another inquiring at *Maison Russe,* then both suddenly appearing on the scene when Samantha threatened them . . . and looking for the film under the guise of drugs.

"They know it all, Ed."

"You and Andy better be careful, you're targets. Make sure you have enough copies of that film and make sure it's safe. It's your insurance. Now back to The Snake. Do you have any ideas?"

"Take your pick. It could be the guy in Andy's building, Ali Sahlool or the guy she met at the party, Farid Majdellani, or about two hundred thousand other guys. Can we start by getting some shots of the first two guys . . . fax them to your friend."

"Won't work, nobody has ever seen The Snake's real face, he is a master of disguises."

"Neat, very neat . . . " He was hungry and wanted to get out, it was becoming very complicated and Eddie really had nothing.

"It's his style," Eddie quickly said, sensing his disappointment. "British ambassador's wife, dead. American ambassador's wife, dead. Our First Lady, dead, with a secret shroud over it. He fits the mold."

Lucien rolled his eyes, not completely convinced. "It's a long shot."

"Not really." He sat up pushing his smelly feet back into his shoes. "My friend gave me a code name."

"Yeah?" This held his interest.

"Casablanca." Their eyes locked as recognition crept into Lucien's face.

"White House?"

"That's what it means. I'm gonna run this by Jack. I'm gonna ask him if we can go to Michigan, to A.L.A. headquarters. I want to do a piece on them. Something flattering, that will gain their confidence. They may appreciate a respected journalist coming to their aid in their hour of need, now that their benefactress is gone."

"No doubt, but who'll come to your aid?"

"You." He pointed a finger at him. "You're coming with me."

CHAPTER 21

The slap left a red mark on Mal's cheek. He jerked his head back in shock, trying to avoid the backhand, but Karl hit him again.

"Don't you ever . . . discuss our private life with anybody, least of all that loser, Philip." His voice was measured and menacing.

"I swear I didn't," Mal protested, the mark on his face becoming angrier.

"Stop lying to me you . . . *mal*content. Stop lying." He grabbed Mal's arm, squinting accusingly at him. "You discussed us with Philip, and he had the gall to intercede on your behalf."

"So what." Mal spoke with a lofty air, jerking his arm away. "You're using me and everyone knows it." Little Karl's gotta have control." He mimicked a little boy. "They all say I can do better."

"Then do it."

After a pleasant evening spent with friends, dining on stuffed quail and fine wines, they ended up sniping at each other. Mal's restlessness was evident; the sniping was becoming more frequent. It was happening after spending evenings out with friends. *Was Mal in love with someone else?* Karl wondered, as he watched his lover confide in somebody else. Mal would always present his case to some sympathetic ear who encouraged him to voice his dissatisfaction with his present arrangement.

"Is Philip your new benefactor?" Karl sarcastically asked, knowing that Philip also lived on the generosity of his wealthy companion. "I know exactly what you want. But suppose you run off with somebody else?"

"Don't start that crap with me. We're together five years and you still don't trust me . . . But you trust that bitch who's worked exactly two years. You trust an employee over me. Where's my security? You refuse to come out even though everyone knows you're an old queen. You live in denial. You don't know who you are or what you are. You're pathetic." He stood his ground, stomping over to the polished bar and pouring himself a scotch, and belting it down in one gulp. He slammed the heavy crystal glass on the bar in defiance.

"I pay all of your bills, and you contribute nothing to this household except your bitching." Karl roared like a lion trying to rattle the man who was perched on the bar stool, with legs crossed, trying to ignore the tirade by looking at the ceiling in a bored manner.

"I make a damned good living, selling to liberals as well as to conservatives. I don't have to flaunt my sexuality, it's nobody's business . . . And I don't need an insecure lover to screw up my income . . . And as far as the *bitch* is concerned, she has contributed more to the bottom line than you will ever imagine . . . So treat her gently." Karl had to keep Mal in his place or he would be destroyed by this appealing predator, so as always, he came up with ways to keep him off guard.

"You know, luv, I'm thinking of having a baby with Andrea."

"What?" Mal laughed.

"You may think it's hysterical, but with our gene pool, we'd have a little genius. I can't do that with you."

"You won't do it with her either." Mal threw his head back and laughed, swinging his body from side to side. "I could see the little nipper, crawling to the lectern with his corncob gavel. *Sold to the dude in the red flannel shirt*," he spoke like a hillbilly hitching his thumbs through his belt loops and hiking up his pants. "Get real, love, stop this shit. Andrea's a hick and you're gay, so that's that."

"But you're not sure, Mal, you're not entirely sure."

"You vindictive bitch, don't make me laugh. You . . . going straight?" He continued in a falsetto voice. "*Queen Karl wants iss.ue in his old age.* Give me a break, you can barely get it up with me. You need friction and tension and drama." He hopped off the bar stool and threw the heavy glass against the wall, leaving a dent, but the glass fell unbroken on the thick carpet. "She'd laugh at you."

Karl's eyes sparked with hatred as he lunged at Mal, grabbing his neck. He gasped for air, without resisting. "Mal." Karl hissed his name as his hands squeezed tighter and tighter. They fell to the carpet, Karl repeating his name as Mal gagged, his face turning beet red. Karl loosened his grip and spit out the magic words, feeling the stirrings of an erection. "*Mal* ... icious; *Mal* ... evolent; *Mal* ... lingerer; *Mal* ... odorous." He felt the erection straining against the conservative pinstripes. He dropped his hands and stopped the verbal assault, trying to release his member, the zipper clawing at his skin. He kissed his submissive lover, probing his mouth with a poker hot tongue. He yanked at Mal's belt and trousers with shaking hands and suddenly they were one. They jolted forward with every thrust, Mal touching himself until they had reached a frenzied climax. They grunted with pleasure dripping in perspiration, rolling over in exhaustion on the soft, plush carpeting, their bodies still quivering for what seemed like ten minutes.

Karl reached over and grasped his lover's hand, squeezing it. Everything had been so good, and in spite of the disagreements and sniping, he loved Mal. He felt content and was starting to doze but managed to say, "Incredible baby." Sleepiness blurred his enunciation.

"You bet," Mal laughed, feeling confident. "Nobody else would put up with you." He rolled over on one elbow, looking squarely into Karl's face. "Karl, I'm asking you for the last time ... Treat me as your equal."

"I do, baby, I do." He wished Mal would sleep a while and not pursue this. "You're well taken care of in my will."

"Thank you." Mal kissed Karl's hand, grateful that he had told him. "I also need to know that you trust me with the safe. It's important for my self esteem."

"You're not an employee, Mal," Karl whispered, wanting sleep more than anything else. But Mal persisted, gazing into his face. Karl's eyes flickered as he tried to succumb to the waves of drowsiness which swept over him. But he saw the handsome, young face over him, and he thought about the sex they had just had. He loved this man and he knew he was right. Nobody else would put up with his peccadillos, he would end up having to pay someone for impersonal sex. It wasn't the best time for decision making, but after weighing the situation for a second or two and after five years of constant pressure, he relented. He gave Mal the security code.

CHAPTER 22

I was pleased with myself, my plan had worked. If I hadn't left my car at work, Lucien might not have driven me home.

"I could get used to this." A big grin covered his face as he stepped out of the shower, vigorously rubbing his body with a fluffy towel. "Even the towels are better."

I yanked it out of his hands and dried his back slowly and languorously. He threw his head back and purred. We barely slept last night, making love, chatting, or just holding each other. I forgot how nice that could feel.

Over coffee, I popped the big question. "Why don't you move in with me?" He held his cup in mid-air and looked intently at me.

"Would you like that?"

"Yes."

"Okay." He leaned over to kiss me and seal the promise. I would never let him go again.

"I'll keep my place though . . . just in case."

"Oh, no, I won't change my mind."

"I won't either, but I'd like to make sure that Samantha is out of my hair. I don't want her threatening you." That was Lucien, worrying about my welfare.

"Let's not let Samantha dictate our lives, and she might be in rehab by now."

"True."

"There's plenty of closet space, you could make another dark room"

"Deal." He tapped my behind. "You have a beautiful ass."

"I've been told."

"By whom?"

"By you."

"Then move it."

We quickly dressed and I grabbed the small package I had prepared earlier. I threw it in my briefcase and we sailed out of the apartment earlier than usual, Lucien going ahead of me to get the elevator as I locked up.

As I approached Frank Landry's door, it opened, and he reached out to retrieve his newspaper. He was still in his pajamas.

"Gotcha," I said, pointing a finger at him.

"Oh, excuse me," he apologized; for what, I don't know. I stopped for a second.

"Actually, you look better than I do on wake up." He laughed, as Lucien called to me that the elevator was arriving. "I'm Andrea, from next door." I extended my free hand and he shook it. It was a firm but friendly handshake.

"I know. Ring my bell soon. Let's have coffee one evening."

"I'll do that, I really would like to speak with you, you're profession intrigues me."

"I look forward to it . . . Have a good one, Andrea."

He was so nice that I felt sad leaving that funny looking, little man. It reminded me of the morning that I opened the door and saw the mystery man in the hall. Perhaps he would tell me. I looked forward to having a chat with Frank Landry.

Since we left earlier than usual, the traffic was light. We were in Georgetown in less than thirty minutes; another hour and we would have been sitting in traffic. We wanted to get to work early to do what we had to do. Then Lucien would go to his place and start bringing some of his belongings to my apartment. A slow move but I hoped it would be a permanent one. Every time I thought of it, a tickle would run through me. It only lasted a second, but it was something I had never experienced before. I guess I was truly happy.

Being the first one on the scene, I switched off the night security system and opened the large safe. I hid my small package with my name and the *"Do Not Touch"* instructions in the far corner of the bottom shelf. I breathed easier, knowing that Madeline's film was safe. This had to be safer than the bank. I knew they could get to the bank, if they hadn't already done so. Those government men can do anything.

I could now relax and think about my handsome, new roommate. I couldn't wait until six o'clock.

I began filling the vitrines and the display cases with our magnificent jewels and artifacts that made *Maison Russe* so special. I touched them lovingly knowing that hours of care and workmanship went into each one, but they felt cold. I had never noticed that before. I remembered a time last year when I had been consumed by my work, neglecting our relationship and Lucien asked me, "Why?"

"I love them, Lucien. I love being surrounded by such incredible beauty. I love my work. Don't you?"

"Yes," he replied. "But not enough to make you second in my life."

"I'm sorry, I can't help it, I just love them."

"It's easy to love an inanimate object, Andrea, they're safe, they can't hurt you. But trust me, I love you. Please trust me."

I learned a hard lesson, and now, I'll never let him go.

◆ ◆ ◆

Lucien called to tell me he was stopping at his apartment to pick up some clothes. He would have to do that gradually as I make room for him. When he arrived at his apartment he was surprised it was single locked. Had he forgotten to use the dead bolt? When he opened his door and switched on the light, he stood there numb, as he looked around and saw the devastation. His apartment had been trashed. The leather sofa and chair were so thoroughly slashed that the stuffing was bulging out of every cut like rising dough. Lamps were overturned, the shades flattened, books were strewn over the floor, blinds were yanked down. Dishes, pots and glasses were smashed and dumped on the small kitchen floor, a mini trash heap. As the numbing effect wore off, his first reaction was to leave, the intruder might still be there. But his concern for his darkroom equipment kept him there as he cautiously made his way to it. His heart sunk, his equipment was destroyed. He felt as though he had been kicked by a mule. *This is no ordinary robbery,* he thought as he inventoried the damage. There was too much destruction. Somebody was looking for the film and tried to make it appear like a robbery. He hurried to the film's hiding place and dragged a chair over, climbing on it. He removed the molding on top of his built-in bookcase. It swung out, revealing a small space about two inches high. Inside he had hidden several important items. He squinted to see if the film was still there, it was. "Jesus, they didn't get it," he sighed, relieved. Suddenly, he heard a sound and turned to see if somebody was still there. Carefully, he took the film and stuffed it in one of the many pockets on his jacket and slid the molding back in place. He had to leave. He stepped off the chair and slid his back against the wall, making his way toward the hallway. He saw a dark figure in the dim light and lunged at it before he saw the flash of steel.

"How could you? How could you?" Samantha Dewar screamed, waving the knife as he tried to hold her arm from coming at him. There was a deranged, far away look in her eyes. "I'm going to kill us both. I can't live without you. Can't live . . . Can't live . . . How could you with that whore?" She was stronger than he had anticipated, and he needed all of his strength to prevent her from plunging the knife into his massive chest. With his left fist he clipped her jaw, knocking her senseless, as she slid to the floor. He disarmed her and called her father.

"Lucien Champier. I want to speak to Senator Dewar, now." The tone of his voice screamed emergency and the Senator got on immediately.

"Hello, son, how are you?" His voice was cheerful, a voice people in denial always use.

"Your daughter just tried to kill me and herself. Didn't you learn your lesson from yesterday? If you're not here in twenty minutes, it'll be on the 11 o'clock news tonight. Not very good for your career."

"We'll be right over, son. Just sit tight."

Samantha stirred and turned her back on him hunching against the wall, her lungs exploding air heavy with sobs. He felt for her, but he didn't hold her, he had to make the break. If he didn't do it now, she'd drag him down with her.

They sat on the floor for over forty minutes, waiting for her father, Lucien trying to convince her to go into rehab. He finally made her face the truth about her future. She would either cooperate with her father or he would call the police and press charges. They waited, his patience running out with her and her family, when his bell finally rang. He stood at the open door waiting for his visitors to climb the three flights of stairs, and he made a silent bet with himself. *I bet the bastard doesn't show.* When they came into view, three of the Senator's household staff stood before him, offering embarrassed apologies for her parents absence.

"The Senator and Mrs. Dewar regret not being able to be here, a conflicting schedule. They are very busy." Lucien won his bet.

"That was expected, Harold. You know politicians never keep their word." At this moment, he felt very sorry for Samantha. In spite of her wealth and glamorous life . . . she had nothing. Nobody cared. He could no longer help her. She needed professional help and he needed Andrea.

"If Miss Dewar isn't in a rehab facility within twenty-four hours, this story and pictures of this mess will be in every newspaper. Tell that to the busy Senator."

"Yes, sir. You may submit a list of damages for reimbursement, Mr. Champier."

"Forget it. I want no further contact with this family." With that, he handed Samantha to them and closed the door. It was a very harsh ending, but it was the only way he could make her understand that it was over! He loved another woman.

He walked into the ravaged bedroom and he looked through his drawers to try to salvage some clothes. He shook his head in disgust at his underwear and shirts which were either stained with urine or feces or ripped to shreds. He riffled through the slashed clothing still hanging and found one undamaged jacket, the rest he would have to buy. Throwing the jacket over his arm he turned out the lights and left. Somebody would have to clean up this mess, thank God he had a new home to go to.

CHAPTER 23

Frank Landry's hand trembled as he held the cassette his cleaning lady had just handed to him. She had found it among the sofa cushions while vacuuming the furniture. "You lose 'dis t'ing, Messier Frank?" She laid it on the table, while he drank his coffee. He stared at it a long time before touching it, afraid it might blow up in his face. But it didn't. The title, *Casablanca*, was hand printed on a white label pressed onto the sleeve. *Somebody must have taped it themselves.* he thought. *Perhaps Madeline or another client lost it among the pillows of his sofa.* Maybe he would watch it when he had time. He hadn't seen that movie in years. While holding it, he became increasingly agitated, yet there was nothing strange about it. It was obviously a self taped cassette of the movie *Casablanca*.

As he held it, strange images flashed before his eyes like a speeding train. It startled him. He saw a movie on his mental screen, of people screaming shrieks of horror. He saw fire and water and terror in their faces. He saw a woman gasping for air with a pair of hands clutching her throat. He saw a dark haired man bending over the struggling woman.

Frank knew this cassette had something to do with Madeline.

He had gone to her memorial service, begging an invitation from her scheduling secretary whom he had known from her visits to him. He paid his respects, feeling uneasy because of the nature of his relationship. He was embarrassed that the President knew of him. But his reaction to this cassette unsettled him. Could Madeline have died here? Could she have been murdered by the dark haired man he had warned her about?

Every time he touched the cassette the kaleidoscope of ghastly images rushed through. "What is this thing?" He shook in fear, but he had to see it alone, not with Georgette around.

"Georgy," he called. "I forgot, I'm expecting early clients, like in twenty minutes. A VIP."

"Who, Mr. Frank?" her eyes bugging out. "I gotta tell my relatives." Frank knew she supported a bunch of them on her small salary, he also knew she was honest and trustworthy.

"Kimmy Cox."

"The rock star? Oh, Messr. Frank, I wish I could stay, just in a closet, maybe?" She laughed.

"Why don't you call it a day." He counted out the bills, paying her for the day.

"I stay longer next time, Messr. Frank."

"No need, darling, no need." He wanted her to leave and he sighed with relief when he heard her call good-bye and closed the door behind her.

He slid the cassette into the VCR and pressed power. A series of numbers appeared. A man spoke in a foreign language, narrating the story which began to unfold. The foreign narration was replaced by a translator's voice in the foreground, crisp, clear English. Frank dropped into a chair, staring in disbelief. He was transfixed by what he saw. *Is this a joke?* he thought. He couldn't figure it out. *Is this some kind of reenactment?* But the narration seemed to be dead serious, it was over in ten minutes.

He tried to rise to rewind the tape and view it again, but he was paralyzed for the moment. Some of the images he had seen in his mind's eye when he first handled the cassette matched what he had seen on the tape. His body trembled as he rose to rewind and replay it again, but the same horror played before him. This was no joke. It was real. "I've got to call those two agents," he muttered, running to his desk, rummaging through the drawers, looking for their cards. Suddenly he stopped. *What if I'm wrong? They'll call me a fool.* He began to have doubts. he had a reputation for accuracy, but on several occasions he did misinterpreted the images. He stood there like a lost child, biting his lip. It was not good for his reputation if he created a stir for nothing and as he debated the pros and cons of exposing this, he half heartedly rifled through the desk drawer until he spotted the agent's card. Drenched in perspiration, he punched in the number to the Secret Service White House Command Post. He was told agents Nichols and Levitt were unavailable, so he left a message to call.

When he hung up he felt he was standing in the path of evil. Perhaps he could do something to reverse things as a calm came over him. He would safeguard this video until it was placed in the proper hands. He calmly placed the cassette back in its sleeve and pressed a white label over *Casablanca,* the video's title. It now became *Exact Vengeance,* a recent movie. He did the same to another. He wrote the title *Casablanca* on a label and pressed it over a goofy comedy, called *The Bow Wow Theory.* The switch gave him some protection. This was too important to fall into the wrong hands. He stacked them among his video collection, at least safeguarding it until the agents arrived.

◆ ◆ ◆

"So what did he find?" Rolland Nichols said.

"A video cassette," Mitch answered, having just returned Frank's call.

"Did he say what was on it?"

"No. He said it was scary and unbelievable."

"Celebrity snuff film?" Rolland laughed, knowing how dramatic Frank could be.

"Don't laugh, the way he sounded, it could be. He wouldn't say over the phone."

"Wouldn't say, huh? Jeez, we looked all through that place and didn't find anything, we left nothing to connect Madeline with that apartment."

"But we concentrated on the bedroom, thinking she died having sex. We didn't know it was murder. Our investigation would have been different if we knew that. This video was found buried under the sofa cushions," Mitch said.

"We sat on that sofa," Rolland said. "Anything could have gotten lost in that goose down."

"We should have been more thorough. I really screwed up."

"Come on, Mitch. Stop that crap."

They fell silent, keeping their eyes peeled for a place to eat. Frank Landry asked them to come by about four. He expected a client earlier, a rock star whom he couldn't cancel. He would cancel his evening appointments and would then be free to show them the film in privacy.

"You ever bang Madeline?" Rolland Nichols was curious about Mitch's relationship with the former First Lady. Mitch looked at him in disgust without answering.

"Okay, okay. Just asking. You've had such a strong reaction to everything concerning this . . . I just wondered . . . "

"It was all my fault, Rollie. I stopped you from checking on her. I was wrong and you were right . . . And you never pointed a finger at me. For that I'll always be grateful. If I had listened to you," his voice drifted off.

"I'm too young, Mitch, you wouldn't listen to me." He laughed, knowing his partner disliked the young people who ran things in Washington.

"Were you in love with her?"

"For God's sake, Rollie, no. She was our charge. It was my job to protect her, and I looked the other way when she had her affairs. And that would have been the best time to get her . . . " He punched his right fist into his other hand. A glimmer of moisture covered his eyes.

"Stop blaming yourself, Mitch. Madeline was one tough cookie and she made it clear that she wanted no interference. She would have booted you out."

"And the President?" Mitch interrupted. "Do you think he knew how casually we treated those assignations?"

"He knew, because that's what she wanted, she always got her way. Charlie was right, not telling him of the murder."

"Maybe," Mitch said, still not fully convinced. They pulled into the parking lot of a fast food joint. Rolland flashed him a sidelong look and saw the pain in his partner's face. He made no attempt to leave the car.

"Mitch, you always did a good job. Let it go. Sometimes fate scrambles things a bit. Sometimes things are just meant to be. Come on." He grasped Mitch's arm, coaxing him out.

CHAPTER 24

The concierge rang up, announcing the arrival of Kimmy Cox, the rock star. As Frank waited at the door to greet her, the telephone rang. He left the door ajar, while he went to answer it. It was a new client, Maxwell Alt, who begged an appointment, as soon as possible, possibly today? Frank refused, but the man continued his plea. "You were referred to me by our late First Lady, my dear, dear friend." The softly accented voice was persistent. "She said you would help me, and I am at the crossroads of my life. I must see you today." There was something compelling in his voice which kept Frank on the line. Any other time, he would have given him short shrift, but this man's voice mesmerized, yet frightened him. He told Mr. Alt to come by at four, he would squeeze him in after Kimmy Cox, but before the agents came by. He was curious, perhaps Mr. Alt had been Madeline's lover.

◆ ◆ ◆

After his call to Frank, Maxwell Alt switched pay phones at the hotel. It was old fashioned, but he found it the safest way to contact. Everything else was traceable, but anybody could have used a hotel pay phone. Even the security cameras couldn't identify him after he switched caps and scarves in the men's room. It was a fast way to do the trick. His second call was made to his contact informing of his appointment, which would give him an opportunity to find the missing video cassette. It was dangerous to have that floating around, he had to get it one way or another.

A calm settled over Frank as he resigned himself to the situation in spite of the warning bells that the caller set off. He felt uncomfortable but the die was cast and his own curiosity got the best of him. So when Kimmy Cox pushed open the unlocked door and flew in, wearing platform boots, she lost her balance, sailing right into a hallway chair which slammed into the wall, making a thunderous entrance. She fell to her knees, her hands gripping the silk seat of the chair, but she kept slipping off.

"That's some entrance," Frank was forced to laugh, forgetting that he had left his door ajar for her.

"Yeah, right. I took a snort. I know you don't like that, but I'm always straight with you, Frank. I need you, baby . . . Christ, how I need you."

"You should have stayed sober, Kimmy. I hate dealing with drugs." He wanted her out of there. His mind was on the caller. But Kimmy rambled on, still trying to rise on the unsteady legs of a new born colt, and never quite making it, her hands slipping off the silk.

"Shit, Frank, fuck it. I ain't movin'. Do me here." She sat there and rested her head on the seat of the chair. "I need to know things Frank. Are my guys gonna split? They've been approached by that cunt at Ersatz Records. Will my contract be renewed? I'm up for a part in a movie. Shit, Frank, don't turn me down. I'll sleep it off. You'll get the vibes, but I need to know these things." She sprawled on the white tiled floor and patted the space next to her. "Here, Frank."

"I'm getting too old for this." Frank groaned as he sat down beside her on the gleaming floor and fanned out the cards before her. "All right Kimmy, with your left hand, choose three cards."

She drew the Page of Pentacles, the Hermit IX and the Three of Cups.

"Kimmy, this year is a new beginning for you. You're growing up, it looks like you will meet an older man."

"Yikes," she screamed. "Tommy Motali? He's free. He's also head of Sing Sing Records."

"I can't tell you that." But the news put Kimmy in a good mood.

As they continued, Frank told her that her new album would be a huge success, even though her lead guitarist was threatening to leave." Your contract will be renewed, but I see another entertainment giant in the picture."

"Tommy," she screamed. "I'm sure."

He gave her a good reading, guessing at certain things, eager to be rid of her. She was elated with the reading. He lifted her spirits, and finally lifted himself and Kimmy Cox. After paying the hefty fee, she kissed him and asked to use his bathroom.

"No drug use in here," Frank warned.

"I swear, Frank, I only gotta pee." When she returned, he stood waiting at the door with a manila envelope. "Give this to the concierge at the desk downstairs. It's important that he get this. You won't forget, now, Kimmy. Don't walk out with it."

"Jesus, Frank, whattaya think I am? An airhead?"

"Do you have a limo waiting?"

"Frank, I always have a fucking limo waiting." She grabbed the envelope very indignantly and kissed his cheek. It was her favor to him for making her future sound so rosy. Twenty minutes later, Maxwell Alt stood in his hallway.

◆ ◆ ◆

Rolland Nichols and Mitch Levitt climbed out of their car, crunching over the hard packed snow, and into the familiar back entrance of Frank's apartment house. When they reached his floor and pressed his buzzer, there was no answer.

"Chicken out?" Mitch asked.

"Beats me. I still have the key." Rolland dug around in his pockets for the small key ring he kept in a plastic bag. When he opened the door, they cautiously entered, calling Frank's name. In spite of the fresh flowers in the hallway vase a sour smell filled the air. As they approached the living room, the smell was heavier. They saw the body sprawled over the yellow silk sofa. Thick vomit clung to the side of a seat cushion. A ring of blood circled the body, the red blood on the yellow silk made some parts look green. Somebody had slit Frank's throat. It was fast and neat and he knew it was coming—he was scared out of his wits. They carefully checked his vital signs, knowing he was already dead.

"He must have been so scared he retched before they killed him," Rolland said.

"Who do we call on this one, Charlie or the cops?" Mitch asked, losing confidence in his judgment.

"Call Charlie first," Rolland said.

◆ ◆ ◆

Charlie would have to see the video cassette before reporting the murder. So the agents looked through Frank's collection, and found it, *Casablanca*, that's what Frank said. They would play it later at Charlie's. But first they checked Frank's appointment book and saw that Kimber Lee Cox, the rocker, and a new client, Maxwell Alt were his last clients. The rest were cancelled. They now were careful not to touch anything and used their own cell phone to contact Ms. Cox, catching up with her in the magnificent suite she rented at the Jefferson Hotel. She was sober and acted properly, hoping this civilized image would help her get a movie part she coveted. She was very cooperative.

"I was on time and he gave me a good reading. I gave him my check and left."

"And was there anything different or out of the ordinary?"

"Well, he left the door open for me, and he seemed in a rush. He hurried through the reading, although it was a good one."

Rolland turned to Mitch. "Did you get Mr. Alt?"

"No. It was a pay phone."

"Did you happen to see the next client?" Rolland said.

"No, that's all I can tell you." She didn't want to get involved in a murder so she deliberately skipped telling them about the manila envelope she left with the concierge. Suppose it was drugs. Forget it. So Kimmy Cox said nothing about her final favor to Frank. It was done, and all behind her now.

◆ ◆ ◆

They couldn't figure it out. What was on this video tape which was so horrible? The three men sat in Charlie's office playing and replaying a video of a goofy comedy, which was clearly marked *Casablanca*. When they removed the pressure sensitive label the actual title was revealed. It was "The Bow Wow Theory."

"Is this a joke?" Charlie asked.

"I don't think so. He was scared shitless."

"Then what the hell is this?"

"I don't know," Mitch continued, "unless he switched the labels to confuse someone. Somebody who knew he had it and he wanted to protect it for us."

"How did he find this mysterious video?"

"His cleaning woman found it."

"Could she have inadvertently told someone?"

"Possibly, but she didn't know what was on it, he said he sent her home."

"She could read. It said, *Casablanca*," Charlie said.

"The video was found this morning, he's murdered this afternoon, who would know all this so quickly?" Rolland said.

"What about Ali Sahlool? He lives downstairs in the building. Suppose he overheard the cleaning lady on the elevator or in the lobby?" Mitch added.

"Then you should check out Mr. Sahlool, the cleaning lady, and Frank's client list," Charlie said.

"That last phone call was made from a pay booth, in a downtown D.C. hotel. The previous call on the message machine was a woman saying she was referred by a client of his, then Frank picked up. We'll check that one too."

"Check them all," Charlie said. "We've got to get that cassette. It might be Madeline and the guy having sex."

"I don't think so," Mitch countered. "He said it was frightening, horrible."

"Having sex with Madeline was probably frightening and horrible," Charlie laughed.

"She was not one of your favorites?" Rolland asked.

"He deserved better. Okay, guys, it's time to inform the police."

CHAPTER 25

I could barely maneuver my car into it's parking space. the place was a sea of flashing lights, making the drab area as exciting as a strobe lighted disco. "What's up?" I asked a young cop sitting in one of the patrol cars.

"A homicide, ma'am." My hair stood on end, I prayed Samantha didn't harm Lucien."

"Who was it?"

"Some old guy, a fortune teller or something."

I dashed inside and picked up my mail, dying to find out the details. I knew it was Frank.

I took the manila envelope that the concierge had handed to me. My name and apartment number were clearly written, but there was no return address.

"Who left this?"

"It was here before I got on. John, the day man, must have gotten it."

I looked suspiciously at the package. "By the way, Miss Evanovich, there are a hundred cops on your floor." I know." I waited for an explanation.

"Mr. Landry, your neighbor. Somebody murdered him."

"Oh, no." My suspicions were confirmed. "Was it a client?"

"The cops don't know yet, and I'll have to ring up and tell them a tenant is coming up." He picked up the house phone and spoke to someone.

It was the second death in that apartment. It was beginning to get creepy.

When I got off the elevator, a cop was standing in front of

Frank's apartment, 7B. The door was open, I hesitated as I passed looking in, exchanging a few words with the cop.

"What happened?"

"It's a homicide, ma'am."

"How?"

"You don't want to know, miss." I felt shaken. These people didn't know the drama that took place just a scant few weeks ago, but I knew. As I spoke to the guard a detective came forward and asked me several questions.

"I left early and I've been in work the whole day. I'm just getting home now." I said nothing about speaking to Frank this morning as I passed his door and I said nothing of the package which had been left for me. I didn't know who left it, it could have been Lucien, leaving me some romantic gift.

"I really didn't know Mr. Landry well. I knew he was a famous psychic, and I knew he had a celebrity clientele, but I never saw too much of him. I'm out all day and very often I go out to dinner after work. I'm sorry I can't help you." The detective handed me his card. "If you happen to see, hear or remember anything unusual, Miss . . ."

"Evanovich, Andrea Evanovich. I'm with *Maison Russe*." I knew that he'd be impressed.

"Am I supposed to know it?"

He wasn't. "It's a very prestigious art and antiques store, in Georgetown."

"Not my style, but maybe you can teach me about it over coffee one day."

He was hitting on me! "That would have been nice, except I'm seeing someone."

"Figures. All the good ones are taken."

"Should I be afraid to stay here tonight?"

"Right now, miss, this is the safest place in town. There'll be a police guard on all night for several days. You'll be fine."

I said nothing about Lucien staying over. When I entered my apartment I did a strange thing. I looked in all my closets and under the bed. I didn't open the package until I felt safe. But was I? What if the package was an explosive. I decided not to open it until Lucien arrived. I tapped his number at work and left a message on his voice mail. I called his apartment, knowing that he was stopping there to pick up some clothes. I left a short message. I would just have to be patient and hope the thing wouldn't blow up in my face.

Lucien arrived about nine. He too, was shocked by the police presence in the parking lot and on the floor, although by this time my floor had cleared except for the guard and a handful of detectives.

We exchanged horror stories. His, about Samantha and the destruction of his home and mine . . . a neighbor's murder. It wasn't your usual dinner conversation, but it was a preview of things to come.

"You're stuck with me, Andrea." Lucien caught me from behind, wrapping me in a big bearhug. He rested his chin on my shoulder while we nuzzled. "God, my place is a dumpsite. There is no way I could go back."

"What about the clean up?" I asked.

"I paid the super to do it and tomorrow I'll call the owner. He'll be glad I'm leaving. He can raise the rent fifteen percent. So m'love, I'm at your mercy, I'm homeless."

I broke free from his hold to pour us a much needed glass of wine. We touched our glasses and our lips as I whispered, "You're not homeless anymore; and you're so easy luv, you don't even need a big closet . . . not with one jacket slung over your arm, plus . . . and this is a big plus—you came in the nick of time. With the murder next door, you'll come in handy." I tried to make light of the situation but I was scared to death.

We sat down to an herb crusted breast of chicken, salad and a good Chardonnay which we already sampled. My eyes stung as I thought about Frank Landry. Lucien stopped eating holding his fork in midair. "What's the matter, honey?"

"Nothing, really." I dabbed the corners of my eyes with my napkin. "I just feel terrible about Frank. You know I stopped to chat with him on my way out this morning. He wanted to have coffee with me one day and I probably would have had a reading . . . and now he's gone. Murdered by some maniac. He was my neighbor for two years, ever since I moved here, and this was the first time I said more than a *hello* . . . on the day he died."

"I'm sorry, kid." Lucien covered my hand with his. "We never exchanged more than a nod, a hello. We could have been friends. Who would do such a thing to that strange little man?"

"I don't know, but I would think that psychics are like psychiatrists, they deal with a lot of nutty people, people on drugs. Someone could have gotten ticked off at him for some imagined slight."

"Slitting his throat is a little harsh for a slight." It had been on the news. "I think it had something to do with Madeline, I don't think it was a client, and what about the mystery man in the hall, maybe he was involved."

"I would keep my mouth shut about him." We finished our dinner and it was nice having his help. He cleared the table while I stacked the dishes in the dishwasher. When we finished we zeroed in on the mystery package. Handling it very carefully, Lucien took it and a sharp knife to the bathroom, and made a slit in the middle of the manila envelope. He slit the side without touching the flap. Slowly he eased out a note and a video cassette titled, *Exact Vengeance*. I opened the note.

> My dear neighbor,
> I may be a tad dramatic and if I am, please ignore this and return it to me in two or three days. On the other hand, if something dreadful happens to me (you'll be the first to know, living next door), please contact the agents on this card and give them the cassette.
> Ever grateful,
> Frank Landry
> P.S. I received good vibes from you.

Lucien and I looked at each other, then at the card. The name on the card read Mitch Levitt. Rolland Nichols' name was scrawled on the back.

"Don't we know these guys?" Lucien said.

"We sure do. Shall we see what's on this thing?" I took the cassette and slipped it into the VCR sleeve. "Okay, I think we should see this before we pass it on." I turned on the VCR. Immediately a series of large numbers flickered by, then disappeared from the screen. A voice spoke in the background in a foreign tongue which sounded like Russian, although I couldn't quite make out the words. Suddenly a male interpreter translated what was being said in the background. The screen was pitch black for a moment as the voice continued, and then the scenario began to unfold. It was awful to watch and absolutely riveting. We sat dumbstruck, and now we knew why Frank had been murdered, he knew too much. Chills swept through me and I shivered uncontrollably. Lucien held me, not saying a word. We knew our lives were in danger holding onto this and we had to get it into the hands of the proper authorities, and we weren't thinking of Mitch and Rolland. This could not be swept under a rug. They would be the last ones we would call assuming that they were involved with Madeline's cover up.

"How about Eddie? He'd know what to do. But we can't use these phones, we've got to use the lobby phone." Before I was through talking, Lucien threw on his only jacket and was heading for the door. "Lock this and don't open it for anyone."

"Wait" I handed him a set of keys. "They're yours."

I sat staring at the empty screen wondering how to handle this bombshell. I quickly found a blank tape and decided to make a copy . . . just in case this one would disappear. I knew I was flirting with danger but I felt compelled to do it. As I taped the ten minutes, I wondered if the mystery man I had seen that morning lived in the building. That would have been convenient for Madeline as nobody would see him coming or going on the security tapes. She used the psychics apartment as a cover, and if her lover lived here, all he would have to do is use the stairs to get to his place. Frank's killer could have done the same. The surveillance tapes would show nothing. The tapes for December 3rd were missing as Eddie and Lucien found out, and the reason they were missing was because they showed a body bag leaving the building. I pondered all these questions, wracking my brain until I heard the buzzer and Lucien's key turning the lock.

◆ ◆ ◆

Eddie Wallace was at our door within the hour. He, too was flabbergasted by what he had seen on the cassette.

"Remember this is a time bomb. Anyone who has seen this, or has this in their possession, is in jeopardy—from unknown sources. It's treachery personified. And they will hunt down each and every copy; where does one keep such a thing?"

We sat in silence, staring into space, trying to think of some way to get it out of our possession and into the proper hands. Finally Eddie spoke. "I think the best plan is to let Jack Stern see it, and have the newspaper take responsibility for it's safekeeping. Unscrupulous people would stop at nothing to get it, and this may be the tip of the iceberg involving Madeline." We couldn't think of anything better. "And you're absolutely certain nobody knows you have this?"

"You read the note. Frank must have seen or felt something to turn to me for help. It was something that forced him to make a quick decision. I don't know if he took it downstairs or if someone else did, but the concierge on duty tonight didn't know who left it, and the police haven't questioned me, so they don't know it came from him."

"Right," Lucien added. "They'd be all over you, they know nothing." Eddie settled in his seat, he was feeling more comfortable now that we came to a decision.

"Okay, Jack Stern must see this and we'll pursue what we started out to do. Dear boy, we'll start our research and do a piece on the A.L.A. We'll shake the bushes and see if we can find the lover, the Snake or some unsuspecting pawn who will take the rap if things get too hot. By the way, Andy, where did you hide the copy of Madeline's film?"

"In our store safe. It's huge and Karl thinks it's just some personal stuff. Legal papers, etc. He thinks we had robberies in the building and now with the murder, he'll really believe it."

I knew Eddie felt the cassette was too hot to leave there. He rose and paced the floor, I could see him thinking, trying to work out the safest way for us.

"Does anyone know you have this?"

"No. I could ask the day concierge who received it."

"Don't. Don't raise any questions or suspicions. Somehow Frank got hold of it, probably through Madeline's use of his place. He knew it was volatile . . . and he knew someone would be after it. But that someone didn't know he left it for you. You weren't even a friend. It was fast thinking on his part if they searched without success, then threatened and killed him for it. The man was a hero, he was truly a hero, and smart. They must have been there before, but they would never dream that this would end up next door."

"Well, they did get in, couldn't find it and murdered him for it," Lucien added.

"True, but he didn't talk and they didn't get it, we did." Eddie quickly grabbed his jacket from the chair he had flung it on.

"I'm going to Jack Stern's."

"Now?" we blurted, checking the time. "It's after midnight."

"Now," Eddie said.

CHAPTER 26

"For Chrissake, what?" Charlie MacIssac looked up from his desk, annoyed at the intrusion.

"The boss needs to see you, big time. Did you hear the news? Madeline's clairvoyant was murdered."

"What?" Charlie acted surprised. He knew about the murder yesterday, but had to go through the motions, so he pushed his chair so hard he almost rolled into the wall behind him. "What the hell happened?" He sounded convincing.

"Don't know, it was just on the news, they found him dead yesterday, his throat slit. The cops got an anonymous tip."

"Okay, I'm coming, tell him I'm coming." He was glad the aide left, he needed a minute to collect his thoughts and not give anything away. Madeline was murdered, now this guy. That place had a treacherous atmosphere. The news of the murder shocked everybody, and he was a spin doctor, so the President would rely heavily on his good judgment.

He rose and walked to the oval office poking his head in the door. "Sir."

"Come in Charlie. You know my good friend, Jack Stern."

"Do I know Jack Stern?" Charlie walked over to Jack and pumped his hand. "We got you elected, right Jack? I just heard the news. Do you want some kind of a statement?"

"No Charlie, Jack's here on other business. Sit down." The President looked at his two loyal friends and wondered, *what now?* "Okay Jack, what's so urgent?"

"I assume I can speak freely in front of your Chief of Staff?"

"Yes, Charlie knows everything. If I were to die tomorrow, Charlie could take over and do a damn better job than Hugh," referring to his Vice-President.

"This is raw, personal stuff concerning Madeline."

"Jack, we know it all. The young men, the affairs... Charlie has gotten me through it all."

Jack rested his elbow on the armrest and propped his chin in his hand, thinking. He was momentarily at a loss. This was going to be a lot harder than he had anticipated, and he wondered if indeed Charlie knew everything.

"Tom," he spoke slowly almost afraid to stray into the territory he would have to go, knowing their friendship was at stake. "Tom, when Eddie Wallace suspected Madeline's cover up, I made him kill the story out of respect to you... but on one condition; that if our national security was compromised in any way, I would allow him to pursue it. Well, now I have proof that Madeline *was* involved in a game of international hardball."

His listeners watched expressionless, waiting to hear what else Madeline had in store for them. "A video cassette has come into our possession," Jack Stern said.

"From where?" Charlie asked.

"I can't reveal the source."

"That's convenient," Charlie snapped.

"It incriminates Madeline," Jack added.

The President was visibly upset, removing his glasses and kneading his eyes with the tips of his fingers. It seemed a sign of hopelessness, a sign that he wished all this would go away.

Jack spoke softly, he wanted to be gentle, delivering such horrible news, but Charlie's usual friendly voice took on a brittle edge as he fired questions at the seasoned newsman.

"Is her name mentioned?"

"Not exactly, but she's referred to."

"Is she on the tape?"

"Not really."

"Does she speak?"

"No," Jack said, wondering why Charlie asked all the right questions placing doubt in anyone's mind.

"Then what do you have?" Charlie continued.

"Incriminating evidence."

"Jack, I can't believe this." The President shook his head in disbelief. "Mady liked men, but she would do nothing to rock the boat. She loved being First Lady."

"Tom, we have proof," Jack said.

"According to the answers you gave Charlie, you don't have proof. Tapes can be doctored up, it's been known to happen to prominent people."

"Okay, then you be the judge," Jack challenged.

"Fine, we have a VCR."

"No, not here. We'll see it at The Herald."

"I don't have time to do that," the President said, clearly annoyed at this latest accusation.

"You'd better make time, Tom, because Frank Landry died protecting this tape, making sure it got into the right hands."

"Frank Landry?"

"Mady's psychic, the guy who was just murdered."

"Well, did the bad guys get it?"

"No Tom, we did."

"Then I'll go, I'll check it out," Charlie reluctantly offered.

"Fine, let's go." Jack rose, grabbing his coat and stormed out of the office, disappointed that his friend chose not to face the bitterest of truths. He wondered if this would finally effect their long friendship and in his heart of hearts he felt it would.

◆ ◆ ◆

They sat speechless. Jack Stern darted looks at Charlie as he stared straight ahead, watching. Jack knew he had Charlie's attention on this one.

When it was over, neither man felt eager to open the conversation. Finally Charlie burst out.

"Jesus Christ, I don't believe this. Are you really going to tie this to Madeline?"

"I promised Eddie Wallace, if the 'Madeline Caper' was more than a tryst I would let him pursue it. He is ready to do a piece on A.L.A. and I'll bet my last buck he'll come up with the truth."

"Do you have absolute proof that she was involved in this?" Charlie said.

"There's enough on these. Eddie Wallace and his Interpol contacts will give us absolute proof, and then it'll never be the same between Tom and me. I'm afraid he'll love Mady, no matter what she did."

"It's called unconditional." Sarcasm cloaked Charlie's words.

"You must have been tired of cleaning up after her," Jack said.

"If you only knew. Tom was too fine a man for her. In some perverted way, I hope she *is* connected with this, maybe it'll force him to see that bitch as she really was. In some ways I hope you're right, I mean that."

"I hope I'm wrong." Jack felt sorry for the brash, young man who sat beside him, using his talents as a spin doctor the past four years, covering up Madeline's indiscretions. Jack could understand how he felt, watching a man he admired being secretly demoralized by the woman he loved. "Did you hate her enough to have her killed?"

Charlie was thoughtful for a moment. "No, without Madeline, I wouldn't have a job. I need my agents to look at this," he said.

"Madeline's men?"

"Yes. They may shed some light on it."

"You mean those luncheons she had? I doubt it, but have them come over."

Charlie pulled out his cell phone and called the command post, instructing the men to meet him at The Herald immediately.

An hour later both men had seen the tape. They said nothing, but they seemed to know that this was the cassette that Frank Landry had called them about the day they found him murdered.

Jack Stern watched all of them suspiciously as they wondered how he got hold of it and who would have murdered the psychic for it. Could Jack be harboring a murderer? He'd never give them his source, so why ask. The reference to Casablanca on the video rang a bell with the agents, who whispered comments to each other. They had seen that name written on a pad in Ali Sahlool's apartment, it was also the title of Frank's mysterious tape that he called them about, and the translation means White House.

"And you men never picked up anything at those luncheons? No clues, not one inkling of what really went on?" Jack asked.

"No," Mitch said, "we try not to listen to private conversations, and we stayed close to the First lady, that was our job, being part of the woodwork, protecting her. But we never saw anything unusual. Shaking hands, introductions, laughing, talking."

"I understand. We're dealing with very slick people here and you can believe it or not, but I hope I'm wrong, and I really hope that Eddie Wallace comes up empty."

He'll have to," Mitch said. "We'll have to take this tape, it's part of our murder investigation. The police can't know about this." Jack handed it over, expecting this.

The agents said nothing until they left *The Herald*, and as they walked to their cars, only then did they tell Charlie that they thought Jack Stern was on to something.

"You might try to find out who else has seen it, and how many copies were made."

Charlie instructed his men, unaware that Andy Evanovich had made a copy.

CHAPTER 27

"Listen, Dickhead, I told you all I know." Kimmy Cox's face was flushed with anger as she spewed out her insults to the questioning officer, whom she knew was a little in awe of her. (He probably had a bunch of her CD's.) So she took liberties. Her attorney placed his hand on her arm to calm her down, but she was still shaking with anger. "I loved Frank, and I miss him already. He guided my career, why would I waste him... and with a knife, ugggh." She made a face and quivered at the thought of the horror. "It doesn't make sense."

"A lot of things don't make sense when you're on drugs." The older detective stepped in now, seeing his partner waging a losing battle with the acid tongued star.

"Prove it." She rose and started for the door, her attorney grabbing at her leather sleeve to stop her, the detectives shouting threats. "I'll piss in a bottle and you check it." She beckoned to the older detective, determined to put him in his place. "Come on, Dickhead." Now he and his partner were on equal ground with her, and he didn't like it.

Her attorney pulled her back into the chair whispering in her ear. "Kimberlee, cooperate with these men... *now*, or I'm out of here. Just tell them the truth."

"I told them the truth."

"Let's hear it again," the older detective said.

"My client is sorry for her behavior, she's very upset. She will cooperate fully. Now Kimmy..." It sounded more like a threat than anything else. Kimmy blew out a noisy blast of air, puffing her cheeks, and tapping the table impatiently with boredom. But she said nothing, she knew her lawyer's patience with her was running thin.

The older detective leaned forward on the table but spoke softly, losing his threatening tone. "You were the last person to see Frank Landry alive. Of course you're a suspect, but it doesn't mean you did it. If you liked this man so much, you should want to help us find his killer." His civilized manner seemed to work magic on her.

"All right." She took it from the top. "When I arrived, Frank was on the phone. He had left the door ajar for me, so I went in and waited in the hall until he was finished, then he gave me a reading."

"Where?"

"At the dining room table," she lied, wondering why that was important. "Then I paid him and left."

"What time?"

"About 3:45."

"And you arrived at three?"

"Yes."

She noticed the younger detective flinch a little, a trace of a smile on his lips, as his partner placed his hands squarely in front of her, narrowing his eye and leaning toward her. "There was no record of any incoming calls at that time. The phone records show the last call he had was about 1:30 pm."

"So maybe he talked for two hours," she snapped, "What do you want from me?" And then she remembered something, something she hadn't mentioned before, but something that might take these 'assholes' off her back.

"He gave me a manila envelope to leave downstairs."

"What?" Both detectives came alive with curiosity.

"A manila envelope. He gave it to me to leave at the desk."

"You didn't mention it before." They looked at her with skepticism, probably wondering what she was up to.

"I forgot. I was excited and scared."

Her lawyer also looked surprised at this sudden turn of events and gestured with empty hands to indicate he knew nothing about it.

"Who was this envelope for?" The cop was now staring holes through her, warning her with his eyes that she'd better tell it straight, star or not, or she'd be charged with obstructing justice.

"I don't know, I just took it and left it with the concierge to mail."

This revelation was the key to Kimmy's release. She was to stay in touch, which her lawyer promised to do, and the detectives quickly dispatched three of his top men to Parker House, where they immediately questioned the help on duty.

The day concierge, on early duty, vaguely remembered an envelope was given to him by Kimmy Cox, whom he admired. He left it for the night man to take care of because he was going off duty at four.

"Was the envelope to be mailed or delivered to someone?" the detective said.

"I guess mailed. It was from Mr. Landry's," he said, "But I was trying to get her autograph at the same time. But she just gave me the envelope and kept on walking, so I left the desk and watched her get into her limo. Gosh, you should see that thing—."

"We aren't interested in that right now," the detective said, knowing how impressed the young man was by her celebrity.

The evening concierge was equally as vague. "I was a little late, and Greg was in a rush to leave. I don't remember if I mailed it. We had a few things to be picked up by U.P.S., but I did have some parcels and envelopes that U.P.S. delivered around 4:30, and I distributed them to our tenants in the evening mail."

"Do you have a list of the tenants?"

"Sure." He pulled a log book from a lower shelf and thumbed through the pages until he found the page in question, turning the book around, showing it to the police. "See? The red checkmarks indicate that those tenants received something other than their regular mail." The page looked like a graph with each floor and apartment number listed. Bright red checkmarks were placed in boxes next to the apartment numbers. They began counting the checkmarks. There were about forty. The men would have to check every tenant to find out what each person received. If the package was mailed through the post office or picked up by U.P.S., they would have to check that too.

They started questioning tenants as they arrived home from work. When Andrea's buzzer sounded, she froze, glad Lucien was home with her. Suddenly, the house phone rang, the concierge informing her that the police were going to question her. She breathed easier now, no longer worried that some lunatic was at her door. When they questioned her, she denied receiving anything.

"But your apartment number was on the list, Ma'am. You received something that day, a parcel, a manila envelope, something other than your regular mail."

"Oh, I remember." Lucien came out of the kitchen wearing a big white chef's apron, carrying his slicing knife. "It was a sex toy we sent for. Don't be embarrassed, honey, they're grown-ups." The cops exchanged looks and left with a smile on their faces. Other people were into that too.

CHAPTER 28

I was at my desk in *Maison Russe*, daydreaming about Lucien, my new sex toy, who saved our asses with his quick thinking. Suddenly Mal's head popped in. I jumped, scared out of my wits. After Frank's death and that tape, I scare easily.

"Don't do that," I snapped.

"Sorry, but are you busy?"

"Can I help you with something?" I remained formal. I knew how erratic his behavior was, so I gave him a wide berth since he became the new kid on the block. To my chagrin, Karl gave Mal a job at *Maison Russe*. Doing what I don't know, but I do know they seemed to be happier with each other and Mal's disposition seemed to have improved. He did try to be friendly; at the same time picking my brain for information that he could pass on to some customer to appear knowledgeable. He seemed genuinely happy when he made a sale to a local society matron. Mal does have a certain smarmy charm compatible with the antiques business, and it seemed to work for him.

His darting eyes took in everything on my desk.

"Is that a good thing to have around?" He pointed to the camera.

"Yes, very good, you never know when you'll find something interesting, a painting or an object you might want to show Karl or a client."

"Or if you need to blackmail someone."

He laughed. I joined him, but I wondered what he meant by that. Perhaps I'm getting a little paranoid where Mal is concerned but I wondered if he had seen my negatives of the First Lady. He was quiet for a minute, as if he wanted to say something unpleasant. He screwed his face like a little boy and blurted, "I've been a rat to you, Andy. I see now how valuable you are to this business and I don't ever want you to feel that I'm trying to displace you."

I was shocked, miracles did happen. Was this really Mal? All he needed was acceptance and attention from Karl to make him into a changed man.

This year, Karl had decided to take Mal to the Grand Faberge auction in Geneva, something I usually attended. This year Karl asked me if I would mind the store, while he and Mal attended the auction, then taking a holiday in the South of France. I didn't mind at all. I couldn't bear the thought of leaving Lucien. So I was surprised to hear Mal say, "Look Andy, you're the expert, you really should accompany Karl."

"That's very thoughtful, Mal, but it's all arranged and you guys have this great vacation planned."

"I could meet him after the auction. I could fly straight to Nice, but at least I won't be stepping on your toes."

Stepping on my toes, I thought. *He finally had a pang of conscience.* "No, Mal, really, it's fine."

"As long as it's your decision, Andy. I know Karl can be very controlling. I want you to know if you change your mind, I have no problem with that." He turned to leave and stopped. "Let's have dinner some evening."

"I'd like that, Mal. I really would." He left, leaving me feeling that I had made the social grade with him. Dinner with Mal? I thought it would never happen.

◆ ◆ ◆

Two days later, Karl came to me, interrupting my morning chores. It's hard to listen to chitchat and keep your mind on arranging beautiful displays.

"Andy, could you go to Geneva—you and Lucien? My treat."

I hesitated because I really didn't want to go, so I quickly said, "Lucien can't go, he's on assignment here and I'd hate to leave him now that we're getting our lives together. What happened with Mal?"

"Mal broke his ankle. He can't go and I hesitate to leave you two alone, you don't exactly hit it off." After he explained how Mal broke his ankle, falling down the steps at home, I assured Karl that Mal had been very sweet to me lately.

"He invited me to dinner."

"When?" a surprised Karl asked.

"We didn't set a date, but Karl, you go. I'll meet him more than halfway. Something has changed his attitude toward me. He's really much nicer and I feel he's sincere."

Karl looked sheepishly at me as I handled a magnificent ruby dagger, laying it on a royal blue velvet background.

"Mal is nicer, Andy . . . he's a much more secure man." I waited for him to continue, curious to know what caused this great transformation. "I made Mal a partner, Andy."

"What?" I almost dropped the dagger, smashing it through the glass shelf. Disappointment written all over my face, it was something that I had expected. "Does he know that much about the business?" There was sarcasm in my voice.

"No, but he's my partner and I love him, please understand. Mal's made my life a living hell until now. But there are conditions to this. If he doesn't show a genuine interest or improvement in six months, he's back to square one."

"Six months isn't a very long time." I found myself defending Mal.

"It's long enough for me to know that the position should have gone to you, and it still might. Forgive me, Andy. You would have done the same for Lucien."

"Lucien wouldn't have put me in that spot." I continued doing my work but I felt royally screwed. Now I knew why Karl wanted to give us the all-expense paid trip. He was shrouded in guilt. But employees can't complain. If things get hairy with Mal, I'll just plan to leave.

At 1:00 pm Mal arrived, hobbling in on crutches.

CHAPTER 29

It was incredible! Mal and I were getting on so well in Karl's absence that I looked forward to seeing him every day. He was turning out to be fun, still acid tongued and wry, but I was no longer a target. Everybody else was fair game and I became his confidante when he made his outrageous remarks. Sometimes I laughed until I cried and in some insecure way, I felt he finally accepted me. I found myself choosing outfits that I felt he would approve of, and he certainly did notice everything I wore.

I could now forgive Karl for making him a partner, it transformed Mal from a mean Mr. Hyde to a fun Dr. Jekyll. I began to wonder if living in Karl's shadow was in some way responsible for his previous ill temper. Left on his own, he seemed to thrive, being a good sport about getting to work on crutches, no small feat in the rush hour. I had offered to drive him, but Karl wanted me in early and had arranged for a driver to ferry him back and forth.

I was at my desk sipping hot tea, trying to quell a queasy stomach, when I heard Mal's crutches clumping along in the corridor. I immediately felt better. Suddenly he was framed in the doorway, a boyish grin on his face, a shock of sandy hair on his forehead. Small, wire rimmed glasses sat on his straight nose, and all I could think of was *what a waste*. His putty colored suit was impeccably tailored. He belonged on the cover of *G.Q.* magazine.

"Andy, I think it's time we had that date. That is if you don't mind hanging out with a cripple."

"Not at all." I was thrilled by the invitation.

"You could fill me in on this business, as well as the other Karl, the one you straight people get to see. He's different on the gay scene."

"Karl is Karl." I didn't want to say the wrong thing.

"He sure is." He rolled his eyes. "How about dinner, tomorrow night and then . . . I'll let you take me home."

"Great." I looked at my schedule. "Lucien is on assignment, it'll be fun."

He turned to leave throwing an aside over his shoulder. "Alone at last."

When Lucien called that night, I told him about Mal's new attitude toward me. It made for a much nicer work environment without the strain of Mal snarling at me. I began to wonder how large a part Karl played in his unpleasant disposition. Why was Mal so transformed in Karl's absence? Was Karl really so different in private life? I thought I heard a hint of jealousy in Lucien's voice when I told him how handsome Mal looked today. I guess he wanted my full attention.

I woke up early and dressed with care, looking at several outfits before I settled on a chic, charcoal, pinstripe pants suit, knowing that Mal would love it. For some reason, I wanted to please him. he projected a certain aristocratic snobbery that was intimidating, I know because I had been on the receiving end of it. But now we have become friends and I wanted his approval.

We had reservations at *Chez La Grande Mere*, a chic bistro in Georgetown frequented by D.C. celebrities, so I was certain we would bump into some of our best customers, making tongues wag.

When I opened the door, an eerie feeling came over me, something didn't feel right. I looked around, and all seemed well. A chill ran through me, and my stomach felt unsettled, as it had been recently. But I had been through a huge emotional strain the past few months so I thought nothing of it. The thought of Frank's murder flashed through my mind. *I wonder if they would ever put two and two together and suspect me?*

We hadn't heard anything more about the mysterious package they were pursuing, perhaps they decided it went through the U.S. mail, and without a receipt, it would be hard to trace. I felt around in my tote bag for the video copy that I had made and which I always carried, afraid to hide it anywhere, I couldn't risk the vault with Mal around.

I turned off the alarm and punched in the security code, eager to get started. I thought of Mal and how insulting he had been to me at our Christmas party, which was held right here. Did he ever think about that? How did he feel now, after getting to know me? I wondered if he could ever change and fall in love with a woman. She would have to be a very rich woman, who could afford his expensive taste.

I unlocked the iron gate that protected the massive safe and I saw my reflection in the shiny steel door. I did look chic, albeit somewhat blurred in that burnished metal. The huge door swung open and I stared straight ahead at empty shelves, which stared right back at me. Was I in the wrong place? I blinked several times to clear my vision, but nothing had changed. They were still empty. We were burglarized. My heart raced, my stomach churned and I felt clammy. I wanted to throw up right there, but somehow I didn't; not eating breakfast helped. I bent down, looking for my personal envelope which I hid, but even that was gone. Everything was gone, and it was a horrible feeling knowing that it happened while I was left in charge.

But why weren't the police here, why no alarm? And then it dawned on me . . . Somebody had turned off the night alarm and opened the safe, and that somebody was my big date for tonight! It had to be Mal. I quickly telephoned him, letting the phone ring off the hook, but there was no answer or answering machine. How stupid I felt. How dumb I was to have fallen for his phony, nice guy act. This was a despicable thing, robbing his partner who entrusted his business to me. He demeaned us both, showing Karl just how clever he is and how stupid I am. Mal didn't change at all.

I hesitated to call the police, I didn't know if Karl wanted that yet. So I decided to try to reach him. I looked at my watch. It would be about three p.m. in Europe, he might be back in the hotel. The sooner the police were involved the sooner they would find him hobbling around at some airport; and then I saw them, carefully placed against the wall. He left a last slap at me, he left his signature; he left his crutches! Jesus Christ, we were had! My heart ached for Karl, how could I tell him this? I thought about my first impression of Mal; you should always trust your first impression. I didn't like him right from the start, he was only nice to me to get what he wanted, when he got it . . . he reverted to type.

I began to get angry. He left me holding the bag, he made me look incompetent. I took a deep breath, while looking up the hotel's number and then I dialed with trepidation the many numbers for the overseas call.

When I heard Karl's voice I had mixed feelings of relief and dread. He sounded cheerful. I just couldn't tell him. We chatted a few minutes and then I forced myself to speak of it. "Karl, brace yourself, something terrible has happened." There, I said it, now it'll take on a progression of words that will tell him.

"Is Mal all right?"

He sure is, I thought. But I said, "I don't know, Karl, we had a suspicious robbery."

"A robbery." He pooh-poohed it, not knowing the extent of it. "What'd they get?"

"Everything of great value."

"Come on, Andy, that's some haul. Nobody would have time to clear out that stuff with the alarm blaring and the police on the way."

"The alarm didn't go off."

"What, did you leave the safe open?"

How clever of Mal. Karl was questioning me. He was obviously in denial and needed a good jolt.

"I have never left the safe open, you know that."

"There's always that first time."

I felt anger which I had to control. "Karl, the alarm never went off because *this* was an inside job."

"You've got to be kidding, you mean Mal?"

"Well, I'm still here, and he isn't."

"Have you tried to reach him?"

"Yes. There is no answer and no answering machine." And then I said nothing.

"Mal, oh my God, Mal." His voice cracked and I felt for him. "Andy." He sounded frightened. "Andy, is Mal all right? Could somebody have kidnapped or harmed him? Forced him to do that?. My God, he might be hurt or murdered." He was a little too dramatic for his own good.

"Karl," I spoke sternly, "knock it off. Mal's crutches were carefully placed against the back wall. He left them there so we would know that he never had a broken ankle."

"How can you be sure of that?"

"Because a broken ankle doesn't heal in a week."

"But . . . "

"Were you there when he fell?" I said.

"No."

"So, he made it up, got someone to put on the cast or he could have done it himself."

There was an uncomfortable silence and then it finally began to register.

"Thank God I'm insured."

"You're not, Karl, not when the safe was opened by an employee who was given the code by you." I was certain the insurance company would fight this.

We ended our conversation with Karl planning to leave the next morning. He would cancel the vacation to the south of France. "How I wanted to show Mal that beautiful place, how I wanted to share it with him." He sounded wistful and pathetic, and I wanted to comfort him in some way. He is my friend and I felt his hurt. I still don't believe he fully realized the impact that this terrible deed would have on all of us. I wanted to get that bastard.

Before we parted, I told him I'd call the police and inform Interpol. Mal will certainly try to dispose of the goods on the black market for a fraction of what they are worth.

"Andy, did they get the Faberge collection?"

"Yes, Karl, *he* got everything."

One thing bothered me, which I did not discuss with Karl, he had enough for one day. But Mal could never have done this alone. Who was his accomplice? He lived with Karl, while romancing someone else. This was clearly a set up, and now he had the loot . . . and a new love.

I phoned the police and waited to speak to an officer in burglary. As I held on, I printed a sign I could put on the door, and I played with it, improving the lettering as I began answering the officer's questions. He knew our store and would be there shortly. Soon our employees would be filing in, our customers would be calling and coming by to browse, buy or exchange. I thought it best not to let the public know, not just yet. So I got up and taped the sign to the big glass door. It was the first time in the history of *Maison Russe* that a sign like that appeared on the door. "Closed for Inventory," it read.

◆ ◆ ◆

So far, Madeline's picture didn't surface on the news or in any tabloid. Mal may not have developed the film or he was so involved with the "big stuff," why bother with some negatives of somebody he may not have even recognized.

The following evening I remained at *Maison Russe* waiting for Karl to arrive directly from the airport. I had to be there when he confronted the reality of Mal's deed. The store was now closed "For Inventory," and the staff who knew the truth handled things well while we tried to regroup. Our customers were understanding, some probably glad they could hold onto their money a little while longer, and several dealers were willing to help us out with some consignment pieces. I was touched by that.

About 8 p.m., I looked up as Karl walked into his ravaged store. I sat there and watched as he viewed the empty showcases and vitrines. I let him be. Later we would have time to talk. He went to the empty safe and looked into the empty offices, perhaps hoping to find Mal sitting there, perhaps hoping that this was just a bad dream. After his tour, he came back into the store and plopped down on the huge green velvet banquette that dominated the floor. He held his head in his hands and sobbed.

"My life's work is down the drain. All for love. I'll never be taken in again. I'm not perfect, Andy, I'm a rat at times. But I did love him and now I know he stayed with me to do this. To ruin me financially. I'm ruined," he moaned.

It was only then, that I went to him and put my arms around my friend and I tried to comfort him. "Karl, you're not." I sat next to him trying to shore up his confidence. "Look, Karl." I placed one arm around his shoulder. "I have money. I could get a loan. We both have contacts. We have a good reputation, we have always paid our bills. *Maison Russe* is a class act. Several dealers have offered consignment pieces and our customers are loyal. We'll survive, and I'll work for nothing. Lucien will carry our bills."

"I can't ask you to do that. Andy, I have nothing. I'm ruined. I've already mortgaged my house to pay for some of the pieces. It was Mal's suggestion, and now I know why. Because he ended up with them. I'll have to put my house on the market. We lived well, I have huge outstanding bills. If I go bankrupt I won't even have credit for years."

"Can your family help you?"

"Andy, family money doesn't last if it's squandered on the good life."

"We'll think of something. Let's try to get some sleep and I'm sure we'll come up with something. The police and Interpol are on the case, they'd like to speak with you. I'm sure they'll find Mal."

But they didn't. He was as elusive as ever. He was a ghost. Curiously, another young man disappeared at exactly the same day. Philip Ashford was another young hustler who lived with an older benefactor. But Philip didn't steal a thing. It was Mal who did the stealing and the planning. He was now in control, playing big shot to Philip, his new love. The police surmised that they may have changed their I.D.'s and left the country, probably having had a private buyer lined up. All those magnificent objects would no longer be seen in public. They would probably end up in a vast private collection, to be seen by very few eyes, probably two.

The following day found us on the telephone calling around the world, asking customers if they wanted to sell any of their previous purchases. We finally hit pay dirt in Europe. Several dealers were interested in working with us. The house of *Maison Russe* had impressed them and Karl once again made arrangements to fly back to England, France, Belgium and Holland.

Lucien and Eddie were preparing to travel to Michigan to interview the people at A.L.A. I was glad he'd be gone for a few days. I could put all my time and energy in saving our beloved store, in trying to turn things around.

CHAPTER 30

The car screeched to a halt at the airline check in. Jack Stern jumped out, opening the back door and pulling Eddie Wallace to his feet, while Lucien lugged most of the bags. Jack waved his driver off to the parking lot while he personally took care of his men. He used his faithful driver and his own car, hesitating to rent a limousine. He trusted almost no one on this important assignment, telling Eddie and Lucien that they just might turn up the missing part to the Madeline puzzle.

Jack spent several sleepless nights trying to figure out a way to get at the truth. They had all seen Andy's video and they knew there was a lot more to this. The tentacles of this treachery reached far and wide into the inner circles of international politics. He decided that they would begin innocently enough, writing a favorable account of A.L.A.'s many charitable activities with only a hint of wrong doing by some anonymous accuser. *They said that you were funneling money into terrorist activities.* He knew it would soundly be denied, but Eddie would have to do a follow up story to prove that those rumors were false. And that's where they would start their campaign against A.L.A. They would check every 'scurrilous attack' on the group, interviewing all the officers and employees, hoping to uncover something. Tax returns, employment records, bank statements, offshore accounts, anything linking them to the horror that they had seen on the video cassette. Bit by bit, layer by layer, they would peel off the respectable facade like an onion skin until they would find the inner core of truth. Jack Stern, a man who was hard to convince at first, now firmly believed Eddie and Lucien. He knew his friendship with Thomas

Chambers would be over. He no longer would protect the First Lady's name. It was the price he had to pay for journalistic integrity.

Today, he took every precaution to insure the safety of his two top men, booking their flights under assumed names, fearing both A.L.A. and the U.S. government, not knowing exactly which one to fear most. "You can't be too careful in the roiling waters of politics." He preached safety and precaution as he used his special pass to guide the men through the huge terminal, almost boarding with them. With minutes to spare, his parting shot was of cautious encouragement. "This could be the biggest scoop of the century. Be careful." They shook hands and he watched them disappear through the gate.

The men found their seats in business class, Eddie opting for the aisle seat while Lucien juggled the bags, locking some in the overhead stow and another two under the seat in front. Eddie's portly frame crowded Lucien, who sat stiffly uncomfortable, waiting for the older man to doze off so he could give him a mild push in the other direction. *He'd never know*, Lucien thought. A little while after take off, Eddie dozed off, a soft buzz escaped his lips as Lucien made some room for himself, thinking of Andy. He would call her when they arrived.

The flight was smooth and uneventful and when the plane landed, they were tempted to applaud, happy that the first leg of their mission was successful.

They were greeted by a representative from A.L.A.

Hamza El Din was a tall, wiry man with thick, horn rimmed glasses perched on an aquiline nose. In minutes, he did a superb public relations job in perfect English.

"We only serve the good of the people." He spoke in the softly accented voice of a man who believed in his case. "We have raised more money for Arab/American charities than any other organization in this country." Eddie was inclined to disagree, but he decided to say nothing. "We fund scholarships, support exchange students and cultural events. We contribute to everyone from AIDS to unwed mothers."

To terrorists, Eddie thought.

"When you finish your article on our prestigious group, I'm certain that more people will respond to our fund raising."

What a bullshit artist, Eddie thought, playing the game and telling his host, "What a great honor it is to be here. Your altruism touches me."

He saw Mr. El Din's face relax as he smiled and bowed his head. He guided them through the crowded terminal, never offering to help Lucien with the bags, as he struggled toward a curbside stretch limousine with its motor idling, a smoky stream escaping the exhaust. The weather was cold and crisp, several degrees colder than Washington, and those few minutes outdoors were bone chilling to the men who had been comfortably warm for the last few hours. Lucien looked like a clothes tree, with a bag hanging from every part of his body, while Eddie carried his briefcase, and did all the talking.

The driver got out and opened the limousine door, helping Lucien with the bags. They leaned into the vehicle and came face to face with an elegant, middle aged man swathed in cashmere and expensive leather shoes. His iron gray hair was styled like a movie star of the forties, and the dark, tinted glasses which sat on his patrician nose made him resemble one. He sized the scruffy pair in jeans with an imperial once over, and Eddie felt he could read his thoughts. *Allah, be praised. These are Pulitzer Prize journalists?* He wasn't too far off base as their mysterious host shielded his eyes and his thoughts. They shook hands with Mohamed Razek, the executive director of A.L.A. Judging from his expensive attire, he did well indeed.

The unsmiling Mr. Razek gave the men his blessing by toasting them with a diet Pepsi. Liquor was unavailable, even though Eddie could have used a good drink. In his accented English he said, "This better be a flattering piece, because if any of our fund raising takes a nose dive because of your article, you'll know about it."

Eddie and Lucien exchanged looks. They were dealing with a

straight shooter . . . Not an old world charmer as they had thought. Any repercussions and they might as well go into hiding.

The hotel suite was big and comfortably modern. It was there that Lucien placed a call to Andy, while Eddie flopped down on the bed for a quick nap. Andy had just gotten home after having taken Karl to the airport, where he embarked on his search for some art objects to keep his business afloat. He desperately wanted to save the prestigious name of *Maison Russe*, it was too late for his house. That would be sacrificed, the bank already planning foreclosure proceedings. A harsh reality that Karl had to face. So far, Mal and the stolen treasures hadn't surfaced. One theory being that he and Philip, his suspected lover, took off in a private jet to Costa Rica, the rich coast where many of the shady rich live. Interpol was in that area pinning their hopes on Philip, hoping he would make a slip and lead them to Mal. The consensus was that Philip was not as clever as Mal.

When Lucien heard Andy's voice the usual thrill ran through him. *It never changes.* He smiled to himself, feeling the pressure in his groin. They chatted as lovers do; he telling her about the trip and their hosts, she telling him about Karl's sadness. She was alone in Washington now and Lucien hated to hang up.

"Lucien, I have something to tell you."

"What?"

"When you get home, we'll celebrate."

"With a wedding."

"Maybe," she said coyly.

"A shotgun wedding?"

"I'll tell you when you get home."

"I thought so, I really did, tell me now. I . . ."

"Don't say another word." She cut him off. "I want you in my arms. I want to see your face."

"I love you. I love you." He sighed, "God, I miss you. Let me get through this, so we can be together tomorrow night."

"I'll second that. Good night, love."

"Good night, sweetheart." They exchanged kisses over the

phone and hung up. Lucien sat there, his hand still on the receiver, his eyes glazed with happiness. *There's nothing better than old fashioned romance,* he thought, as his dream was finally coming true. He would marry the woman he loved.

The following morning they were up early, ready to tour the executive offices of A.L.A.

"We're finally allowed in the inner sanctum," Eddie laughed. "Keep your lens open to anything. I don't think they'll have the nerve to restrict us in any way, not after we lulled them into a false sense of security. They think we love them," Eddie said. "And we are representing a liberal newspaper from D.C., Madeline's stomping ground."

"Yeah, funny her name hasn't surfaced yet."

"It will," Lucien said.

True to his word, Mr. Razek's limousine was waiting, ready to whisk them to the huge beige brick building just a few blocks away from the hotel.

"If it wasn't so cold we could have walked," Eddie said.

"Sure," Lucien shot back. "You're only carrying a briefcase."

When they arrived they were greeted in the large, modern lobby by a coterie of executives welcoming the pair.

"We are honored, a Pulitzer Prize team from a Washington newspaper has expressed such interest in us."

"Our First Lady gave the Arab/American causes much of her attention. It is only fitting that we do a follow up story." Lucien's camera was flashing lights all over the place, causing the group near blindness, all except Mr. Razek who continued to wear the tinted glasses. He tried to catch those hollow eyes on camera, there was something sinister going on behind that tinted glass, perhaps the camera would capture the truth.

After a tour and a lecture on the accomplishments of the organization, the men were introduced to a number of employees at a luncheon reception in the building's special events area. Some employees seemed studied, careful in what they had to say. There was no frivolity, no disgruntled employees, there was nothing but glowing remarks being said about A.L.A. and its executive directors. Finally Eddie was ready to interview Mohamed Razek privately, as Lucien continued to take roll after roll of pictures trying to catch something . . . anything . . . on camera.

The interview went well. Eddie was careful not to antagonize Mr. Razek with any direct accusations. But it was time to address the rumors surrounding A.L.A.'s role in funding international terrorism. He handled it well, wisely discussing the issue beforehand, telling his interviewee that they could not possibly ignore that rumor. "Let's discuss it openly, and put it to rest," he said sympathetically, hoping to take Razek off guard. This was as much a trap as it was an interview, but Mohamed Razek beat him to the punch, inviting him and the U.S. government to check anything they wished; their books, employment records, background checks. They were an above board and open charitable organization. As far as Mohamed Razek knew, A.L.A. was a gift from God.

While Eddie tried to pierce the inner circle of the group, Lucien mingled and chatted with the young student volunteers and employees, taking pictures, passing out his cards, hoping that somebody would be brave enough to contact him. He spoke of the rumors and what a raw deal it was to the group. He watched facial expressions, which told him more than words. He saw something in one man's face—a young man whose interest in photography sparked a conversation.

"Come down to D.C. I'll take you around, show you everything. I also give a course at a visual arts school." The young man was very interested and asked for Lucien's card. When Lucien heard he was with the accounting department of A.L.A., that interested Lucien, who was not able to communicate this to Eddie, who was now surrounded by his new friends. Lucien felt there was more to the young man than met the eye. He felt a nonverbal communication between them, although nothing specific was said or indicated. He seemed afraid to say more than he should. If Lucien could get to him, he would work on him. Being in accounting could prove valuable to their investigation, perhaps shed some light on where their money went. If it went to terrorist groups with respectable fronts, they would find ways of checking on it. They were grasping at straws, but that's all they had right now. This and the video cassette.

◆ ◆ ◆

They were packed and ready to leave when the phone rang and Lucien answered, hoping it might be Andy. But a man's voice spoke in a slow, accented voice, clearly a Mid-Eastern accent.

"I am a friend. You are in grave danger, so heed my advice and do not travel on flight 4949. A black Chevy sedan is waiting for you in valet parking. The ticket is with the concierge in your name. If you want to live, use it."

"Who is this?" Lucien's voice grew louder as Eddie stuck his head out of the bathroom, but the caller had hung up.

"What's going on?"

"I don't know." He stood there trying to collect his thoughts. "We just had a strange call." He told Eddie what the caller had said.

"What did he mean, 'don't fly'? They gonna blow up the plane or something?"

"It's been known to happen. And we're dealing with suspected terrorists. He knew our flight number."

"You think we touched a nerve with that interview?" Eddie said. "You think they're on to us? Know that we're full of shit?"

Lucien shook his head. "I don't know. The guy I met today, the one interested in photography, seemed interested in our welfare. He asked intelligent questions, at times, too intelligent for small talk, and he's in accounting, but eager to meet me in D.C."

"Interesting," Eddie said, raising his eyebrows. "You think he's one of our guys or a turncoat? Was he the caller?"

"Couldn't tell, the call was brief. He has a car for us in valet parking, and said we'd better use it if we want to live."

"I don't get it. The interview went well, they know nothing of our planned exposé."

"Oh no?" Lucien whispered, placing his finger to his lips. It had just dawned on him that the room might be bugged.

"Come on, Lucien, you're being dramatic. This was a crank call, someone having fun with us."

"I don't think so, you saw that video, these guys have no conscience. I say forget the flight and drive back."

"That's a helluva drive," Eddie protested. "And I sure as hell am not going to use a car someone else arranged for us. That's stupid."

They continued packing, stuffing their clothes into the bags, checking the drawers, and the bathroom as the debate continued.

"We'll take turns, it won't be bad."

"My body can't take it," Eddie said. "And I thought you were so hot to get to Andy?"

"I am," Lucien said. "But I want to get there alive."

The debate continued over breakfast in that cheery, sun filled room located in the atrium of the hotel. They were so intense that the waitress hesitated to break in.

"No, no, it's okay, darlin', we're ready to order." Eddie put her at ease.

As they ate breakfast, they lobbed ideas back and forth until Eddie insisted on one. They would advise the airline and airport security of the call, and let them handle it. This didn't suit Lucien, who felt the terrorists had such sophisticated weapons that the airline could do nothing to protect them. Finally Lucien deferred to Eddie's wishes, himself eager to get back to his love.

When they finished breakfast they stopped at the concierge out of curiosity. True to the caller's word, the envelope holding the valet parking ticket was there.

"Do you remember who left this?" Lucien asked the brunette beauty in the navy blazer.

"I'm sorry, I don't remember. There are so many people leaving items," Miss Malouf apologized, giving Lucien the creeps when he saw her name tag.

Is this like some kind of underground, he thought.

They went to valet parking and handed in the ticket, waiting approximately fifteen minutes until the black Chevy sedan shot up from the belly of the hotel. The keys were inside, as well as a map on the front seat with the route from Detroit to Washington penciled in. Lucien inspected the car for any tracking device. He knelt down and felt around the tires as Eddie looked under the hood. All seemed well. They asked the attendant if he remembered who drove it.

"There are six attendants. I don't remember bringing this down," he explained.

"Forget about the license, it's probably bogus," Eddie said, not wanting to waste time. "We won't be using this now, so repark it."

They made their way back to the room to pick up their gear. "We'll take a cab to the airport, and that's that."

They stood in a cab line inching forward, as more people joined it. Eddie flashed a bill to the dispatcher, who quickly grabbed their bags and walked them over to a cab that had just pulled in, not joining the line. They jumped in as the driver tucked their luggage in the trunk, and off they went.

"Money talks," Eddie said.

"Is that what did it? It happened so fast, the others never had a chance to get pissed off. I was even surprised," Lucien answered him, as he noticed the driver's profile when he turned to them. *Had he seen him before? Could he have been there last night?* He looked up at the man's name and number; Mustafa Aheg. It didn't ring a bell. *They all look alike,* he thought.

They drove through the center of town, then passed through a deserted industrial section on the outskirts. Soon they would be on the interstate, heading for the airport. The cab began to slow down, and as they rounded a curve, the driver suddenly opened the door and rolled out onto the road, the car continuing toward the concrete wall.

The explosion ripped the car to shreds, hurtling the tangled metal and mangled body parts into the air and smashing them onto the frozen pavement. Red streamers of blood flew in every direction like splattered paint, and two friends were joined in death, their body parts mingled, indistinguishable from one another.

The fire that followed shot thick acrid smoke into the air, and a watchman in a nearby building took cover as his windows shook from the blast, the acrid smoke enveloping the buildings in the area. Cautiously peeking out of a window at the grotesque sight the watchman yelling, "Emergency" before dialing 911. He continued yelling and dialing at the same time until someone came on the line. By the time he had called his wife to tell her, he heard the fire engines and police sirens approaching, and Farid Majdallani was blocks away, driving out of the area with his partner.

CHAPTER 31

Jack Stern was on time. He paced the arrival area, checking his watch. His men must have missed the flight, but they hadn't called; he thought that strange. He called his wife again, but they hadn't called. He checked with the airline.

"The gentlemen missed the flight, but they didn't book an alternate," he was told. He called the hotel, confirming their check-out. He tried A.L.A. headquarters, but got a recorded message saying they would be open for business at 9 am Monday.

He left the airport dissatisfied, driving back home and calling Andy on his cell phone to know if Lucien had called.

"No, I spoke to Lucien last night."

"Doesn't help now," he brusquely said, hanging up. A strange feeling gripped him . . . He was a tough, hard-nosed, ex-Marine, whose stomach was churning.

He parked his car and dashed inside to his study. "Did Eddie call?" he yelled out to his wife on passing. Her answer panicked him. Eddie always called, always kept in touch, something was wrong. He picked up the phone and dialed the operator. "Please connect me to the Detroit police, any precinct will do." The calls flew back and forth and finally he had his answer within the hour "I'll be there on the next flight out of D.C." He hung up and ran to the bathroom, retching his meal.

His wife, who stayed in the background now helped him pack a small bag, calling his driver and alerting his editor to meet him at the airport for instructions. He was ready to leave but he felt he must make one more call.

Andy had been preparing a romantic dinner for two, which was now warming in the oven. This was a special homecoming.

She had special news to tell her love. They probably missed the flight, or traffic is bad. She sat around waiting, filing her rough nail with an emery board, looking through the Sunday paper again. She jumped when the phone rang, grabbing it on the second ring.

"Andy, Jack Stern, brace yourself. I have some terrible news." Her head spun. *What was he talking about? There was no plane crash, there was nothing on the news.*

"Andy, we have to wait for a forensics report, but I've been in contact with the Detroit police. I'm certain that Eddie and Lucien were in a terrible car accident." he would save the gruesome details for later, discouraging her from accompanying him.

"Andy, listen to me. It appeared to be an accident but they may have been murdered. We're in jeopardy, because we're the only ones who saw that video cassette and somehow they can't take a chance with us. Look behind you and trust no one. I'm sorry, kid, but I have to go to Detroit." He hung up, pacing the floor as his wife silently watched him, knowing he didn't like to talk in difficult times. Seeing his impatience, she went to the window looking for his driver to arrive when the phone rang. He knew it would be Andy, the news finally penetrating, he didn't expect what he was about to hear.

"You're next, Jack," the voice said. "You and the girl are next."

"Who *IS* this?" Jack roared, shaking the very foundation of his big house. But the caller hung up, he was yelling into a dead telephone.

◆ ◆ ◆

"Andy, we're on the list. I just had a threatening call. Something must have gone wrong with the A.L.A. interview. Pack a bag, we'll pick you up in twenty minutes. I want you here with my wife. I don't trust anyone in government. I'm calling DELLCO International, the top security firm. Don't leave the apartment until I get there, and if you happen to have a copy of that cassette, hide it."

Andy immediately threw some essentials in a bag along with

some jewelry and cash. She quickly tore the hem of her coat lining and stitched the cassette inside; the weight of the long coat hiding it. Then she waited.

On the ride to Andy's apartment, the car went around a curve in the road. The driver was blinded by the setting sun directly on his windshield. He didn't see the white catering van which came up behind them, out of nowhere, picking up speed and riding the sedan's tail. With one quick thrust it bulldozed the car right over the steep embankment, where it rolled and bounced several times, smashing into a stand of trees, bursting into flames. Jack Stern, a thinking man, never had a minute to think.

Andy paced the floor for over an hour before calling Jack's house.

"The Señor and Señora were not home," she was told by their maid. She turned on the radio to hear if there were any traffic tie-ups and that's when a news flash told her: "Jack Stern, the publisher of the *Washington Herald* and his driver were killed in an automobile accident late this afternoon. Police believe that another car was involved, possibly making it a hit and run. They are investigating."

◆ ◆ ◆

"What? What?" I leaped at the radio, frantically twisting the dial until I heard it again. I stood paralyzed, trying to absorb what had been said, while the newscaster droned on. "Oh my God. Lucien and Eddie, and now Jack. Who are these people?" Those were no accidents, I was certain of that. I've never felt more certain, or so completely alone. "Bastards," I screamed as I lost control. "Fucking bastards, I hate you, I hate you," I kept screaming, as I dropped to the floor. "You've taken everything from me! They're gone, they're all gone," I sobbed, writhing with emotional pain. Suddenly I stopped. I sat up, holding onto a chair. "Oh, my God," I whispered, "I'm next."

CHAPTER 32

December 3

Mitch Levitt and Rolland Nichols had escorted Mrs. Chambers through the side entrance of Parker House. The management knew of Mrs. Chamber's monthly visits to her psychic, so her presence there on a gloomy Thursday morning didn't create a stir. They gave her the privacy she needed. The security cameras would show the trio entering and leaving the building and nothing would be made of it; the Parker House staff would be discreet. For the past two years, ever since they played host to Mrs. Chambers visits, they no longer had any code violations. It helped to know powerful people.

The two agents walked their charge down a corridor to a bank of elevators which were lined up waiting for business. Within seconds, the doors opened and the trio entered the empty car, which moved swiftly to the seventh floor.

"I'm fine, gentlemen," she said leading them down the corridor, giving them notice that this was as far as she wanted them to go. From this point on she wanted to be alone.

"Shouldn't we go inside, Mrs. Chambers, you know, to check things out for you?" a playful Mitch Levitt asked (having an idea of what went on behind those closed doors and knowing what her answer would be).

"You're just nosy, Mitch." She tapped his nose with her finger, reducing him to mush. "I'll call you when I'm through with my reading." She winked at Mitch, dismissing them. She slid the key in the lock and slipped inside, turning the lock until it made a loud click, shutting them out of her secret life. A triumphant look crossed her face as she tossed her hat and flung her coat on the yellow silk sofa. She reached into her tote bag and took out a black, rectangular object which she shoved between the lush pillows. Satisfied that the object was out of sight, she strode across the living room, removing her clothes, dropping them in a trail to the bedroom where her lover waited. First the blouse came off, as she deftly unbuttoned it. Then she unfastened her skirt, which slid down around her ankles. Stepping out of it, she shook out her elegant blonde hair, running her fingers through it, bending her head and shaking it again. She resembled a jungle cat searching for prey. The black lace bra and panty smelled of her body creme, a heavy musk. The black thigh high hose left a generous slice of ivory skin between the black lace garments.

She leaned against the doorjamb, posing seductively while her naked lover lie on the bed, waiting. The attraction was so overwhelming that she succumbed to that heady rush that totally took over her body. For now, she was his slave, dropping to her knees, and crawling to him like the jungle cat she was. She clawed up the side of the bed, crawling over him and feeling every part of his hard sinewy body, comparing him to the handsome, young agent who escorted her upstairs. She wondered why she thought of him now, finally deciding that her lover was smaller framed. And as they made love, Rolland Nichols once again crashed into her thoughts. She thought of the convenience an affair with Nichols would be, and Mitch would say nothing. She had trained him to keep his mouth shut. But she was here and Farid Majdallani was a good lover, she might as well enjoy.

"I missed you, darling," she murmured dreamily while squirming over him. Her lips wrapped around each word with studied sexiness. "Tell your contact, I'll give him what he wants for what I want. A fair exchange, no?"

"How can you speak of deals now, my golden girl?" Her dusky lover spoke in the softly accented voice of the Middle East. He caressed her body licking her neck and ears.

"I'll speak of anything I choose, I'm not your slave."

"No, I am yours, my love." He massaged her anus with his finger as she felt the slight contractions.

"Farid, I have some serious business to discuss, something that has me concerned."

"And what is that, my love?" He was in a playful mood.

"I was able to get a bootleg copy of that tape and if they want it, they must pay me a hundred times what I paid for it."

"You are punishing them?" Majdallani said.

"Yes, I am. They're putting me in jeopardy; if this should fall into the wrong hands..."

"I don't know if they will take kindly to this kind of... thing?"

"Why not? I give them credibility and dignity. They no longer do business in alleyways and park benches and they'd better stop the leak in their organization before the whole thing comes to a screeching halt. If I can get a copy, someone else can." She purred her ultimatum.

"It's done, sweet, I'm your slave, you know that." He jumped off the bed, clowning around, pulling her legs over the side of the bed and dropping to his knees, kissing her private parts. An electric shock ran through her as he continued teasing her quivering body. He removed the remaining garment and fell onto the bed again. She rolled over on him, once again assuming the superior position.

"Where is the tape?" he asked.

"You don't have to know," she answered.

"But I do."

"I hid it," she said.

"Here?"

"No, in my private quarters." She lied, having hidden it among the sofa pillows.

"Your private quarters belong to me." He sucked her nipple and rubbed her vigorously while she squirmed like a tadpole, pushing into his hand. They made love and climaxed, relaxing in each other's arms. Again, he tried to find out where the purloined tape was hidden, but she refused to budge. She wanted her money and she wanted to teach them a lesson. She could not jeopardize all she had because of their lax security. They'd better tighten up or lose her involvement.

It was almost two hours before he realized she was playing hardball to the end. They sipped champagne and then he rose to get her dessert from his pocket. He handled the ampule carefully, knowing it was time to do his work.

In less than five minutes she would be dead.

He braided his fingers through her hair and yanked her head back, licking her neck. She groaned with pleasure.

In four minutes she would be dead.

She deserved a passionate kiss before she died, and he kissed her passionately.

He crushed the ampule between his fingers and shoved it under her nose, instructing her to sniff, then breathe deeply.

"The next climax, my darling, will send you to paradise." He accurately predicted as she obeyed him. She inhaled and moaned, undulating like a bitch in heat, arching her back and rubbing her vagina against anything she could, calling out obscenities to him. Her lips parted in sensual abandon as she threw her head back, sending her hair cascading over the side.

In less than three minutes she would be dead.

She rode him like a bronco, screaming in ecstasy, not getting enough. He lie there, looking up into that distorted face; waiting. Her climax was thunderous as she clutched her chest, gasping and swallowing huge gulps of air as the excruciating pain shot down her left arm. Her lower jaw ached as she fell over him. He rolled her onto her back and shimmied out from under, feeling her pulse. She had none. He dressed quickly as the telephone rang and the message machine kicked on. It was Madeline's Secret Service agent, concerned about her lateness.

Majdallani stuffed the champagne flutes into each pocket and combed through her tote and her pockets, looking for the incriminating cassette. Perhaps she was telling the truth, perhaps she did hide it in her private quarters at the White House. He would have to get someone to look. His blank expression had twisted in frustration. He grabbed the bottle. After a year of role-playing, he finally did his job; but where was her videotape? He scanned the bedroom. They couldn't have Frank Landry stumbling onto it, but he found nothing. His eyes darted around the living room, not knowing that what he wanted was just yards away from where he stood, not knowing that she had hidden it among the soft sofa cushions, only to be found weeks later by Frank Landry's housemaid.

CHAPTER 33

Rolland Nichols tried to have a conversation with his partner. He sipped his hot coffee while making small talk, but he was talking to himself. Mitch Levitt stared ahead, deep into his thoughts. His coffee remained untouched. He just picked at his food when they stopped for lunch and he spoke when absolutely necessary. There was a drastic change in his behavior and appearance. What once was a robust, lively man was now a shadow of himself. His face drawn, his eyes hollow, his clothes ill fitting. Everything about him was flat, that's why a drive to Fort Marcy Park seemed like a good idea. It gave them some privacy in the open air. It wasn't busy and Rolland found a good place to park. Nobody would bother them. He tried to cajole his partner out of his dark mood. It wasn't like Mitch, to be quiet and withdrawn, and everything the younger man suggested was met with silent resistance.

For the past few weeks Rolland noticed the gradual change and watched closely for signs of drug or alcohol use. He ruled both out. Something else was eating at him, like a terminal disease, first attacking his confidence, then eating away at his personality and self esteem. Mitch always behind the wheel, now left the driving and the decisions to his partner. Mitch Levitt became a shell of a man.

He sat there picking at his cuticles, muttering to himself.

"What'd you say, Mitch?" Rolland asked to no response. It was obvious that the man needed help and Rolland would speak to his superiors. He wondered why his wife ignored the call for help. Why would she pretend that all is well? He missed the man who shared part of his life the past year. He missed his corny jokes and lusty laugh. In the bullshit world of D.C. politics, Mitch was real; with a wife, kids, a house and mortgage. They shared Thanksgiving dinner. At Christmas they theorized about the First Lady's death, and buried deep in his heart, Rolland knew that Mitch was his anchor to reality.

The usual silence surrounded them, as an occasional tear would scramble down Mitch's cheek, losing momentum as it raced to his chin. Maybe the department psychiatrist could dig it out of him. Rolland would arrange it.

"Hey, buddy." He spoke with forced cheerfulness. "We've been through a lot together, but you seem so 'serious' lately." He made fun of the word serious, trying to make light of it, trying not to put a gloomy spin on it. "Come on, guy, what's up?"

"Yeah, yeah, Rollie, yeah, yeah. Something's bothering me." He spoke quickly, staccato paced. "I fucked up, that's what. *I fucked up!*"

"Come on," Rolland protested.

"You know I always did a good job, took pride in my work. But . . . " His voice cracked and his lips quivered. "I can't do it any more. I'm a phony. I'm taking a check every week and I'm not doing the job, and I haven't been doing it for the last couple of years. I'm quitting this game."

"Why quit, you did nothing wrong," Rolland said.

"Nothing wrong? I'm the senior agent, and you, kid . . . you have more brains in your ass than I have in my head. I let it happen. I let her manipulate me into getting her way and she died because of it. If I had done my job, she'd be alive, the President wouldn't be involved in a cover-up."

Rolland could no longer keep the secrets he had lived, locked up. He could no longer allow Mitch to feel that he was inept, when it had all been planned, everything was beyond his control.

"No, Mitch, you did nothing wrong. There were tremendous forces against you." Rolland looked at the untouched container of coffee. He thought of Mitch's decline and he wondered how he could fix it. *Was it really his fault that Mitch was falling apart? How the hell can I fix it?* he thought. *By being straight with him. By telling him the truth.* "Mitch." He took a deep breath. "There was an insidious plan and I was part of it."

"Plan, what plan?" Mitch showed interest for the first time and Rolland felt encouraged that he was on the right track; he had to continue now, he had to salvage his friend, his own anchor to reality.

"Madeline died because she was involved in terrorist activities. She was killed."

Mitch, slowly and eerily, turned to face him. "Why?" he whispered.

"Sahlool and Majdallani are double agents who got firm evidence that she had to be taken out. They're working for us. We're C.I.A., Mitch, State Department, not Treasury."

"Oh, my God," Mitch whimpered, shaking his head in denial. Rolland continued to explain as fast as he could.

"They choose Majdallani for his looks and he fucked her royally. During this liaison he collected enough evidence to connect her with the new Soviet nations and every rogue nation that could scrape up enough cash to buy black market weapons, plutonium and other deadly shit. Madeline was a well paid power whore. That's what this First Lady was about." His voice rose as he tried to convince Mitch that she deserved to die. "Majdallani firmed our suspicions when Madeline showed him a book. *Investing Your Money in Offshore Money Havens.* He immediately informed us and we began digging. That, and some numbers someone found, led us to several offshore accounts under an assumed name." Mitch began to tremble. Rolland reached over and turned the heater on, hoping the brisk winter weather was the reason why he shook.

"All this took place under my nose . . . and I smelled nothing." The revelation was too much for him. He opened the car door and let in the cold.

"Please, Rollie, let me be, this is too much. I was duped by everyone. You, Madeline, Charlie. My God, what must you think of me? Was I singled out for this? Did they say, 'Get that asshole, Mitch. He'll never know what goes on.' ?"

"No, Mitch, it was never like that. I wanted to tell you."

"Yeah, sure." He climbed out of the car and slammed the door.

"Leave the gun, Mitch," Rollie called out, quickly rolling down the window on the passenger side.

Mitch lowered his head and shook it. "That's funny. That's really funny."

He walked down the footpath, disappearing into the woods, a certain resignation in his step as Rolland watched. *He should have left his gun. I don't like this. Maybe he needed time alone, maybe he'll be all right, maybe all he needed was the truth and some time alone to digest it.* But Rolland still felt concern as he left the warmth of the car, turning up his collar and following Mitch's trail down the footpath.

◆ ◆ ◆

The shot rang out as Rolland ran toward it, yanking out his cell phone, dialing 911 on the run. He wanted no more secret ambulances. This he had to handle legit. He looked left and right, trying to spot Mitch, but the trees and brush obstructed his view. He stopped running, looking all around him, but he saw nothing. He scanned the ground, perhaps he was lying somewhere in the brush. He raced up a knoll and then he saw him, crumpled in a heap on the frozen ground. Rolland yelled for help, hoping a security guard would hear him and come to their aid. He continued running toward the heap and slid to a stop, dropping to his knees, removing his coat and covering the wounded man. He took his pulse. He was still alive. He tried to stem the flow of blood pouring out of his chest. He wondered why he didn't aim for his head. He held Mitch as his life ebbed away. *Poor Mitch*, Rolland thought. *He couldn't even do this right.* Madeline had compromised him. She had another notch in her belt.

"Jesus, Rollie," Mitch sputtered, "Don't tell me you're The Snake?" It was difficult for him to speak, but he had to know.

"Majdallani came in as The Snake, and infiltrated A.L.A. He gave her some shit to bring on the heart attack."

"And if I had gone with you, like you said, we might have saved her," Mitch said.

"It would have happened sooner or later. You can't prevent the inevitable."

"The psychic?" he whispered. It was becoming more difficult for him to speak.

"When the psychic informed us about the video he found, I called Majdallani on one of our pit stops. He did the rest. He had to kill the psychic because he had seen the video and wouldn't give it up. But Majdallani never found it." The wailing of the ambulance siren was heard in the distance.

"Rollie." Drained of color, Mitch struggled with his words, knowing that death was moments away. "Who . . . was behind it all?"

"It was a C.I.A. thing, Mitch."

"Was that bastard Charl . . ." His voice drifted into nothing as he took his last breath, cursing his nemesis. He made one more exhaling sound, a gurgling noise and then his eyes became fixed. The ambulance came into view slowing down, crawling toward them. The paramedics bolted out, wheeling the stretcher down the footpath to where he lay. Rolland wondered why Mitch didn't speak of his family, why he didn't leave a final message to them. *I guess he only had so much time, and knowing this was more important than anything else.* Mitch would never have admitted it, but Rolland now knew what he had suspected, that Mitch had been in love with Madeline.

CHAPTER 34

Rolland Nichols sat pillar-straight in his chair waiting for his meeting with the President. He was summoned without explanation knowing that eventually this meeting would take place. After waiting twenty minutes, the door flew open and agent Nichols rose, only to be stopped by the President's hand, signaling him to remain seated. He nodded 'hello' on passing to his desk. A profound tiredness pulled at every stride he took toward his desk, and as he settled into his chair an uneasiness seemed to wash over him. There was no small talk about the weather or health, he came directly to the point.

"Is it safe to speak?"

"Yes sir, I swept the room, everything will be off the record."

"Then we'll have a frank and final discussion. After this . . . the matter is closed." He steepled his fingers and rested his head against the back of the tall leather chair, peering at the young man in a thoughtful manner. There was an awkward silence, as one waited for the other to speak. Finally the President broke the silence.

"You know I invoked my right to executive privilege."

"I know, sir."

"Under current laws, a president has the right to withhold secrets from Congress for national security reasons."

This was not what the agent wanted to hear as another awkward silence filled the room. Finally Rolland said, "I liked Mitch. I liked him a lot. It hasn't been easy for me."

"I'm sure. But he was getting dangerously close to home, suspecting Charlie."

"Yeah, poor Charlie."

"Yes, poor Charlie indeed, always taking the blame." The President's mouth curled as he recalled some incident when Charlie gallantly took the heat.

"But I faced a moral dilemma, I had to choose between my wife or the good of the people. Remember, I gave her this powerful position, and I loved her, but she was evil, and she didn't even know it. She thought it was one big drama and she was this charismatic leading lady, and she would have gotten away with it. I had to take action." The young man nodded in agreement. "I felt the end justified the means, because there's something I learned through the years and it's that . . . you can't change the music of the soul; you just can't." The lines in his face deepened as he pondered what he had said and Rolland Nichols thought of all the good people who died because of her or was it because the President decided to handle it his way. He had to bear some responsibility. But in the end, Rolland agreed, that it had to be. "Madeline really wanted to be President, but she ended up being First Lady," the President said.

"And that wasn't enough for her?" Rolland said as his mind wandered to the only marketplace luncheon he had worked at.

◆ ◆ ◆

He was selected from an elite group of young C.I.A. operatives. The timing was right. John Stanger, the First Lady's personal agent for almost three years, retired, leaving a vacancy that agent Nichols had been recruited to fill. He was told everything about her; now only five people knew of the operation "Em Pea" (*MarketP*lace). The President; Howard Baskin, the head of the C.I.A.; Rolland Nichols; and double agents Farid Majdallani, and Ali Sahlool. Rolland had been on the job a short time when he worked at Madeline's final "marketplace" luncheon.

It was picture clear in his mind as he escorted the First Lady into the dazzling gold and white room, standing near as she greeted her guests, while white jacketed butlers circulated with gold trays of champagne, vodka and foie gras. A string quartet played Mozart in a far corner, the music mingling with the delicate scent of the lily centerpieces on each table, but the music and the flowers weren't enough to cover the stench of evil that prevailed in that room.

"Not too close kid," Mitch warned. "She wants privacy with her guests, otherwise you're history."

I know why, Rolland thought. But he nodded his thanks for the advice. He couldn't risk getting transferred. He spotted double agent Majdallani chatting with Madeline as she shimmered in a white satin top and black slit skirt which exposed a well shaped leg. *How could anyone so exquisite, be so bad* Rolland thought, trying to eavesdrop without success.

She worked the room like a butterfly, moving from guest to guest. Flirting, joking, introducing the buyers to the sellers, and all of them mingling with legitimate business people.

"Igor darling, come with me," she spoke in a breathless voice, leading a Soviet ambassador by the hand to a dusky complexioned man in a well cut suit, whom Rolland knew to be a black market arms dealer. She focused her attention on him, sliding her hand under his arm, squeezing his muscle. His lips curled into a half smile as he looked directly at her cleavage. Others swarmed toward her, kissing her hand, angling to catch her attention or an approving glance.

Is pussy that powerful? Rolland thought. *I guess it is.* He answered his question wondering what these guys *really* thought of her. He watched her manipulate those men and he glanced at Mitch who seemed to be getting a kick out of the way Madeline controlled the situation.

She complimented Mohammed Razek, for his good work with the A.L.A. , that Goddamned front for terrorists, Rolland thought.

"Ah, Madame, you are the loveliest of First Ladies," the foreign minister of the Ukraine kissed her cheek while his handsome aid added, "Jackie wasn't bad."

"But what about Barbara, could she turn you on?" Madeline said.

"No, but you could." They burst into co-conspiratorial laughter throwing back their heads, white teeth flashing as Rolland stood by knowing that she had had a fling with him.

He knew of the affairs; of her involvement with the arms dealers. He knew she had arranged to seat the buyers with the sellers so they could finalize their deals and she would be assured of her cut. Agent Nichols knew everything. *She must be getting a tremendous high pulling this off right under the nose of the most powerful man in the world,* he thought as that man's voice brought him back to the room.

◆ ◆ ◆

"She waged war on her own people for a price. She manipulated and deceived in such a way . . . that would have been dazzling if it wasn't so vile."

His calm voice with its cold analysis pleased the agent. *He was in complete control,* he thought.

The President reached for the cut crystal decanter which sat on a silver tray. He slid it toward him, removing the sparkling stopper and carefully poured two snifters of brandy. Cradling the drink in his hand he rose halfway to serve it. Rolland reached for it. There was a slight tinkle as they touched snifters then sipped the golden liquid, feeling it coursing down.

"You know I stalled signing of the anti-terrorist bill because of Madeline. She argued against it citing our openness to multiculturism and she begged me to give it a favorable bent. She gave me all kinds of politically correct reasons why decent Arab/Americans would be offended by it." He gave a bitter laugh, shaking his head in dismay. "I wonder how much she got for that?"

"You did sign it, sir."

"Only after she lost her grip on me."

"How, sir?"

"Blood pressure pills."

"Pills, sir," Rolland said.

"Yes, thank God, pressure pills. I was becoming impotent because of them. No Viagra for me, I saw a way to finally free myself from this woman. I shook myself free from her grasp and I stepped back and saw my life with her. If I allowed her to continue, she would have sold us to the highest bidder, probably to the Chinese."

"How did you come to suspect her?"

"Little hints, here and there. A stray name, a few clues, rumors of the marketplace luncheons, and that video. Then one day I was in the ground floor corridor, you know, the Hall of the First Ladies. Security had found a snippet of paper with a name and some numbers written on it. They gave it to Charlie. The name on it was "Magdalena Casablanca" and the numbers were 7034. They'll be graven in my mind forever. Something rang a bell with that name and I searched my mental file, and I finally remembered Madeline humorously referring to herself as "Magdalena Casablanca," when I spoke to our Hispanic constituency. Immediately I felt an ominous overtone. When you live with a Gemini you can expect anything. It could have been another affair but I felt it needed checking. I called your chief personally at the C.I.A., I didn't even tell Charlie. Howard agreed with me, knowing Madeline's fondness for young men and Arab causes but I was more concerned with her being used for access to the White House. So we pursued it, being the only two who knew." The President took a long sip of brandy, heaved his head back and closed his eyes for a minute, as agent Nichols sat in silence, waiting for more. When he opened his eyes, he seemed refreshed, ready to continue without missing a beat.

"The Russians who were the sellers used various aliases to wire money through a complicated route via the West Indies, the Cayman Islands, then to Ireland and finally to the Isle of Man, an offshore haven where banking is secretive. One name kept popping up. Howard ingeniously traced that name and those four numbers to two offshore accounts. He played with thousands of combinations using those four numbers before he hit, and he found millions of dollars in those accounts and he was able to trace the convoluted trail of aliases back to Madeline. We had absolute proof that she was the one. Handwriting analysis, Frank Landry's apartment in Virginia, we had the goods on her, and I forced myself out of shock when we discovered who it was who was paying her. We had to act, and the plan went into effect."

"Couldn't you just confront her, sir?"

"No, she would have lied or charmed herself out of it, but we needed to know more. Howard recalled double agent Farid Majdallani from the Middle East where he had infiltrated and killed The Snake and his men, taking on his identity. He then infiltrated the A.L.A. ranks here."

"And nobody knew?" Rolland Nichols said.

"No, because nobody knew what The Snake looked like. He was a master of disguises. We gave him a business front, the Taxi and Limo Service, invited him to social functions where he made contact with the Russians and Ukrainians. Soon after that he made Madeline fall hard for him. But Majdallani is like a trained police dog, young, virile, controlled and loyal. Soon she involved him in international intrigue to broker deals which produced huge rewards for her. We rented the apartment in the psychic's building for agent Ali Sahlool, which gave Majdallani easy access to both apartments, the psychic's and his hiding place, without having his name on the lease or anyplace else. If she tired of him, you were chosen to take over and become involved with her. But clearly you were chosen to finish the job . . . in case he failed."

"I did, sir, I did finish it," Rolland said.

"I thought so." They were two men with the bond of murder between them and now they were perfectly at ease with this discussion.

"It was good that Mitch decided to wait in the car that day rather than accompany me upstairs. Majdallani was leaving as I arrived. He had given her the amyl nitrate to sniff and she had a coronary, which is what he wanted, but she wasn't dead. I had to finish the job with a pillow."

At that moment Rolland searched the President's eyes and

wondered what kind of a man sat before him. Why didn't he just expose her, turn her into the Attorney General or just resign from office, leaving her powerless. He wondered if it was payback for all the past hurt and humiliation she had heaped upon him. His mind continued to probe as he heard the answer.

"It had to be this way. I've asked myself, 'was this a personal thing?' I can't honestly say, but I don't think so. We were helpless in preventing this over U.S. Airspace. The country would have been in chaos and Madeline would have been thrown in prison, she couldn't have handled that. The party would have been destroyed along with it's President. I could never finish what we've started and I would have been remembered only for this tragedy, not for anything else."

"So it all boils down to politics," Rolland said.

"To a degree, but don't forget what she was involved in. Here . . ." He rose and removed the video cassette from his pocket. "Let's play this, just in case you feel some guilt. It works for me." He slipped the cassette into the mouth of the VCR and pressed a button. He returned to his seat watching the young man's face more often than the screen.

A series of large black Cyrillic numerals flashed by. A distant voice became audible. The man spoke Russian. The screen suddenly showed a view of the coast, with lights dotting the shoreline like a sparkling garland. Suddenly, an English translator's voice overtakes charge as the Russian is barely audible in the background.

"Good evening and a special thank you to Señora Casablanca, our beautiful hostess from Washington."

The President interrupted. "They tie her into this on the record, just in case she decided to walk away or turn them in."

"Blackmail, sir."

"Of a sort, since they all know whose code name it is." Their eyes returned to the shoreline on the screen. The invisible translator continued.

"We are in a boat off the coast of Long Island. This is a popular and frequently used air corridor for New York's largest airports.

While we wait for our one time only demonstration, I will give you a rundown of facts that have led up to this exciting moment. Years ago . . ." the voice droned on, "Soviet scientists experimented with scalar or telsawaves. The Soviets were terrified of the destructive capabilities of the Star Wars defense system which gave the United States the capability of showering the Soviet Union with nuclear weapons shot from the earth's orbit. In 1986 the Soviets were advancing in the development of an energy beams weapons system to counter Star Wars. Upon breakup of the Soviet Union, Soviet scientists involved in weapons development, including nuclear ones, suddenly found themselves out of work. Some were reduced to smuggling plutonium, as we know, while others have tried to sell their knowledge of a powerful weapons system to the highest bidder, and that is why you are here tonight . . . that bidder is . . . *you*.

We will record for you tonight, the one time demonstration. This will be the *first* and *only* time we will demonstrate the capability of this weapons system; this supreme device of destruction, this potential darling of terrorists, and now . . . we begin.

Suddenly there was silence as the camera focused upward into the inky night. The voice resumed. "Within seconds, you will see a mighty American aircraft gaining altitude from takeoff at a nearby airport. This is a passenger plane heading toward Europe. Watch closely the streak of light targeting the plane as it ascends. Now you see it, now you don't."

The President watched his visitor flinch. He had seen this before, but he still reacted.

A streak of light shot forth and pierced the black sky literally breaking the aircraft in two. It was a hideous, surrealistic sight that was over in seconds. The split aircraft was now in flames, plunging and crashing in a fireball into the black water. The voice continued in its slow, businesslike monotone.

"This targeting beam is followed within less than a split second by a second energy wave which tore apart this jumbo jet. We are most sorry for the passengers, the sorrow and the inconvenience this has caused." The voice was remorseless as he continued. "This real demonstration was absolutely necessary to prove to you that we are legitimate arms dealers, this is not a set up, and that we are capable of delivery. Now, please bear with us as we leave this location immediately." The roar of the engine drowned out any conversation as the boat sped away from the scene.

When they finally stopped, far enough away, the voice continued its sales pitch. "Another good feature of this weapons system is that the aircraft's black box will reveal no clue. Telstar waves immobilize all electronic devices. You will read all about this 'accident' in the news for years to come. The highest government agencies will review many theories but their findings will be inconclusive. There will not be enough supporting evidence to show that there was a mechanical failure, a bomb on board or that the plane was targeted by an explosive projectile. Some people may claim to have seen a sharp beam of light shooting towards the jet, but I guarantee . . . that their findings will be inconclusive. After years of investigation, the jury will still be out on what caused this aircraft to crash.

Our system comes with a guarantee, training and instruction manual translated to the language of choice. The bidding will begin at five million U.S. dollars. Sealed bids will be taken at a private luncheon, better known as the market place, compliments of Señora Casablanca, who will issue a formal invitation to all interested parties. It has been a pleasure introducing our weapons system to you. Thank you . . . until we meet."

The screen was blank as the President rose to turn it off. "He was right. This was a callous, cold blooded demonstration to impress buyers."

Rolland sat quietly. He was trained not to react, but he felt an inward disgust toward Madeline, her deceit and all the people who lost their lives because of her. "And you never suspected those luncheons?"

"That market place for death," the President interrupted him. "No, I never did. It gave her something to do, to get involved with some legitimate cause. They dined, drank, flirted and had a big laugh at the stupid American President whose wife was a terrorist mole, the Señora who got her cut."

"All those guests were checked, we did some of the background checks ourselves. How did they slip through?"

"You know that most of them were respectable and the others were escorted through on Madeline's orders and some gave huge donations to the party allowing them access. She played a high stakes game of international intrigue and lost. Nichols, you deserve a medal." Bitterness covered his words, the bitterness of having been deceived by the woman he loved.

"I murdered your wife, sir."

"You saved us more heartache, be content in knowing that." He began tidying up his desk as Rolland leaned forward and placed his snifter on the silver tray. The meeting was over. "Is there anyone else who knows?" the President asked.

"The young woman."

"Does she have a copy of this cassette?"

"I'm not sure but she might."

"Then you know what to do."

Rolland's eye twitched uncontrollably as he answered, knowing exactly what he must do. The President rose, signaling the meeting's end. The young agent popped up out of his seat, his shoulders straight back as he saluted his commander-in-chief. He turned on his heels and left without further ceremony.

President Chambers removed the cassette, holding it close to him as tears streamed down his face, his body barely moved as those tears fell and beaded on the plastic cover. "I'm sorry, my love, I'll never understand . . . why. I only know it had to be," he explained to her for the last time. Later, in the privacy of his quarters, he would destroy the monster he held in his hand, and move on to other business.

CHAPTER 35

It was the crossroads of late night and early morning as I sat in a hotel lobby in Pentagon City, trying to stay alive. Why I chose this hotel, I don't really know, except that it was right under their noses, while they probably watched every road and terminal out of D.C. I had to remain vigilant and proceed with extreme caution. So far, so good.

I had dumped my B.M.W. at the dealership, telling them I was ready for a trade-in in a day or two. Then I cabbed it to the hotel. I'm certain that there was a silent, all-points bulletin out on my car and that they'll find some way to involve the local police. They will also act slowly and thoroughly and in the end, like Lucien and Eddie, I will be exterminated. Somehow I've got to live, for my baby. If the baby lives so does Lucien. I had enough cash to help me for a while, but I couldn't go home and jeopardize my parents, and that's why I never called them.

Karl would have helped me if he was here, but he was traveling in Europe trying to gather enough merchandise on consignment to put him back in business again. Karl was bankrupt and brokenhearted; his house was in foreclosure, his life was a mess. I wished that I could help him in some way. It was unlikely that the insurance company would come through because he had willingly given the security code to Mal. Interpol was on Mal's trail, but so far, no Mal, and none of the stolen treasures have surfaced. I felt that Mal sold those gems to a private collector through an underground agent. There was a market for all things beautiful, and there are enough wealthy eccentrics to make that market profitable and untraceable.

I sat in a huge leather chair staring at nothing in particular. There were very few people in the lobby and nobody had checked in for a while. I was feeling very much alone thinking about my life and Karl's heartache. I knew he would be happy about the baby, Karl would love to have a child around, and if all went well, he'll be the Godfather. I wouldn't allow myself to think of Lucien; if I did, I'd crack, and I had to keep my wits about me. I didn't know what to do or where to go, so I just sat there and did nothing, paralyzed with fear. I might have made it to one of those survivalist groups or militia camps, I'm sure they would have believed me. I thought of buying a weapons magazine to seek out one of those groups in West Virginia.

Slowly, I had begun making changes in my hairstyle, combing my bangs off my forehead, then streaking it with some makeup foundation. The beige color gave my hair a graying look. I had a scarf wrapped around my neck to cover the jawline, but in spite of this, I had a nagging feeling that I would be dead soon . . .

I rose, and walked to the dimly lit bar which was frequented by drunken military. Several men were still hanging onto the darkly polished mahogany bar. I craned my neck pretending to look for someone as several bleary eyed men looked up from making love to their drinks.

It was a man's bar, the walls were paneled in wood and adorned in art. Hunt scenes covered the walls. I could understand its appeal to the military crowd, but it was a little too somber for me in my present state. I sauntered back to the lobby, and walked past the closed lobby stores, window browsing at the clothes. I needed a room and I knew they would ask for I.D., something I couldn't risk. I finally walked over to the reservation desk and out came some bullshit story about a lost wallet. "Everything was gone," I told her. "Credit cards, driver's license, I.D., everything. Thank God I still had some cash in my pocket." When she heard "cash," a sympathetic look crossed her face and check-in was no problem. I gave her a phony name and address and got the room. I walked through the lobby, picking up a discarded newspaper on the way to the elevators. I made certain the elevator was empty before I stepped in, and I found my room on the fifth floor, halfway down the hall. I slid the small plastic card into the slot until the green light winked at me, then looked back before I entered, making certain I was still alone.

The room was dark, even with the lights on. The carpeting was dark green, the furniture was dark wood and the draperies were a rose and green floral. Hunt scenes with dark green matting hung on the wall. I checked the bathroom and closet before I locked the door. I discovered a thick, white, terry cloth robe in the closet, with a tag saying I could use it or buy it. I decided to use it, throwing it over my clothes for added warmth; I had to be ready for anything. I pulled off my boots and plopped in the chair, sitting there, trying to warm up. I thumbed through the paper and started to scan it with bleary eyes, rapidly blinking to clear my vision. I glanced through the first few pages, looking for something about Lucien and Eddie, but there was nothing. Was the *Herald* in on it as well? Why these deep, dark secrets; and will my death be termed an accident as well?

As I perused through the local news, an article written by a political correspondent jumped out at me. "Mother of God," I said as I read and reread the piece, finally tearing it out. "This could be my only chance." I was relieved for the moment, at least now I had some kind of a plan. I must have dozed off, because I don't remember any more, but I was awake at dawn, ready to go and on the move by seven.

◆ ◆ ◆

As the cab rounded a corner, I realized I was near Lucien's old apartment. It wasn't a very good area and when we got to my destination I hesitated to leave. The driver sat silently drumming his fingers on the steering wheel waiting to be paid. "Madame, we're here." He spoke in a soft Caribbean accent. I peeled off several bills and dashed inside before I could change my mind. My idea didn't seem that good right now. Everybody was Afro-American. Now I know how they must feel living in a Caucasian society. Several volunteers were pushing wheelchairs while others were supporting pathetically emaciated people dragging along on sticks of legs. They all resembled death camp victims, and my heart bled for them. This is an AIDS Hospice and all these people are in the final stages; this is their last stop. I quickly forgot my own horror; at least my death would be quick.

I went to the front desk and I was greeted with a happy, moonfaced woman whose mahogany skin was polished to perfection. She added a cheerful note to the stark, sterile surroundings. In this house of death, this woman was the picture of health. The smock she wore was a candy floss pink with the requisite red ribbon pinned to her lapel.

"Is Samantha Dewar in? I'd like to see her." I had read where Samantha was a volunteer, working every day since her drug rehabilitation. It was part of her sentence, doing community service. She beat jail time doing this. No wonder Lucien hadn't heard from her, if this wouldn't change her, nothing would.

I pulled out a twenty, folded it lengthwise and forced it into the contribution can.

"Thank you," the receptionist nodded, impressed by the amount. She leaned over to look at a schedule taped on one side of the desk. Her finger followed a line until she found the day. "Yes, Sam's on early duty, upstairs. Are you a relative?"

"A friend." I crossed my fingers. About ten minutes later, a heavier, plainer Samantha got out of the elevator and went to the desk. I had stepped away and I stood near the window where a stream of human traffic passed by, some with nose studs and trapeze size earrings. I would never have recognized her in her baggy pants and signature pink smock with the ribbon pinned to it. Her glamorous blonde hair was darker and it was pulled tightly back in a ponytail, a rubber band around it. She wore no makeup except a light lipstick, and her once flawless skin had a blemish on her chin, which she did nothing to conceal.

My stomach did flip flops as she leaned over and spoke to the receptionist who nodded her head in my direction. Samantha turned to look and I smiled as she came toward me. My heart stopped beating. "Remember me, Samantha?"

"No." She screwed up her face trying to place me. "Sorry, but I meet so many people. Can I help you with something?" I removed the head scarf and finger brushed my bangs into place. "Wait a minute." Recognition came into her eyes, then shock. "Lucien's girl? The other woman?"

A chill shot through me. "Yes," I meekly said, then asked myself, *why did I come?*

"What are you doing here? What do you want?" She was direct and to the point. I drew her to a corner for a smidgen of privacy. "Samantha, I have some devastating news." We stared at each other, unspeaking, while she waited to hear. The look in her green eyes pierced my skull, questioning me.

"It's Lucien," my voice cracked. I lowered my head and covered my lips to stop them from quivering. She touched my arm to console me. That touch gave me the courage to continue. "Samantha . . . Lucien is dead." My voice broke. A gasp escaped her lips as she steadied herself against the wall, her eyes filling with tears, as human traffic bumped into us on passing.

"Was he on assignment?"

"Yes."

"Bosnia?"

"No, Michigan." It was almost funny if it weren't so tragic. "He and Eddie Wallace uncovered some horrible secrets concerning our national security. They were blown up by some lunatic terrorists who made it appear like an accident. It just happened yesterday on their way from A.L.A. headquarters in Detroit. It isn't on the news yet." I decided to hold off telling her about Jack, she didn't mention it, so I assumed she hadn't heard it.

"I just can't believe it. I'm numb. I can't even think straight. What's your name?"

"Andy."

"Oh yes, Andy . . . I don't watch the news anymore. This job is all consuming, so I usually don't care to hear any more bad stuff.

But Lucien was important to me. I really loved him . . . you know how that feels." She closed her eyes holding back the tears. I know she would have wanted to be alone, to cry her heart out, but I had one more thing to say. "I'm having his baby."

"Pity," she said, I was shocked at her response.

"Pity I was so screwed up at the time. If he saw me now, he'd love me again, I'm certain of that." She was deep in thought. It was more wishful thinking than anything else and my survival instincts told me to say nothing.

"Lucien's baby?" she finally said wistfully, lowering her head.

I told her the terrorists wanted me dead because I knew too much, but I didn't have a chance unless she helped me. She continued staring at the floor and I became nervous.

"Why should I help you?" I didn't answer because I had none. She was right. Why should she help me? Finally she looked up at me. "What do you need?"

"A car," I said.

"A car?"

Yes. Would you make an exchange with me? My BMW for whatever you have."

"A Volvo. Why don't we just exchange plates?" She saw the disappointment on my face, then said, "Oh, what the hell, I'll do it. But will I be in danger?"

"No, because they know what I look like. They want me."

"All right, I'll do it."

I gave her a bear hug and told her where she could pick up the car, and to tell them that she had bought it from me because I was leaving the country. That put her in the clear and she is a senator's daughter, she'd be fine. We hurried to the locker room where we exchanged our keys and registration. "You'll love my BMW, it's a great car."

"The Volvo won't let you down. Remember the red Jag?"

"Do I?" I laughed, remembering the ramming she gave us. We used the side exit and went to the parking lot, shivering from the damp cold. I could smell snow in the air.

She used the remote, then handed it to me while I familiarized myself with the car and she cleaned out the glove compartment, placing a cap on my head. "Wear this." She covered my hair with it. "Where will you go?"

"Perhaps Europe, perhaps Mexico, I don't know. I can't go home and expose my family to danger."

"They'll be watched." She caught on fast.

"I know they will. I don't know what to do or where to go." There must have been such a forlorn expression on my face, because suddenly she hugged me.

"Andy, I'm doing this for Lucien, and his baby."

"I know you are. Thank you."

"I know he loved you. You were balanced and I wasn't."

"Sam, if he knew you now, he never would have left." I was sincere as I looked at this woman, this rival, who is now, my only hope, my only friend. "I'll never forget this, Samantha. "

"Can I be the Godmother?" she laughed.

"You can be nanny." We laughed and cried together, thinking of our lost love, we two strangers who loved one incredible man. She started to shiver as she pulled her sweater tightly around her, preparing to slide out into the dank, cold day.

"If you make it, call me." She closed the door, then tapped on the window as I fumbled with the buttons trying to lower it.

> "Life is merely froth and bubble
> Two things stand in stone
> Sorrow for another's trouble
> Courage in your own."

"It's beautiful, who wrote it?"

"An Aussie bush pilot," she said, running inside as I sat there and fumbled with the instruments to get the car going.

I drove off, praying she wouldn't have a change of heart and mess me up, like report her car stolen. That would have been the ultimate revenge on a woman who took her man. Every time I thought of it, I shook, gripping the wheel until my hands hurt. I was traveling too fast. *Slow down, slow down,* I told myself. *Don't get stopped for speeding. You're going nowhere, Andrea, you have no plans or destination, slow down.*

I started to cry, I felt so alone, but the little voice inside kept egging me on. *Pray, Andrea, pray . . . God is with you. He'll help you. Reach into yourself and find His strength.* I hadn't prayed in years and I didn't even remember how. But slowly I started to remember fragments of prayers, the "Our Father," the Apostle's Creed. They didn't sound right as I stumbled over the words and rearranged sentences, forcing myself to remember. I grasped at these words like a drowning person, hoping that somehow, they would rescue me. I repeated them over and over until the right words crept back into my memory and fell into place. I begged Him for help, as I checked the rearview mirror. I begged Him for mercy, for my unborn child, and I prayed that Samantha Dewar truly changed her life.

CHAPTER 36

Like a homing pigeon, I headed north, knowing I couldn't go home. But like a huge magnet, something was pulling me there, to the safe haven of my youth; grandma's farm. I drove at a steady clip, hoping my enemies wouldn't know of it, but in my heart of hearts I knew that they knew everything about me. I began having second thoughts, feeling guilty for putting that dear old woman in harms way, but grandma always had good solutions. Maybe she would come up with one now. If she didn't, I'd leave.

I knew the secret enemies had limited manpower and I still had my copy of that horror video tape that I might exchange for my life. I drove past a mall and decided to stop. I was hungry and I needed the ladies' room. The racket of canned music blared through the mall as I escaped to a small pastry shop. I sat down and eyed the glistening pastries in the cabinets, but I settled for tea and toast. My stomach couldn't take those whirling desserts. I sauntered through the mall, feeling secure with all the mothers dragging their sullen children, through cliques of noisy teens. But I had to continue my trip, hoping to find some shelter for the night, hesitating to ask anyone. A light snow had dusted the area as I pulled off the main road and luckily I found an obscure motel. Several trucks were parked in the lot, so I assumed it was all right. Truckers have a way of seeking out decent places. The room was plain, but clean, with a disposable cup, tightly wrapped in plastic and the disposable floor mat was made of a heavy paper. At least the towels were terry cloth. I slept in fits and starts, not wanting to fall into a deep slumber and when I finally awoke, my eyes were red rimmed and heavy but I was still alive and hungry . . . ready for the final leg of my journey.

It was an iron chill day, the air feeling colder as I approached Montrose. The area looked bleak with nothing but snow as far as the eye could see. Snow covered everything; roofs, sheds, tree skeletons, land. A winter storm system had settled over the entire area. I was glad that the roads were cleared as my tires held and kept going. This was a good storm weather car.

I could hear the ghostly stillness muffling every sound, even that of the snowplows somewhere in the distance. I saw several farmers trudging laboriously from their barns, probably soaked with perspiration inside their parkas and wet with melting snow on the outside. I swung off the blacktop onto a stretch of country road leading to the farm.

As I was about to make a left at grandma's mailbox, I stopped . . . to look into the wide open mouth of the box. Somebody had forgotten to close it. The gaping hole revealed a stack of mail inside. I guess her neighbors hadn't passed by in a day or two to help her. I checked my rearview mirror then climbed out to get it, leaving my motor running. I glanced up at the house which loomed on the rise like a huge, abandoned carousel. It was octagon shaped and painted the same greenish gray color she had for years. We all begged grandma to change it to white with a crisp green trim, but her answer was always the same. "It don't show the dirt," and it didn't. A stand of fir trees lined the drive, across from the entrance of the house, their boughs drooping from the weight of the snow. In the distance sat the vacant sheds and barns. A fleeting thought scrambled through; why not change my identity and open up an antiques shop right here. It was a presumptuous thought for someone targeted for murder. I looked down the road from where I came and I saw a dark car swing onto it from the blacktop. I grabbed the mail, clumsily holding onto it while I steadied myself against the car, struggling over the mound of snow left by the plow. My foot slipped but I caught my balance and held onto the car door, sliding into the seat, slamming the door and stepping on the gas. My wheels spun as the dark car quietly crept up on me.

"Oh, God, I shouldn't have stopped," I muttered, desperately trying to get traction, but the wheels just spun hysterically and went nowhere. I checked the mirror again and saw the driver watching me. I thought of making a run for it, but I wouldn't get very far.

The man opened his door and struggled out. I locked my doors, the click louder than usual in this stillness. The hair on my neck stood out as he approached the car and tapped on the window. "Need a push?" I looked up into the weather-beaten face tightly protected inside his parka hood. I almost laughed. This was not the face of a killer, this was a farmer from down the road doing his neighborly duty.

"Yes, thanks," I said, opening the window.

"Hold on." He climbed back into his car and gently nudged me out of my dead end. I moved a little, then a little more and finally my tires caught traction and I turned left. The farmer honked his horn, waved and moved straight down the road as I began to get closer to what used to be my summer camp. Whenever I spent a summer on grandma's farm, I would return to school and mesmerize them with such tales, that all my friends wanted to spend their summers with me and eschew the tony camps in the Poconos.

Slowly I made it up the long drive leading to the nineteenth century octagon shaped house. Several pieces of frozen laundry hung stiffly from the clothesline on the porch. As I turned off the motor, I lowered my head and peeked, hoping grandma would welcome me after all this time. I saw the lace curtain move as the old lady peeked out at the strange car in her driveway. I waited for the barking of the dog, but everything was strangely quiet. I looked around before leaving the car and grabbed my tote, locking the door and struggling up a small incline, my feet slipping from under me, but I made it. When I reached the porch, the door swung open.

"Andrea, Andrea, oh." She clutched her heart. "Malishca, my Malishca . . . you finally come to see me."

"Babulia, it's so good to see you."

I hugged her gently, afraid to break something in that frail body. She felt warm and safe and her hair smelled of consommé. "Oh, it's good to see you." I hugged her again and kissed her withered cheek. "I'm sorry I've been so selfish the past years."

"Never mind, you young, you have lots to do besides talk to an old lady."

And that's what I loved about grandma. She never held a grudge. She never made you feel guilty, she was just happy with whatever came her way.

She looked frailer than before. The tip of her nose hung like a little ball, gravity having tugged at it for ninety years, but her small green eyes sparkled with merriment in spite of the crepey skin drooping over them. Her face was kind. She had known love and it showed on that wonderful face, and right now, grandma was the most beautiful woman in the world.

"Come in, come in." She grabbed my sleeve pulling me inside, out of the cold. The warmth of the kitchen hit my face and the sweet aroma of fresh baked bread warmed my cold nose. I removed my coat and I stood in that familiar old kitchen, a small puddle of water forming around my boots. I had forgotten to wipe my feet. In the old days there would have been hell to pay, but today, she didn't even notice.

"Where's Skippy?"

"He's gone, last month to doggy heaven."

I remembered the old spotted mongrel who chased chickens for sport, never harming them, but he would tear you apart if you were a threat to his mistress. I wished he were with us now.

Grandma scurried about like a little bug wearing her pink duster with snaps down the front, high socks and scuffies. She looked cute.

"Will you get another dog?"

"Oh yes, all the neighbors have doggies for me. In the spring, I pick one. You must be hungry, Andrea? Are you hungry, Andrea?" She was excited having company.

"Yes, Baba." Lunch was long gone, but several pots with leftovers still remained on the stove. She heated up soup and chicken and insisted that I eat everything while she sat there watching me wolf down what would have been her supper.

I looked around the cavernous kitchen where most of farm life took place and nothing much changed. Ribbons of slime still shimmered on top of the water in a large plastic salad bowl, a makeshift vaporizer. From time to time, grandma would rise and clear a dish or bring me seconds and whatever she brought, I ate. Finally she sat down long enough to have a cup of tea with me, in tall glass cups, Russian style. We chatted and reminisced, and then I remembered her mail and retrieved it from my tote.

"Later, later." She waved me away while she sat down again chatting over a second cup of tea. She was enjoying this and so was I. We talked about my job, and Karl, and trips to Geneva to the Faberge show. She relished all of it. She spoke carefully, almost haltingly, not used to conversation, and I felt guilty for having neglected this wonderful old lady for so long.

"Now tell me, Andrea."

"Yes, Baba, what?"

"Why are you here? I know you wouldn't visit me in the middle of winter," she said looking directly into my eyes.

You couldn't fool her, she always knew. How could I possibly begin to tell her of this bizarre tale. But her eyes held steadfast and her jaw was set; I didn't want to frighten her, but I had to tell the truth.

"Baba, somebody is trying to kill me."

"Why?" She furrowed her brow.

"Because we uncovered a terrorist plot involving the President's wife."

"The one who died?"

"Yes. She was no good. These people have killed my fiancée and his boss and now they want to kill me." I lowered my head, ashamed that this prompted my visit to her, bringing her danger. She leaned over and gently raised my head.

"What more?"

"I'm carrying his child, the man I loved. I don't want to die, Baba, I don't want to die." Tears stung my tired eyes as I lay my head on the table and sobbed.

"Oh, you not gonna die." And that was that. She spoke with finality and conviction that even I believed it and I stopped crying. She didn't comfort me nor was she shocked at anything I said.

"I don't want to bring you trouble, Baba, but I had no place to go. I'll leave tomorrow."

"No, you stay. I like this stuff, you know, figuring things out, outsmarting them. You think they gonna look here?" She rose to check the locks on the door.

"I don't know."

"The car." She pointed to my car as she looked out the square of glass on the kitchen door. "We gotta hide it."

"I couldn't get it to the garage with all the snow," I said.

"Okay, then tomorrow, we change the license plate from my old car inna garage, okay?"

"That's good, Baba, because they don't expect me to be driving a Volvo."

"Good. If they come, they not gonna find you. Come."

She took my hand and led me up the stairs to her second story bedroom. It was exactly as I had remembered; comfortable and pleasant.

Suddenly she leaned toward me, whispering in a confidential tone, "My whole life, we have prepared for this day, grandpa George and I." She went to the peach and white striped wall, slowly running her hand over a section of it, like a blind woman trying to find her way. She seemed to be looking for something. Her hand stopped and she slid a two foot panel of the same wallpaper, which covered a small opening. It blended in so well I would have never seen it. Grandma held onto the wall and edged her way in sideways. I followed. We stood in the cutest pieslice of a room with a little bed, a commode and a washstand, with a pitcher and basin on it. I was stunned. How I would have loved this secret room as a child and yet I don't remember ever having seen it before.

Old books and magazines were piled in one corner. A *Godey's Ladies Book of Fashion* from the turn of the century was sitting on top. I picked it up, curious, perhaps Karl could sell it. It was so old, bits of it broke off and flakes of paper twirled to the floor like dried moth wings. Pity it wasn't in mint condition.

"Baba, why this room?"

"Grandpa George made it for me," she proudly stated.

"Why? To get away from your kids?"

"No." Her eyes sparkled with excitement. "The Bolsheviks." She lowered her voice. "He was always afraid they would find me and kill me."

"Why?" She saw the confusion on my face as I wrestled with the possibility that her imagination had run away with her. She tried to explain to me, in her softly accented voice, the Russian easing in and out of her conversation.

"The Bolsheviks, because my papa was Admiral Dvornetsky, Commander of the Black Sea Naval Fleet, the Czar's Admiral. Papa was in charge of the U-boats during the first big war and he helped some White Russians escape, so . . . they didn't like us very much."

I almost fell over. I had to plop down on that little bed. Everybody thought that grandma was raised on a farm in Russia. "How old were you?"

"Nine, ten." Suddenly she took off into her bedroom and returned holding a sheaf of handwritten papers. "It takes me a long, long time, but ever since grandpa George died, I write a little every day. I have lots of time to do that. My children, grandchildren, great-grandchildren, like your little one will now have a family history. I wrote it."

It was hard to see in that light so we returned to her bedroom and I glanced through it. It began, *I, Irina Djornetsky Petrov, was born on February 8, 1910 in St. Petersburg, Russia.* She went on to share the milestones of her ninety years. Her childhood in Czarist

Russia. Her visits to the summer and winter palaces of the Czar. She played with the young Czarovich and his sisters. *He was spoiled, she wrote. But looked nice in his white sailor outfit. He jumped in the mud puddle to splash our white dresses and then he stood there and laughed.*

I couldn't believe this. Perhaps it was pure fiction, an old lady's imagination running away from loneliness, giving her something to do, but I couldn't be sure. She claims to have met all of the royal family and even played with Anastasia, whom she thought died with the family but at another location when the guards discovered her diamond filled corsets. When the revolution began, grandma and her family escaped with several grand dukes and duchesses, traveling through Turkey, paying their way with portable treasures. *My father was well respected because of his reputation with that strange contraption that moved under the sea. The peasants thought he was blessed with some supernatural power. Lucky for us,* she wrote, *we met some God fearing but greedy soldiers who let us pass for the right price.*

The text was crude, riddled with grammatical errors and improper punctuation, but it was a dynamic revelation. In her youth, grandma spoke French, German and Russian, and was as well-educated as any upper class Russian child.

She held her wedding picture in front of me, interrupting my reading, showing me grandpa George who was tall and handsome, wearing white gloves and a flower in his lapel. He stood proudly next to a pretty, young grandma. He had been through it all with her, having been the son of a naval officer. They traveled together and married in Binghamton, New York, not far from where they made their life together.

I was touched by his devotion to her, his loyalty was unending. It was still there, helping me. "You actually knew the Czar?" I asked incredulously.

"Yes, yes, I grew up with them. Everywhere around them was beauty . . . palaces, art, flowers, furniture, jewels, clothing . . . beauty everywhere."

"Is that where you learned about antiques?"

"Sure," she said with confidence. "English, French, Italian, artists and craftsman, all came to work for the Czar."

"A lot of young Russians are now showing an interest in the Czar."

"Good. He was a kind man, slow to act, completely dominated by his wife, who was a little stupid."

This whole episode took my mind from my problems. It was such a fantastic discovery I felt dizzy from the bombardment of surprises. I could hole up here, get a computer and rewrite this whole family history for her. The more she talked, the clearer her English became. Her eyes shined with excitement as she watched me approve what she had written. I became lost in her life's story. When I looked up, grandma had disappeared. She went back into that tiny room, her safe haven that grandpa George had made for her, and now I was reliving her worst nightmare. I shook my head at the irony of it. She quietly popped through the secret door again, back into her peach and white bedroom. She stood there holding something just like a little kid showing company her new toys. I began to look closer at the emerald green object she was holding. It startled me. There she stood, holding a magnificent bejeweled egg. "This gets better and better," I whispered, holding my breath, afraid to ask . . . but could this possibly be a Faberge egg from Alexandra Fyodorovna? I reached out with both hands and gently caressed it, holding it like a newborn, while grandma stood proudly by, hands clasped behind her back, looking up at me, waiting for my reaction. I went closer to the lamp on the night table and examined it, looking for the mark. My heart stopped when I saw it. The green jewels sparkled like the sun on dewy blades of grass. I'm in the business but I had never heard of this particular egg and yet I felt I had seen it before.

"Where did you get this, Baba?" It was an incredible find.

She didn't answer. "See," she said as she pushed a button and the top of the egg flew open. Two tiny mechanical monkeys slid up and down on a delicate gold pole while a tinny tune tinkled away. One tiny monkey was dressed in a ruby jeweled vest and tambourine hat, the other wore yellow sapphires. The rest of it was gold and silver. This was an incredible find. As I scrutinized it in that dim light, grandma took it from me and placed it on the nightstand. She had something to tell me. "Andrea, when you were little and very sick, I let you see this. Nobody ever saw it but you." She covered her mouth and giggled. "You thought the monkeys came from the fever." Then I was right. I had seen those monkeys recently when I was sick. They must have been locked in my subconscious, but now I know they weren't a dream, they were real. This was grandma's big secret which she shared with me. But why did she have this?

"Baba, how did you get this?"

"I took it."

"You stole it?" I can understand how a little kid could be drawn to it.

"No, she didn't want it."

"Who?"

"The Czarina." She sounded annoyed, like I should have known. I waited for an explanation. "They were going to throw it away, so I took it and protected it all these years."

"Why would they *throw out* such a magnificent piece?"

"Superstitions," she snapped. "I told you she was a little stupid. The Czar always gave these eggs. The Czarina thought it was made of emeralds, which she liked."

"But it isn't." I looked again. I know malachite was considered the stone of the Czars, but in this light . . .

"No," she explained, "the werkmeister made it in green demontoid, a stone the superstitious Czarina didn't want around her. She called it the Demon's egg and begged her husband for a new one. Nobody wanted this, it was to bring bad luck to the owner, but it proved to be lucky for us; we lived." I was mesmerized and I wanted to hear more. "They told my father to lose the Demon's egg in the bottom of the sea, but I liked those little monkeys so much, I begged him for it. Even as a child, my papa saw I was not superstitious, neither was he. So he gave me the egg to hide from everyone, even Mama. And he put a real egg in a box and dropped it into the sea. He told them he buried the egg in the ocean. He didn't lie and only papa and I knew the truth." This was an incredible story. I took the egg again and examined it. On closer scrutiny I could see a slight difference distinguishing it from the coveted emeralds, but it was still a magnificent work of art, and it had the mark of Faberge werkmeister Henrik Wigstrom, 1862-1923. If I could reach Karl, this would make his year. I salivated at the thought of it. Here was Karl traveling through Europe, looking for treasures and we had one right here. Of course, grandma would have to approve. All of this took my mind off my trouble and I did something I hadn't done in years. I thanked God for his help. I thanked Him for guiding me back to this farm.

Grandma took the egg and ordered me to bed. She was tired from the day's excitement, she needed her rest. So I showered and slipped into one of her flannel gowns and kissed her good night, fondling her soft upper arm, remembering when I cradled it like a baby, the skin hanging loose now.

"Tomorrow we work on the car." Fatigue blurred her enunciation as she nodded off to sleep.

I found my bed in the pieslice room and crept under the covers. It was pitch dark with the door closed but I felt safe. Tears sparked under my eyelids as I closed my eyes. I was still alive. I gently massaged my abdomen, my baby was asleep and soon after I followed. I slept soundly for the first time in weeks, with grandma just yards away guarding me, fast asleep.

When I awoke, it was still pitch black. I had forgotten where I was and I felt disoriented, and then I remembered. I rose and found my way to the door, opening it and peeking out. The sharp light hurt my eyes. I squinted until my eyes adjusted. The leaf patterned lace curtains dappled the room with sunshine and once again I was drawn to the Demon's egg still sitting on grandma's nightstand. By daylight, in the sunshine, it was sensational. A burst of the most magnificent color. The find of the century. A forbidden Fabergé egg, unrecorded and thought to have been destroyed, but any expert would have known it.

I heard the phone ring and the muffled sound of grandma's voice. It was probably some neighbor checking up on her. I heard her step creak on the cellar stairs and I smelled the coffee, bacon and eggs. I hadn't eaten that in years. Her purple velour robe was thrown on the bed, so I slipped into it and started downstairs, startled to see her climbing toward me.

"Good morning, Baba." She waved me to silence. "Go to the room, to the little room," she whispered. I knew better than to ask any questions, so I quickly retreated to the secret room. Unable to find the camouflaged door at first, I waited, holding my breath when I heard voices downstairs. I worried that I might have left something around, but it was too late to do anything, I'd have to rely on grandma's quick thinking. About twenty minutes passed before I saw the sunlight of the bedroom, and heard grandma's voice sifting into the darkness.

"It's okay, Andrea. My neighbor come by to bring me cake. I tell him the car is mine, I get it second hand from my son who lives in Washington."

"Did he believe you?"

"Why not. Why should I lie about a car?" She laughed. "It's better he not see you or know you're here. Now come downstairs and eat." I couldn't wait, after having smelled that glorious food all morning.

She set down a breakfast made for a stevedore and I ate it all . . . all the forbidden food we health nuts shun. Grandma busied herself at the sink and stove, never joining me. She seemed to be deep in thought. Was she nervous about my being here? Afraid I would bring her harm? I was just about to tender my resignation to her when she barreled in on my thoughts.

"Andrea, I want you to have that egg. You'll know what to do with it. It is yours to do as you like. The others will get the land. Lot's of money they'll get." My head reeled with the thought of such a magnanimous gift. I started to protest.

"Baba, sit down, we'll talk about it." Grandma sat down and poured herself a cup of coffee, stirring in her sugar and milk. I was amazed at how steady her hand was, and her voice was even steadier.

"No, there is nothing to talk. I want you to have it, that's it, finished business." I rose to thank her and kiss her. She held me for a moment. "That egg brought me good luck. It brought me my good husband, my children, my farm and my good health, now you need luck." She cherished the simple things, finding the key to happiness. Her cross was balanced. Lucien would have loved her.

"If you like, I'll stay here awhile and I'll rework your book."

"Good, that would be good."

"I don't know what to say about the egg."

"Say nothing, do what you like, it now belongs to you."

She rose and cleaned the table while I went upstairs to dress. When I returned, she was busy at the kitchen table, writing out checks in her scratchy hand, licking the envelopes, stamping the letters. I went to the window and looked out. Everything was white as far as the eye could see, even the pines had every bough decorated with white frosting. "Can the mail get through?"

"Oh, sure, we used to snow up here, the road is plowed."

"Can I take those to the mailbox for you?" I reached for the pile of mail.

"Oh yes, before my electric gets shut off." She laughed.

"You must leave out the red flag so he knows there is mail to get."

I looked out the window squinting at the sun exploding onto the white landscape, but nothing looked suspicious. There were no strange vehicles or footprints, there was only my car waiting for its bogus license plate. I pulled on my boots and slipped into my coat and tied a scarf around my head. When I opened the door a blast of cold air hit me, the sunshine was deceptive. I quickly shut the door behind me and stood on the porch checking the surroundings, my eyes swept the area looking for intruders, but everything was untouched . . . if only this was the end of it. I could make my life here, with grandma and my baby. The egg would fetch a tidy sum and Karl could be our agent. Nobody need know. I could finally see it working out.

    The two minute trudge down the long drive invigorated me after yesterday's exhausting trip. I needed this walk. I began to remember things from my youth. I had made this trip so many times, the red flag, signaling the mailman to stop. I had also fetched the mail, and had waited for a letter from my parents or some other relative who knew I had been grandma's summer companion. I carefully stepped over the mounds of snow and I left the mail in the box and put the red flag up. I turned and saw grandma standing on the porch, holding her sweater tightly wrapped around her. She was still guarding me in this bone chilling weather, as the sunlight glistened on the snow covered tree limbs. A warm feeling settled deep in me. Suddenly, I heard a car. I quickened my steps, but it drove by. I trudged back through the deep snow, picking my way. *I must change the license plate*, I thought as I looked toward my car and then I saw him, as he stepped out from behind the shed. I froze like a doe caught in the headlights. His features were visible as though he wanted me to know his identity. My heart thumped wildly in my chest and I now knew who was behind it all; agent Nichols.

    He was more than six feet away and I still felt the cold steel which was pointed at me. Icy shakes descended in waves through my body as my terror filled eyes pleaded with him not to kill me. I didn't think, I didn't move, I didn't breath. I just heard my heart pounding. We stood there eyeballing each other. He, motionless and unflinching, staring me down, holding me hostage with those eyes, rooting me to the spot. Cold smoke billowed from his nostrils like a dragon and I was suspended in time, knowing that this was the end for me.

    We faced each other for an eternity, as he held me with his hypnotic gaze. I heard the groan of the storm door as it was slowly pushed open. *Stay inside, stay inside, Baba,* I silently screamed inside my head. I saw his eyes shift beyond me toward the porch.

Go inside, get help. Please, go inside. My ears strained to tell me something . . . anything; and then I heard the click of the lock and I almost buckled with relief. *Now get help, Baba . . . Call for help.* But his eyes remained fixed on the porch, then finally he blinked, breaking the spell. He muttered something to himself, but I couldn't hear. He took several steps back and lowered his gun, walking behind the old shed where he disappeared from view. I was paralyzed, not knowing what he was up to, but when I heard his labored steps across the field of snow, I felt a glimmer of hope. He came into view again, turned and stared at me. I could almost read his thoughts. *I know where you are. Talk and I'll come back and kill you.* Then he struggled toward the bare boned trees of the forest, out of sight and hopefully out of my life forever; the decision to kill me or not, all came down to the blink of an eye. My teeth chattered, my stomach churned and the sour taste of my breakfast reached up into my throat. It made me gag. I tried moving, but my legs buckled as I fell into the brittle, cold snow. The tears that poured freely, felt like icicles on my cheeks. I thought of Lucien and Eddie; why didn't they get a break? Or Jack and his driver? Why was I spared? There was no answer to that as I remained there, swallowed up by the snow, a shivering wisp of humanity, grateful to be alive.

Grandma's sharp voice carried through the stillness. "Andrea, come," she commanded, and she was right; I was still a sitting duck for a legal madman. I staggered to my feet, trying to keep them from slipping out from under me, trying to keep my balance as I started toward her, digging my heels into the snow for support. I looked up, and saw grandma standing there with her legs apart, hoisting an old shotgun on her hip. Her mouth was set like a steel trap around a squirrel's leg, a glittery challenge in her eyes. I stopped, to watch her, standing like a statue. *My God!* I thought, *the gun was what I heard; a Mexican stand-off.* Her courage made me feel giddy. My mouth stretched into a grin at the sight of her; that old woman who remained fearless, her eyes still pierced the distance toward the woods as she spoke without moving them from his direction.

"Come."

I moved faster, making it to level ground, running to her.

"Baba, you're my angel, a saint . . . you're Joan of Arc . . . Calamity Jane!" I shook my head and stepped back, and roared at the sight of that brave old lady who could barely lift that heavy, old gun.

But her scowl was fierce and I had confidence in her marksmanship. "I would have knocked him to hell," she said never once cracking a smile. "Grandpa George teach me good." Only then did she release the gun to me and I hugged her, grateful to be alive. "I don't know if I scared him or not, but he let you be." I didn't know that either, but he must have known that the kick would have knocked her off the porch. Perhaps he was tired of killing or perhaps he couldn't risk getting killed with the questions that would follow: I don't know . . . I'll never know. Perhaps he'll be back.

"Come, come." Grandma rushed me indoors "Put this in the pantry in the back against the wall and lock the door." She handed me the old 12 gauge Remington and we scurried inside, following her instructions. She didn't relax until she heard the click of the lock. "Is there someone who can help you?"

"No, Baba, I don't know of anyone I could trust besides you. People high in government, must be involved, that's why I can't go to the police or the F.B.I., I'm afraid to."

"Then come," she said, now busying herself at the stove, putting that episode behind her, not wanting me to live in fear. "I made good barley soup. You eat."

I looked at her and felt grateful to have come from her stock. Joy fringed my sorrow. Two days ago my haunted future seemed stark but now I was still alive, carrying my baby. Karl was still my friend and we will be back in business, big time, thanks to grandma. Everything was thanks to grandma.

I went to the telephone hoping the line hadn't been cut. It wasn't. I felt secure hearing the steady hum of a working phone. I watched as she carefully balanced the steaming bowls of soup from the stove to the table.

"Andrea, we still better change the car plates," she said, as she looked out the window surveying the landscape. She stood there watching.

"Okay, Baba." She was right. Was this the end? Or will it go on? I knew who was behind it, but who was behind him? The video might be my life insurance or it may not. My life is full of uncertainties. But somehow I must try to live a normal life, if not for myself, then for my child. I dialed the rotary phone, watching those numbers spin into place trying to forget his face, and then I waited until it was answered.

"Sam, thank you . . . this is Andy."

"Andy," she happily yelled.

"I made it, Sam, I made it. You're going to be a Godmother."

◆ ◆ ◆

The President's private line rang, interrupting the meeting with his aides. Charlie MacIsaac threw him a glance, expecting the nod from him to pick it up, but President Chambers answered it, excusing himself. The caller was brief.

"Everything's been taken care of, there is nothing more to worry about."

"Thank you," he said. "Thank you so much for taking care of it." He hung up and turned to his aides. "Now, gentlemen." He looked at Charlie. "Where were we?"

Thomas Paine

Common

Thomas Paine, the son of a Quaker, was born in Thetford, England, in 1737. His mother, using the Bible as a textbook, taught him to read at home. Later he attended a private boys' school where he became an exceptionally good student.

When he was thirteen years old, his father started to teach him to become a staymaker. He found his work very boring and became eager to see more of the world. Finally he enlisted as a seaman on an English privateer, where he served about a year.

Back in England he worked for several years in different towns as a staymaker and afterwards became an excise officer. While engaged in excise work, he happened to meet Benjamin Franklin, who interested him in coming to America.

In 1774 Paine sailed for America, where he immediately became involved in the cause for freedom. Within a few months he wrote a small book, called *Common Sense*, which clearly spelled out the rights of the American colonies to become free and independent. His book caught on and helped to build up sentiment for signing the Declaration of Independence. Later he wrote a series of pamphlets, called *The American Crisis*, which promoted financial aid for American soldiers taking part in the Revolutionary War.

Following the war, Paine returned to England where he wrote *The Rights of Man* attacking the power of royal government. For writing this book he was forced to flee the country. From England he went to France, where he participated in the French Revolution and was put in prison for opposing acts of violence. While in prison he wrote a book called *The Age of Reason* based on the Bible, which aroused the ire of clergymen in both Europe and America.

In 1802 Paine returned to America, but his last years here were saddened because many old friends turned against him. Federalist leaders condemned him for having opposed some of their policies. Clergymen continued to attack him for having written his book on the Bible. He died in New York in 1809. Today historians rate him as one of the truly great founders of our country.

Illustrated by Robert Doremus

Thomas Paine

Common Sense Boy

By Elisabeth P. Myers

Bm

The Bobbs-Merrill Company, Inc.
Indianapolis / New York

COPYRIGHT © 1976, THE BOBBS-MERRILL COMPANY, INC.

ALL RIGHTS RESERVED

PROTECTED UNDER UNIVERSAL COPYRIGHT CONVENTION

AND PAN-AMERICAN CONVENTION

TRADE ISBN 0-672-52189-X

EDUCATION ISBN 0-672-71323-3

LIBRARY OF CONGRESS CATALOG CARD NUMBER: 75-12448

PRINTED IN THE UNITED STATES OF AMERICA

To my brother
Edward Foote Perkins

Illustrations

Full pages

	PAGE
"What is this hole for?" he asked.	47
"Your teacher will be my assistant."	58
It completely hid his other clothes.	67
"See those old earthworks?" he said.	94
He sat cutting and sewing cloth.	104
He lingered by the coffee houses.	125
He offered it to his former employer.	153
He wrote it in the form of a letter.	162
The Academy reported favorably.	178
They had many good talks together.	189

Numerous smaller illustrations

Contents

	PAGE		PAGE
Tom's Hiding Place	11	The Lure of Life as a Seaman	109
Deep Thoughts for a Small Boy	25	Working Again as a Staymaker	121
Learning to Read	39	Busy Years in Excise Work	131
Enrolling in School	52	"Common Sense" for America	142
Tom's First Day at School	62	The *Crisis* Papers	155
Comforting Words	74	Champion of New Causes	168
Good Companions	87		
A Young Apprentice	99	Final Years in America	184

Books by Elisabeth P. Myers
DAVID SARNOFF: RADIO AND TV BOY
EDWARD BOK: YOUNG EDITOR
F. W. WOOLWORTH: FIVE AND TEN BOY
FREDERICK DOUGLASS: BOY CHAMPION OF HUMAN RIGHTS
GEORGE PULLMAN: YOUNG CAR BUILDER
JOHN D. ROCKEFELLER: BOY FINANCIER
KATHARINE LEE BATES: GIRL POET
PEARL S. BUCK: LITERARY GIRL
THOMAS PAINE: COMMON SENSE BOY

★ # Thomas Paine

Common Sense Boy

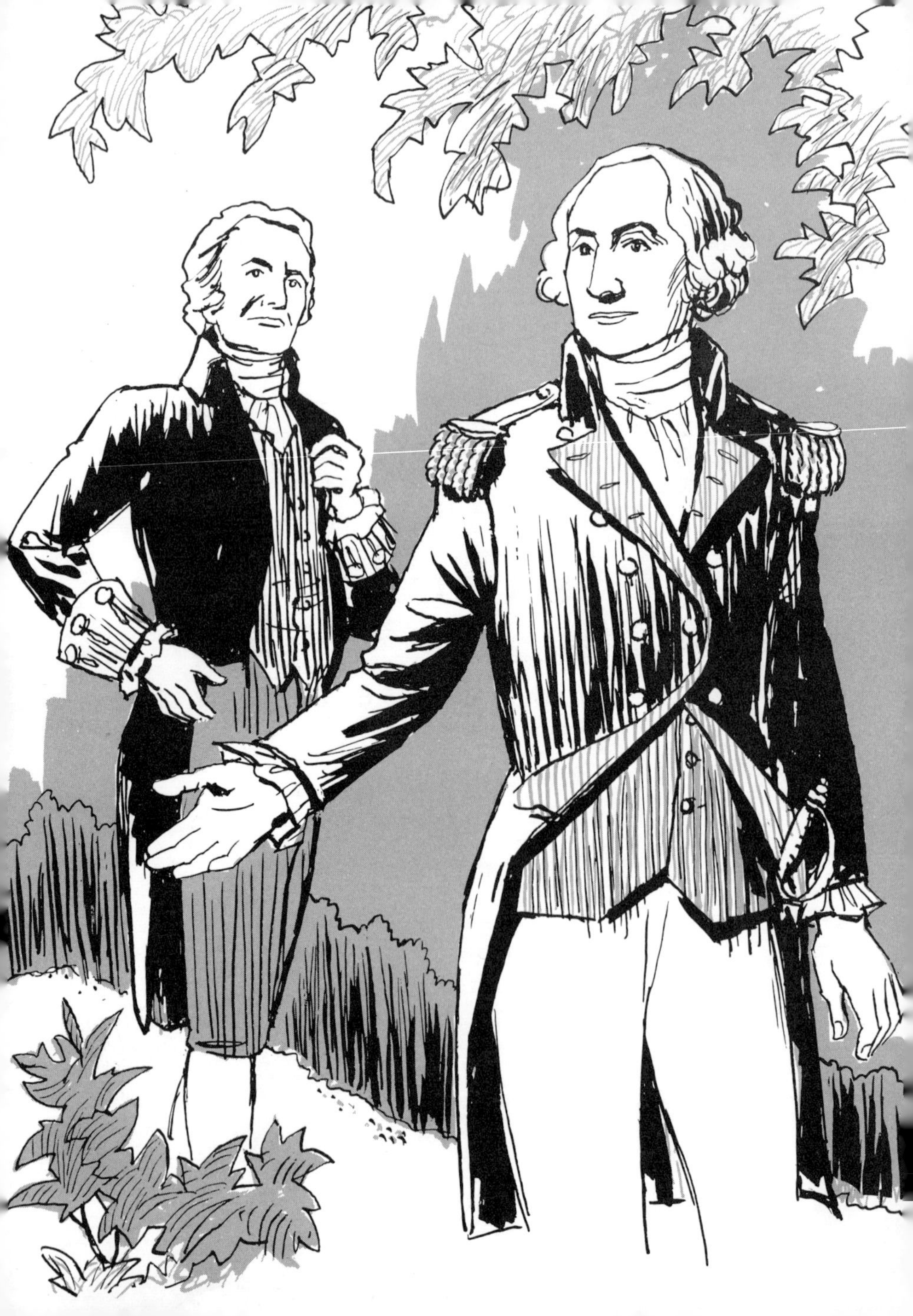

Tom's Hiding Place

ONE LATE spring day in May in Thetford, England, Frances Paine was busy sweeping the living room floor. As she swept, straws from her broom came loose and littered the floor. Her five-year-old son Tom followed her about the room and picked up the straws.

Soon she stopped to examine the broom. "I'll have to mend it before I use it again," she said. "Now that you are five years old, maybe you can mend it for me."

"I'll try, Mother," said young Tom.

Frances Paine brought some fresh straws for Tom to put in the broom. She asked him to climb up on a chair so he could hold the broom between his knees to work on it. Then she showed him how to stick new straws into the broom.

Tom started to work happily. Breezes blew in through the open window and fanned his cheeks as he worked. Before long his mother said, "While you are busy I'll go downstairs to talk with your father. I won't be gone long, but I have something to talk over with him."

The Paine family lived on the second floor of a two-story house on the top of a hill. Tom's father, Joseph Paine, ran a small workshop on the first floor of the house. In those days in England many people had small shops in their homes where they made things to sell to people who lived nearby.

Joseph Paine was a staymaker. He cut whalebone into thin strips which he used as stays or stiffeners in making undergarments for women. He had a good business and made a good living for himself and his family.

When Joseph was married, the church recorded his family name as P-A-I-N-E. Later he dropped the final *e* from the name and taught Tom to do the same thing. After Tom came to America, however, he restored the final *e*.

Joseph was a descendent of the Vikings from Norway who had invaded England centuries before. His wife, Frances, was of English descent. Her father was a prominent lawyer who lived in the neighborhood.

As he let the pleasant breezes fan his cheeks, Tom took deep refreshing breaths. He could almost smell the perfume of the many flowers that carpeted the heath in May. Thetford was a town of about two thousand persons located in eastern England. It was a friendly, prosperous little place, surrounded by a beautiful countryside. The land around the town, which was dry and level, was called a heath. It was covered with shrubs and grass, good for pasturing sheep. Many sheep roamed the heath nibbling the shrubs and grasses.

Before long Tom stopped work to enjoy the fresh country breeze. He climbed up on his knees before the open window and thought of how beautiful everything must be out on the heath and wished he could go there. He could picture the tall, blue-flowered viper's bugloss and the purple musk-thistle. In addition he could almost see the wild mignonette with its sweet greenish-white blossoms. He imagined he could hear the humming of honey bees, the whirring wings of low-flying birds, and the bleating of black-faced sheep.

The five-year-old boy sighed. He hadn't been out on the heath yet this spring. "Oh, how I'd like to be out there roaming about," he whispered to the breeze.

He turned away from the window and looked down at the broom. Then he smiled. "Why, it's almost finished!" he cried. "After I put in a few more straws I'll be through with my work. If I get done before Mother comes back, I'll go roaming on the heath."

If he didn't succeed, Tom knew his mother would not release him. She would find something else for him to do around the house. "Man must 'eat not the bread of idleness,'" she was in the habit of saying to him.

This was one of the many Bible-based quotations Mrs. Paine had ever-ready on her tongue. She was a member of the Church of England and believed it was her duty to proclaim the written word aloud. Her husband Joseph, on the other hand, did not believe in giving quotations. He was a Quaker and believed that messages from God came silently into a person's mind, telling him how to act.

Tom was still too young to understand much about religion. Right now he was only interested in finishing his work on the broom. In a few minutes he was through and looked the broom over carefully. Then he picked up the scrap materials from the floor and threw them out the window. "Now Mother will be pleased," he said to himself. "I'll put the broom where she'll be sure to see it."

He carried the broom into the kitchen and hung it on the peg where it belonged. From here he could hear his parents talking directly below. Now he was sure his mother wouldn't be coming back for a while.

The stairway to the lower floor was in a hall beside his father's workshop. Tom hoped that he could get down before his mother started to come back upstairs. The quickest way was to slide down the railing, but he knew that he might be caught and punished.

Fortunately he knew where the steps creaked and where they were firm. He began to move down them cautiously. Now, much to his surprise, he could hear his parents' voices even more clearly than before. This meant that the door between the workroom and the hall was open. He paused to listen and discovered that his parents were talking about him.

"I want my son to become a member of the Church of England," argued Frances Paine. "My father belongs to this church, I belong to this church, and now I want my son to belong to this church. I have discussed this matter with my father and he feels the same way. Remember, he is a prominent lawyer here and knows what's best for our son."

"I respect thy father's judgment, but as thy husband I disagree with him in this matter," Joseph Paine replied quietly. "As my son, Tom must become a Quaker."

"I know how you feel, but remember that the Church of England is the official church of the kingdom," Frances added. "Why should Tom grow up outside this church when he can gain so much by growing up within it?"

"The answer is simple," Joseph calmly explained. "Under English law, as thy husband I am head of our household and entitled to tell our son what to do. I want him to become a Quaker and so it must be."

"Well, you have the right to decide about his future, but I think you are making a grave mistake," said Frances sadly.

Joseph Paine made no reply but kept right on working. He wasn't the kind to argue once he had made a decision. He never spoke angrily to his family or anyone else.

Tom, out in the hall, now could tell that the talk had ended and realized that he must leave as quickly as possible. He got outside safely but changed his mind about where he wanted to go. After listening to his parents talking about him, he wanted to find a quiet place where he could go to think, as in a church.

Instead of turning left and heading for the heath, he turned right and ran down Bridge Street to St. Peter's Church. This church belonged to the Church of England, but wasn't the one his mother attended. She went to St. Cuthbert's, which was farther away, because she liked the clergyman there better than the one at St. Peter's Church.

The church sanctuary wasn't Tom's real destination. He was headed for the belfry, which he could reach by climbing a circular staircase. The belfry was like a little porch. It was square and had half-walls on all four sides. Hanging from the roof was a large bell. It had a great clapper with a heavy rope attached to it. The sexton of the church rang the bell every

Sunday before church services. He was an old man and hardly ever climbed the tower, but he had given Tom permission to do so whenever he liked. No one else knew Tom ever went there.

Tom was out of breath when he reached the belfry. Panting, he stood directly beneath the bell and looked upward. There under the bell he saw spider webs, one of which contained a large blue-bottle fly buzzing angrily. He watched it struggle for a minute. Then he said, "You're trapped, poor fly. I feel sorry for you. I'll help you get loose, if I can."

The fly seemed to buzz even more loudly after he had spoken to it. He looked around the empty bell-chamber and spotted a chunk of stone that had fallen to the floor. Quickly he picked up the stone and tossed it toward the spider web. His aim was good. The web broke and the fly flew safely away. Tom laughed and his laugh echoed strangely and loudly from the hollow of the bell down through the circular staircase.

Soon he moved out from under the bell and went to lean on one of the walls. This was his favorite view, for he could look down over the town of Thetford. It was a pretty town, with rows of houses close to the streets. But when he was down there he felt tiny beside the tall houses and public buildings. From the belfry the town looked tiny, instead. The buildings looked like toys—things he could handle and move around, if he wished.

He moved over to another side of the belfry. Now he could see the green banks of the Little Ouse River, crossed by the Town Bridge with its single arch. Also, he could see other bridges, both up and down stream. In addition, he could see the paper mill and the turning sails of distant windmills. He could even see the place where the Little Ouse merged with the River Thet. He never had visited that place yet, but he hoped to one of these days.

Yet another wall let him gaze down on the chalk mound known as Castle Hill. From this wall he was certain he could see the outline of what had been a real castle. People had told him that this castle had once been taken over by the Vikings when they had invaded England several centuries before.

Slowly he walked down the steps from the belfry and found the sexton working below. "Did you have a good time up there, my boy?" asked the friendly old man.

"Yes," replied Tom politely. "I looked out to see things in all directions. Besides houses and other buildings, I could see Castle Hill and the rivers, Little Ouse and River Thet. From up there all the houses looked little, just as if they were toys."

"I'm glad you could come," said the sexton. "Come again whenever you can. You're always welcome here."

Happily Tom started on home. Along the way he happened to remember that tomorrow would be First Day or Sunday. This meant that he would go to the Quaker Meeting House with his father. Every First Day his father took him there without fail.

Before Tom reached home his happy feelings gave way to fear. He was afraid his mother would punish him for leaving without getting her permission.

"Where have you been?" she asked coldly when he entered the living room.

"To St. Peter's," he replied.

"Oh, good," she said in a mellower tone of voice. "I'm glad you went there. I would like to see you grow up in the Church of England."

Deep Thoughts for a Small Boy

THE NEXT MORNING, the Paine family started off for church together. Frances Paine was dressed in her Sunday finery. She wore a tightly laced purple velvet gown with an elegant hooped skirt. On her head she wore a white lace cap, and over her shoulders a black fringed shawl.

Joseph Paine and Tom also wore church-going clothes, but theirs were black and very plain. They wore black hats, which they would keep on their heads even in the Meeting House. "Quakers or members of the Society of Friends do not doff their hats," Joseph Paine often explained to Tom, "except when praying to God."

The most prominent person in Thetford was the Duke of Grafton, who was fabulously wealthy. He not only controlled the politics in Thetford but in other cities and towns as well. These places were known as his "pocket boroughs," meaning that he had them "in his pocket," or in complete control. He appointed his own friends as town officials. He handpicked the men who represented the towns in the House of Commons in Parliament. He even had great influence with the King of England.

Joseph Paine always kept his hat on while he was in the Duke's presence. The first time this happened, Frances Paine censured her husband for being so impolite. "There's no wonder Quakers are the subject of so much criticism," she said bitterly.

Joseph Paine took his wife's comments calmly. "Let me remind thee of what happened when William Penn, the founder of the colony of Pennsylvania, came to call on Charles II," he said. "When William Penn first visited the court after becoming a Quaker, he advanced with his hat on his head to meet the King. The King, noting this, removed his own hat.

"'Friend Charles, wherefore dost thou uncover thy head?' Penn asked in surprise.

"'Friend Penn,' replied King Charles, 'it is the custom in this court for only one man to wear a hat.'"

Joseph Paine often told Tom this story to illustrate how steadfast Quakers were in refusing to "doff their hats" as a gesture of honor in the presence of others. "In God's eyes, men are equal," he said. "Never forget this very important fact."

Today the Paines walked slowly along Bridge Street. Joseph and Tom had to suit their pace to Frances' pace. She had trouble walking on the cobblestones in her thin-soled slippers.

St. Cuthbert's was on King Street beside the Guildhouse or City Hall. The Quaker Meeting House was on Cage Lane, near the town jail. It was called Cage Lane because there was a barred cage in front of the jail where prisoners often were put on public display.

The Quaker Meeting House was a large, plain room with a center aisle and hard wooden benches. The men, all dressed in black, sat on one side of the aisle. The women, all dressed in gray, sat on the other side.

All business affairs connected with the church were held in the Meeting House. Each month the members conducted a business meeting which was held at any time other than on a First Day. At each meeting anybody was allowed to speak his mind, and nearly everyone did. All ideas were discussed fully, until some agreement was reached. A clerk kept a record, but there was no voting.

"That's what we believe is the fair way of doing things," Joseph told Tom after he had taken him to one of the meetings.

The Quaker meeting for worship was quite different. The people entered the meeting house and sat down in complete silence. This silence lasted until some person felt carried upon to pray aloud, to read some sacred verse, or to preach a short sermon. Sometimes the meeting lasted a very long time.

This morning Tom sat still as long as he could on the hard bench. Then he just had to move, so he raised his body to change his position. Immediately, his father put out his hand to pull him down.

Tom sat quietly for a little longer. A few moments later, he raised his hand to loosen his tight collar. This time his father whispered softly to scold him. A neighbor heard it and Tom could see his look of reproach.

Fortunately, just then a church member behind them spoke up. "Let us pray for a quick return to peace and the safe return of our countrymen," he said solemnly.

This was the third year of the War of the Austrian Succession and the fourth of the War with Spain. Englishmen were fighting and dying in both of these wars under the banner of King George II of England.

Someone at church had offered a prayer for peace every First Day as long as Tom could remember, although no Quakers were in the armed forces. Violence was against their way of life. Further, Tom knew that there weren't any men from Thetford, even from the Church of England, fighting in the war, so this morning he didn't pay any attention to the prayer.

As Tom bowed his head he thought of the conversation between his parents which he had overheard the day before. Why did his mother care so much which church he attended? Once, he knew, Quakers had been imprisoned in England for their beliefs. Their property even had been taken away, and often they had been stoned or beaten by mobs. Quakers had been punished even though the charges against them hadn't been the truth. "What do Quakers really believe?" Tom had asked his father.

"They believe that all who do the will of God are brethren of Jesus in the Spirit," Joseph had replied.

During the past fifty years or so, since the joint reign of William and Mary, Quakers had been treated better than before in England. The meeting which Tom was attending proved this to be true. It included many familiar citizens of Thetford. For instance, the shoemaker and the blacksmith were there, and the paper-miller and the harness-maker.

"Just let Thetford try to get along without

these important citizens," Tom thought to himself. He glanced sidewise at his father, understanding why he was proud to be a Quaker.

At that moment people began to shake hands at the front of the room. This was the signal that the Quaker Meeting was over. Now everyone would shake hands with the person sitting beside him. Then all would file silently out of the house of worship.

On the way home Tom and his father walked past the two-storied, gabled jail near the Meeting House. They noticed that there was no prisoner in the cage, but Tom was horrified to see a girl standing in a pillory nearby. A pillory and stock were two other devices for punishing people in common use in Thetford. The pillory was a wooden frame behind which the prisoner stood with his head and hands sticking out through holes. The stock was a similar wooden frame, behind which a prisoner sat with his hands and feet sticking out through holes. "Oh, Father!" cried Tom, his deep blue eyes filling with tears. "That's Sukey Ames in the pillory! She's not much bigger than I am. What could she have done to be punished?"

Joseph's face was sad as he glanced at Sukey. "I don't know, Tom," he replied, "perhaps nothing more than talk sassily to her father."

"Then why didn't he just scold her?" said Tom. "Or send her to bed without supper, as Mother once did to me?"

"I do not know," said Joseph Paine again.

Tom realized that his father didn't want to talk about Sukey any more, but he was still curious. If he could have, he would have let her loose, just as he had the fly in the belfry. "Please tell me why the jailer punishes such a little girl in this way?" he said. "It isn't right to do such a thing, is it?"

"Praise the Lord, no," replied his father, "but

Sukey's father is one of the Duke's Selectmen. If he wishes to shame his daughter publicly, the jailer doesn't dare refuse."

"That's not fair!" cried Tom, his blue eyes blazing with anger.

Just then Sukey called out something faintly. Without thinking whether he should or not, Tom walked closer to her. "Do you want something, Sukey?" he asked.

"Water, please," begged Sukey. "For the love of God, bring me water."

Tom didn't wait to look at his father but ran to a nearby well. Suddenly he stopped, remembering that he had nothing in which to carry water. Luckily, he thought of the clean handkerchief which his mother had given him that morning. Quickly he soaked it in water and ran back with it to Sukey. "I couldn't find a cup," he said, "but maybe this wet handkerchief will help you a little."

Sukey moved her helpless hands. "You'll have to squeeze it into my mouth," she said.

Tom squeezed the water from the handkerchief. Then he turned toward the well again, but his father took him by the arm.

"Come on, now," he said. "That was a humane thing to do for Sukey, but many will criticize thee for thy act."

By this time Tom noticed that quite a crowd of people had gathered near the jail. He could hear some of them muttering angrily about what he had done. He looked sadly back at Sukey and found her smiling at him. "Thank you," she called, "and bless you, Tom Paine."

Tom and his father walked on toward home in silence for a time. Near the Town Bridge, they passed the Bell Inn, which was a very old building, dating from 1493. Its walls were made of wattles-and-daub, widely used for building in the fifteenth century. Wattle consisted of sticks intertwined with vines. Daub was a mixture of lime, sand, and water which hardened slowly as it dried.

To Tom, the interesting thing about the Bell Inn was a colorful painting on the outside walls. This painting pictured scenes from the accession of Henry VII, the first monarch of the House of Tudor, in 1485. The colors of the paintings had dimmed through the centuries, but they were still remarkably clear.

The scenes in the paintings always interested Tom, but today he looked at them more seriously than usual. "Father," he said, "you have said that King Henry was the first absolute monarch. What did you mean?"

"I simply meant that he had the power of life and death over his subjects," replied his father. "What makes thee ask?"

"Because I don't understand why a king should have so much power," said Tom.

"Power may be either good or bad," said Joseph. "If kings are just men they will rule wisely and well. But, of course, kings are human. They can act unwisely and do much harm, as we Quakers have found out."

"So has Sukey Ames," said Tom soberly.

Joseph Paine stared at him. "What dost thou mean?" he asked.

"I have heard you say that a man is absolute monarch of his household," replied Tom. "Selectman Ames, as monarch of his household, has acted unwisely. He has done Sukey much harm by putting her in the pillory."

"That is Selectman Ames' own business," replied Joseph. Then a worried look came over his face. "Thee thinks too seriously for one so young, Tom. Wait until thou art a few years older to think of such things."

"It is not fair for one person to have so much power over another," repeated Tom stubbornly. With these words he turned his back on the Bell Inn and started rapidly toward home.

Learning to Read

ONE MORNING, when Tom climbed out of bed, the Paine family's day began as usual with their breakfast of thick barley porridge and goat's milk. Immediately afterward, Joseph Paine went downstairs to his workshop and Frances Paine cleared off the table. Tom inspected the water buckets, to see how many trips he would have to make to the well. Making sure that all the buckets were full was one of his daily chores. Keeping the fuel basket filled with peat was another daily chore.

Today two buckets were empty. Tom picked up one of them in each hand. "Use the yoke,

Tom, for carrying the buckets," ordered his mother. "It will make your task easier."

The yoke was a frame fitted to a person's shoulders which was used for carrying pails suspended from each end. Joseph had made a yoke for Tom fitted to his shoulders, but Tom didn't like to use it. He much preferred to carry pails of water with his hands, so he could set them down on the way from the well. He liked to tarry along the way and spend as much time as possible outdoors.

Tom paused and looked at his mother. "Please let me carry the pails in my hands," he said. "I'll only need to make one trip to the well to get water today."

"No, because I want you to return as quickly as possible," his mother replied. "I have something planned for you."

Once more Tom looked at his mother. He noticed that she had a very serious look on her face. "Why do you want me to hurry today?" he asked. "What have you planned for me?"

Tom's mother didn't answer his questions. "I simply want you to bring the two pails of water without wasting any time," she replied. Then she glanced at the peat basket by the hearth. "You won't need to bring any peat today as the basket is almost full."

Frances picked up the yoke and put it across Tom's shoulders. Next she picked up the two empty pails and hung them on the ends of the yoke. "Hurry back as soon as you can," she said.

Tom realized that his mother still hadn't answered his question. Why did she want him to hurry? What did she have planned for him? Keeping secrets from him wasn't like her at all!

Tom's curiosity made him wish he had wings on his feet. Outdoors he found the cobblestones wet and slippery from a misty rain. He had to watch his footing carefully but hurried to the well as fast as possible.

"You were quick!" his mother said approvingly, coming to take the yoke from his back. "Put the pails in the storage cupboard and come to me in the sitting room. Then I'll tell you what I have planned for you."

Tom put the pails in the cupboard and covered them with clean cloths. Now he was so filled with curiosity that he could hardly wait to find out what his mother had in mind for him. He hurried across the kitchen and on into the sitting room.

His mother was seated in her special chair. Once this had been just an ordinary oak chair, but her husband had fastened large canvas bags on both arms. Frances used these bags for storing personal things such as her Bible and her sewing materials.

When one of Joseph's friends had first seen

these bags, he had said, "These bags are a good idea, Mr. Paine. You should make up some more of them to display in your shop. People would want to buy them and you could sell them for a good price."

Joseph had brushed the idea aside. "I merely invented them for my wife," he had said, "not to sell in my shop."

The friend had shaken his head. "You Quakers are always modest about your accomplishments, but I think you have a good idea here," he argued. "You can make and sell them to a good advantage in your shop."

"I appreciate your comment but have no desire to make and sell them," Joseph had replied, ending the conversation.

Frances kept the bags on her chair in constant use. Usually when she sat in the chair she took out her Bible or needlework from one of the bags. Today when Tom entered the room he found her holding the Bible in her lap. "Here I am, Mother," he said excitedly.

Frances stroked the Bible. "My plan for you is in this book," she said. "It is the official book of the English church."

"Yes, I know, Mother," he said. "I often find you reading it when I come into the room."

Tom's mother held up the Bible. "This Holy Book is the Word of God," she said. "It was translated from the Hebrew in which it was written. The task was accomplished by many learned men by command of King James I. This task took them seven years."

She lowered the Bible to her lap. "I am going to teach you to read, so that you may read the holy words yourself," she said.

Tom's heart leaped, because he wanted to learn to read. He knew that his father would be pleased too because all Quakers favored education. For a moment he stood thinking, however, because he knew his father would object to his using his Mother's Bible as a textbook. "Come, let's get started," said Frances. "Draw up a chair and sit beside me."

Tom pulled up a cane chair and sat stiffly beside her. Frances reached into the bag where she kept her Bible and brought out an object which looked strange to Tom. He gazed at a thin square piece of blue-gray stone. "What is that?" he asked curiously.

"This is a piece of slate on which I will print letters of the alphabet for you to learn," his mother answered.

"May I hold it?" asked Tom.

His mother handed the slate to him. It was frameless and had a hole punched at one side.

"I have never seen anything like this before," said Tom, holding it carefully.

Frances smiled proudly. "Neither have most people in Thetford, because slates are newfangled tools for reading and writing. Your Grandfather Cocke bought this one for you at a bookshop in Stockton."

Tom started to examine the square piece of slate. He turned it upside down and round and round in his lap. Curiously he looked at the hole in one side of the slate. "What is this hole for?" he asked.

Frances reached into one of the bags on her chair and pulled out a slate pencil for writing on the slate. "The hole in the slate is for tying this pencil to the slate with a string," she explained. "Once the pencil is tied to the slate, it will always be handy for writing and not likely to be lost."

"I have some string in my pocket," said Tom. "May I tie the pencil to the slate?"

"Yes," replied his mother, "but tie it on tightly. You'll need only enough string to allow a person to use the pencil in writing."

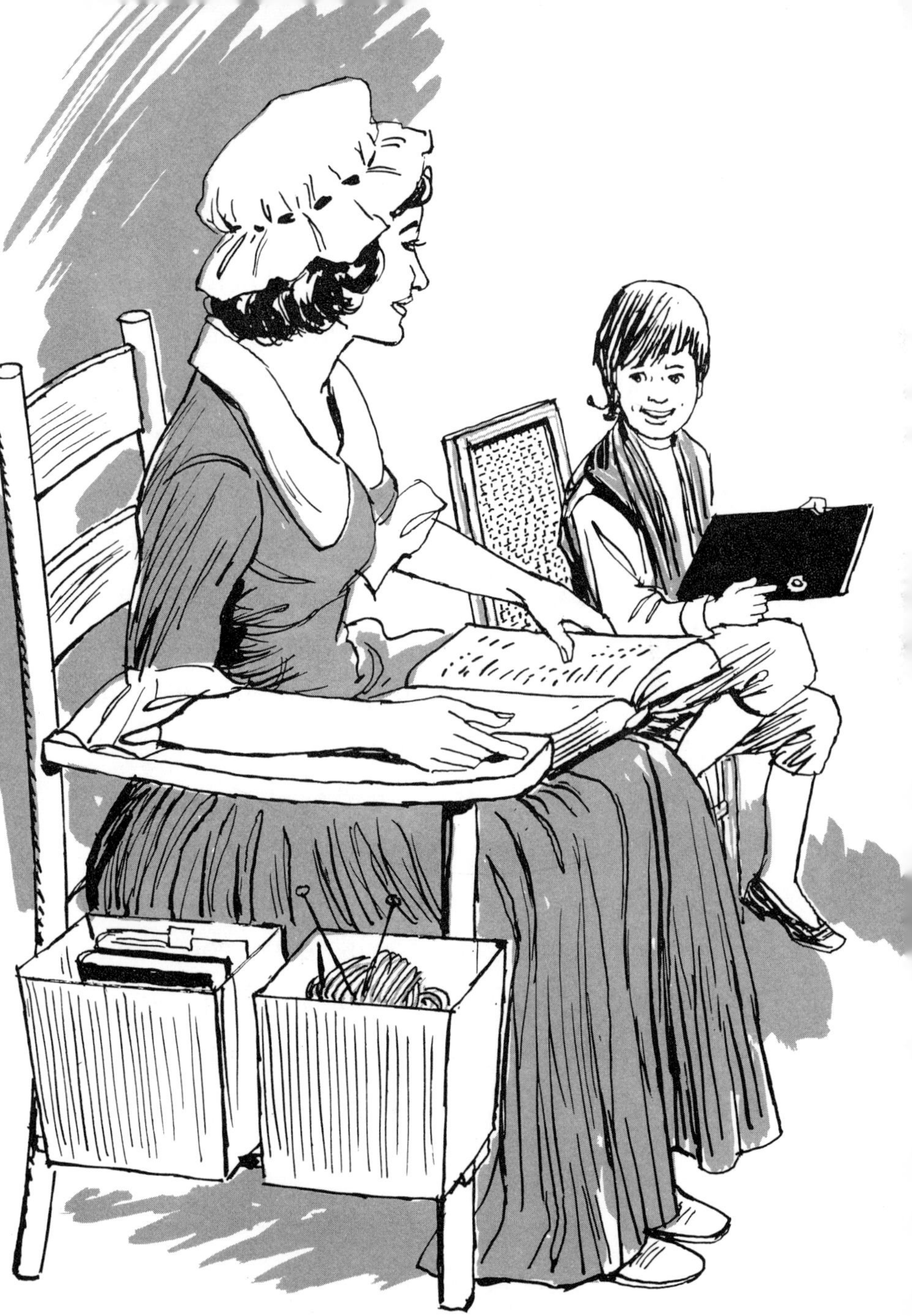

Tom reached into his pocket and brought out a piece of string. He carefully measured the length of string that he would need and snipped it off with his mother's scissors. Then he tied one end of the string to the slate and the other end of the string to the pencil.

His mother watched him proudly as he worked. Then she reached for the slate. "Now we'll begin your lessons," she said.

She printed *a, b,* and *c* in both large and small letters. She named them and asked Tom to repeat them several times. Finally she had him copy them on the slate.

After Tom learned to read and write these three letters of the alphabet, she printed the next three letters, *d, e,* and *f,* for him to learn. Before long she said, "I will leave you alone now, while I prepare our noon meal. Keep on studying *d, e,* and *f* until you know them, and then put the slate back in my bag."

"All right, Mother," said Tom. "I'll keep on studying until I know them."

Tom kept on studying the second three letters of the alphabet until he could read and write them well. Next he wiped the slate clean and wrote all the six letters, both capitals and small letters, which he had learned. As he gazed at them, he felt elated. "I like the looks of these letters," he said to himself.

Moments later he took the slate to the kitchen to show the letters to his mother. "Excellent," she said, giving him a pat on the head. "Tomorrow I'll teach you some more letters and we'll keep on until you come to know all the letters of the alphabet. Then you'll be ready to read from my Bible."

Tom proudly took the slate back to the sitting room, wiped it clean, and placed it in one of the bags on his mother's chair. He was happy about learning to read but was still afraid to tell his father, because he wouldn't approve of him using his mother's Bible as a textbook.

Tom learned to read quickly because he was eager to learn. His mother worked with him until he was able to read the Garden of Eden story from her Bible without making a mistake. From then on she had him sit down each day to read the Bible all by himself.

He read the Bible all the way through once. Then he went back and read certain favorite stories and poems over and over again. He learned great portions of both Testaments by heart.

Tom's mother was pleased with how rapidly he learned and how much he enjoyed reading the Bible. With his early knowledge of the Scriptures she felt sure he would grow up to be a righteous man. "Now the word of God will remain with you always," she said.

Tom read and reread the Bible for two main reasons. First, because it was handy to find in the sitting room. Second, it contained exciting stories and poetry that sounded much like music when he read them aloud.

All the while neither Frances nor Tom told Joseph that he was learning to read. Frances hoped that by reading the Bible he would grow up to become a member of the Church of England. Tom was afraid to tell his father because he knew that his father expected him to become a Quaker. Sometimes when he and his father were out walking his father stopped to read notices and signs, but Tom pretended that he didn't know what they said.

Enrolling in School

When fall came, Tom's father made a sudden announcement. "Tom," he said, "I'm going to enroll thee in the Grammar School."

"Husband!" cried Frances worriedly. "Remember that this will cost money."

Joseph frowned. "I know, but I can readily pay it. At present my business is good. Besides, we must be ready to sacrifice if necessary to prepare Tom for the future."

Even though Frances was surprised, she was pleased by Joseph's announcement. Grammar School was a private boys' school and boys from some of the best families went there. It had been founded some years before by a rich landowner. At first boys could go there free, but now they had to pay a small tuition.

"I'll be glad to have Tom attend the Grammar School," said Frances. "If he applies himself, he may rise to fame in the world."

"I especially want him to learn to read and write and do sums, so he can start to work for me in my business," said her husband.

"Boys from all around the area attend the Grammar School," Frances said to Tom. "They come from Brandon, Euston, and even from places farther away. You may hold your head high as you associate with these boys."

"Come, wife," scolded Joseph. "Don't lead Tom to have false ambitions and desires. Rather let him be content to cast his lot with plain folks right here in Thetford."

The next morning Joseph took Tom to the Grammar School, which was across the Ouse

River from Thetford. Tom had seen the Grammar School often, but never had looked at it carefully before. It was a gray stone building thickly covered with green ivy. It was located in a stone-covered courtyard shaded by huge branching lime trees. There was a large arched gateway in front of the courtyard.

Joseph led Tom through the archway and across the courtyard. They entered the front door of the building and stepped into a hall. There they came to a closed door with the name of the headmaster on a brass nameplate.

Joseph rapped on the solid oak paneling of the door. After a moment, the headmaster opened the door and stood there before them, elegantly dressed. He wore a maroon silk coat and a waistcoat embroidered with flowers. The cuffs of his white ruffled shirt were banded with lace. His black breeches, which came just below his knees, were met by white silk stockings.

The finishing touch was his shiny black shoes, which had enormous brass buckles in front.

Tom had never seen anyone so elegantly dressed before. He merely stood and stared at the headmaster, even though he knew it was rude to do so. Finally his father tapped him on the shoulder as a warning to quit staring.

The headmaster, meanwhile, kept looking Joseph and Tom over, too. As always, both wore Quaker plain clothes, though not their First Day best. Today they wore gray suits without buttons or lapels. On their heads they wore broad-brimmed gray hats.

The headmaster seemed surprised to see Joseph and Tom. "Pardon me," he said, "but I was looking for Squire Grimes and his son this morning. He wants to enroll his son in our school. What can I do for you?"

Joseph took a step forward. "I am Joseph Paine, a freeman of Thetford," he explained.

He laid a hand gently on Tom's shoulder and added, "This is my son, Thomas. I want to enroll him as a student in thy school."

The headmaster's face brightened when Joseph said he was a freeman. In England at that time being a freeman meant possessing a certain standing in the town. It meant that a person had certain civil and political rights not enjoyed by every man who lived in the area.

"So you wish Thomas to become a student here," said the headmaster. "Do you want him to take the classics course or the ordinary course?"

"Kindly explain the difference," said Joseph.

The headmaster walked over to his writing table. Then he waved his hand at two nearby chairs. "Please be seated," he said courteously.

Joseph and Tom promptly seated themselves. They sat up stiff and straight in their chairs and folded their hands in their laps.

The headmaster put his hands flat on the table and leaned forward to speak to them. "I teach the classics course," he said proudly. "This course includes a thorough grounding in Latin and Greek. If a boy completes it, he will be prepared to go on to Oxford or Cambridge to continue his education."

Joseph shook his head. "I do not want Thomas to take the classics course. The Society of Friends does not approve of studying history or languages of ancient non-Christian countries. Rather we want our boys to learn to read, write, and figure for everyday living."

"I know," said the headmaster, "but I urge you to let Thomas take our classics course. He will profit much from the broad knowledge which he will receive. He may even become a better Quaker by taking this course."

"No," replied Joseph, "my mind is made up. I want Thomas to take the ordinary course."

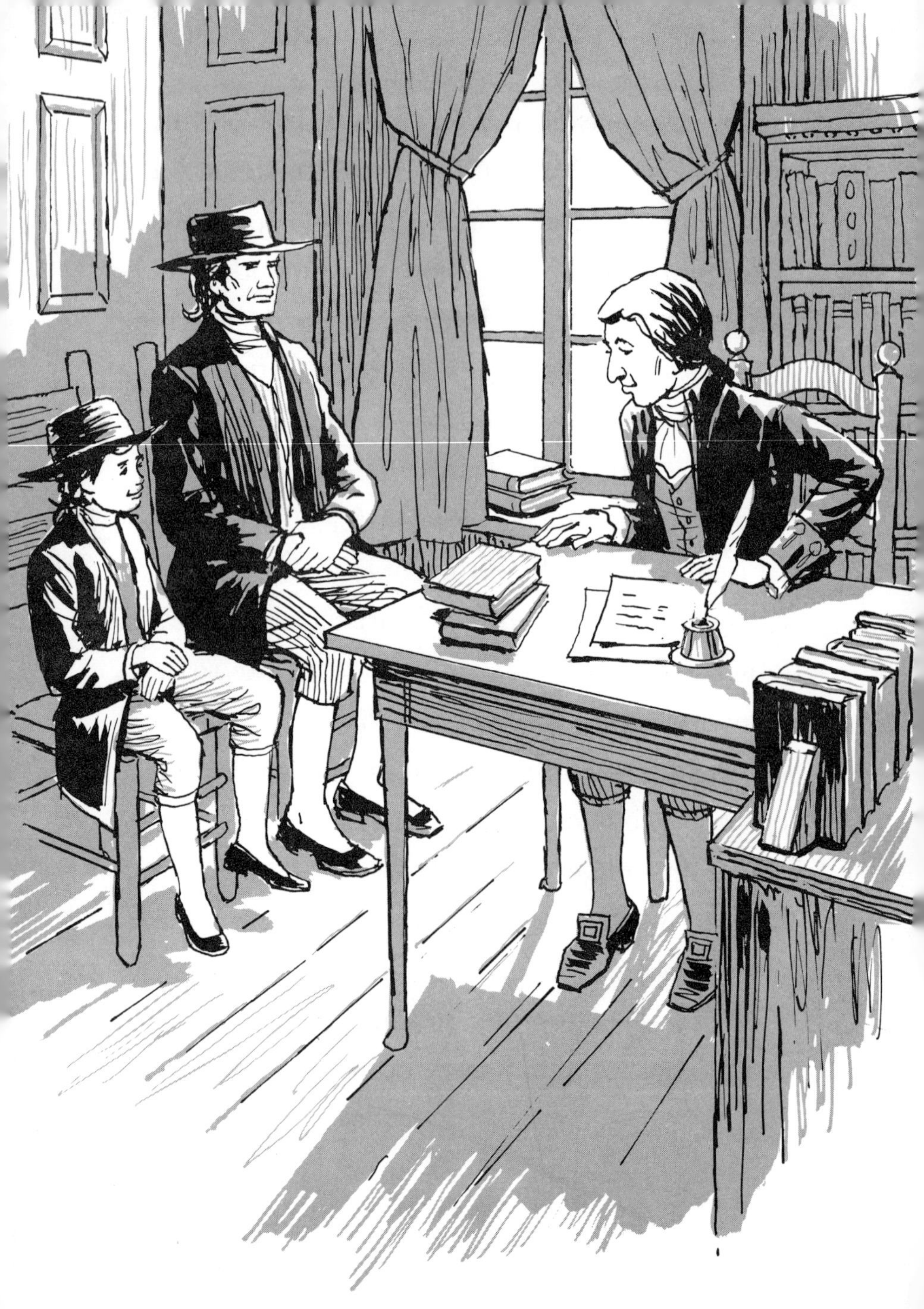

The headmaster shifted his gaze from father to son. "Well, then, Thomas, you will not be privileged to have me as your teacher or guide," he said. "Your teacher will be my assistant, Mr. William Knowles."

Tom bit his cheek in order to keep his feeling of relief from showing in his face. He was thankful to learn that the haughty headmaster would not be his teacher. Now he wondered what Mr. William Knowles would be like. "May we meet him?" asked Tom's father.

"No, this is vacation time and Mr. Knowles is not here," replied the headmaster. "I would not be here myself except to meet Squire Grimes and his son. I wonder where they are? They are late for their appointment."

Joseph and Tom arose and started to leave. "We'll keep you no longer," said Joseph. "When should Thomas begin his studies?"

"Classes will start at eight o'clock next Monday morning," replied the headmaster. "Have Thomas report directly to Mr. Knowles."

"Thomas will be here in good time," Joseph assured the headmaster. "Now, son, we must bid the headmaster farewell."

Tom knew from the tone of his father's voice that "farewell" was all his father wanted him to say. "Farewell, sir," he said in chorus with Joseph on their way out.

As Joseph and Thomas went through the archway in front of the building, a handsome coach drew up and stopped. "That probably is Squire Grimes arriving with his son," said Joseph, nodding in the direction of the coach.

"Oh, may we stay and see what his son looks like?" asked Tom.

"That would not be good manners," replied his father. "Come on, let's go home."

Joseph and Tom walked silently all the way home. Joseph never said anything just to make conversation. As for Tom, his mind was awhirl with questions about the school, but he knew that now wasn't the time to ask them.

Joseph went at once to his workshop. Tom hurried upstairs, where his mother was waiting to learn about his visit to the Grammar School. She began to question him the moment he appeared. He described the headmaster and told how elegantly he was dressed. He explained that he would take the ordinary course of study and that Mr. Knowles would be his teacher.

Frances seemed excited over Tom's report of his visit to the school. "Your Grandfather Cocke will be pleased to hear about this," she said. "He will approve of your father's decision to send you to the Grammar School."

"Tell him that I'll start to school next Monday. That's only a few days from now," said Tom.

Tom's First Day at School

ON MONDAY MORNING, when Tom came near the Grammar School, he heard laughter and voices inside the school courtyard. The closer he came, the louder they sounded to him. "What is going on?" he wondered.

He stopped at the archway and peered into the courtyard. There he found it crowded with boys of all ages and sizes. Some of the older boys were standing in small groups, laughing, and others were running here and there, playing with hoops, sticks, and balls.

Tom was surprised to find the boys so happy and carefree. He had expected to find them trying to be as quiet as possible. School, he had thought, was a serious place for studying books, not for playing with hoops, sticks, and balls.

He stepped cautiously into the courtyard. For a moment he stood wondering how he could reach the school building. He wanted to report to his teacher, William Knowles, but was afraid to walk through the crowd of boys. Finally he decided to follow the courtyard wall around to the building. He hoped that he wouldn't be noticed.

Along the way, an older boy spotted him and called to him, "Hey, there, Quake! Where do you think you're going?"

Tom stopped and glanced at the boy. "I'm going to my first day of school," he replied, starting on toward the building.

"What's your hurry?" asked the boy sneeringly. "Are you looking for someone?"

"Yes, the Master, Mr. Knowles," said Tom.

"He answered me without quaking!" said the boy in a jeering voice.

"Or shaking either," said one of his friends.

"Couldn't be he's faking," said a third boy.

Tom bit his cheeks. He realized the boys were poking fun at him, but he didn't dare display any anger. He remembered the warning in one of the proverbs from the Bible that he had memorized: "He that is slow to anger is better than the mighty." Tom felt thankful for remembering this proverb.

The boys stared speechlessly at one another. They were baffled by Tom's calmness even though he was only about half as old as they were and half as big as they were. His calm actions caused them to be ashamed.

Just as Tom reached the door of the building a big boy stepped out with a large bell in his hand. He had come to ring the bell to call the boys from the courtyard to their classes. When he saw Tom he said, "Step inside before I ring this bell. Otherwise you may get caught in the crowd. I'll hold off to give you a start."

Tom didn't wait to ask any questions but stepped into the hall, calling "Thank you" over his shoulder. Luckily, he soon spotted a half-open door with the name WILLIAM KNOWLES printed on a panel. He gave a quick knock and cautiously stepped inside.

Just at that moment the big boy began to ring the bell in front of the building. Soon after came the thud of many running feet as the boys streamed into the building from the courtyard. "Shut the door behind you, lad!" yelled the room's other occupant.

Tom obeyed. The closed door cut off most of the noise in the hall and he turned to face the person who had spoken to him. He saw a large, broad-shouldered man with a weather-beaten face, wearing shabby dark clothes.

"I'm looking for Mr. Knowles," Tom said, feeling sure he had made some mistake.

The man smiled. "Well, you're in the right place. I am William Knowles, Assistant Master of this school."

Tom's cheeks flushed with excitement. He swallowed but could think of nothing to say. Mr. Knowles looked so different from what he had expected a schoolmaster to be.

Mr. Knowles stood up and took a black scholar's robe from the back of his chair. When he put it on, it completely hid his other clothing. "Now do I look more like a schoolmaster?" he asked with a pleasant smile.

"Yes, sir," Tom managed to reply.

Mr. Knowles smiled again, "Good," he said. "I take it that you are Thomas Paine, who is to be in the lowest form here."

"Yes, I am Thomas Paine, but I don't understand what you mean by the lowest form," said

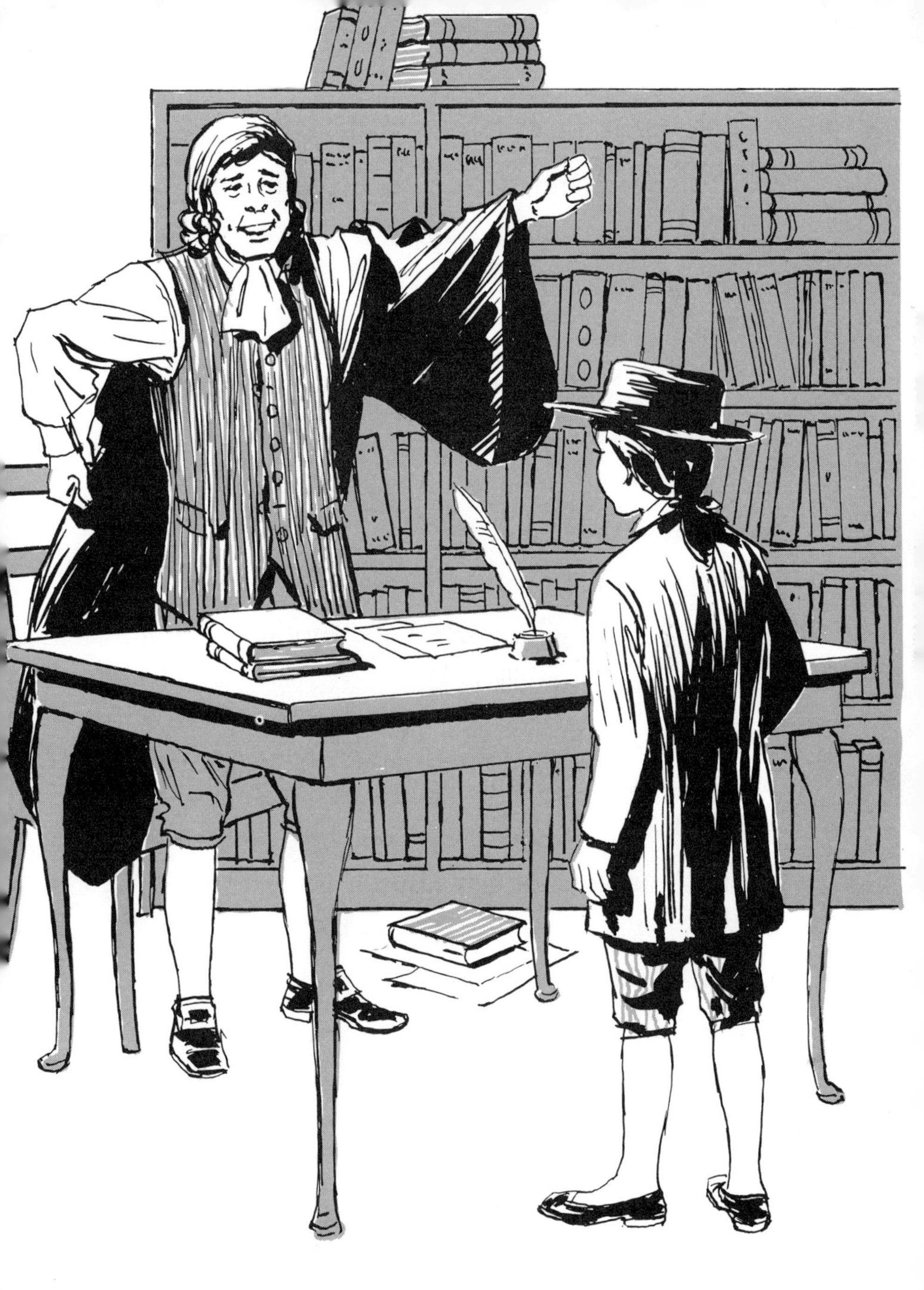

Tom. "My father, Joseph Paine, wants me to learn to read and write and do sums so I can help him later in his shop."

"That's sensible of him," said Mr. Knowles.

"Since you will be my teacher, I have a secret to tell you that even my father doesn't know," said Tom. "My mother has taught me to read and write and I have already read her Bible from cover to cover."

Mr. Knowles' eyebrows rose as he glanced at Tom's Quaker clothes. "Your mother's Bible, did you say?" he asked.

"Yes, my mother is a member of St. Cuthbert's," replied Tom. "From my reading her Bible she hopes that someday I'll want to become a member of her church too."

"Well, I'll put you with the low form until I find out what you can do," said the schoolmaster. "Come on now and follow me."

They walked together to a large room filled

with benches and tables. Boys sat stiffly waiting on the benches with their hands folded on the tables in front of them. Tom looked them over rapidly and was glad to see that none of his tormentors were present. He saw several boys he already knew, among them Nip Tanner, son of the town turnkey or jailer.

Mr. Knowles stood at the front of the room and looked the boys over carefully. Then suddenly he nodded to Tom and said, "Take the empty seat in the second row left. You and Peter Colbert will get along well together."

Tom promptly obeyed. "Good morning," he whispered softly to Peter.

Peter looked slyly at Tom. "Are you a cripple?" he whispered in return.

This question startled Tom. "No, why do you ask that?" he replied.

"Because I'm a cripple," explained Peter. "I have a gimpy leg and a weak back. From what

Mr. Knowles said I thought you might be a cripple, but maybe I am mistaken."

"Well," said Tom, thinking quickly, "I'm not a cripple, but your being a cripple won't make any difference to me. We'll get along well just as Mr. Knowles said we would."

Peter smiled. "Thank you," he said. "I'm glad to have you sit by me."

Mr. Knowles now called the room to order.

"It's time to get down to work," he said. "We'll soon find out what the summer holiday has done to your brains!"

He walked to the back of the room and began to question some of the older boys. At first Tom tried to listen but couldn't hear what they said. Once more he thought of Mr. Knowles' comment about getting along with Peter. Was it because he was a Quaker that he thought they would get along well together?

Mr. Knowles walked over beside Tom, but

Tom was so deep in thought that he didn't notice him. "Thomas Paine," said Mr. Knowles, putting his hand on Tom's shoulder.

Tom jumped up so quickly that he banged his knee against a table leg. "Yes, sir," he said.

Mr. Knowles handed him a small book. He looked at the book curiously. "Read the title of the book," ordered the schoolmaster.

Tom looked at the cover and read, "*A Book for Boys and Girls, or Country Rhimes for Children.*"

"By whom was it written?" asked the schoolmaster.

Tom opened the book to the title page. "By John Bunyan," he replied.

"Yes," said Mr. Knowles. "Bunyan was a religious man noted for his common sense."

Tom now started to sit down. Suddenly, however, Mr. Knowles said, "Face the classroom and read the first page aloud."

Tom's heart pounded as he looked at the room full of strangers. Mr. Knowles noticed that he was frightened and turned him around. "Now start to read," he said.

Tom took a deep breath, held the book firmly, and began to read the following lines:

"To those who are in years but Babes I bow
    My pen to teach them what the letters be
    And how they may improve their A.B.C.
Nor let my pretty Children them despise.
All needs must there begin, that would be wise,
    Nor let them fall under Discouragement,
    Who at their Hornbook stick, and time hath spent,
Upon that A.B.C., while others do
Into their Primer or their Psalter go."

"You read very well, only a little too fast," said Mr. Knowles approvingly. "You are a good reader and should get along well with your studies here in the Grammar School."

All the boys in the room listened closely as Tom read. They were astounded to find that such a small boy could read so well on his first day at school. Some of the older boys felt ashamed since they realized that he could read better than they could.

"May I take my seat again, please, sir?" asked Tom after he finished reading.

"Yes," replied the schoolmaster. "You have finished your task." He walked away quickly to another part of the room.

Tom nervously sat down. Peter Colbert looked at him a moment and moved over beside him. He said nothing, but having him near was comforting to Tom. "Mr. Knowles was right," thought Tom. "Peter and I will get along famously sitting here together."

Comforting Words

WITHIN a few days, Mr. Knowles asked Tom to wait after school to talk with him. "Tom," he said, "you have demonstrated that you can read and write too well for the lowest form. But unfortunately you don't know how to work with numbers. I must keep you in the lower form until you can get started in arithmetic."

"Yes, sir," said Tom. "I understand."

"Well," said Mr. Knowles, "I'm sure that if you study your numbers hard you'll soon be ready to move up."

"I'll study them hard," said Tom. "I want to move up as soon as possible."

The children in the Grammar School had no textbooks in arithmetic. They had to learn the different number combinations by rote, that is by saying them over and over. For instance, the teacher said, "Two and two make four." Then the children repeated this combination until they knew it by heart.

Tom learned the number combinations faster than most of the other pupils. He spent many hours repeating combinations that he already knew by heart. Soon he felt that he was wasting time and decided to have another talk with Mr. Knowles about his arithmetic work. "I've learned all the number combinations," he said, "and now I'm ready to learn how to use them. I want to learn to figure."

Mr. Knowles broke into a hearty laugh. "You certainly are a sensible boy to want to figure things out with numbers," he said. "What you really want are some problems to solve."

"Yes, sir," said Tom. "That's what I mean. I want some problems to solve."

"Well, I have a book on my shelves called *Wingate's Arithmetic*," said Mr. Knowles. "It includes problems to solve and contains tables of measures and other things to use in working with numbers. It provides much information which you will find helpful in the future."

"Oh, good!" cried Tom. "May I borrow it from you for a while?"

Mr. Knowles thought about Tom's request for a few moments while Tom watched him hopefully. "Yes, I'll be glad to lend it to you because you are so eager to learn more about numbers," he said. "Besides, it will help you to make good use of your idle time."

Tom fully expected Mr. Knowles to give him the arithmetic book, but instead he held up a sheet of paper which Tom readily recognized. It contained a bit of verse which he had made up while some of the other pupils were reading haltingly from their primers. Somehow the paper had disappeared and he was wondering what had become of it.

Mr. Knowles wore a broad smile on his face as he held the paper before his eyes to read:

"Here lies the body of John Crow
Who once was high, but now is low.
Ye brother crows, take warning all,
For as ye rise, so must ye fall."

Tom's face flushed with embarrassment. "I'm sorry, sir," he said, hanging his head. "I shouldn't have written it."

"Oh, I'm not objecting to your writing it," said Mr. Knowles. "I just wonder why you chose to write about a dead crow. What made such an idea occur to you?"

"Because I noticed a dead crow on the way to school this morning," replied Tom.

"I'm surprised that it bothered you," said

Mr. Knowles. "Seeing dead animals around here is a common occurrence."

Tom shook his head. "To me death is never commonplace," he said. "It always bothers me."

The schoolmaster stared at him. "Young Paine, your thinking is most unusual, and with your intelligence you can go far in the world. I hate to think of you wasting your time in your father's workshop."

"Well, I need not work in my father's shop forever," explained Tom thoughtfully.

"You may be right," replied Mr. Knowles. "I started out as a common seaman, but left the sea to become a minister in a church. And now here I am a schoolmaster."

"Were you really a seaman?" asked Tom in great surprise. He often had wondered why the schoolmaster's skin was so weatherbeaten. "How exciting! Tell me more about it."

"Yes, life on a man-o'-war was exciting, a

little too exciting sometimes," explained Mr. Knowles. "For instance, we faced tense moments when we heard the drums beat ordering us to our battle stations and we knew that we would soon do battle with the enemy."

"What happened when you went to your stations?" asked Tom, looking up eagerly.

"Many things," replied Mr. Knowles, "some of which were too horrible to describe. As you say, Paine, death is never commonplace."

The schoolmaster turned to his bookshelves, took down the arithmetic book, and handed it to Tom. "I hope you enjoy studying this book," he said. "If you need any help, don't hesitate to tell me so. My door will always be open whenever you wish to come here."

"Thank you, sir," said Tom, clutching the arithmetic book. For now he was dismissed, but he knew that the would often return to the schoolmaster's study. He felt that he and Mr.

Knowles were more than just schoolmaster and pupil. They were close friends.

As the days went by Tom's friendship with Mr. Knowles became very important because most of the boys were downright unfriendly to him. Some were still resentful because he could read so well when he first started to school. Mostly, however, they belong to the Church of England and disliked him because he was a Quaker. Tom could understand the first reason but not the second.

He decided to talk the matter over with his crippled friend, Peter Colbert. "I thought that people here in England are free to choose their own religion," said Tom. "Why should anyone be against me because I am a Quaker?"

"They don't really care about your religion, Tom," said Peter. "They simply plague you because of certain things you do, such as wearing plain clothes instead of fancy clothes as the rest of them do. They make you a target because you seem different. I ought to know because before you came I was their target."

Tom was shocked to learn that Peter had been mistreated. "Do you mean that the boys made fun of your crippled leg?" he asked. "Did they tease you because you couldn't move about as they could?"

Peter nodded. "Yes, they even used to trip me just to see me fall and try to get up again. They watched me struggle just as if I was a turtle turned wrong-side-up. One of the worst teasers was Nip Tanner."

Tom's blue eyes blazed with anger. "How could he be so cruel to treat you like that?" he asked. "I suppose he gets used to cruelty because his father is the town jailer. That's a job no Quaker would want."

"Don't Quakers believe that persons who do wrong should be punished?" asked Peter.

Tom thought a moment before he answered. "Of course we believe that persons who do bad things should be punished, but we don't believe they should be mistreated. For instance, my father believes that we shouldn't use such shameful devices as cages, stocks, and pillories to punish people, and so do I."

That very afternoon, on his way home, Tom found a person known as Jackie locked in the stocks. He recognized Jackie as an idiot, a man with the brain of a little child, who often was put in the stocks to keep him out of mischief. Today Tom was shocked to find Nip Tanner throwing chunks of dirt at Jackie. Worst of all, he seemed to be aiming at Jackie's eyes. The poor fellow was completely helpless to cover them and was crying pitifully.

When Tom saw what Nip was doing, he rushed up to him and shouted, "Stop that! How can you be so cruel to him?"

Nip turned fiercely on Tom. "Keep out of this, Quaker!" he shouted. "I dare you to stop me, if you can."

Nip wore his hair long, down to his shoulders. Tom grabbed him by his long hair, which was the easiest thing for him to reach. He merely intended to pull Nip away from the stocks so he could talk and reason with him.

Nip misunderstood Tom's actions and thought he was starting a fight. He prepared to use the weapon which led people to call him "Nip." He let Tom draw him close and sank his teeth deep into Tom's ear lobe.

Tom screamed in pain. He let go of Nip's hair so he could use his hands to protect himself. He tried to push Nip away, but Nip held on with the persistence of a bulldog. He didn't let loose his bite until Tom punched him hard in the stomach. "I didn't think you Quakers would fight," Nip gasped, holding his stomach.

"We don't like to fight and I didn't want to hit you," said Tom. "I just wanted to get you away from Jackie."

"Well, you hurt me anyhow," said Nip weakly. "From now on I'll leave Jackie alone if it means that much to you."

By now blood was dripping from Tom's ear and he started to walk over to a well. He wanted to wash his ear with cold water. He half expected Nip to follow him, but Nip turned away. When Tom looked back Nip was gone. At the same time, much to his surprise, Nip's father was releasing Jackie from the stocks.

When Tom reached home his mother was horrified to see his injured ear. She smeared it with some homemade salve. "That Nip must be an animal instead of a boy to bite you like that," she cried in anger. "He's nothing more than an animal to treat you that way."

Tom explained to his mother just what had happened. He told how he had tried to stop Nip from throwing chunks of dirt at Jackie in the stocks. Then Nip had bit him in the ear and he had hit Nip to make him let loose.

When Tom's father came upstairs for supper

Tom had to repeat the whys and wherefores of the affair again. "Well, you did no wrong, son," said his father. "You had to hit Nip to make him let go of your ear. Not even Quakers turn the other cheek forever."

These words were comforting to Tom and helped to relieve his guilty mind. He vowed to remember them the rest of his life. Later he often repeated them as an important lesson that he had learned from his father.

Good Companions

Tom made frequent calls on Mr. Knowles in his office. At first he pretended that he wanted to ask him questions about mathematics. Mr. Knowles always answered these questions promptly and soon they began to talk about other things. Often Tom asked a question about a book which he noticed on Mr. Knowles' bookshelves. Once he asked such a question, his schoolmaster was ready to keep on talking.

As the weeks passed, Tom stopped almost daily to see Mr. Knowles and to examine the books on his bookshelves. These books covered a wide variety of subjects, including history, science, and literature. Mr. Knowles was always willing to lend Tom any of these books.

Mr. Knowles' library contained certain works translated from Greek and Latin. Under Quaker beliefs Tom was not supposed to read Greek and Latin works. Since Mr. Knowles' books had been translated into English, he felt that he wasn't doing anything wrong.

One of his favorite Latin books was written by Virgil. "I like him because he writes so many sensible things," said Tom. "He says things that are helpful in everyday living."

"Yes," agreed Mr. Knowles. "I remember one of his sayings that especially applies to you."

"What is it, and how does it apply to me?" asked Tom anxiously.

"That persons 'can because they think they can,'" replied Mr. Knowles. "It applies to you because you seem to be able to do almost anything that you set your mind to."

Tom was surprised and pleased with the schoolmaster's statement. "That may be right," he said, "but I have to want to do something in order to get it done."

"I've noticed that," said Mr. Knowles.

The years went by rapidly in this way until Tom was thirteen years old. Finally, just before the brief spring vacation in 1750, Mr. Knowles asked Tom whether he would like to go on an overnight walking trip while the school was closed.

Tom's eyes sparkled with joy. "Where will we go?" he asked eagerly.

"We'll go into the area of Breckland north of here," said Mr. Knowles. "We'll visit a part of England which is very rich in history. Also, we'll see a large flint mine, one of the largest in the world."

"Oh, how exciting!" cried Tom. "I only hope that my father will let me go with you."

"Well, there's only one way to find out," said Mr. Knowles. "You'll have to ask him."

That very night when Tom went home, he asked his father for permission to go on the overnight walking trip with Mr. Knowles. His father considered the request in a thoughtful manner, while Tom waited, all but holding his breath. At last Mr. Paine spoke, but what he said came as a great surpise to Tom. "I haven't told thee before, but I plan to withdraw thee from school at the end of this term," he said. "Now at age thirteen it is time for thee to begin thy apprenticeship with me."

"Oh, my!" exclaimed Tom, the shock of this news almost choking him.

"Since thy schooldays are almost over," said Mr. Paine, "I see no reason to deny thee this last chance to take a trip with thy schoolmaster. Thou may go with Mr. Knowles."

One morning soon Mr. Knowles and Tom set

out together, each with a small bag strapped on his back. The bags contained bread, cheese, and meat for their food, and changes of clothing which they might need. They would use the bags as pillows while they slept on the ground under the stars at night.

At first they walked over heathland which was familiar to Tom. Soon they came to country which was very strange to him. It was covered with old, wind-bent, eerie-looking trees such as he had never seen before. "Their twisted limbs look live evil arms that might reach down and grab me," he said.

"Don't harbor such thoughts," said Mr. Knowles. "You may expect to find several things that look eerie to you on this trip."

"Of course," said Tom. "I must expect to see things that I won't fully understand."

The two of them kept on walking until they came to the large flint mine which Mr. Knowles had mentioned. Tom was surprised to find that the mine was called Grimes Graves. He was further surprised to find it was managed by the same Squire Grimes whom he had almost met when he first enrolled in the Grammar School.

Mr. Knowles explained that this flint mine had been opened thousands of years before. Prehistoric men had found the flint embedded in layers of chalk deep in the ground. They started to mine the flint to made crude tools and weapons for themselves.

"How deep did they have to dig to get the flint?" asked Tom curiously.

"They dug down about forty feet and then extended tunnels in all directions," explained Mr. Knowles. "You might think that after all these years of mining the flint would be gone, but not so. This mine is still the center of the flint mining industry in the world."

"Can we go into the mine?" asked Tom.

"Yes, by all means," replied Mr. Knowles. He talked briefly with a mine worker who gave him a lantern and directed him to a mine shaft.

Mr. Knowles and Tom backed slowly and carefully down steps cut into the chalk. Soon Mr. Knowles held the lantern high and said, "There, Tom, is what I want you to see. Behold the altar which prehistoric men once erected here to honor the chalk goddess."

Tom looked and saw crude carvings a short distance away. They looked meaningless to him, but he finally managed to say, "An altar to the chalk goddess. How wonderful that it has lasted all these years!"

That night they slept on the ground near the flint mine. The next morning they started to walk leisurely back toward Thetford. Along the way Mr. Knowles told Tom interesting bits of history about this part of England. At one point he called his attention to some ridges

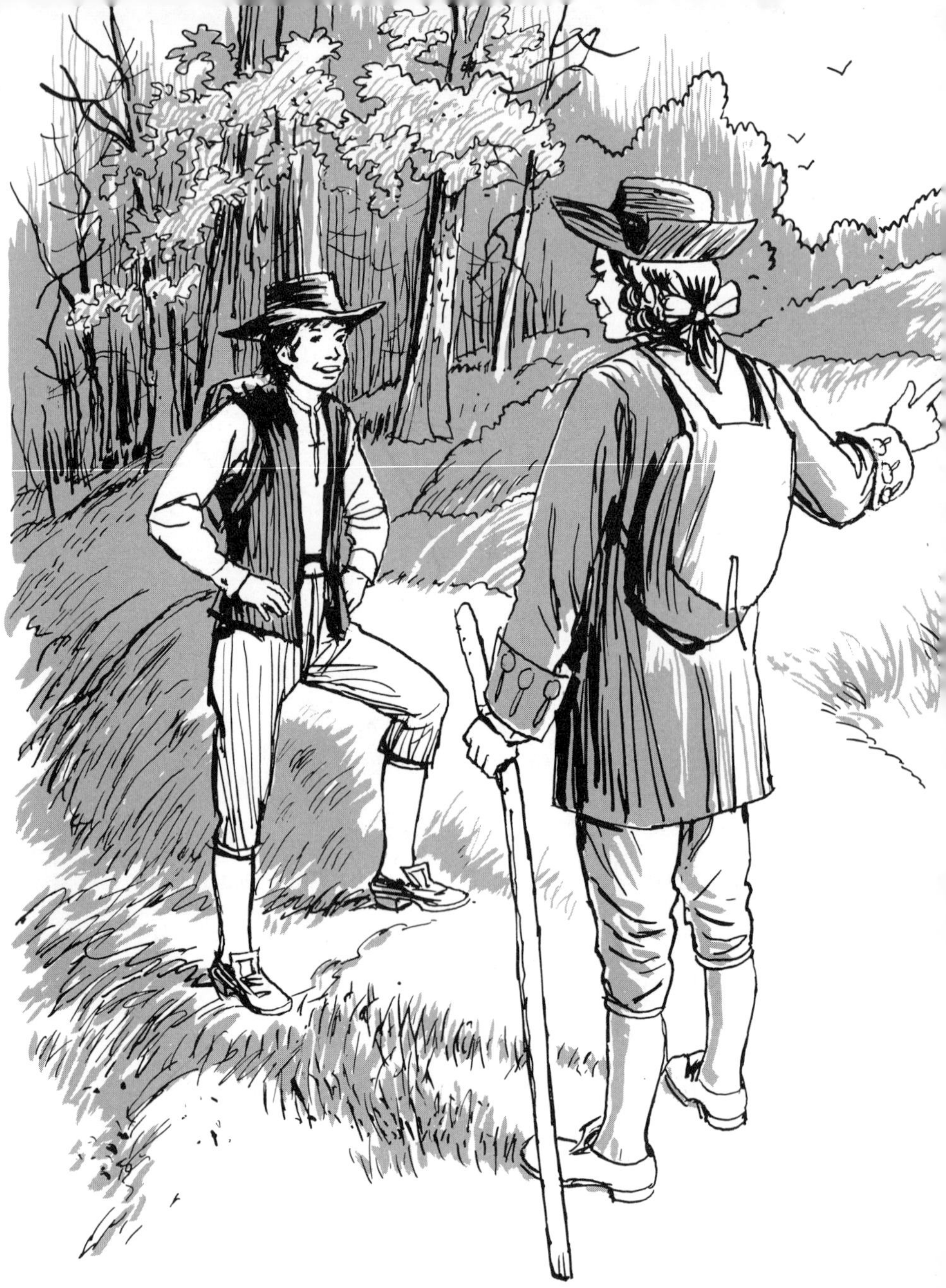

of earth nearby. "See those old earthworks?" he said, pointing in their direction.

"Yes. What are they?" asked Tom.

"They are the remnants of a battle which the Iceni tribe of early Britons fought against the Romans in 61 A.D.," Mr. Knowles explained. "Formerly Britain was made up of different tribes or groups living in different parts of the island. Each tribe had its own ruler and made its own laws.

"In 55 B.C. Julius Caesar, a Roman general, started an invasion of Britain, which continued until the Romans conquered most of the island. Some of the tribes combined their forces to try to drive the Romans out. In this part of Britain, when the Roman governor tried to take over the Iceni tribe, their ruler Queen Boudicca fought back. She sent out a call for help to all the other tribes in southeast England. She felt certain that they would join her, because they had come to hate the Roman conquerors just as she herself had.

"The different tribes united and converged on the Romans in hordes. They destroyed Roman military posts and burned several cities where many Romans lived. They finally lost, but not until they had killed more than 70,000 Romans and Britons who had sided with them."

"What became of Queen Boudicca?" asked Tom, interrupting the story.

"She took poison," replied Mr. Knowles. "She preferred death to slavery, as did thousands of her loyal subjects."

"What a shame!" cried Tom. "All this happened simply because the Romans were unjust."

"Yes," agreed Mr. Knowles. "Most wars in the world happen because people on one side or the other are unjust."

"Fortunately we Quakers don't believe in war or any form of violence," said Tom. "At the same time I don't think we would have criticized Queen Boudicca harshly for what she did. As my father often says, not even a Quaker turns the other cheek forever."

Mr. Knowles nodded. "I know," he said.

When they reached Thetford and Tom saw the Grammar School ahead his heart was heavy. He felt almost overcome with the thought that his school days were over. Most of all he wondered how he would get along without seeing Mr. Knowles day after day. He knew that he should tell his schoolmaster that he wouldn't be back after vacation, but he just couldn't make himself do it at this moment.

For a few minutes they walked along side by side in silence. Finally Tom stuck out his hand and said, "Thank you, sir, for all you have done for me. I've had a wonderful time on our overnight walking trip."

Mr. Knowles shook Tom's hand vigorously.

"I'm glad, but why are you so serious?" he asked. "You have been a fine companion. It isn't often that a boy and his schoolmaster hit it off as well as we do together."

"You're right," said Tom, "and I'm serious because I hate to leave you and bring such an enjoyable trip to an end." With these words and a heavy heart, he called back, "Good-by, sir," as he turned to leave for home.

A Young Apprentice

THE VERY NEXT DAY after Tom returned home from the walking trip with his schoolmaster he started to work in his father's shop. Now at age thirteen he was facing a great change in his life. No longer would he be poring over books at school, but would be learning the stay-making trade from his father. From now on he would be known as an apprentice.

In England at that time it was customary for boys to become apprentices. They agreed to work for older persons in order to learn various trades. Usually a boy entered into a contract to work for a tradesman for a period of seven years while learning to do a certain kind of work. His only pay consisted of board, room, and clothing.

Since Tom lived at home, he was not a true apprentice. Even so, he knew he would have to work in his father's shop for seven years in order to be accepted as a tradesman. To a growing boy who loved to read and explore the outdoors this seemed like a real hardship.

Tom tried to make the best of his situation. From the very first he worked hard for his father and tried to learn what he needed to do. His father watched him with pride and often praised him for his work. "I don't wish to make thee overproud, Tom," he said, "but I am pleased with thy efforts."

After Tom had worked for a few months, his father began to give him greater responsibilities. He wanted him to learn everything about his business. "When thee finishes thy apprenticeship as a staymaker, I'll take thee in as my partner," he said. "Then later I'll turn the business over to thee."

Tom realized that this was a good opportunity, but he wasn't enthusiastic about it. He couldn't bear to think of spending his life in this workshop or even in Thetford. Instead he wanted to get out and see the world.

Soon after Tom quit going to the Grammar School, Mr. Knowles left the school to become a vicar or clergyman in the Church of England. He became vicar of St. Cuthbert's church, which Tom's mother attended. Now she was pleased to have Tom go to visit him. Every few evenings Tom went to the parish house to talk with Mr. Knowles.

These evenings together were highlights for both Tom and Mr. Knowles. They talked about any number of subjects, including the new English colonies in North America. Mr. Knowles constantly bought books about these colonies which he lent to Tom. One of Tom's favorite books was *A Natural History of Virginia*. He borrowed this book so often that Mr. Knowles finally gave it to him.

From time to time Mr. Knowles told Tom about his service in the Royal Navy. He recited one adventure after another but hardly mentioned the hardships which he had endured. "That kind of life is just the ticket for the soup, for a young man," he declared.

"What do you mean by 'ticket for the soup'?" asked Tom, looking up curiously.

Mr. Knowles laughed heartily. "That's a sea-faring term, my lad, which means 'just right,'" he explained jovially.

Tom nodded. "It sounds like a sea-faring term to me," he said.

"In the Royal Navy you get to see far-off lands and strange people," continued Mr.

Knowles. "Besides, you have great comrades, or friends, among the navy men. The best of all, however, is your feeling of freedom at sea."

"Is it something like being alone on the heath, sir?" asked Tom.

"Yes, and yet different," replied Mr. Knowles. "On a naval vessel there's nothing about you but water, and there's no noise except the sound of waves slapping the boat and wind striking the sails."

"That sounds exciting, but don't seamen have work to do?" asked Tom. "Don't they have to keep house on a vessel, and do such things as sweep the decks and look after the sails?"

"Of course, because you can't expect the officers to do the housekeeping," replied Mr. Knowles. "The important thing to remember is that all the work is outdoors."

Tom listened to all of Mr. Knowles' tales of sea-faring life with great interest. He realized

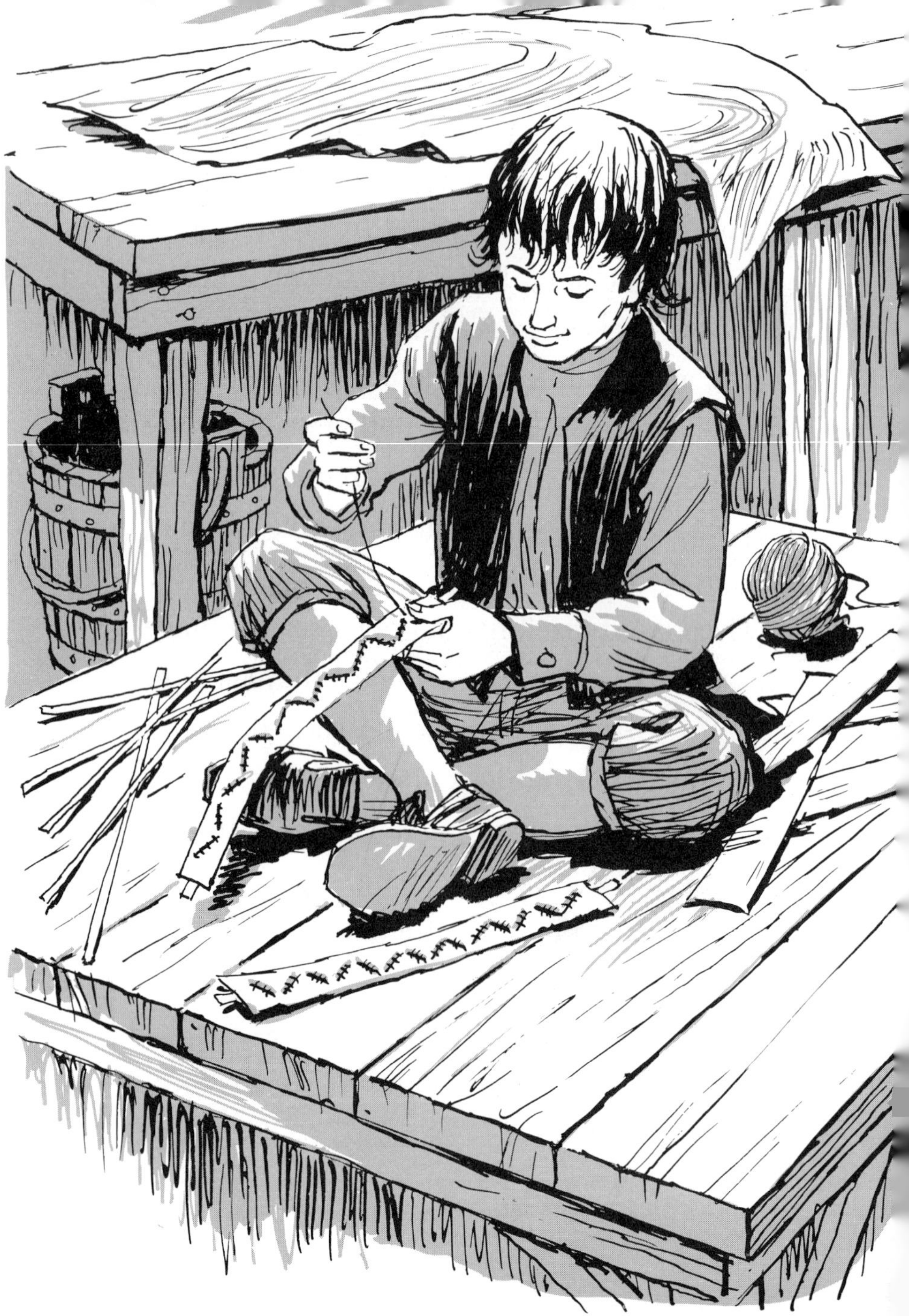

from his reading that seamen endured many hardships, but he was lured by their outdoor life. After spending all his daylight hours cooped up in a windowless workroom, this seemed very enticing.

All the while he worked as an apprentice in his father's workshop, he led a very lonely life. From morning until evening, for six days a week, he sat cutting and sewing cloth at a table. Hour after hour he sewed cloth around pieces of whalebone, making stays, or stiffeners, for ladies' undergarments.

As the only child in a hardworking family, he had seldom had opportunity to talk or play with other children. Now as an apprentice he talked mostly with his father in the workshop and with his mother when he went upstairs for meals. Occasionally his father allowed him to talk with customers.

From his talks with his parents he formed

serious questions about their religious beliefs. He felt that his mother's church, the Church of England, conducted too many ceremonies which were empty and meaningless. For this reason he doubted whether the members of her church were filled with religious fervor.

He was critical about his father's church because he felt that it was too solemn and passive. He liked the down-to-earth services but felt the church should be more active in the affairs of everyday living. Of the two churches, he much preferred his father's church to his mother's church.

When Tom first started to work as an apprentice, his parents refused to let him leave home in the evenings. After a year or two they relented, but this was of little help to him. For one reason, most people in the village went to bed soon after sundown and few people could be found on the streets. About all that a person could do was to take lonely walks out over the heath. For the most part Tom was regarded as an outcast in the village. Many young people were scornful of him because he was studious and eager to learn. Some of the elders who couldn't read and write even thought there was something wrong with him. Others in the village avoided him because he was a Quaker. As members of the Church of England they feared all people in their midst who belonged to other religious groups.

Tom's only close friend in the village was Mr. Knowles. He enjoyed talking with the vicar and borrowing books from him. Sometimes when he borrowed a book he stayed up most of the night to read it.

Tom continued to work at his apprenticeship until he was seventeen years old. He became very good at staymaking. Still, the idea of staying indefinitely at the job didn't appeal to him.

More and more his thoughts turned to the exciting lives of men on ships at sea.

In the spring of 1754 Tom felt that he could no longer stay cooped up in his father's shop. One evening he packed a few things into a sack and dropped them out of his bedroom window. Then he went outside, picked up the sack, and strode off with it in the dark.

He headed at once for Harwich, a port about thirty miles away. There he hoped to follow in Mr. Knowles' footsteps by enlisting to serve for a time in the Royal Navy.

The Lure of Life as a Seaman

At first Tom walked slowly, letting his eyes get accustomed to the darkness of the night. There was no moon, so his only light came from the stars.

As he walked through the country toward the port of Harwich he often looked up at the stars for guidance. He felt grateful to Mr. Knowles, who had taught him how to use stars to tell directions. Astronomy, the study of stars and other heavenly bodies, had been the subject of many discussions between pupil and teacher. Mr. Knowles had told him that seamen were stargazers who often had to depend entirely on stars to steer their ships at night. Now as Tom walked along by himself he felt almost like a seaman.

After he had walked a few hours, he lay down to sleep. Then he wakened at the first light of dawn and started off again. Shortly he came to a stream where he stopped to drink some water and eat some bread and cheese which he had stuffed in his pocket.

Within a few hours he reached the village of Stowmarket. It was market day in the village and he found a great many people strolling in and out of the town square. Since most of them were carrying bundles, he was able to pass among them unnoticed. "That was a streak of luck," he said to himself when he was clear of the village.

Outside the village he saw a sign, shaped like a hand, on a post beside the road. He looked up and read the word Ipswich, which he recognized as a town near Harwich. This, he felt, was another omen of good luck, for now he knew for sure he was on the right road. He had read much about Ipswich in a history book. It was an old city where several famous people had lived. One of them had been a trusted advisor of King Henry VIII. This advisor's house still stood in Ipswich, and Tom wished that he had time to see it.

Now that he was in open country he walked along rapidly with his sack over his shoulder. He still had some distance to go, but he hoped to reach Harwich while daylight still lingered. Hour after hour he trudged along, spurred on by the thoughts of becoming a seaman.

He got his first glimpse of Harwich and its harbor from a hilltop. His heart beat fast as he looked down at all the ships tied up at the wharf. "Surely one of them can use an extra man in its crew," he said to himself.

When he reached the harbor he walked up and down the wharf looking at all the ships. At last, he spoke to a fisherman who was sitting on a post mending a fishnet. "Do you know whether any of these ships can use an extra hand?" he asked anxiously.

The fisherman nodded. "Yes, there's one of them signing up a whole new crew," he said. "I expect the captain can use you."

"Is it a Royal Navy Ship?" asked Tom.

The fisherman shook his head. "No, there are no Royal Navy ships here now," he replied. "If there had been you wouldn't have had time to ask to become a seaman," he added with a grin. "You would have been gobbled up the moment you stepped on the wharf."

Tom was stunned. He stood for a moment, too disappointed to speak. His plan to join the Royal Navy wasn't going to work out after all. Finally the fisherman broke the silence by asking, "Aren't you interested in becoming a seaman on the ship which I told you about?"

"Yes, I am," replied Tom. "Tell me more about it. What kind of ship is she?"

"Her name is *Terrible,* and she's a privateer," explained the fisherman." She's about ready to set off to raid French shipping lanes."

This was supposed to be a year of peace in Europe, but the English and French had frequent skirmishes at sea. They fought over land in America, which they both claimed as colonies. One of these areas in America was the Ohio country, which now was being explored for settlement in the future.

"Is the *Terrible* getting a crew for herself or on behalf of the English?" asked Tom. From his reading he had learned that privateers were sometimes pirate ships.

"On behalf of the English," answered the fisherman. "Besides, she's one of the best raiders at sea. You can feel very proud and happy to become one of her seamen."

"Where will I find her?" asked Tom.

The fisherman waved his hand in the direction of a ship with a red figurehead. "Yonder she is, waiting for you," he replied.

"What's the captain's name?" asked Tom.

"His name is Death," said the fisherman.

"Death!" repeated Tom in surprise. "Is that his real name?"

"Yes, and you'll find him very much alive," replied the fisherman with a smile.

Tom thanked the fisherman and took off for the privateer *Terrible*. As he came near he found the figurehead on the ship was a devil's face. He shivered, partly from excitement and partly from fear. Bravely he walked up the gangplank, where a sailor was leaning over a rail of the ship. "Are you the captain," asked Tom. "I want to join your crew."

The sailor grinned. "No. I'm the boatswain," he explained. "My job is to keep the ship in good running order. You'll find the captain right over there." He pointed in the direction of a nearby cabin.

"Is his name Death?" asked Tom.

"Yes, it is, and the French have reason to know that he lives up to his name," answered the sailor with another grin.

Tom walked to Captain Death's cabin. The captain looked him over curiously and carefully. "You don't look like seaman stuff to me," he said. "Why have you come here? Have you run away from home?"

"Yes, sir," said Tom. "I want to become a seaman. I'm strong and healthy."

"Well," said the captain thoughtfully, "we're short of crewmen, so I'll take you on." He pushed a paper in front of Tom. "Sign your name here," he continued, "or if you can't write, just put down an 'X' and I'll write your name beside it."

"Oh, I can write," said Tom proudly. He signed his name big and black, but he noticed that many other young men who had signed up had merely put down some "X's."

"Now go below and have some food, Thomas Paine," said the captain after looking at Tom's signature. "You look hungry to me."

Tom went below and ate heartily of a hot meal. Since leaving home he hadn't had anything to eat except the bread and cheese which he had stuffed in his pocket. Just as he was finishing the boatswain came to get him. "Captain Death wants you," he called out. "Get up there as fast as you can."

Tom rushed up to Captain Death's cabin, still chewing the last bite of his meal. When he reached the door he was astonished to find his father sitting inside. "How did you find out where I am?" he asked.

"I just guessed where thee were," his father replied. "When thee suddenly left home, I went to see the Reverend Mr. Knowles. He guessed what thee might do, so I came here. He blames himself for the whole thing."

Tom was still too astonished to talk, but Captain Death broke the silence. "I didn't know you were a Quaker or I wouldn't have taken you on," he said. "This is a fighting ship and Quakers aren't fighters." He pulled the register toward him, crossed out Tom's name, and added, "You are no longer a member of our crew on our privateer."

Mr. Paine and Tom left Captain Death's cabin and walked down the gangplank off the ship. There they mounted an old horse which Mr. Paine had borrowed to make the trip. Tom sat back of his father on the horse as they slowly wended their way home. Both of them were silent most of the way.

The next day Tom was back at the workshop, continuing his apprenticeship to become a staymaker later on.

Now that he had had a taste of life away from Thetford, however, he was more restless than ever. He managed to stick it out for two more years. Then he stole away again to try to become a seaman.

This time he went to a port which was farther away than Harwich. There he went on board another privateer called the *King of Prussia,* where he talked with Captain Mendez. "I'm a Quaker but I want to join your ship," he said.

Captain Mendez looked up in surprise. "Surely you know that this is war time, that England is engaged in a war with France and Austria. Why do you expect me to take you when Quakers don't believe in fighting?"

Tom already knew about the war which later was to be called The Seven Years War. He looked at Captain Mendez and said, "Yes, I'm aware of the war with France and Austria. As a Quaker I'm against fighting, but I'll do anything else aboard."

Captain Mendez hesitated briefly. "Well, we need men to take care of the ship and you look strong and willing. I'll take you on, but your life won't be easy for you, lad."

"I don't expect it to be," said Tom. "Just give me a chance."

The captain shrugged his shoulders and pushed a sheet of paper toward Tom. "Sign your name or make an 'X'," he said.

Once more Tom wrote his name in big bold letters on a ship's list. That night the *King of Prussia* sailed out to sea with Tom on board.

Working Again as a Staymaker

TOM SOON found that life at sea was entirely different from what he had pictured it. He had to learn to scamper up masts in all kinds of weather, even in freezing rain. He had to help scour the wooden decks at least once a day with a holystone, a kind of sandstone used for scrubbing purposes.

Besides caretaking, Tom had many other jobs on board ship, one of which was to stand watch on deck. On his first night watch, he fell asleep after standing for several hours. For sleeping on watch, he was flogged with a cat-o-nine-tails, a whip made of nine knotted cords. Following this flogging he had a mighty sore back for several days and never went to sleep while he was on watch again.

Even the food on the ship was very disappointing to Tom. Mostly it consisted of strongly salted meats and flat heavy biscuits, called hardtack. The only liquid to wash it down was stale water. Tom often longed for some of his mother's cooking and a drink of goat's milk, such as he had had at home.

The *King of Prussia* never caught up with a French ship, so Tom never witnessed a fight at sea. In the spring of 1757, after almost a year at sea, Captain Mendez gave up the chase. He brought the ship back to Gravesend, a port at the mouth of the Thames River. There he dismissed the members of the crew.

Tom and some of his shipmates made their way up the Thames River to London. He realized that soon he would have to look for a job, but he wanted to get acquainted with this big capital city. With money which he had received for his work at sea he rented a sleeping room at a sailor's inn near the docks. From there he set off on daily wanderings through the streets of the city.

He explored all parts of London. He visited the Parliament buildings, where the House of Lords and the House of Commons made laws for England. He saw the Tower of London, the fortress where many famous people had been kept in prison. As he gazed at this fortress, he thought of Sir Walter Raleigh, who had been shut up there for eighteen years. From his readings he recalled how Raleigh had conducted experiments in chemistry and written a *History of the World* while he was in prison. "He certainly was a great man," Tom said to himself. "All the while he was locked up in prison he kept right on working."

In some sections of London Tom glimpsed palaces and elegant homes. In other sections he found poor people living in filthy houses not fit for animals. He passed theaters and opera houses, gambling dens and coffee houses. Often he lingered by the coffee houses, because he knew that intelligent men came there to talk just as he had once talked with Mr. Knowles. He missed these talks more than anything else from his life in Thetford.

Soon the time came for him to look for a job and go to work. He hoped to get a job where he would have a chance to get some schooling on the side. He applied for work as a clerk in law firms, as a helper in print shops, and even as an usher in music halls. Unfortunately, however, nobody would hire him.

Despite these setbacks, he kept on trying until he was almost penniless. Finally he spotted a staymaker's shop where he applied for a job.

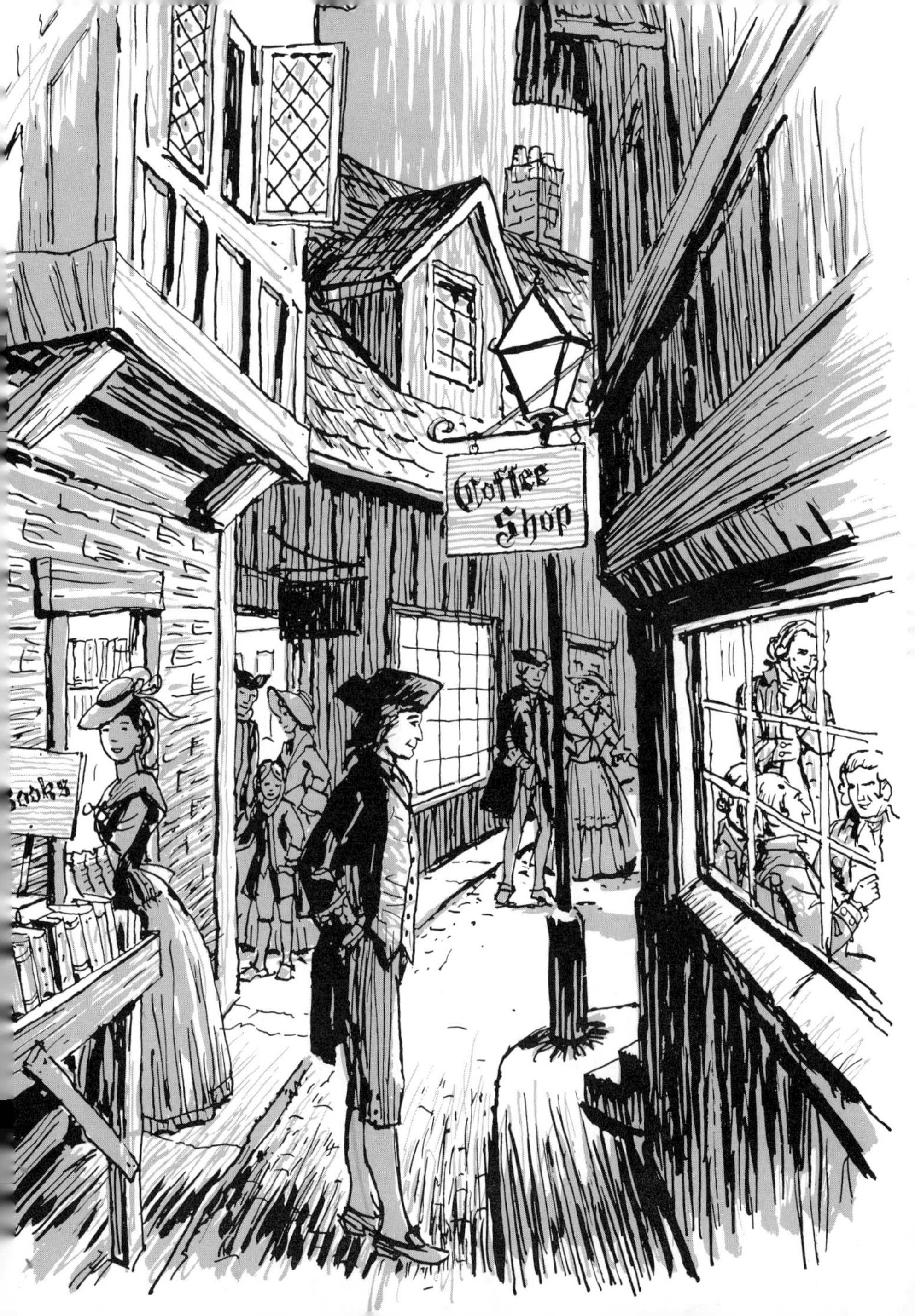
Coffee Shop
Books

The owner, Mr. Morris, was glad to take him on since he was an experienced worker. He readily agreed for Tom to be free in the evenings so that he could attend night lectures.

Soon Mr. Morris suggested the Royal Society as a place where Tom could hear interesting and instructive lectures. "It was founded to spread knowledge of the world and to aid would-be explorers and inventors," he said.

"That sounds wonderful to me," said Tom, "but how can I get in?"

"Well, the husband of one of my customers is an astronomer and a member of the Royal Society," replied Mr. Morris. "His name is Bevis, and I am sure that he will help you."

A few days later Tom had a meeting with the astronomer. The two of them got along together famously. Mr. Bevis was highly impressed with Tom's ability and knowledge and readily agreed to sponsor his membership.

Tom could hardly believe his good fortune. Now he wished that he had had the good sense to apply to Mr. Morris for a job at once, instead of wasting time seeking jobs for which he wasn't trained. He resolved to make the best of this new opportunity.

At the Royal Society, he attended lectures in geography, astronomy, and philosophy. In his philosophy group, both the leader and the listeners talked freely about what it meant to lead a good life. Always there were as many ideas as people in the room, and Tom left each session with his mind in a whirl.

Besides attending lectures on weekday evenings, Tom spent Sundays at the Royal Society. He busied himself reading in the library and examining maps and globes in the map room, and looking out at the sky through a telescope. He often became so interested in something that he was studying that he forgot to eat.

As soon as he had saved enough money he bought a globe so he could study about the world in his room. After that he bought second-hand books on various subjects which interested him. Soon he had a shelf full of volumes to stand beside his favorite volume, *The Natural History of Virginia.*

Except for the Royal Society, Tom cared very little about London. It was too large and noisy to suit him. After working there for about a year, he decided to move to Dover, a much smaller place. In Dover he at once took a job as a staymaker.

Dover was located on the English Channel, directly across from France. As Tom stood on the white cliffs there he could see the coastline of France. "That coastline is only twenty-one miles away," said a fellow walker who had joined him on the cliff.

Tom nodded. "Now I understand why so

many invaders have come across the channel to England," said Tom. "The first was Julius Caesar in 55 B.C., who started the Roman invasion. Next came the Angles, Saxons, and Jutes."

The stranger gazed at Tom in wonder. "You surprise me by how much history you know," he said. "I can tell you something that you probably don't know."

"What's that?" asked Tom excitedly.

"Well, two galleons of the Spanish Armada were wrecked on the sands just a little way out there in the channel," said the stranger. "People still think that much treasure went down with them."

"That's interesting," said Tom politely. "I have read how Sir Francis Drake in 1588 led the British fleet against the Spanish Armada. In that great sea battle, over a hundred Spanish vessels were sunk or wrecked right here a short distance away in the English Channel."

Tom liked Dover better than London and thought of going into business here for himself. He was tired of working for someone else and talked the matter over with his employer. "I enjoy working for you, but I would like to have a shop of my own," he said.

"Dover doesn't need another staymaker," said his employer, "but you might start one over in Sandwich. If you want to go there I'll even lend you money to set up a shop."

"Thank you," said Tom with a broad smile on his face. "I'll accept your generous offer and will go to Sandwich. I'll start as soon as I can get my things together."

"Good," said his employer. "I'll give you all the help that I can."

Busy Years in Excise Work

SANDWICH, where Tom moved to set up his business, was even smaller than Thetford. It consisted of a network of narrow streets, lined with houses made of native yellow brick. In the heart of the village was a tiny oblong park called a square.

As Tom looked over the village he said, "London was too big, but Sandwich is too small. I doubt whether there'll be enough business here to make my shop worthwhile."

Despite the outlook for business, young Paine opened up a shop in Sandwich. Before long, just as he had feared, his business dwindled because there weren't enough customers in the village to keep it going. This lack of customers made the situation look hopeless.

Tom scolded himself for starting the business, but one good thing came from it. He fell in love with one of his customers, named Mary Lambert, the daughter of an exciseman or tax inspector. Paine and Mary were married but lived in Sandwich only a short time. As soon as Paine could dispose of his shop, they moved to Margate, a short distance away.

Margate was a larger town than Sandwich. Paine set up shop there and his business started off well, but he soon faced trouble at home. Mary was not strong, and she died giving birth to his child. The baby died, too, and Paine could not bear to stay in Margate. He decided to leave and give up the staymaking business.

Through his wife's father, Paine became interested in excise work. Excisemen were government officials who checked up on taxable goods sold in stores and other places. They were assigned to districts and made regular rounds to conduct inspections.

Applicants for excise positions had to take a difficult written examination. Paine went to London where he obtained books and papers which he could read to prepare for the examination. The information which he needed to know was new and challenging to him, but he would have to study hard and long.

"I think I'll go home to Thetford, where I can study in peace," he said to himself. He knew that his mother would approve of his plans for the future, because she would think that a government job was much better than staymaking. His father would be happy to have him home whatever the circumstances.

He returned home and spent about a year with his parents. Late in 1762 he passed the excise examination with high marks. He had hoped to be assigned to a permanent post immediately, but unfortunately there were no such positions open at this time. Thus he had to travel about the country and fill in as a temporary helper. His pay was poor, and the people he called upon didn't like dealing with a substitute. Often he wondered why he had ever thought that working as an exciseman would be good.

In 1764, he finally was appointed to a post or station centered at Alford, in Lincolnshire. His territory covered a wide stretch of land along the North Sea. His work was dangerous because it involved catching smugglers. These smugglers tried to sneak goods in by boat without declaring them for tax purposes.

The excisemen who had preceded Paine had closed their eyes to much smuggling. They had accepted bribes to forget the excise taxes. This practice shocked Paine's Quaker soul and he was determined to stop it.

The business people who bought smuggled goods became angry at Paine. "Your interfering costs both us and our customers unnecessary money," they argued. "What the government doesn't know won't hurt anybody."

"Well, it's dishonest," replied Paine, who would not give in to their demands.

"Then you'll be sorry," they threatened.

Paine ignored their threats and tried hard to stop the smuggling. One day soon, however, when he was overworked, he was caught in a trap. He accepted a grocer's word for what taxable goods he had in stock and stamped the papers to show his approval.

The grocer gleefully told his friends. They reported to the government and Paine was called to London to explain. "Is this rumor about you a fact?" asked the authorities.

"Yes," Paine admitted with deep shame.

Following this frank admission, he was dismissed from office after only a year's work. Now once more he was in London without a job. He applied for a position to teach English grammar in a private school. His application was accepted and he taught there for a period of several years.

Even though he was a successful teacher, he was eager to return to excise work for the government. He kept after the authorities to reinstate him. Finally, since his crime had been so minor, the authorities yielded to his request. In 1768, he was appointed to a post or station in Lewes in southern England.

Paine liked Lewes and the people there liked him. Soon he became very popular and the leading spirit in an important intellectual club. All the members of this club were readers and thinkers who held debates and wrote papers on various issues of the times. The warmest debates were usually about English politics or economic problems.

Always Paine participated strongly in the debates and arguments. His quick mind and background of knowledge made him stand out among the other members. He stated his points of view clearly and simply, yet never tried to make a good impression by using big words or complicated sentences.

When Paine first came to Lewes he boarded with a family named Ollive. This family included Samuel Ollive and his wife and their daughter Elizabeth. Mr. Ollive operated a tobacco shop on the first floor of his house. He bought leaf tobacco which was raised in America and prepared it to sell in his shop. Most people in those days used tobacco for smoking in pipes, chewing, or snuffing.

Mr. Ollive died in 1769. Before he died he asked Paine to remain in the house to assist his wife and daughter in running the tobacco shop. Paine agreed, later married Elizabeth and continued to live there. Then he helped in the tobacco shop as much as he could without taking time from his excise duties.

Gradually Paine became a leader among the other excise officers in England. In 1772, when they decided to plead for an increase in wages, they chose him for their spokesman. Afterwards he spent several months preparing a paper called *A Case for the Officers of Excise.* This paper contained arguments to justify the requests which the excisemen were making.

In the winter of 1772–1773 Paine went to London to campaign for Parliamentary help on behalf of the excise officers. His campaign was a failure, but his efforts in London were not wasted. He met many important people there and became a welcome member of daily coffee house gatherings.

One of the most important persons whom he met was Benjamin Franklin, official representative of the American colonies in England. He and Franklin became close friends and had many interesting talks. He showed Franklin his paper *The Case for the Officers of Excise.* Franklin was very much impressed with the arguments for justice which Paine had included in the paper. "You would fit very well in America at this time," he said seriously.

A short time later, when Paine returned to Lewes, he found that once more he had been released as an excise officer. The government claimed that he had taken time off from his post without securing a leave of absence. The real reason, however, was for conducting the excise officers' campaign.

When he was dismissed, he recalled his conversation with Benjamin Franklin. At once he decided to make arrangements to go to America. He talked over his plans with his wife, Elizabeth, but she decided to stay in Lewes with her mother. Thus their marriage of only a few years ended in failure.

Paine now returned to London, where he had

another talk with Benjamin Franklin. He told Franklin that he would like to go to America and requested help. After he felt certain that Paine was sincere in his plans, Franklin wrote to his son-in-law, Richard Bache, in Philadelphia. In his letter he described Paine as an ingenious, worthy young man who wanted to go to America. Further, he wrote:

> "He goes to Philadelphia with the view to settling there. I request you to give him your best advice, as he is quite a stranger there."

Paine had very little money but enough to purchase a first-class passage on an early ship leaving London. With great hopes he sailed for America in September, 1774.

"Common Sense" for America

ON PAINE'S way to America a serious disease, probably typhoid fever, swept the ship. There were no doctors or nurses aboard to take care of persons who became ill. Many who took sick simply died and were buried at sea.

When the ship reached Philadelphia, Paine was exceedingly ill with the disease. A doctor named Kearsley came aboard to check him and the other ill passengers. The captain of the ship told Dr. Kearsley that Paine carried a letter from Benjamin Franklin to his son-in-law Richard Bache. This information led the doctor to take Paine home with him for treatment.

Under the doctor's medicine and care Tom slowly recovered. After a few weeks, he asked for a pen and some paper. Then as he sat up in bed, he wrote an imaginary dialogue between General Gage, the English commander in America, and General Wolfe, who had died during the French and Indian War. This essay had a very pro-American and anti-British flavor, showing how Benjamin Franklin and Dr. Kearsley had influenced Tom's thinking.

Dr. Kearsley liked the essay. He sent it to a local newspaper, where it soon appeared unsigned. Immediately it attracted wide attention and led people to stand on street corners to talk about it. There in black and white were the words that many people thought but dared not speak. It stated that the people of America were ready to reject laws made by Parliament in England and throw off British rule.

Paine was excited when he discovered that

his essay had been printed. He was more excited when he found out how much people liked it. This caused him to think that possibly he could turn to writing to earn a living.

By mid–January, 1775, Paine was feeling strong again. The doctor agreed that he was well and ready to take up his new life in America. "I'll try to repay your kindness someday, sir," he said, shaking the doctor's hand.

"Just be a good American and I'll feel fully repaid," replied the doctor.

Paine now went to present Benjamin Franklin's letter to his son-in-law Richard Bache. Bache read the letter with great interest. "Dr. Franklin wants me to give you aid and advice here in America," he said. "Therefore I'll help you to meet people who may be useful to you."

"I thank you, sir," said Tom, feeling grateful for this generous offer.

Bache, who had married Franklin's daughter

Sarah, was a prominent person in Philadelphia. When he recommended Paine, people accepted him without question. After they learned that he had once been a teacher, several of them hired him to tutor their sons.

Paine accepted these tutoring jobs because he needed the money. He wasn't happy with teaching, however, and wanted to become a writer. He told a friend of his, named Robert Aitken, about his interest in writing. Aitken was the owner of a bookstore to which Paine had been drawn like a duck to water.

Aitken was pleased to learn of Paine's ambition. "How lucky!" he exclaimed. "I need an editor for a monthly publication which I have just started. I can't spare enough time or energy to manage it myself."

The new publication which Aitken had started was called the *Pennsylvania Magazine*. He wanted it to be a magazine which Americans could enjoy for leisure time reading. He intended it to be a thoroughly American magazine, independent of England for content.

Unfortunately, this was a bad time to start such a publication. Now persons who might have contributed adventure stories, essays on nature or other subjects, lyric poetry, and the like were devoting their thoughts entirely to colonial rights. The First Continental Congress had already sent to England a list of what Americans considered their rights to be. Among them were the right to tax themselves, to choose their own political leaders, to be tried in courts by their own people, and to be free of British soldiers stationed here.

This action by the Continental Congress had been taken because of certain so-called "Intolerable Acts" passed by the English government. The first had been the Tea Act, which gave the British-owned East India Company the right to sell tea duty-free to the colonies. The merchants of Boston had felt that this act was very unfair to them. To protest the act, a group of patriots had dumped three shiploads of tea into Boston Harbor. This bold action had become known as the Boston Tea Party.

The Tea Act had been followed by the Boston Port Bill, and then by the Quartering Act. The Boston Port Bill had been designed to punish Massachusetts for the Boston Tea Party. It prohibited ships from using Boston harbor until the tea was paid for. The Quartering Act permitted British troops to stay in private homes, inns, and other places in the colonies.

Along with the lists of the colonial rights, the Continental Congress had passed a resolution stating that if England refused to respect these rights by December 6, 1774, the colonies would cease to import or consume goods coming from Great Britain or the British West Indies. This date had gone by without any official reply from the British government.

As Paine discussed the *Pennsylvania Magazine* with Mr. Aitken he said, "America is on the brink of a precipice. People here are upset and uncertain about the future. They are in no mood for pleasant leisure reading."

"I know," Aitken said, "but I should like to sidestep controversial issues. Surely we can find other topics to attract attention."

Paine agreed to follow Mr. Aitken's wishes and started to request articles and poems for the magazine. Most of the contributions he received were unusable, and he had to write much of the content himself. He signed various pen names to the articles and poems so readers wouldn't know that he had written them.

The magazine prospered, but Paine soon became tired of writing on non-controversial topics and began to lash out at England. Also, he gradually changed his style of writing. Instead of using language which only educated people could understand, he began to use simple sayings. Some of these sayings were: "Let every tub stand upon its own bottom," and "Like sailors, we must swab the deck."

For the July, 1775, issue of *Pennsylvania Magazine,* Paine wrote a poem entitled "Liberty Tree." One verse from this poem which readers especially liked went as follows:

"With timber and tar they Old England
 supplied
 And supported her power on the sea;
Her battles they fought, without getting
 a groat,
 For the honor of Liberty Tree."

This poem, which was very popular with the magazine's readers, displeased Mr. Aitken because Paine accused England of using tyrannical powers in America.

"Well, I can't keep from doing it any longer," replied Paine, "so I'd better resign and devote myself to America's cause."

To him, that cause was liberty for America. He still hoped that liberty could be brought about peacefully in the Quaker way, even though there had been open fighting at the Battle of Lexington. The trouble was that many colonies were afraid to break their ties with England. They would be content merely to have their rights respected by England.

Paine thought this matter over. "I must write something to stir people up," he said to himself. "As my father said, 'Not even a Quaker can turn the other cheek forever.'"

For six months Paine spent most of his time writing a book which he called *Common Sense*. He wrote this book so simply that every reader could understand it. He explained why it was foolish for strong, self-reliant Americans to obey whatever orders came from a nation across the sea. He pointed out how these orders showed complete ignorance of the problems facing America. He called heathen a system that allowed a king to rule over human beings.

One of the most forceful paragraphs from his book reads as follows:

> The heathens paid divine honors to their deceased kings, and the Christian world has improved upon the plan by doing the same to their living ones. . . . In England, a king hath little more to do than to make war and give away places; which, in plain terms, is to impoverish the nation . . . a pretty business indeed, for a man to be allowed 800,000 pounds sterling a year for that, and worshipped into the bargain! *Of more worth is one honest man to society, and in the sight of God, than all the crowned ruffians that ever lived.*

After Paine finished writing *Common Sense,* he had trouble finding a publisher. He offered it to his former employer, Mr. Aitken, who called it treasonable and refused to have anything to do with it. Finally a friend sent him to a Scottish bookseller, named Robert Bell. Bell offered to publish the book only if Paine would agree to stand any losses and give Bell half of any profits.

Common Sense was published on January 10, 1776. This first edition did not list Thomas Paine as author. The title page merely stated that it had been written by an Englishman.

The book became an immediate best seller, the first in American history. During the first six months after publication more than 100,000 copies were sold. Afterwards many editions were brought out, some by other publishers besides Bell. In those days there were no copyright laws to prevent other publishers from taking over books. Probably more than 200,000 copies were published by outsiders.

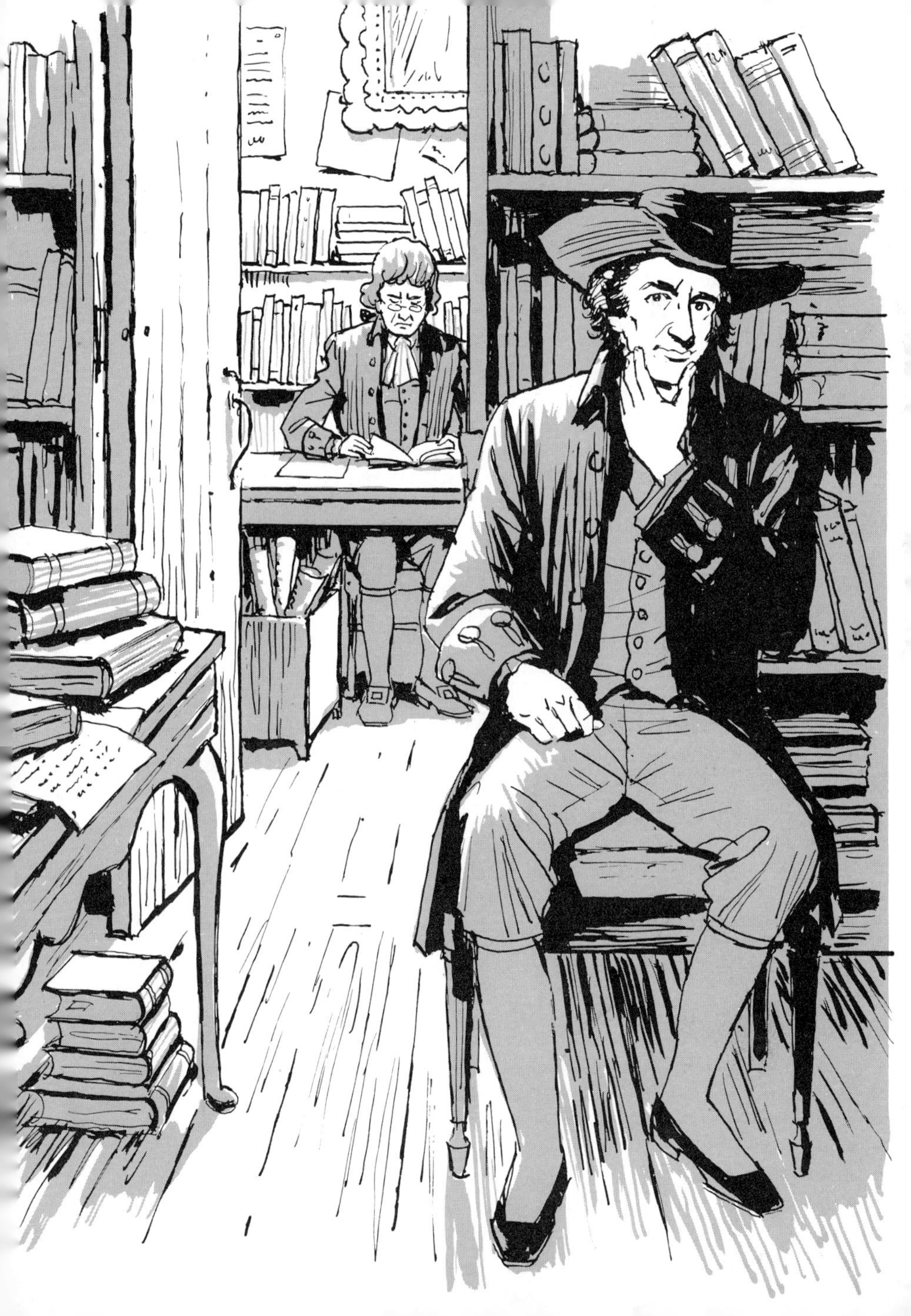

Paine's name appeared on the third edition of the book and on all future editions. Now people seemed to take greater interest in the book than ever. They read it while standing on street corners, sitting in their homes, and even while working at their places of business. Persons who could not read asked others to read it to them. In the Continental Army the officers read it aloud, while the men stood at attention, listening to every word.

To Americans the author Thomas Paine and his book *Common Sense* became inseparable. George Washington was one of many to praise Paine. "His *Common Sense* is working a wonderful change in the hearts of men," he said.

Paine might have become a rich man from the wide sale of his book, but he turned all the money which he earned over to the Continental Army. "This is the least I can do for the cause of American independence," he said.

The Crisis Papers

WHILE PAINE was writing *Common Sense,* he had written short articles for the newspapers of Philadelphia in order to earn a living. These had included articles against slavery, cruelty to animals, and the lowly status of women. They had aroused wide discussion among readers, but the one on slavery had received most attention. Shortly after it had been published the American Antislavery Society had been formed in America.

When Thomas Jefferson wrote his first draft of the Declaration of Independence, he included anti-slavery expressions from Paine's article. Later these expressions had to be omitted because certain members of the Continental Congress objected.

The Declaration was signed on July 4, 1776. Two days later Paine entered the military service of the Colonies. He became secretary to General Daniel Roberdeau, head of a group of volunteers known as the Flying Camp. This group moved from place to place to help out in emergencies but did no actual fighting. After an emergency was over the volunteers could go home or not, as they chose.

Paine first served with General Roberdeau's volunteers at Perth Amboy, New Jersey, about twenty miles south of New York. They were supposed to keep an eye on British troops under General William Howe, who were threatening to invade New York. They were to report any troop movements to General George Washington, in charge of the American troops there.

Soon the British troops began to move toward New York and Roberdeau sent a warning to General Washington. Unfortunately, the colonial forces were far outnumbered. Howe's army consisted of 20,000 well-trained and well-armed men. Washington's army included only 8,000 poorly trained and poorly armed men. He held out as long as he could, but the American losses were tremendous. He finally abandoned New York to the British and fled with what men he had left across the Hudson River.

General Roberdeau now returned to Philadelphia to await his next orders. Most of his volunteers went back to their homes. Paine, however, offered his services to General Nathanael Greene, the commander at Fort Lee on the west bank of the Hudson. Greene, who was well acquainted with *Common Sense,* was glad to add its author to his staff.

General Greene had important services in

mind for Paine. "You can be our field correspondent," he said. "You can publicize our exploits in the Philadelphia press. Our boys need a little puffing up to encourage them."

Paine sent many articles to be published in Philadelphia newspapers. Always he was careful to include the names of men who did anything to help the cause.

Soon General Washington visited Fort Lee. Greene proudly introduced Paine to Washington, who said, "Before your *Common Sense,* the idea of revolution was merely a thought. Your book made it an action."

"My pen actually is my only sword, sir," Paine graciously replied.

"Still, it's one of the best weapons we have," said Washington. "I hope you will continue to wield it for us."

In November, 1776, the British troops crossed the Hudson River and forced the American armies to retreat to New Jersey. Now the cause of American independence looked very black. Soldiers were almost ready to give up.

At this point, Paine wielded his mighty weapon, the pen, again. He wrote the first of a series of pamphlets, later to become known as *The American Crisis.* His purpose was to revive the spirits and courage of the American soldiers and inspire them to believe that eventually they would be victorious.

In *Crisis I* Paine used words that went straight to the hearts of readers as follows:

> These are the times that try men's souls. The summer soldier and the sunshine patriot will, in this crisis, shrink from the service of their country; but he that stands it *now* deserves the love and thanks of man and woman. Tyranny, like hell, is not easily conquered; yet we have this consolation with us, that the harder the conflict, the more glorious the triumph.

As in all his writings, Paine made reference to the wisdom of God, saying:

> My opinion has ever been, and *still is,* that God Almighty will not give up a people to military destruction, or leave them unsupportedly to perish, who have so earnestly and repeatedly sought to avoid the calamities of war by every decent method which wisdom could invent.

This first pamphlet had exactly the effect that Paine had intended. It put new heart into the fighting men and inspired them to show great courage in their next military effort. This was the noted Battle of Trenton.

By now the American army had retreated westward across the Delaware River into Pennsylvania. At the same time the British troops controlled portions of New Jersey, including Trenton. When Washington's men were encouraged from reading *Crisis I,* he decided to take a spectacular chance. In bitter weather on Christmas night, 1776, he and his army crossed the Delaware River in rowboats and took the British troops in Trenton completely by surprise. They were so fired up following this stunning victory that they pushed on to Princeton, where they again were victorious.

Paine's *Crisis II* appeared about three weeks later. He wrote it in the form of a letter to the two Lord Howes. General William Howe was commander of the British land forces in the colonies. His brother, Richard Howe, was commander of the British fleet in American waters. Admiral Richard Howe had recently returned from England with an offer of full and free pardon to American troops who would lay down their arms and pledge allegiance anew to King George. The Admiral also threatened dire punishment to every soldier in the American army who continued to defy royal authority.

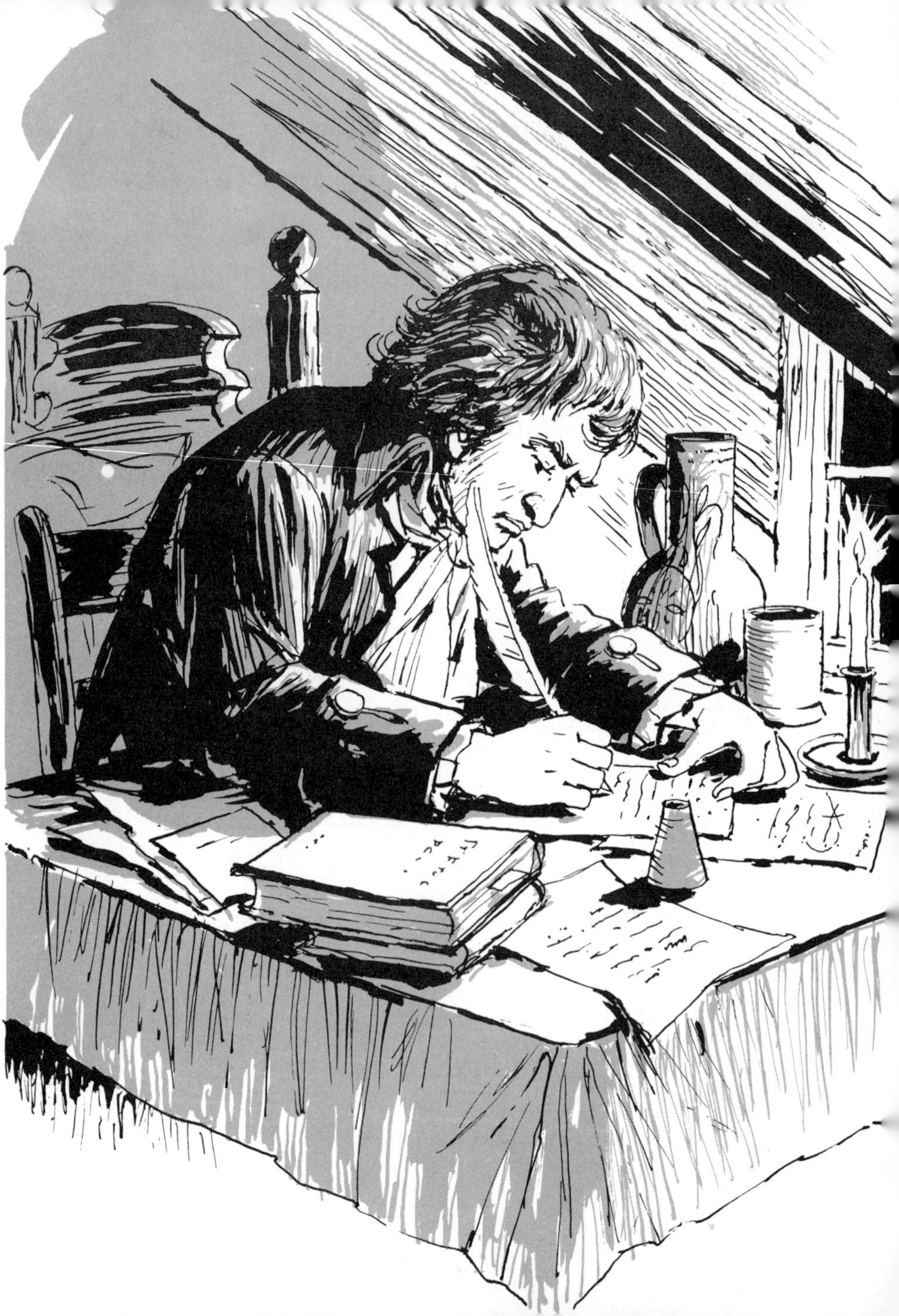

While serving in the Flying Camp, Paine had witnessed the first arrival of Admiral Howe's fleet about six months before. At that time, the combination of land and sea forces under the two Howes had looked unbeatable. Now, the recent American victories at Trenton and Princeton had changed this gloomy picture. From this background of knowledge he wrote:

> By what means, may I ask, do you expect to conquer America? If you could not effect it in the summer, when our army was less than yours, nor in winter, when we had none, how are you to do it? . . .
>
> What we contend for is worthy the affliction we may go through. If we get but bread to eat, and any kind of raiment to put on our backs, we be not only contented but thankful. More than that we ought not to look for, and less than that heaven has not suffered us to want. . . . What are salt, sugar, and finery compared to the inestimable blessings of Liberty!

At once Paine bound his two *Crisis* papers together and sent them to Benjamin Franklin in Paris. Franklin had gone to France to try to secure financial help and possibly naval help from the French government. Paine knew that England and France were constantly at odds with each other. He hoped that his *Crisis* papers would be pleasing to the French and help to make Franklin's mission easier.

Paine kept on writing *Crisis* papers whenever he felt that the cause of American independence needed a boost. He wrote thirteen *Crisis* pamphlets in all, ranging from 1776 to 1783. He ceased writing only after the American Revolution was over.

In his *Crisis* papers Paine was the first to use the expression "The United States of America." In his *Crisis II* he declared, "The United States of America will one day sound as pompously in the world or in history as the Kingdom of Great Britain." In *Crisis XIII*, he stated, "In short, we have no other national sovereignty than as United States. . . . As the United States we are equal to the importance of the title, but otherwise we are not."

All the while Paine was badly in need of finances. He took no money personally from the sale of either *Common Sense* or the *Crisis* papers. He had received only expense money from General Roberdeau and only food and lodging from General Greene. "I want no pay for myself while the army is without sufficient shoes and food," he declared.

Finally in 1777 the Continental Congress formed an important committee to be known as the Committee of Foreign Affairs. It appointed Paine as secretary of this committee at a salary of seventy dollars a month. When informed of his appointment he asked, "Will my taking this job keep me from writing what I wish?"

"You may write about anything that we members do not classify as secret information," replied John Adams.

Paine held this position as secretary for a period of two years. During this time he worked hard to promote the cause of the American Revolution. He became a trusted friend of members of the Continental Congress.

In 1776 the Continental Congress had sent Silas Deane to France to serve as an agent in securing war materials. He was to receive his expenses and 5% on all the materials he obtained. Later it became rumored that he was charging commission on actual gifts from both the French and Spanish governments.

As secretary of the Committee of Foreign Affairs, Paine investigated the rumors about Deane and found them to be true. In 1778 the Continental Congress ordered Deane to return to America to give an accounting of his work abroad, but after hearing his testimony it took no action against him.

Paine was not content to let the matter drop. He began to publish articles criticizing Deane for profiting from his work while American soldiers were living in rags. He signed the articles "Common Sense," which angered certain members of the Continental Congress. They accused him of violating his promise not to write articles on confidential subjects. He explained that the information about Deane had not been classified as secret, but this explanation failed to satisfy his accusers.

In the midst of this turmoil some of Paine's friends on the Committee of Foreign Affairs advised him to resign. He accepted their advice in January, 1779, and in submitting his letter of resignation he explained that he felt no guilt under God for having done anything wrong in violating a trust.

Champion of New Causes

WHEN PAINE resigned as Secretary of the Foreign Relations Committee he was almost penniless. His salary had been barely enough to cover the cost of renting a room and buying food, clothing, candles, and writing materials. Soon after he resigned his post he began to look shabby and scrawny.

Many people at this time wondered why he was poor. They felt that he must be earning money from his books, which still were selling well. Only a few persons knew that he donated the earnings from his writings to the American cause for freedom. At last a friend who understood forced some money on him. "I'll take it only as a loan and will pay you back," Paine said flatly.

Before long a Philadelphia merchant named Owen Biddle offered him a job as clerk at a small salary. This salary would pay for his food and rent but would not allow him to buy new clothes. Still, he accepted the offer.

Later in a letter to a friend Paine said, "It matters not what I look like, just so I have the strength to keep on writing. My employer will provide me with pen and paper."

In writing Paine felt that his real purpose was to build up support for the American Revolution. He realized that Washington and his troops were in dire need of financial help. By his writings he sought to make those who held the purse strings come to their aid.

In November, 1779, Paine's widespread popularity led him to be elected clerk of the new

Pennsylvania State Assembly. He was delighted with this appointment because he felt that he now would be in a better position to plead for aid to the army. He soon learned, however, that the state was in bad financial trouble, but that some of the members of the Assembly were very well off. For this reason he would have to seek help from them personally.

A few months later Paine received a letter from General Washington explaining the deplorable conditions which his men had to endure. Paine, in turn, read the letter to the Pennsylvania State Assembly.

> Every idea you can form of our distresses will fall short of reality. There is such a combination of circumstances to exhaust the patience of the soldiery that it begins at length to be worn out. We see in every line of the army the most serious features of mutiny and sedition.

The members of the Assembly listened closely as Paine read Washington's gloomy letter, but they hesitated to vote state money for relief. Still not willing to give up, Paine took a different step in his appeal for money. He went to the State Treasurer and withdrew $500 from the amount due him for his services as clerk. Then he used it to head a subscription list for relief of the army.

This bold step brought the desired results. Two prominent members of the Assembly, Robert Morris and Blair McClenaghan, promptly pledged sizable amounts in actual money. Others made pledges and soon making contributions to the cause became a popular movement.

Soon the women of Philadelphia became eager to help the movement. They started an organization known as the American Daughters of Liberty to serve as a collection agency. They roamed the streets, where they gathered not only money but food, clothing, and other useful articles. Nearly everybody contributed.

The fund which Paine had started grew and grew. Finally it totalled the unexpected amount of over 300,000 pounds. A special bank, the Bank of Philadelphia, was organized to handle and distribute the money.

In November, 1780, Paine resigned his position as clerk of the Pennsylvania Assembly. He now had saved a little money and wanted to take time to start writing a history of the revolution. He barely started to write, however, before something happened to alter his plans.

Congress decided to send Colonel John Laurens, a member of Washington's staff, to France to ask for more active help from that country. Benjamin Franklin, Arthur Lee, and John Adams already were in France, but they were not in close touch with the army's needs. They didn't realize how desperate these needs were.

When Colonel Laurens was asked to go to France he said, "I'll go only if I can take Thomas Paine with me. I may need his help."

Congress agreed and Colonel Laurens and Paine set out for France. Paine turned out to be an able helper to Colonel Laurens. His *Crisis* letters had been published there and he was favorably received as their author. As a result, the Laurens-Paine mission was successful.

Laurens and Paine returned in August, 1781, on a French ship containing 2,500,000 livres in French money. Accompanying this ship were two others loaded with French troops and supplies to assist the American army. Up to this time, only a few Frenchmen had been militarily active in America. One was the Marquis de Lafayette, who had been of great assistance to General Washington.

The Laurens-Paine achievement was the major factor in bringing the Revolutionary War to an end. General Washington's nine thousand men, now well-clothed and well-fed, and the new French recruits combined to attack British General Charles Cornwallis at Yorktown, Virginia. Soon Cornwallis realized that his situation was hopeless. On October 17, 1781, he agreed to surrender and two days later the British Army laid down its arms. Now at last the Revolutionary War in America was over.

Washington traveled to Philadelphia where he was welcomed by the Continental Congress for his victorious efforts. Huge crowds of people greeted him on the streets and acclaimed him as the Father of American independence. At last after years of suffering and privation, he and his men could lay down their arms.

Now once more Paine was out of a job and penniless. He appealed for help to Washington, who brought the matter to the attention of the Continental Congress. Finally, through the efforts of Robert Morris, the Congress voted in February, 1782, to give Paine $800 a year. This amount was to be paid out of a secret service fund which Morris administered.

With this money, Paine proceeded to purchase a small home in Bordentown, New Jersey. Unfortunately, however, this government help was short-lived because, about one year later, Morris resigned and the agreement came to an end.

Soon Paine's plight came to the attention of the New York legislature. In the spring of 1784 this legislature gave him some good farm acreage and a house near New Rochelle, New York. The Pennsylvania legislature, not to be outdone by a neighboring state, later the same year voted him a gratuity of 500 pounds.

Finally the Continental Congress took steps to compensate Paine for his long-continued service to the American cause of freedom. In

October, 1785, it passed a resolution of gratitude for "early, unsolicited, and continued labors of Mr. Thomas Paine, in explaining and enforcing the principles of the late revolution by ingenious and timely publications upon the nature of liberty and civil government." Then it instructed its treasurer to pay Paine $3,000 as a gratuity.

Now at age forty-eight, Paine for the first time in his adult life was free from worrying about money. He decided to settle down in his new home in Bordentown, New Jersey. There he hoped to carry on some inventive activities which he had long had in mind. He had always been able to use his hands deftly in delicate work such as repairing brooms, making neat stitches in cloth, and repairing clocks.

At this time he wanted to invent an iron bridge. He got the idea because people in Philadelphia were discussing the need for building a bridge across the Schuylkill River. At present the only means of crossing the river was by ferry boat. Various designs for a bridge were submitted, all to be built of wood except Paine's. Up until now all bridges had been made of wood.

"Your bridge won't stand up," people said as they looked at Paine's model.

"Yes, it will," he said.

To prove his point, he built a thirteen-foot-long model and secured permission to set it up in Benjamin Franklin's garden. Then he invited visitors to walk over it and stamp hard. Hundreds accepted and crossed in perfect safety.

Still, the Philadelphia city government could not be convinced. In March, 1787, Franklin advised Paine to take his model to the Academy of Science in France. "If the Academy there pronounces it safe, the Philadelphia city government will be receptive," he said.

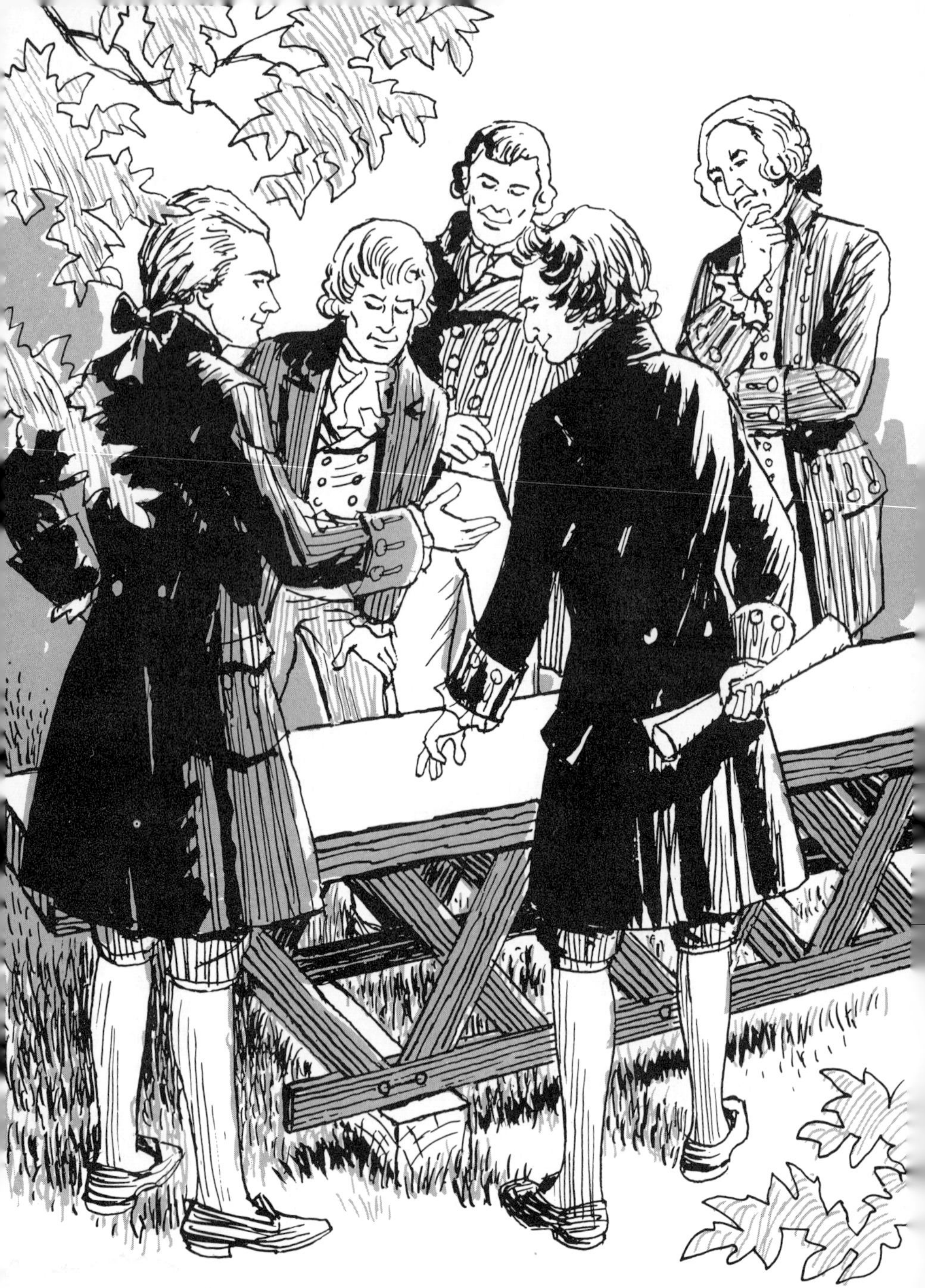

A month later Paine sailed from New York to Paris with his model. Soon after he arrived he called on Thomas Jefferson, who now was the American minister to France. Jefferson, who also was mechanically minded and inventive, was very much interested in Paine's model. He promised to add his recommendation to Franklin's endorsement to get Academy approval.

Several months later the Academy reported favorably on the plan of the bridge but doubted whether it would be successful in a large structure. Paine was greatly discouraged. "Take your model to England," said Jefferson. "England is a great iron-producing country and British iron-masters may be interested."

This was a welcome suggestion to Paine. He had wanted to go to England anyway to see his parents. About a year before he had received a letter from his father saying, "Once more I'd like to clasp thy hand."

When Paine reached Thetford he found that his father had already died and that his mother was living alone in the family home. While there he arranged for her to have a small weekly income for the rest of her life.

As for Thetford, Paine found that it hadn't changed. It still had little contact with the outside world. The people there had never heard of his *Common Sense* or his *American Crisis*. The English government had banned their sale throughout the country.

For the next couple of years, Paine shuttled back and forth between France and England trying to promote interest in his bridge. During this time he was well received in the capitals of both countries. By now the leaders in the English Parliament realized that America was fast becoming a power to be reckoned with. They felt that Paine could be of great help to them in maintaining friendy relations with

America. In France Paine was known as the close friend of both Franklin and Jefferson. When these men returned to America, Marquis de Lafayette became his chief advisor.

In both England and France there were currents of dissatisfaction with their governments. In England the chief political leader was Edmund Burke, a brilliant orator and writer. He headed a liberal movement for the people but felt that the monarchy should be preserved. In France, on the other hand, most people felt that the monarchy should be overthrown. In fact, a revolution was almost under way.

Paine aligned himself with the revolutionary movement in France. Soon afterwards Edmund Burke wrote a book condemning the revolution. This angered Paine, who retorted, "It's a trumpet call to privilege and power, the very things we fought against in America. I thought Burke was more liberal than that."

Paine hurried back to England to answer Burke. He wrote a small book which he called *The Rights of Man*. In this publication he spelled out these rights in words that the poor and downtrodden could readily understand.

This book alarmed British government authorities, who concluded that he was a dangerous man. They decided that he must be imprisoned before he could incite Englishmen as he had Americans. Some of his friends warned him and he escaped to France.

The people of France acclaimed Paine for writing *The Rights of Man*. They made him a member of important organizations involved in the Revolution. He threw himself heart and soul into this new cause but differed from some of the leaders. He allied himself with the party which was opposed to violence. He was horrified when the radicals executed persons whom they deemed enemies of the revolution.

Paine pleaded with the leaders of this party to use peaceable means to promote the cause, but they would not listen. He urged them to allow the king and his family to go into exile, but they refused. As a result the king and queen were beheaded.

One after another, many prominent persons were led to the guillotine. Even Lafayette had to flee to Switzerland for his life. Finally Paine and other semi-conservatives were put in prison for opposing radical acts.

To occupy his time in prison, Paine turned to writing. This time he wrote a book called *The Age of Reason,* based on the Bible. All his life he had been eager to clarify some of the incidents and passages in the Bible which seemed vague or conflicting. Now with ample time on his hands, he undertook this task.

Final Years in America

As a prisoner in France Paine escaped execution by accident. Definite arrangements had been made for him and several other prisoners to be killed. On the night before, guards came to mark X's on the doors of the condemned, but fortunately Paine was not in his cell. The head jailer had taken him to help quiet a hysterical boy, and the door to his cell stood open, flat against the wall.

In the dim lantern light the jailer who was marking the doors didn't realize that Paine's door was open and marked it on the wrong side. When Paine was returned to his cell and the door was closed the X didn't show from the outside. For this reason when the executioner came the next morning he passed Paine by.

A short time later Paine became seriously ill of typhoid fever and almost died. While he still lay sick, President Washington sent James Monroe to Paris as the new Minister to France. In assuming his duties Monroe came across some old letters which Paine had written requesting help. He investigated and arranged for him to be released in November, 1794.

Monroe took Paine to his own home so that Mrs. Monroe could help nurse him. He soon improved with good food and care, but never recovered completely. Although he was only fifty-seven years old, he had lost much of his former vigor and strength.

As soon as he was able he moved from Monroe's home to a lodging place of his own. He hoped to return soon to America where the new

United States government was getting under way. He read all he could about the new government to find out how successful it was. He was interested to learn that two political parties had been formed. One was the Federalist Party, headed by Alexander Hamilton of New York, which supported President Washington. The other was the Democratic-Republican party headed by Thomas Jefferson.

Paine felt that the Democratic-Republican Party was much closer to the people than the Federalist Party. He wrote letters to Washington and others criticizing some of Washington's policies as President. These letters irritated Washington and many of his friends. As a result, there was little hope for Paine to return to America at this time.

In 1797, Washington was succeeded by John Adams, another Federalist, as President. Not until 1801, four years later, when Thomas Jefferson was elected President, did the situation change. Late that year Jefferson wrote Paine a letter offering to let him come to America on an American warship about ready to sail from France to the United States. Paine was grateful but did not accept because Jefferson was severely criticized for making this offer. An article had appeared in a Federalist newspaper in Baltimore condemning Jefferson and picturing Paine as a dangerous individual. Besides, many religious leaders still attacked Paine for having written *The Age of Reason.*

In October, 1802, he arranged to sail to America on his own. At this stage in his life he was desperate for a place to spend his declining years. He felt that he couldn't stay in France because he had lost favor and been imprisoned there for opposing violence in the French Revolution. He couldn't return to his home country of England because government authorities there would seize him and punish him for having written *The Rights of Man.*

On the way across the Atlantic Ocean he could hardly wait to arrive, but the people of America greeted him with scorn. The Federalist politicians were still angry about the letters which he had written criticizing Washington's policies. Clergymen preached against him in their pulpits, urging their congregations to avoid him as if he were Satan.

The only place in America where he seemed to be welcome was the White House. President Jefferson invited him to stay there for a while as a guest. During this period he and Jefferson had many good talks together and he enjoyed several entertaining social events.

In February, 1803, he left Washington and traveled to Philadelphia and New York. In these cities he looked up former companions, but many turned their backs on him. Next he

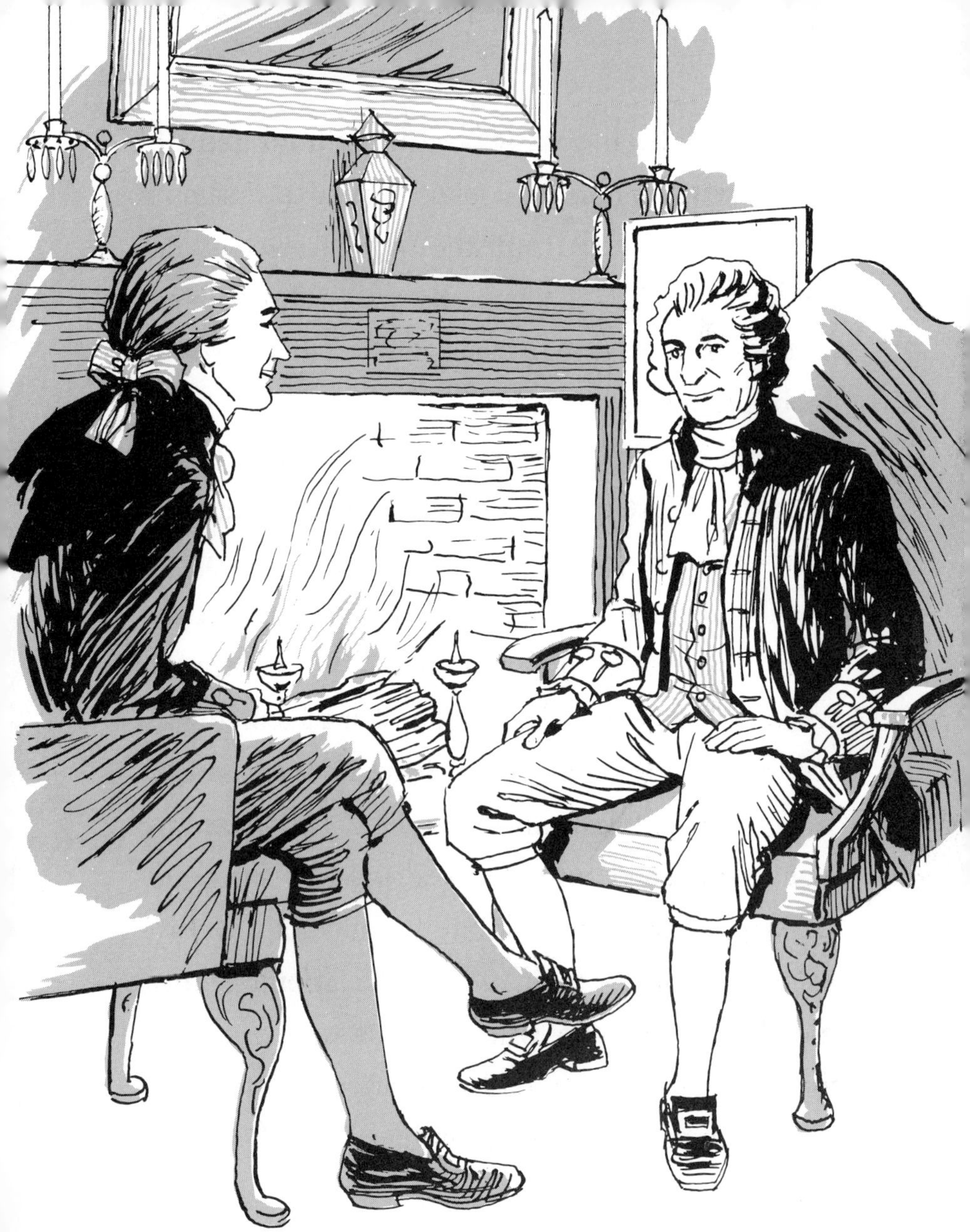

went to Bordentown, where he still owned his little house. There he looked forward to seeing his old neighbors, but they too turned their backs on him. The only persons who treated him kindly were two men who had helped him to build his iron bridge.

He now gloomily retreated to his lonely farm house near New Rochelle. There, in beautiful surroundings, he planned to turn to writing again. Soon he discovered, however, that partly from infirmities and partly from his treatment in America, he had lost much of his former will to write. He was only 66 years old but a broken-down old man far beyond his years.

For three years Paine lived in New Rochelle like a hermit. He seldom traveled anywhere except to New York, where he spent a few months during the winters. He wrote only a few letters because had few friends left with whom to carry on correspondence.

On election day in 1806 while he was at New Rochelle, he dragged himself to the voting place. Much to his surprise the supervisor, who was a Federalist, refused to let him vote. "You are not a citizen of this country," he declared flatly and coldly.

This was a final blow from which Paine could not recover. Even though he had given himself body and soul to the cause of freedom in America, he was not allowed to vote here. Instead, he was told that he didn't belong here.

Feeling unwanted and disowned in New Rochelle, he moved to New York. There he was fortunate enough to find lodging with kind-hearted people who cared for him during his few remaining years. He died June 8, 1809, ending the saddest years of his life.

Today historians give Thomas Paine his rightful place in history. They realize that except for his pen the United States of America might not exist. He bolstered the cause of freedom when it was most needed to win the American Revolution. Proudly we honor him along with Benjamin Franklin, George Washington, John Adams, Thomas Jefferson, and others as one of the founders of our country.

Many tributes have been paid to Thomas Paine. One appears on a bronze plaque in his home town of Thetford, England, which reads:

TOM PAINE, 1737–1809
JOURNALIST, PATRIOT AND CHAMPION
OF THE COMMON MAN

and, after listing his writings, adds:

THIS SIMPLE SON OF ENGLAND LIVES ON THROUGH THE IDEAS AND PRINCIPLES OF THE DEMOCRATIC WORLD FOR WHICH WE FIGHT TODAY. IN TRIBUTE TO HIS MEMORY AND TO THE EVERLASTING LOVE OF FREEDOM EMBODIED IN HIS WORKS, THIS PLAQUE IS GRATEFULLY DEDICATED.